FALSE COLORS

An M/M Romance

BY ALEX BEECROFT

RUNNING PRESS
Philadelphia • London

9   8   7   6   5   4   3   2   1

Digit on the right indicates the number of this printing

Library of Congress Control Number: 2008939355

ISBN 978-0-7624-3658-3

Cover design by Bill Jones
Cover illustrations by Larry Rostant
Interior design by Jan Greenberg
Typography: New Caledonia and Amigo

Running Press Book Publishers
2300 Chestnut Street
Philadelphia, PA 19103-4371

Visit us on the web!
www.runningpress.com

◖◗ CHAPTER 1 ◗◗

HMS Termagant, *standing out from France—1762*

Beneath the *Termagant's* imposing side, the newly captured *Météore* wallowed like a discarded boot. John Cavendish, however, standing by Admiral Saunders' shoulder, gazed on it with as much satisfaction as a returning husband might gaze on his young wife. Around him, the fume of smoke blew away in dirty yellow tendrils across the Bay of Biscay, revealing the squadron; a thicket of masts, a white foliage of sail as the ships filled and backed, holding station around the flagship.

After Admiral Hawke had so gloriously trounced the last invasion fleet at the battle of Quiberon Bay, Saunders' squadron had been sent to cruise the French coast and discourage the formation of another. The little French convoy of merchant ships with their escort of two-decker and gun-boat which they intercepted this morning had put up a brave, despairing fight, but it had been all over by lunchtime. Various lieutenants, more senior than John, had been dispatched already to take the more valuable prizes back to England. But the *Météore*… the *Météore* was to be his.

"Your temporary papers." Admiral Saunders took the hastily written page from his flag captain and handed it to John. "Well done, Mr. Cavendish."

"Thank you, sir." John's breast filled with happiness. It was all he could do to keep a reasonably straight face—the smile would keep trying to escape. As he folded the paper and tucked it into his waistcoat, his joy got the better of him and he could not help repeating, "Oh, thank you."

Saunders, a florid man with piercing blue eyes, paled and gave John an uncomfortable look. He pushed back his wig and rubbed at the line indented across his forehead. "Walk with me a moment."

At this hint, the captain and the midshipman of the watch strolled away, leaving John and Saunders in virtual privacy on the windward side of the quarterdeck. Silence fell, as Saunders looked out on the fleet, watching replacement yards being rigged on the *Juno*.

Snatches of fife music skirled shrill across the water as the distant *Hebe*'s men stamped and turned the capstan to raise a new foremast. On the flagship itself the carpenters were hard at work plugging shot holes. But down on the *Météore* the sparse crew stood about, idle, waiting for someone to tell them to bend on a new suit of sails; to get the gore and body parts of the previous occupants off the deck, and clean her up. John itched to be there, getting on with it, as soon as was decently possible.

"Well," Saunders sighed. "No need for thanks. You weren't my first choice, after all."

"I understand, sir. A shame about Mr. McIntyre." Rightly reproved, John sent up a quick prayer for the second lieutenant whose right it would have been to have this prize, this chance. Cut in half by a French cannon ball and heaved over the side during battle, McIntyre currently lay in two pieces on the ocean bed.

"Fortunes of war." The Admiral waved that aside with a chubby hand, a long, long history of sudden death at sea summed up in his slight shrug. "It don't do to pretend otherwise. Good man, 'tis a shame he's gone, but we won't bring him back by moping, eh?"

"No, sir."

On the flagship's jolly boat, rowing towards the *Météore* with midshipman Smythe in its bow, one of the oarsmen caught a crab. The oar tangled with his neighbor's, knocking both men from their seats into the bilge. They picked themselves up with a roar of oaths, then launched themselves at one another. Smythe shouldered into the midst of it, yelling obscenities in his clear, boy's voice, indiscriminately slashing both men with his cane until they separated and settled grudgingly back to their benches.

Watching this, Saunders shook his head. His gaze skittered across John's face and a thread of anxiety began to wind its way through John's elation. "Your crew may be a little…less than ideal, Mr. Cavendish."

"I understand, sir," John replied promptly. "If I were a captain, asked to make up the complement of a prize, I'd use the opportunity to get rid of my troublemakers too."

"You *are* a captain," Saunders pointed out, with a flash of ferocity from beneath his tufts of pepper-grey eyebrows. "At least for the duration of this voyage. Afterwards too, maybe, if you can pull this off."

"Yes, sir." *Don't smile!* Glee returned, intensifying beneath John's ribs until he was sure his chest should be glowing.

His face probably was, for Saunders gave a reluctant smile. "Well, don't thank me again, until you hear what 'this' is. I'm about to give you something to do with this new ship of yours, Commander Cavendish. And it won't be easy. D' you understand me? I'm not offering you any kiss-my-hand sinecure here. I'm setting you a challenge."

"I am quite ready for a challenge, sir."

But Saunders' smile faltered again and, as he fidgeted with his watch fob, that pinprick of anxiety drove further in through John's joy, puncturing it. John's feet, once floating, seemed to settle back to the deck and his weight to bear down on him as he slowly deflated.

Saunders glanced sideways, eyes dulled with distaste. He

lowered his voice. "You're a religious man, aren't you?"

John straightened up, defensively proud. "Yes, sir. Very much so."

"Well, that may help." The Admiral reached out and patted the *Termagant's* railing, as if he comforted her. Above, the sun came out, lighting up the naval equivalent of carrion crows—a towering spiral of seagulls. They soared above the fleet, silver and raucous, fighting over scraps of dead men in the water.

From a splintered gun port below seeped the heathery, bitter smell of tobacco as the master carpenter leaned out to assess the damage to the hull, pipe between his teeth.

Saunders looked up. "I'm unleashing you on the heathen, lad. While we've been patrolling here, trying to keep Louis' hands off London, the Barbary Corsairs have had a free run at the coasts. Devon and Cornwall devastated; thousands of English men and women stolen away to become slaves; uproar in Parliament; papers proclaiming the end of the world. The King himself asking pointed questions of the First Lord of the Admiralty. Something has to be done."

"Yes, sir." The glory of captaincy faded in the light of its responsibility, and John looked at the *Météore* with a new eye. She might be his—and marvelous because of it—but she was totally inadequate to the task being set. "Do I comprehend you correctly, sir? I am to take on the armed might of the Ottoman Empire *in a bomb ketch?*"

From ill at ease, Saunders turned instantly harsh. "Are you questioning your orders, Mr. Cavendish?"

"No sir! *Clarifying*, sir. Forgive me."

"What is there to make clear? Stop them, Cavendish. Talk to them. Blow them up—that's what you have a damn mortar for! I don't give a fig how you do it, but *stop them*. Afterwards you may rendezvous with the rest of the fleet at Gibraltar. If you pull this off, you'll be a hero from Cornwall to the Orkneys, with mothers of Christian babies kissing your feet wherever you go. I'd like to see the Admiralty turn you down for a ship after that."

John studied the *Météore*, examining her eight guns and the two stubby mortars which weighed down her bows. The racing currents of the Channel met the deep waters of the Atlantic here and choppy waves broke over her rail, washing some of the filth from her decks. '*Purge her with hyssop and let her be clean,*' he thought, surprising himself, '*wash her and let her be whiter than snow.*' He could only imagine she was being sent as a sacrifice, and all her new crew with her. No wonder she was being fitted out with the rejects of half a dozen ships—the men no one minded losing.

"I understand, sir," he said, sober at last.

Saunders bent a little at the waist and peered at John's face. Then he smiled. "I see you do. Well..." Straightening his wig once more, he placed his hat carefully atop it. "I can at least give you a lieutenant to serve under you. He'll be some use to keep your untried crew in order. A volunteer, no less."

"I had rather not, sir." It was the closest John could decently come to acknowledging the reality aloud, but he'd be damned if he took a fellow lieutenant with him on what must surely be a doomed mission. One victim was enough.

"You were not asked for your opinion, Mr. Cavendish. If I deign to give you a lieutenant, you will take a lieutenant and be grateful for him, God rot you."

In the face of such a command what could he do? *A volunteer? Who would be idiot enough to give up the prospects of advancement that came from a ship of the line in order to volunteer for a position on a bomb ketch, under a man with little more seniority than himself?* Perhaps such a prodigy had been sent for the purpose by God himself. *Perhaps the Navy was better off without so great a fool?* Whatever the case, he could not turn down a direct order. Better to die in the execution of his duty than to be hanged for mutiny. He bowed his head. "Aye, aye, sir."

Eighty pairs of eyes watched John as he came up the side and strode stiffly to the *Météore*'s small quarterdeck. Taking off his hat, he turned to face his crew, noting the slack, bruised faces of men with scurvy, the nose-less, crusted features of those whom pox was slowly consuming from within. The Master was barely being held up by his mate, his linen drabbed with wine stains. The single midshipman picked his nose as he slouched by his division, then spat over the side. Only the new lieutenant stood straight and alert, in newly laundered dress uniform, his wig powdered, his buttons gleaming and his pale brows arched a little in amusement as he watched John struggle with hat and paper in the increasing wind.

John fumed inwardly at the slackness, the disrespect as well as the waste of lives. Opening Admiral Saunders' letter, he read it aloud in a firm, positive tone, reading himself in as captain, telling them whence his authority came and warning that he had the right to govern and punish as he saw fit. Some of his anger wound its way into his voice, making it snap like the cat, and the more alert members of the crew stood straighter by the end of it.

Hoping to find at least one other person aboard competent to do their job, John was about to quiz the volunteer, when his thoughts were instantly dashed as the huddle of warrant officers parted to reveal the modest black dress and white lace bonnet of an elderly lady. John bowed over the twigs of her fingers, reeling. "The Doctor's wife, Mrs Harper," a voice informed him, and "Charmed," he said mechanically. They'd sent a woman on board! In God's holy name—knowing what they knew—they'd allowed not merely a woman, but a lady on board! The blood drained from his face, then returned, thundering and stinging in his ears. *A victim. Are we to put up a plucky resistance and then be sunk, so that the outrage may provide an excuse for war? So that the First Lord may say, 'See, we don't scruple to spare even our women in the pursuit of this menace?'* It was despicable.

His head throbbed suddenly, pain winding up from his

clenched teeth to lance through his temples into his eyes. Giving orders to set sail, to clean the decks, and paint a properly anglicized *Meteor* over the name on the stern, he waited until the life of the ship around him settled into its routine, then ducked into the captain's cabin to think. But the ruin he found seemed to mock him. The French captain's cot lay slashed on the floor, stern lockers and all the chests broken open and ransacked.

"A right fucking pig's ear they've made of this, sir," the voice of his steward grated along his spine, making him straighten up, instinctively. Turning, he found Japheth Higgins looming behind him with John's portmanteau propped against his hip and his sea-chest dragged by one handle from the other hand. An orange brute, Higgins had a tendency to appear out of random shadows, like the Borneo wild man.

"I thought I told you to stay on the flagship, Higgins."

"You was having a little laugh, though, right sir? 'Cos you wouldn't leave me behind, not was you Admiral of the White." Higgins dropped the sea-chest by way of final punctuation and scratched his ginger sideburns with a tobacco-stained finger.

John laughed around the queasiness in his throat. Higgins made an unusual fairy gomother, to be sure, but it was true. Assigned to him as a sea-daddy on his first ship, set by the captain to teach the infant young gentleman the ropes—and to make sure he was not too homesick, too lonely, or too much picked on—Higgins had been with him ever since. Now he couldn't even say "I was trying to keep you safe, you fool," without spreading rumors he did not need the rest of the crew to hear.

"Not a very good joke, I'm afraid," he said instead. "I'm sorry Higgins. I'm glad you're here. See what you can do to sort this mess out, would you? I'm going for the tour."

Choosing not to notice the Master retching into a bucket as he passed, John paced the length of the gun-deck. Lighting the lantern he had taken from the midshipmen's berth, he descended to the lightless lowest deck, past the carpenter's workroom and the gunner's stores, and so back again to the grated area where the anchor cables were laid to dry. Trying to calm his mind, he strode out nervous and filled with a lightning of energy he had to out-walk before he could think.

On the cable tier, absolute darkness pressed inwards around the circle of his light. Water trickled, glistening, down the *Meteor's* flexing sides, the sound of it sweet in the silences between waves. A stench came from the hold, seeping up through the holes of the deck. Below the latticework of planks on which he stood, the ballast of gravel below stirred with a great hiss, like the tide rolling over a beach. Not all the anxiety in the world could prevent him from making a note to order the pumps set working at once.

Around him, on either side, the anchor cables lay coiled, water dripping from them, falling as an indoor rain through the gratings to join the water in the hold beneath his feet. Footsteps knocked on the deck above him, but down here the dark, quiet, and solitude calmed him. Breathing in, he sighed, the spring of his anger easing enough to allow thought. It was too early to despair. Somehow, he would complete this mission and return as the hero Saunders described. Or at the least, he would complete the mission while keeping his crew alive, from the old lady to the youngest powder monkey. Here in this waiting space, this space between worlds, as he thought of it, it was easier to believe.

Straightening his back even further, an ache like a fist between his shoulder blades, he picked his way back through the coils of hawser. They rose like cliffs on either side and, as he walked, his lantern light mingled with a growing brown gloom that spilled in from the doorway. There, in the narrow gap between John and the main companionway, stood the volunteer— *Lieutenant Donwell,* he reminded himself from the orders—with his wig off and his bold eyes glimmering gold as John raised his lantern to look at him. Walking forward, John expected the man to yield, to step back and let him out. Mere inches separated them by the time it dawned on him that Donwell was not going to move. Confusion striking through him, he pulled himself back from a collision only just in time. The skirts of their coats brushed, sending a jolt of invasion through him from thigh to shoulders. *What the devil?*

His mouth dried as a wave of prickly embarrassment swept over him, bringing guilt in its wake. Yet what had *he* done wrong? It was Donwell who should flinch, who should feel guilty, *who should not be smiling so!* John could not wrench his gaze away from Donwell's face. Limned with gold, it was perfectly nondescript; round, pleasant, and completely lacking in self-conscious guilt. Donwell's mouth quirked up at one side into a slow, charming smile. And his presence! It was extraordinary. It beat on John's skin like strong sunshine. He fought the urge to close his eyes and bathe in it. His pulse picked up, waiting, waiting for something....

Returning sanity hit him in the face. He snapped, "Get out of my way! Don't you know who I am?"

Donwell's smile only broadened. John thought the man would at least salute, but he just passed a hand through the loose blond curls of his hair and stepped away. "I'd know you anywhere, sir."

"I'll have a little more respect from you in future, Mister."

"You may have whatever you like."

Speech deserted John once more. Aware he should act now to regain the initiative, he had no idea what to do. Instead he pushed past, feeling the man's gaze on the back of his neck like warm breath, and tried to tell himself that he made a dignified exit. But if the truth be told it was a flight, spooked as a partridge from the covert.

"Anything I can do for you, sir?"

Having gone to ground in his cabin, where—his writing slope on top of a couple of casks and a plank—he was trying to come to terms with the endless paperwork, John looked up, glad for the interruption. Glad for a second chance to establish his authority—to do this *right* this time. When he saw Lieutenant Donwell standing entirely too close, sleeves rolled up to bare tar-smudged forearms, he did not wait to wonder why it was hard to draw breath, but raised an eyebrow. "Did your last captain have a lax attitude towards dress, Mr. Donwell? Because I do not. Nor do I consider it appropriate for you to enter my cabin uninvited."

Donwell duly straightened up, rolled his sleeves down and said, "My apologies, Captain," in an unruffled, cheerful tone. John noticed that he had not been mistaken in his first impression. The young man's healthy vigor seemed to radiate from him like warmth from a fire.

"But is there nothing you want, sir?" Donwell asked with a wry, friendly grin.

John set down his quill, flipped the top of his inkwell closed, and rose to meet the smile as if it was a challenge. It must *be* a challenge of some sort, even a threat, for some of the exaltation of battle—a death or glory brilliance—colored his reaction as he replied. "I assure you I am not without a servant, Mr. Donwell. If you can curb your sudden desire to be my steward, I suggest you go about your business."

"Aye aye, sir." Bowing with an easy, indolent grace, Donwell turned away and shut the door behind him as he left.

Walking over to the stern gallery, John looked out into a black night that turned the glass into a wall of mirrors. Rather than lose his troubles out there on the waves, he found himself gazing at a floating lighted image of himself and the captain's cabin around him. It seemed appropriate. His thoughts too, searching for inspiration, kept being flung back upon themselves as if by a wall of mirrors. There had been such a comfort, in many previous tight spots, to firmly believe that his captain had a plan. He wondered if, each of those times, the captain had in reality felt like this: paralyzed by responsibility and doubt.

Returning to the desk, he gathered the papers into a bundle, tapped their edges together and stowed them in the slope, before pulling out his personal journal. The cane seat of his chair sagged beneath him, half the latticework cut away by a pike, but he perched on the edge, dipped his quill and wrote:

> *If ever a man needed divine guidance, I am he. It*
> *matters not in the great scheme of things, I know,*
> *if this small vessel never returns from Algiers. If*
> *she is sunk, it will serve the Admiralty's purpose*
> *well enough. But it will not serve mine. There must*
> *be some means to accomplish this task without the*
> *loss of any of the lives that have been given into my*
> *care. I will strive with all my might to find that*
> *means, and I pray that God will deliver us all from*
> *the mouth of Leviathan.*

Dipping the quill again, he watched the excess ink bulge into a droplet and splash into the inkwell, tempted to write nothing more. But he must not be a coward.

> *What is it in me that makes the nearer problem*
> *seem so much the sharper? I find myself grateful to*
> *Mr. Donwell. His unaccountable behavior occupies*
> *my mind and drives out thoughts of the future. I*
> *am mystified by it, and yet strangely comforted.*
> *Do I take him into my confidence? I would wel-*
> *come a friend's counsel. But how can I call him*
> *anything of the sort, while his actions dance on the*
> *very edge of insubordination?*

"What am I to do?"

Closing the book, he tucked it into his pocket, took down the lantern that swung overhead, and ducked into the tiny cubby-hole to starboard that was his sleeping cabin. The wind was blowing about four knots, beautifully steady just abaft the beam, and the newly renamed *Meteor* murmured in return. Her creak of ropes and timbers had a cadence specific to herself and John listened to her voice with proprietary interest, learning what she sounded like when she was running sweetly happy before a fair wind.

If he strained his ears he could also hear the far off sounds of the men of the Royal Ordnance Corps, keeping themselves to themselves, somewhere beyond where the wardroom would be. But the wardroom itself was hollow and silent as a grave.

Perhaps, with only the warrant officers for company—on this ship as disagreeable a set of swabs as ever struggled up through the hawse hole—Donwell was just lonely. Perhaps he had sensed John's preoccupation, and sought only to encourage him to speak? Or perhaps he thought himself better suited for captaincy, and was testing how far he could go before John would punish him. *Bucks vying for territory, heads dipped and antlers locked, testing one another's strength? If that is the case, let him watch himself.* John would not stand for that.

Yet… yet it was also possible that John was making too much of simple friendliness.

And at this moment he had a great need of a friend.

◖ CHAPTER 2 ◗

Alfie Donwell reported for his watch just as the sun came up. The bell sounded out, sweet and forlorn, ringing across the deep water of the Bay of Biscay, and the midshipman on the quarterdeck stifled a yawn as he saluted.

"Nothing to report, sir. No sail sighted. Wind's held steady all night."

They stood in silence, watching as the sun's early rays made the sea at the edge of the world glow green. The thankless to and fro of patrolling the French coast lay forgotten behind them, and Alfie smiled as he looked up at the headsails, pointing like arrows toward a new horizon.

"Very well then. Goodnight, Armitage."

The boy favored him with a look of disapproval, as if to say that whether he had a good night or not was none of Alfie's business. But he rubbed a hand over his pimply chin and gave a grudging, "Night, Sir," before departing to his hammock in the solitary splendor of a midshipman's berth that contained only himself.

Armitage's surliness did nothing to dampen Alfie's mood. It might be his general contrariness, but he liked the foreign-made *Meteor* with her bow-heavy mortars and her awkward aft-stepped masts. While he was aware that below decks men from ten different ships were eyeing each other speculatively, not knowing what to expect, he rather liked that too. Better than being trapped in a regime of singular cruelty. There was time yet for hope, time to set an example of kindliness and expect it to be followed. Alfie knew that his own preference—formed by his first captain—was for a style of command so unique he could not hope to meet it anywhere else in life. But still, Cavendish did not seem the sort of man to stamp on every spark of life, as long as the job was being done.

He had them throw the log, measured off speed and time and wind direction, penciling in the dead reckoning, to be checked by noon observation, and thought about the captain.

John Cavendish! Everything from his name on down was elegant. Unhappy with the tight discipline, the unbending rigidity and the lack of respect for the men on his own ship, Alfie might have volunteered for service on the *Meteor* anyway, but once he had seen its captain to be, they could not have paid him to stay away.

Oh true, I am an abomination, a sinner, a boil on the backside of polite society, but is it any of their business? And how could any of them find it in themselves to rebuke me? Have they not seen the man? With his classical Greek looks, the wing-like black brows over pewter eyes that he kept narrowed, and the pale scar that glimmered on his left cheek, as if to make the point that this was a fighting man's beauty, not that of a fop. With his posture and his well bred nerves and that slight uncertainty that just begged to be taken advantage of....

If there was a man in the world who could look at that and not be stirred, well, Alfie felt sorry for him, his must be a poor life.

But how to act, now he'd seen what he wanted? Checking the compass again, he had a word with the steersman, who admitted to being grudgingly pleased with her lack of leeway. Then he leaned on the rail and devoted himself to wondering what he ought to do now.

It would have helped had he been a man of some grand accomplishment—handsome as the devil, powerful as the First

Sea Lord, influential as an Earl with a father in Parliament and a brother the archbishop of Canterbury. But he was not. An old country lawyer's son with nothing more to his name than his sea-chest, he would have to do this the way he did everything—by hard work and charm.

Yet it's sheer folly to try at all. All the men of his persuasion Alfie had ever known—bar one—insisted it was too dangerous to try anything at sea. An unspeakable vice carried on in the dark could protect itself, to a certain extent, by the willingness of the respectable not to speak of it. But when it began to show in one's daily actions, one's choices and career, it had an unpleasant habit of becoming visible enough to condemn.

Even Alfie—the kind of man who would take a lit candle into the powder magazine, confident in his natural invulnerability—found himself unwilling to risk everything on unsupported desire. But, he smiled into the rising sun, remembering that moment down on the cable tier, his desire *had* support. What devil had got into him then, urging him to press his suit so early, he didn't know. He snorted in soft laughter at the line of foam curling away from the *Meteor*'s plunging bow. *Now that is not true, Alfie. It was the same devil as always—your own damned impulsiveness. One of these days it will get you hanged.* Still, thank God he had yielded to it in this instance. For the world had seemed to stop around them both, drawing in to intimate solitude, while Cavendish stood, dazed by his resistance, lips slightly parted and breathing hard, exactly like a man expecting—hoping—to be kissed.

Alfie re-lived that moment on a regular basis, taking the step, pulling the captain close by his lapels, making him drop the lantern in shock and kissing him there in the utter dark until he stopped struggling and started begging for more.

Only dreams, of course. In truth, if Cavendish had rebuked him then, and really sounded like he meant it, that would have been the last of it. Even on Alfie's reckless nature, the threat of the noose worked a certain restraint. But he saw neither revulsion, nor anger, nor even indifference. When he ducked into cover beyond the door, let down the shutters on his dark lantern and looked back, concealed, he had seen—just for one instant— Cavendish's fierce expression melt into a puzzled smile, and his long, slim fingers reach up to adjust the bow in his hair, even as his worried frown returned.

So, not disgust by any means. Alfie rather thought it was innocence. The innocence of a man who did not know what had just happened, but who liked it nevertheless. Doubtless Cavendish thought of inverts as mincing, womanish creatures, easy to spot by their affected gestures and foppish clothes. Really the broadsheets with their satires of the "third sex" formed an honest sod's best defense. No one expected it, Alfie smiled wryly, in so bluff and manly a chap as himself.

But it did add a hundredfold to the difficulties of courtship. Though Alfie very much hoped to be the one who turned Cavendish's naivety into experience, who showed him what his nature clearly yearned for, it would take gentle handling and a great deal more caution than came naturally, if he was not to go too far too early, and altogether frighten the captain away.

Four hours of watch ended in as much peace as they had begun. Alfie handed the quarterdeck back to a sleepy Armitage and went below to the wardroom, where Mrs. Harper, the Doctor's loblolly girl, was laboriously serving tea from the mess's big brown pot. Her arthritic knuckles were twisted and bleached as driftwood. Her hands trembled, and tea spattered over the tablecloth. It did not give him great confidence in her ability to hold down a shrieking sailor for amputation. But he said nothing and accepted a half full cup with thanks, while the wardroom servant brought in a breakfast of hard tack fried in slush, and a glorious dish of bacon from the galley.

From the gun-deck, further forward, separated from the officers' mess only by a canvas screen, came the homely sound of spoons scraping on wooden plates, and a periodic roaring of laughter as the off-duty watch shoveled up their porridge.

Slumped in a chair by the door, filling the room with the scent of stale rum and staler smoke, the Master punctuated his snoring with retching coughs, but did not wake. The Boatswain haunted the deck already with his mates, looking for someone to hit, and Hall—the Purser—would not rise for another three hours, thank God.

It is a good time to be here, Alfie thought, listening to Mrs. Harper's account of the various accidents of the night—two bursten bellies and a wrenched wrist caused by almost falling from the rigging. With no one but the pleasant old relic for company he could forget the shortcomings of his other colleagues and concentrate on his own thoughts.

Cavendish will be getting up around now. Alfie wondered about the man's routine; did he sleep in his uniform in case of emergencies, or in a nightshirt? Did he mumble into his pillow and rise groggy, having to be revived by coffee, or was he one of those cheery souls who hummed an aria while they shaved?

Alfie wanted to know. He wanted to know if John Cavendish preferred Handel to Bach, if his parents were alive and whether they were close, if he had had a puppy as a child and if so, what it was called. Where he had been schooled, what made him laugh, which books to read to engage his mind, how he could bring back that furtive but unconscious smile, and broaden it.

"You look happy, Mr. Donwell." Mrs. Harper pushed away her plate to make room for a ghastly pickled thing in a glass jar, just as her husband dithered his way through the door and favored all three of them—the two humans and the tadpole-like creature with a human head that swam in its bottle between them—with a near blind but benevolent smile.

"I am," Alfie agreed. "I've put a right hard horse of a captain behind me, and I love the beginnings of things; when it's all to do, and you can believe this time... this time it's all going to work out fine."

"Ah," Harper gave him a dusty smile, "the optimism of youth."

"But sometimes it does go well, my dear." His wife rose to give him the brush of an age-worn kiss on his cheek, her hair white and shining as his powdered wig. "Sometimes it does."

Alfie's heart twisted, seeing what he wanted, so close and yet—for him—so seeming unattainable. A life-long love. Even if he could take advantage of Cavendish's innocence to seduce him, how likely was it still that the man would want *him* to grow old with?

Passing through the straits of Gibraltar into the heat of a Mediterranean summer, the *Meteor* left behind the fog and cloud where the North Atlantic current met the coast of Morocco. After a morning spent trimming the sails to catch every elusive breath of breeze, John leaned against the rail of his small quarterdeck and decided to allow the men to enjoy this last day of peace before Algiers. There would be tension enough tomorrow. For today, let them drift easily and gently east on the warm African current.

Over the past weeks, sailor-like, he had achieved a certain detachment from the future. Today's tasks demanded attention today, whether or not there would be a tomorrow. The period of grace thinned. It drew to a close. If he let himself, he could imagine the future as a reef and feel the breakers surge towards it. Yet even now there was nothing at all to be done to mend the situation. Over the past few nights he had studied his maps and pondered until sleep overset him, left him slumped over his plank desk, hair-ribbon in the ink. He knew the disposition of the harbor, the currents, reefs, rocks and even the color of the sea-bed in exhaustive detail. He had done all he could. Worrying would not achieve any more.

Setting aside the problem of Algiers until such time as he could act on it, he fetched a crowbar from his cabin and decided to check the provisions which Hall, the purser, had suspiciously condemned. How likely was it that all the beef brought aboard—

the beef that had weathered three months patrolling with little more than a change of color—should have become inedible overnight? More likely the man intended to sell it and line his own pocket as soon as they made port.

Meteor trotted through the seas like a well-bred horse. Even at this relaxed pace, with a following wind, she dug her head into spray with each wave. Beneath their lashed tarpaulins the mortars glistened like basking seals by her bow. In a cabin below decks someone played a flute. A thread of music wound its way up the stairs. So quiet at first, it could have been the *Meteor* herself given voice, echoing with breathy woodwind sweetness in the hollow spaces of her hold.

Resting his crowbar on his foot, John listened, enchanted, as the melody bundled together the sunshine and the spray, ran up into the sky with them and burst in a firework of notes. When the passage ended, John's cheeks ached with a smile. *Thank you*, he addressed the empty horizon, and the Spirit who rested between earth and sky, God and man, life and death. *Thank you for this moment; for the knowledge that you are here with me.*

He'd thought the piece ended, but now it came again; a rush of notes like a dryad shaking out the leaves from her hair. Even the impulse to pray deserted him in the desire to laugh aloud for joy. Only the knowledge that the men would think him insane restrained him from doing so. Instead he padded down on carefully silent feet onto the *Meteor*'s one gun deck, stalking the music.

Tables hung from the deck above on ropes, and with the off-duty watch drinking their grog, smoking their pipes, and telling tall tales, the long room had something of the look of a summer pub scene. Reflections from the sea dazzled through the open gun ports, through which fresh air also streamed, cutting through the usual reek of wet wool and unwashed sailor. The sound of the flute—louder now—trailed from aft, high and sweet—complex with a mathematical perfection that John's navigationally trained instincts sensed with delight. He continued his pursuit.

Donwell's door stood slightly open—it had to, for sitting on his sea-chest, he couldn't fit his outstretched legs into the tiny room otherwise—but his eyes were closed and he frowned with concentration as he played the rosewood flute. Charmed, John drifted closer until he could prop a shoulder against the frame of the door and settle into silent appreciation.

With a strong love of music, but raised in perfect ignorance on the subject, he could not think of anything intelligent to say. Nor would he have wished to interrupt the piece's transcendence with mere speech. But its rushes of notes, and the long, strong passages in between, resonated through him like the power of a full spread of sail. As always, his ignorance and the enchantment combined to open up a world of light beneath John's breastbone, to fill him with awe and incompleteness combined. A sweet torment; for if he was seeing angels dancing, he had not the wings to join in.

Donwell's wig lay crumpled on the mattress, beside a book, an old shirt and a half eaten ship's biscuit. Brilliant sunshine gave the whole scene the oil painting vividness of a Dutch masterpiece, outlining Donwell's hands, the turn of his throat, his messy flaxen hair as though they were numinous.

As everything paused on a high note, clear and perfect, John's delight escaped in a gasp of breath, and at the sound Donwell's eyes snapped open. With a convulsive heave backwards, he drew the flute to his chest as if to protect it, slamming his heels into the sea-chest and scrabbling to rise. "Oh! Oh, I'm…I'm sorry, sir, I didn't know you were there!"

"No need to apologize, Mr. Donwell." John smiled, not only the music making him radiant. It was pleasing to have the upper hand for a change; to wrong-foot his over-bold lieutenant. "Rather I should ask your pardon for disturbing you in the middle of a performance. I have a most untutored reaction to music. What was it, may I ask?"

"Surely you know Telemann, sir?" Donwell's sandy brows

arched with surprise as he straightened up, freeing space enough for John to walk in. In his new mood of confidence, John did so, and found it pleasant to revert to the comradely visiting he had done on board the Admiral's first rate. There, they had been in and out of one another's cabins all the time, borrowing books and stockings, taking a cup of coffee or a glass of wine with each other. It had been, indeed, a little too sociable for John's tastes, but now, after a fortnight of solitude, he thirsted for company.

"It is not possible to underestimate what I know about music." The canvas partition wall creaked beneath John's weight as he cautiously leaned against it. A small part of him quailed at opening the details of his family life to such a stranger, but Alfie's honest, good-humored amusement encouraged him. Whatever else he felt—this itch of over-awareness which made every conversation a little too intense—distrust was not part of it.

Indeed, the desire to put Donwell on the next ship to China weighed equally against the desire to tell him all and keep him close. If it puzzled John which instinct to trust, he thought he should probably choose the more humane. "My mother did not approve of it. 'Snare of the devil,' she said. It was not played in our house."

"Your mother did not approve of *music*?" Donwell had clearly been very startled indeed; his face only now began to change from boyish openness to the urbanity of an adult. In all the layers thus revealed, John was startled to see pity.

Instantly his temper flared. "Why should she? Is it not used to set the scene for debaucheries? Balls, where young people may lose their innocence. Theatre and opera and dancing that dazzle the senses and make the heart forget true morality? It would be a more steadfast, sober world without music."

In his zeal, John stepped forward. Donwell did not retreat, but stood there, apparently relaxed, his thumb moving gently over the curve of the flute. "And a poorer one."

Fists tightening almost against his will, physical fury swept through John, clear and glorious as the music. Breathing hard, he could almost feel the smack of his knuckles into Donwell's mouth, where a small, startled smirk turned in the end of the man's lips. Infuriating! *How dare he? How dare he laugh at me?* They stood so close he could feel the warmth of Donwell's thigh against his own.

Watching that little knowing smile light up Donwell's smoky amber eyes, John breathed in sharply and turned away, fighting down the urge to wrap his hands around the other man's neck and choke some reason into him.

What the…? Where had such violence come from? Shame flooding him, he stepped back, head bowed, appalled at himself. It wasn't even as though he didn't agree.

"Forgive me. 'And a poorer one, *sir*.'" Donwell too retreated, hopping up to sit on his cot, ceding John the two paces of floor and the sea-chest seat.

For a man who has given in, he looks altogether too triumphant, John thought, sitting down on the chest with trembling legs and a tender conscience. "You might be right." As his racing heart slowed, he attempted a reassuring smile. God alone knew what Donwell must think of him! He himself had no idea. "Though it shows a filial impiety in me to allow it."

John's mother disapproved of many things in which he himself could not see the harm. Had the music not—only a moment ago—made him feel closer to God? Prompted him to worship? How then could anyone say it was a snare? It disturbed and grieved him that she made her life more unhappy than it needed to be, but at times it was hard to avoid the thought. "I do sometimes fancy it is ungrateful—in our quest for purity—to disallow ourselves the things which were created to give us joy."

Alfie licked his lips. Cross legged, sheet music bundled in his lap to hide his inappropriate state of arousal, he tried to get his breathing under control. Just for a moment there, he'd thought…. Oh! How glorious to find that the captain's uncertainty covered such passion. Misdirected passion, true. But that could be remedied.

"I couldn't agree more," he said at last. "Would a good God have created an appetite within us and then forbidden us to satisfy it? Would he have given us no choice but to hunger and then demanded that we starve? I think not."

"My mother would say the appetite itself was debased." John looked up. The blaze had died from his eyes; they were now dark grey as his wig, from which all the powder had been blown by the morning's breeze. The right hand side-curl unraveled, strands hanging down to brush his jaw. "'Man does not live by bread alone, but by every word which proceeds from the mouth of the Lord.'"

Alfie tugged his shoes off and dropped them over the side of the bed. He wriggled his toes in luxurious freedom, digging them into the coarse wool of his blanket and smiling at the tickle. The cot bumped against the hull as his movement set it swinging, and he wrapped his hands around the supporting ropes to still it. From here he was looking down on Cavendish, which was also an amusing luxury. *What a man!* Nervy and sharp and on some deep emotional level just aware enough of what was going on to react against it with terror. A pox on it, but he'd set himself quite a task here! If he had any sense he should give up now. He really should.

"Perhaps," he said. "But then again man does not live by the word of God alone, but also by bread. She was very religious then, your mother?"

"Still is, as far as I'm aware." Now they were unable to touch one another, some of the tension in the room ebbed. John relaxed enough to lean back against the hull, and a softer side of him shone out as he looked up at Alfie with a wry smile.

"I didn't mean…I'm sorry," Alfie said, unused to thinking of parents in the present tense.

"She is a member of the Society of Friends," John admitted, unexpectedly, scratching his jaw. Taking off his wig, he looked with faint distaste at the state of it, winding the horse-hair around his finger before pushing it back into its curl "And believes in silence, sobriety, hard work and the scriptures."

A Quaker? Alfie looked down at the bent head and rueful smile, the chocolate-dark hair modestly, severely cropped. Oh, but that made a lot of sense—restraint, restraint and restraint, all their passion channeled into one stream, making their piety roar like a mill race. "Yet you plainly admit you love music yourself," he said. "Are you then terribly lapsed?"

The wig on his knee like a sleeping cat, John rested a hand on it. He scrunched his face together, pulling his generous mouth into a grimace that conveyed how difficult it was to explain. "My father," all the lines hardened for a moment, implacable, "is Church of England, naturally. And so in theory am I. In truth, however, I am some mixture peculiar to myself. If one can lapse from the most permissive church in the world, my father managed it. It isn't given to every son to be embarrassed by the ridiculous behavior of his parent."

Alfie put down the music gently, no longer needing its shield. He recognized the look on Cavendish's face—the steel and ice in those gray eyes. No pain in the world equaled that which your family could inflict. *I should say something, but what? What could I say that would not be trite? 'I understand'? But I don't. He is at least still in possession of parents.*

"Yet," John interrupted his musing with a sudden smile, "when he brought his whores and actresses to the house, and I was still a child, I would creep from my bed, downstairs, to listen to the music through the closed doors of the ballroom. And if I would be switched soundly for it in the morning, all that achieved was to give it a certain illicit thrill. I could not be stopped."

"I can picture it." Alfie smiled, seeing in his mind's eye the small form of a barefoot boy, draped in a white nightgown, like a stained glass saint, trapped between cheerless piety and cruel mirth. The thoughts conjured up as a result gave him a pang. "Should you like to sing?" he asked, feeling his way between the two extremes. "This is a *cantata.* I'm told it's very suitable, sacred music. I can't aver it positively, though—I don't understand a word."

John's eyes widened. He drew himself together, very prim and contained, but Alfie didn't miss the flickering glance at the stacked white pages on his cot. Picking up the top sheet, Alfie raised his head and sang the melody in his own inadequate bass, then held it out in offering. "It's a hard piece—it's not within anyone's range of course, because…."

Standing up, solemn as a choirboy, John breathed in and sang, and Alfie's apology stopped mid-sentence. For a moment he floated, born up like a petrel on a storm, for the captain's voice—untrained, unsure—rang out in perfect counter-tenor, plumb square within the middle of the range for which the piece had been written. An inhuman voice; all the sweetness of a woman's combined with the strength of a man's. If there truly was a music of the spheres, this perfect, sexless cadence was it; honey and swords, snow and summer, male and female alike reconciled into a sound more complex and beautiful than either. Speechless, Alfie fumbled for the flute, picked up the golden thread and wound about it his own more earthy notes. Bodiless for a moment, reduced to glorious sound.

Then John struck a flat note, coughed, and the world settled itself back into the mundane. "I cannot remember how it goes on."

Certain that the cabin should be glowing, the water-stained brown canvas walls and the grey wool blankets of his bed washed clean and covered with white seraphic feathers, Alfie gave a shaky laugh. "By God, you'd be a sensation in Italy, sir. The girls'd be running after you down the street, ripping into one another behind your back to be the first to demurely say 'good day' to you, clipping little pieces out of your coat for souvenirs, and offering to bear your children whether you would or no."

"I thank Providence I'm not in Italy, then," John laughed, raising a skeptical eyebrow. "But you exaggerate, Mr. Donwell. It is a weak, unmanly voice, unsuitable for an Englishman."

"I've never heard the like." Alfie's tact rose to the occasion; he did not mention that the counter-tenor voice was so prized on the continent that—being in nature so rare—men emasculated themselves to achieve it. He doubted the argument would have an encouraging effect. "May we practice the piece, though? Tomorrow, perhaps? If you have the taste you claim to have, you must have heard how incredible that was."

Sitting down again, John studied his hands, frowning. Wondering what moral scruple afflicted him now, Alfie was not prepared when, after a brief silent struggle, he looked up and said quietly, "I would be glad to know there would be a tomorrow. For us, at least."

"Sir?"

"The Admiral has sent us to find a way of dissuading the Dey of Algiers from engaging in the time-honored piracy he regards as a divine right of his nation. A piracy—preying upon the Infidel—he undoubtedly feels is his religious duty. We must put it to him that Britain wishes him to stop his sovereign activity on the sea. And we must represent this to him, while having under arms approximately eighty men, boys, and one old woman, and in the proud possession of one rather elderly bomb ketch."

Having been momentarily displaced, Alfie's stomach caught up with him, lurching into place as though he had just jumped a high wall on horseback. "Oh…best not to make plans then?"

"Indeed." But John's small smile had elements of amusement and even triumph. "There are some consolations in religion after all, Mr. Donwell. Whatever happens, I have no doubt it will all work out for the best."

◖◕ CHAPTER 3 ◕◗

The Casbah, Algiers

"You will come with us please." The Janissary officer was one of the most opulent things Alfie had seen in his life. He might have been inclined to laugh at the tall, white, wimple-like hat, and the sweep of scarlet robe with—God love him—an embroidered apron on top, had not the man's heavily bearded face been grave and proud and very obviously accustomed to command.

"I'm not at liberty to do so, sir," he said, putting down the bread he had been haggling over and drawing himself up, with unconscious respect, one soldier to another. "If the Dey has finally agreed to a meeting, then I am obliged to him. I will return to my ship and tell my commander at once."

He didn't like the way the troops surrounding the red-coated man eyed him. They too might have looked amusing in a painting, with their dome-like turbans and ballooning pantaloons, but Alfie had seen enough strange things in his life to recognize the look of a well-drilled and trained body of killers, no matter what they were wearing. With a nervous glance, he searched the market for his own men. Armitage had been buying sweets, his fingers sticky with rose-flavored jelly, his sullen eyes all the darker when Alfie called him to heel. Alfie didn't know if he should be furious or relieved to find the youth had disappeared again. Hopefully he would have the sense to lie low and avoid whatever trouble this looked like becoming.

Mr. Hall, the purser—trying to buy enough green-stuff to stave off scurvy for eighty hungry men—had also mysteriously melted from view. But Kelly, one of the tars he had brought with him to carry burdens, stood in the sharp shadow of the awning, with a peach in one hand, a plum in the other, plum juice down his chin and fingers, and a sudden worried look that must, Alfie thought, be the mirror of his own.

"You will come with us."

The soldiers closed in, not comical at all any more, their hands on their long, curving scimitars, their faces grim.

"My captain will gladly talk to the Dey or his representative," Alfie tried again, keeping his voice from rising into a squeak of panic with some effort. If half of what everyone "knew" about the Turks was true, then placidly going with them was the last thing he wanted to do. "He said as much a fortnight ago and you've done nothing but fob him off since. I do not have the authority to negotiate for him, and I am under orders to report back at once if the situation should change."

His answer was the nudge of a rifle in his back. "I also am under orders," said the officer, with a gleam of cold humor, "and your captain must be taught that the Dey has better things to do than to jump at the command of every British Lieutenant with nothing but a gunboat and his arrogance to his name. We can make this point peacefully, or with bloodshed. It is your choice."

Alfie licked his lips—his mouth suddenly dry as the desert sand on which he stood. Not for the first time he damned John's Admiral; the one who expected miracles and provided a pittance to achieve them with. This Janissary officer was right, Admiral fucking Saunders should have sent more than one little ketch to do this job. From the Dey's point of view it must look like an insult, and from his own it looked like suicide. "I'll come then," he said, even as two of the janissaries got him by the arms and made the agreement moot. "But you're making a mistake. You don't insult the British Navy and get away with it. If you don't treat with the captain of the *Meteor*, next time it'll be fourteen ships of the line and there won't be anything left of your city."

"We too are a proud maritime nation." Beneath the extravagant mustache the officer's smile twisted with anger. "We were a proud maritime nation when you British were painting yourselves blue and hunting heads like savages. Enough!" He gestured, and the guards' grips on Alfie's arms shifted to press tendon to bone. He swayed, knees almost buckling with the pain, and struggled long enough to lock gazes with the able seaman, who had dropped both fruit and stood with fists clenched.

"Kelly! Tell the captain!"

"Aye sir!"

As he fled, one of the janissaries raised his rifle and sighted.

"No, Abdy." The officer pressed the barrel down. "Let the infidel be our messenger. He can spare us the unpleasantness of further dealings with these dogs."

That told me, Alfie thought, filled with ridiculous, terrified laughter as they dragged him away. *You don't reason with dogs. But what do you do with them? What are they going to do with me?*

God, he hoped Cavendish would think of something, before he had to find out!

◖◗ CHAPTER 4 ◗◗

The Algerian ship—a long, sleek galley, her great banks of oars beating like a fish's fins—turned to cut across the *Meteor's* course. She maneuvered like a fish, John thought, nimble and fleet. *Or more like a shark.* Barely a hundred feet of sea separated him from his counterpart on the enemy deck. He could feel the mouths of a score of muskets trained on his face, see the pirate gun crews mustered about their cannons, standing ready, slow match smoldering in their hands. The Algerian captain made a gesture with his forearm that required no translation and the laughter of her crew floated over waves stained red with sunset.

"Fucking rag-head," Sergeant Richardson muttered with indignation beside John. "One mortar, sir. Just the one, that's all I'd need if we aimed it right."

Behind the galley he could see the *Meteor's* pinnace tacking for another attempt to slip past. Hall was just visible in the bow, clutching a writhing goat to his buff waistcoat, his powdered face whiter still with fear. A net full of chickens squawked at his feet among the baskets of oranges and green-stuff, eloquent of a successful reprovisioning trip now gone horribly wrong.

"They're playing with us." John ground his teeth with a little squeaking noise. "I am so tempted to do as you suggest, Sergeant. But if it's war they want, let them start it themselves. I'll not be goaded into ceding the moral high ground."

The wind veered. Kelly, in the pinnace, put her about in a flash and surged past the stern of the galley, the little craft heeling so that the boom almost trailed in the sea and water ran clear like varnish down her port gunwale.

"Stand by to haul those men aboard. Lively now!" cried John, watching the scramble on deck with a slow inward burn of annoyance. By the time the boatswain had whipped some order into the brawl of over-eager hands the pinnace lay alongside and the galley had turned about her centre, coming straight for them. Bleating and kicking on the end of a rope the goat swayed in mid air, and men hauled hand over hand to bring the pinnace aboard, Hall and the boat crew scrambling up the side like reckless monkeys. Closer now, oars beat against the water as the beakhead of the galley drove like a spear at the *Meteor*'s head.

"All aboard!" Armitage shrieked.

"Go about!"

Turning away from the harbor, John put the *Meteor* before the wind, spreading all the sails she would carry. For ten long, humiliating minutes, the galley kept pace, but then even her seasoned oarsmen began to flag. The ketch—still gathering speed—pulled away. *Running away*, John thought sourly, out into the safety of the open sea. Not a shot had been fired, but it was plain from the crew's ugly faces and bitter whispers that they too felt the sting of defeat.

Wondering if he could call honor satisfied now, head to the rendezvous at the naval base in Gibraltar and report to Saunders that he had tried—and failed—John looked down into the waist of the ship. The goat *baa*-ed at him indignantly then made herself universally beloved by butting the boatswain. Hall brushed himself down with a sniff of distaste, while Armitage put his hand in his pocket and quickly pulled it out again, sticky pink jelly coating his fingers.

"Where is…?" asked John in sudden panic, checking again, just as Kelly ran up the quarter-deck ladder and strangled his woolen hat between his hands.

"Oh, sir! They've taken Mr. Donwell, sir."

"You ain't gonna leave him there." Higgins brought in a ridiculously elegant tea tray complete with green and gold trimmed white pot, water jug, milk jug, sugar basin, tongs, Sevres porcelain cup delicate as sea foam, and a pewter spoon that John remembered seeing last in the doctor's jar of leeches. Despite the fact that livery would make him look like a performing ape, Higgins fancied himself as a footman and had made up for John's poverty by persuading various members of the wardroom to donate their treasures for the captain's use.

"I am not." John took a cup of tea, poured in milk and sniffed. "The goat's settled then?"

"She's champion. Two pints this evening and she ate the ribbons off Jack Nastyface's trousers, the darling. The boys are saying we're gonna sail back in tonight and flatten the bloody Casbah."

"The 'boys' have not taken the trouble to consult me," John replied mildly.

"Ah well, they did ask me to come up and see how the land lies. We're none of us too pleased at being shown the finger by the likes of them Barbary pirates."

John looked down at the map he had spent all evening drawing. Jotting down a line of figures, he did the calculation in his head then marked the final arc of fire on the paper. He felt…blank, empty. "Why do they do it, do you suppose?"

With the lines and angles of fire of each of the harbor's batteries plotted, John dipped his pen again and marked a tiny cross in the centre where all the arcs of fire just failed to intersect.

"Beg pardon, sir?"

"Why force a confrontation when we might have talked? For that matter, why steal slaves from Britain, when the African nations are all too willing to sell them? Does he expect us to swallow this insult and simply leave? Or can he really think I'm going to come crawling to him, begging for the return of my man?"

Higgins did his best to look deep for a moment, then turned away to pick John's folded coat from the back of the chair and stow it in a newly repaired stern locker.

"I think not," John answered himself, straightening up. "Bring me the Greek brothers, Dion and Cosmo Macronides. Also Duman Naftali and the other Duman—the one with the eye patch. Black Jacob too, if he thinks he'd be safe. Anyone who can pass as not being British.

"Aye sir."

The great cabin filled with nervous tars. Acrid with fear, their reek seemed to touch the walls. Crowding together in the center of the room, they looked at John with painfully false innocence, obviously wondering what they had done wrong.

"Men," he began, standing up too, in an effort to put them at ease. "I understand your desire to make the Dey regret he ever chose to treat with us thus. But if we sail into the harbor now and set it alight, the result will be death for Mr. Donwell. First things first. We will get him back, and *then* we will make them pay.

"You will be landed just to the East of Cape Matafou. From there—passing as Turks—you should proceed on foot into the city, where you will make every effort to discover the where-abouts of the Lieutenant. I imagine—after that debacle this morning—it is a popular source of conversation in the market-place.

"The *Meteor* will stand in to shore every night. Once you have him, or know where he is to be found, return to the cove where we set you down and signal with a lantern. The pinnace will pick you up. Any questions?"

Dion, a young man who tried to hide his startling beauty beneath an aggressive beard, looked up with cunning eyes. "We will need money for bribes."

"I understand," said John, a slow thud of heartbeat breaking through his white calm. Nausea swept over him unexpectedly and his skin prickled with cold sweat. "You may draw upon Mr. Hall for five hundred pounds. If he objects, send him to me."

"Aye, aye, sir."

Ten days… John's nib spattered blots over his diary as his hand shook. He frowned at it, rolling his shoulders to try and unwind the sinews that kept him on edge—tight as an ill-tuned violin just before its neck breaks.

> *And no signal. It was a fight just to get the mission underway: Hall assured me the seamen would just take the money, spend it on liquor and whores, and then desert. Such a greasy fellow! Were he to swim in the slush he could not be more slippery. I represented to him that I could have him discharged for corruption, and he released the money with no more protest. It troubles my conscience to thus blackmail him, but I conceive it to be necessary under the circumstances.*

The same tea-pot stood on the table, the same water jug next to it, John's reflection looking strained and wild in its side. The same sunlight lay in the same arc across the newly painted oil-cloth of the floor. Ten days of standing out to sea in the day, gently, cautiously sliding in to shore at night. The shadow of the headland falling over them as they worked the sails by starlight, commands whispered, footsteps dulled, until they felt like the ghost of a ship, eternally imprisoned by an impossible vow.

> *"Money thrown away upon untrustworthy tars and foreigners," Hall called it, and though I thought him meanly pinched at the time, I must begin to ask myself if he was right. To prevent the Devil from making work for idle hands, I have*

> *exercised both watches on sail drills until they*
> *are almost fit to serve aboard a First Rate Man of*
> *War. Both sides can now run out, fire, and reload*
> *their guns in under two minutes. But the crew re-*
> *sents the delay, the sight of land on which they*
> *may not set foot, and above all the many Barbary*
> *ships we could have taken as prizes, but had to*
> *let slip so that the Dey would not be alerted to*
> *the fact that we were still here. I do not think the*
> *men's temper will bear much more waiting. Yet*
> *then what? Do I return to the harbor and risk us*
> *all meeting the same fate? Or can I....*

He told himself that his emotion was quite disproportionate to the loss of a single officer; that he should pass over it with the sang-froid of Saunders waving aside McIntyre's death. The echo of remembered flute music would not leave him, though he stuffed his fingers in his ears to try and keep it out.

> *Or can I leave him here and sail away? The*
> *thought oppresses me with far greater power than*
> *it should. I cannot reconcile myself to it, and I do*
> *not know why not.*

"A light, sir!"

Turning his own glass on the spot John could see it, a strange yellow star fallen on the edge of the sea. It dimmed, went out, and returned, twice. *Thank God! Oh thank you, God!* "Man the pinnace! Kelley, Higgins, with me. Armitage, the ship is yours until I return."

A shallow, murmuring swell carried the little boat to ground over coarse sand. Dion ran out to catch the thrown rope, his big grin rivaling the moon for brightness.

"He is found," the man panted. "Many Greeks in the Janis-saries. *Paidomazoma*—taken as tax by the child gatherers...They are not all traitors. But it takes slowly, slowly to find out…to arrange to make work. We go now! We have brought clothes."

The scarf around John's face chafed as his breath came fast, dampening it. As they strode out on the long walk into Algiers he could see very little through the long wound cloth and hood that concealed him. Glimpses of white buildings glimmering under moonlight, lattices and mellow windows whose panes were the shape of tiny stars. Colored lanterns lit tea-shops where men lounged, smoking their hookahs and playing trictrac, laughing. They seemed convivial as they might be in any coffee-house in England, though less drunk than the English.

Young boys, sitting among the men, fluttered their long eyelashes at Dion as he passed, making him laugh and wink back. John, trying not to trip over his flowing robe, while the hand on his sword hilt slipped with sweat, almost wished they would be challenged, so that he could fight someone, anyone, to take the edge off his anxiety

Down into the marketplace they went. A shadow beneath an archway moved, became an emaciated creature in a wrapped ochre garment made for someone thrice his size. His waxed, pointed beard and the jaunty red fez that sat atop his turban gave the impression of a man either intent on rising from his natural place, or in the process of falling from it. His right hand fingered the pistol thrust through his sash, and keys dangled on a ring from his left. "Nesim."

There was a brief exchange of what sounded like pleasantries even to John's ear, unfamiliar with whatever dialect of Arabic or Ottoman Turkish was spoken here. Then Nesim unlocked the door behind him and lead them into the slave pens. Walking silently past the bound and wretched forms of his countrymen—and worse, his countrywomen—their eyes raking narrow trails across his skin, imploring him for help, John half drew the sword twice before prudence drove it back each time. Horror started as a prickle on his lips and a weight on his limbs, drove inwards with every breath of the rank hot air, until it squeezed his heart like the dark pressure at the abyssal depths of the sea.

"Nesim is in debt," Dion whispered, falling back for a moment to walk beside John. "They will chop off feet of him, if he does not pay."

Pressing the hated headdress against his nose, John nodded. The huge pens stank. Within them, prisoners lay crammed together in their own ordure, sharing their misery and whatever comfort they might give one another. That was horrible enough, but then John noticed the edges of the pens were ringed with tiny cisterns in the shape of ovens. "The bad slaves, they go in there," Dion explained. "No room. Very hot."

Cursed with a vivid imagination, John could almost feel it himself: the claustrophobia, the itching insanity of being unable to sit or stand, not even to move an inch; encased in a clay oven with the African sun crushing down like a tide of molten lava.

From one of these cells a hand and arm had been thrust out into the comparatively cooler air of the main pit. With a wheedling speech in a tone that mixed servility with arrogance, Nesim smacked his stick down on top of a collection of other bruises visible on the pale arm. Dion said something in reply, and grudgingly the man unlocked and pulled the bars away, allowing them to lever out the semi-conscious form of Alfie Donwell.

Stripped of most of his clothes, the thin shirt did not conceal the all encompassing burns. His face was so swollen from heat and thirst, so black with bruises that he could not open his eyes. When John stepped in and tried to get an arm over his shoulder, pull him upright, Donwell buckled in pain, whining like a kicked dog. Looking down, John saw that his beaten feet were leaving prints of blood on the sand.

Nesim protested, violently slashing both Donwell and John himself with the cane. Turning to shield his lieutenant, John caught Higgins' eye. As Nesim's attention flickered between John and Dion, Higgins moved with cat-footed stealth behind the jailer's back. "He say he did not know we meant this one," Dion translated, his lip curling at the obvious lie. "He say he have some pretty young boy, just for you. Sweet like apricots. But for this one three hundred is not enough. He wants one thousand."

As Donwell leaned limply on him, John could feel the heaving breaths through his own ribs. The man's burned skin was feverish against his own. He could feel too the thinness of the wrist he held, the skeletal lightness of the chest beneath his other arm. Donwell's hair and ten day growth of beard stood out in heavy spikes, stiff with blood. John's heart smoldered in his chest like one of the ovens, but the smoke of fury mingled with a perverse pride. *They couldn't tame you, could they? I thought as much.* "Higgins," he said.

As Higgins' pistol nudged him in the back, Nesim stiffened comically. "Explain his position to him, if you please," John said. "I believe he has misunderstood my terms."

In the end it was far easier than John had feared. Clasping Nesim in a brotherly embrace that kept the concealed pistol pressed meaningfully into his spine, Higgins' dumb eloquence proved persuasive.

"Out through the graveyard, I think," John instructed, lifting the long robe from Naftali's shoulders and wrapping it around Donwell to conceal him. "There, he looks like just another dead slave. Nothing to worry about. Kelly, Naftali, you carry him. Dion, scout ahead. If the pistol in his back is not argument enough, I will also cover Nesim. Please tell him that if he opens his mouth, even to breathe, I will shoot."

Donwell made a terribly convincing corpse as they walked out of the pens as unchallenged as they had entered. Tension crushed John's back and shoulders as he waited for an outcry that did not come. A smell of cinnamon and sweat drifted from Nesim, whose cheek glimmered wet in the moonlight.

The tension wound to a pitch as they passed the pit where the city's dogs dug and fought over bones. Sordid little monuments topped with spat out date stones loomed, crumbling, in the night, and still silence followed them. As they crossed to the parks and silent, cube-like mausoleums of the well-to-do, shadows moved as vagrants laying in the well-tended doorways scrambled out of their way. Despite the lack of pursuit, fear, primeval and irrational, made John's spine tingle cold in the sweltering night.

The locked gate of the city wall yielded to a crowbar. He shut it behind them with sweaty hands and led the rescue party on its long, burdened walk back to the cove, the threat of discovery padding behind like a hunting lion.

They left Nesim on the beach, fingering a small bag of gold and looking like a man who feels a change of career coming on. Then, dawn rising on their left, they sailed out for two hours, until—half way to Tizi Ouzou, it seemed—a glass showed the off-white triangles of the *Meteor*'s sails coming to meet them.

Sunrise's bright citrine light danced on the water. Armitage's face, for once open as he reveled in being left in charge, looked over as they hailed.

"A rope here!" shouted John, making it fast under Donwell's arms to pull him on board. As he did so, Donwell stirred, leaning into him, gingerly settling his swollen face on John's shoulder.

"Captain?" His small whisper, dry and cracked as picked bone, plucked at John's heart.

"You're safe now, Lieutenant." A wave of pity and strange tenderness washed over him. Then he stirred himself, made the rope fast with a hitch, and signaled for the crew on deck to pull the man on board. By the time he had run up the side himself, they had lowered Donwell down into the main hatch, and all he saw was the lace on Mrs. Harper's bonnet, white as the spray, disappearing after him.

John straightened up, looked at the grim faces that surrounded him, and grinned. The expression spread, until finally the ship's crew put him in mind of a pool of piranhas gently holding station as they watched the descent of an unwary foot.

"We will bend on the red sails," he said. "And then you may clear for action."

By the following night all was ready. At the rim of the world the sinking moon extinguished itself in the sea, and in the starlight the

Meteor's black painted hull and ochre sails were all but invisible. Brass guns lurked without a gleam under a fresh coat of brown paint. The mortars, uncovered, squatted like gargoyles peering over her prow, their great black mouths gaping. Standing next to them, the men of the Ordnance Corps deigned to smile, gloating over their bombs.

Only the bow wave caught the occasional glimmer, dimly shimmering as the *Meteor* forged her silent way into the vast bowl of the harbor of Algiers.

Map in one hand, the other on the compass binnacle, John whispered his instructions to the helm. Ship's boys raced on soundless bare feet to relay commands to the captains of the main and mizzen masts.

"Prepare to heave to. Helm a lee. Back the main sail. Boat crews, row out the spring anchors."

Groaning, the braces of the masts so tight a little rain of dew squeezed out of them, the *Meteor* slowed, turned up into the wind and stopped, holding her position, balanced between the backward push of her backed mainsail and the forward thrust of the other sails. Like a dancer balanced and still on the tip of one foot, it was a poised, precarious stillness ready to swing back into motion at any moment.

First to one side, then the other, the boat crews slid the spring anchors gently into the water. John felt them take—the deck beneath his feet shuddered slightly then firmed, losing its easy responsiveness to the waves. Fixed now on the one point in the harbor where, in theory, the cannons of the shore batteries could not reach, the *Meteor* waited.

Theory is a fine thing, John thought, surveying the vessels at rest within range, *now to put it to the test*. He slid his spyglass closed with a metallic rasp like the sound of a sword being drawn. The heels of his shoes rapped like pistol shots in the silence as he walked the length of the deck to the mortars.

"Sir?" said Sergeant Richardson, a dark bulk quivering with keenness beside his beloved weaponry.

"The galleys must go first. After that anything fast enough to follow us. We only have a few moments. Make them count."

"Aye, aye sir!"

Richardson directed his crew with a low muttering. The bomb clanked against the mortar, and the dull thud of the rammer sounded apologetic, as if it cleared its throat in church. The slow-match glinted like a mad red eye. Richardson sighted along the barrel. "Winch her two points to leeward."

The capstan rumbled. Winched towards one anchor, away from the other, the whole ship turned—there being no other way to aim the weapon—and "Fire!" bellowed Richardson, full throated, even as the slow match descended on the touch-hole. A moment's fizzling, a hollow *whoom!* deep enough to steal the breath from John's lungs, make all the bones in his body tremble, and with a shattering roar the first bomb exploded among the moored galleys. The second mortar roared and spat as the first team wormed and sponged; raking out and quenching any smoldering wadding that might remain to set off the next charge too early.

Lights kindled on every vessel lining the shoreline. John could almost hear the running feet and shouting in the fort, and then the shore batteries erupted in red tongues of flame and twelve-pound shot pocked the dark water an inch before the windward side. Satisfaction gleamed as pretty as gold in John's heart as he realized his calculation had been true. The shore batteries could not quite reach the *Meteor* here. He had perhaps five minutes before the ships at anchor could man their guns and become a threat. But he could do a great deal of damage in five minutes. Roaring splendid destruction saw galleys bursting into tumbling jigsaws of pieces, drifting away from their snapped cables to tangle with each other, furled sails on fire.

Wounded xebecs tried to bring their guns to bear on the *Meteor* only to find themselves hulled by the fire of their own fort. Masts tumbled, and the water reflected flame. Richardson whistled as he worked, and the men at the capstans cheered each shot when it went home. As they swung back to bombard the vessels on the other side of the harbor, a ball from the shore knocked the head and ample bosom off *Meteor*'s figurehead, the impact making John lurch to the rail. Before him the harbor of Algiers lay crammed with sinking, burning hulks of pirate ships. The shore seethed black with men scrambling into rowing boats. Caught up in the action, he laughed for joy before seeing from the corner of his eye the first of the moored ships slip its anchor and begin to work its way upwind towards them.

"Loose the anchors!" cried John, hacking through the windward cable with an axe, "Make sail!"

Freed from the anchors, the main topsail put before the wind, *Meteor* whispered forward once more. As soon as she answered to her helm, John put her about. Setting every scrap of canvas she carried, racing through a hail of hot iron as they left the sheltered spot and dashed for the harbor mouth, they fled for their lives, grinning.

ᨕᨙ CHAPTER 5 ᨙᨓ

"How is he?"

True to his orders, Richardson's barrage had spared only those ships which could not keep up with the *Meteor*. But it was a near thing; the chase had gone on for three days. When—on the morning of the fourth—the lookout reported no sail in sight, John celebrated by shaving carefully, putting on a new uniform, and going to visit Lieutenant Donwell.

By dint of moving the canvas panel of the wall to include cannon number seven–Roaring Jack–Alfie's cabin had been enlarged. Under doctor's orders, the gunport stood open to let fresh air into the cabin, revealing dawn's light just turning from pink to pale, and smooth, green seas, their rounded backs swelling and creaming into foam down the *Meteor*'s sides. The cabin smelled of sunlight and fresh paint. Reflections from the water swept rhythmically about the walls.

By contrast to all this glory, Donwell himself looked terrible; a shape mummified in bandages and curled protectively into the furthest corner of the room. Mute, white and bloodstained, he watched Dr. Harper with wary eyes, tracking every movement.

"Well enough to speak for himself, I think." Harper picked up his bag and packed away a variety of blue glass bottles, radiant as sapphires in this light. He looked about vainly for his glasses, which perched on top of the cannon, one arm shoved into the touch-hole. Taking them from John's offering hand he tried to put them into a pocket, scraping them against the hideous screw end of a trepanning iron which poked out, cutting edge up, from the flap.

Once he had collected all the doctor's items together and ushered the man out, John felt quite exhausted and doddery himself. He sat gratefully on the gun-carriage and hoped the light and silence would calm his almost physical anguish of pity.

Donwell sighed, uncurled a little, hesitant, as though he feared to offend. "There's...pills," he whispered. "Here under the...He can't read his own writing."

Getting up, John felt under the board and thin mattress of the cot. He fished out a double handful of pills and a dust of herbs and simples where more had been crushed. Shaking his head in exasperation over the wasted medicine, he put it out of the gun-port nevertheless. Doctor Harper was a good man, no doubt about it, but—too old and absent minded to be relied upon—he had already been known to mistake arsenic for antimony with unfortunate results. It might be the captain's job to ensure his people took physic when needed, whether they wanted to or not, but in this case he felt he might make an exception.

"I ought to rebuke you, lieutenant, except that I should have done the same myself. How are you?"

"I could get back on duty, sir, if you'd give me a couple of fellows to lift me up and down to the deck. Let me serve in a chair. I know you've needed... ."

Donwell's spurt of energy ran out mid sentence. Closing his eyes, he leaned his head back against the wall and seemed about to fall asleep, jerking awake with a frantic, frightened look just before John thought of tiptoeing away.

"I won't say we haven't needed you." John took the excuse to come closer, so that he could examine Donwell's face—now a patchwork of green and purple bruises, red, angry burns, and cuts that had healed into black scabs. It was at least no longer swollen; he could see the lineaments of the man he knew there once more. And the voice, though weak, had regained some of its harmony—like an oboe whose shattered reed still draws at least one or two notes. "But we have managed, Mr. Donwell. You are not yet completely indispensable."

Donwell flinched and looked away. Though the cabin was full of cool light, his eyes retained the fetid darkness of the slave pits. "I learned that, sir. I learned it very well."

"You misunderstand me!" It occurred to John that he didn't know the man at all; that a few charged encounters, a moment of sublimity shared, did not amount to very much. "You are not indispensable—quite the opposite. We went to great trouble to get you back as we knew that leaving your troublesome person among the Turks would constitute an act of aggression far more grievous than bombing their fleet."

Obligingly, Donwell raised the ends of his mouth at this witticism. It could hardly have been called a smile, though he made the effort. "They tamed me soon enough."

In the silence that followed, John felt the weight of each word, the weight of Donwell's casual brokenness, turn the sparkling air into a mockery. He recalled the horror of the pens and tried not to think about what it would be like to be so reduced to worthlessness. Instinctively, he reached out and took hold of the lieutenant's least maimed hand, the touch startling Donwell to look back up.

Their eyes met and John saw terror—fear of all mankind, fear of living in such a world—before Donwell again closed his eyes and turned away, hiding.

"I…" John attacked the terrible void with words, lest it should overwhelm him too. "I…How about some music, Mr. Donwell? We have that cantata to finish, do we not?"

At the change of tactics, Donwell's face smoothed. He raised his hands to his head, the pads of his fingers raw where the fingernails had been torn out, and unwound the bandage which sat like a fashionable lady's turban on his scalp. John thought to protest, but stifled it, not wanting to provoke bad memories with unnecessary orders. Donwell looked more human with his corn-silk hair curling about his face. When he opened his eyes, John was pleased to see a hint of humor had dared to venture back; frail but promising, like the seedling of an oak.

"Still hunting those illicit thrills, sir? I'll see what I can manage."

Every step rolled his foot over broken glass, sliced into his heel, speared through his instep, sawed through the abused, tender lit-tle bones of his toes, trapping them against the unyielding leather of his shoes and ending with a pain as eye-watering as a mouthful of lemon. Every step, the same progression of injuries repeated. With every step came the same reminder of being held down, the canes, the struggling, the cursing, and the wild belief that this could not happen. Not to him. Every step was a reminder of humiliation. By the time he walked from his cabin to the wardroom, his spirit, as raw as his feet, flayed and tender, could barely support another breath.

Alfie fell into his seat, gasping as if he'd run from Marathon to Athens. His hands trembled on the table so hard they made a staccato drumbeat, and he felt the eyes of all the company on him. Sympathy and resentment were equally unbearable. Tuck-ing his hands into his armpits to still them, he raised his head, surprised and pleased to know there was still some defiance left in him.

"Christ! They made a mess of you," said Hall with satisfac-tion, reaching up to fiddle with the paper securing the lefthand curl of his carefully dressed hair. When Alfie didn't answer, Hall took up his fork again and speared a lump of boiled salt horse, nibbling on it with fastidious distaste. "Wouldn't lie down and take it, eh? Can't say I blame you. We've all heard what those heathens like to do with a fresh piece of Christian arse...." He smiled. "But then you'd know more about that than we would, eh? Surprised you can sit down."

The Master laughed. Down at the end of the table, Armitage

gave a shocked, delighted titter. Rage rose up from the brutal-
ized soles of Alfie's feet through every aching, shamed particle
of his body in a tide of burning pitch.

Anger was better than laudanum for making him forget the
pain, for re-knitting bone and sinew. He had risen and crossed
the room before he even felt the fireworks of agony through his
blood. The sudden panic in Hall's eyes as he grabbed the forni-
cating cunt by his foppish hair and slammed his face into the
table was more of a balm for all those days of fear than any of
Harper's pills. Shouting, Hall tried to stab him with the silver-
ware. Armitage yelled something behind him while the Master
laughed until he sent himself into a coughing fit.

Alfie grabbed Hall's knife hand and ground it beneath his full
weight, forcing the fingers to open or to break. Knocking the
knife away, he sent Hall's chair after it, kicking it from underneath him. As the purser dangled from his hair, shrieking as the
roots began to part in weeping clumps, marines came running
through the wardroom door, rifles in their hands. Alfie lifted
Hall's head up, smashed it into the table again and let him slide
ignominiously to the floor. Only then did his own knees buckle
and the swinging lanterns blur in his sight to floating clouds.
Pride got him to a chair, where he could collapse, shaking like an
opium addict in the throes of withdrawal, the cold black mouth
of a marine rifle pressed to his temple.

Just possibly, he thought, he had got himself into very deep
trouble, but he didn't give a damn. *That felt so much better.*

John poured himself a glass of brandy and drank it down straight,
watching the wake stretch out behind the ship, straight and seemly;
a triumph of order against the chaos of the natural world. A foot
dangled into his vision, and he recalled with annoyance that he had
ordered the ship repainted. Fleeing from the Corsairs had taken
them out into the Gulf of Sirte, where they were now making a
wide circle in preparation for sailing back to Gibraltar.

By now the Dey would have repaired what could be repaired.

Nor could it be assumed that all his fleet had been in the harbor to be destroyed. Undoubtedly his greater ships already patrolled the Sicilian Channel with a detailed description of the *Meteor* and a burning desire for vengeance. So John had given orders to change the *Meteor's* color-scheme. Instead of black with a faint red stripe, she gloried in a spring-like green, with port-lids like squares of pressed daffodils against her verdant sides.

The mortars he had ordered unbolted from the deck and brought below, since every last bomb had been fired. The rigging of the main mast he'd overhauled entirely, giving her a square main sail. With the addition of a new name painted on the stern they no longer looked like the bomb ketch *Meteor*, but like an entirely different class of vessel—the innocent brigantine *Aetna*, sweeping for small pickings off the shores of Sicily.

Although he nodded with satisfaction at the evidence of industry, the last thing he wanted was for some inquisitive tar to lower himself down and watch this interview through the windows. *Gossip all over the ship!* The strains of so small a community magnified any dissension out of all proportion. Hall's unpopularity with the crew meant the rebuke he *had to* administer to Donwell would be all the more resented by the people. He could just imagine the factions forming, the ill words and blows, as the ship's company that had so recently and so splendidly come together fell apart as men lined up behind captain or lieutenant, taking sides.

Putting the brandy glass carefully down, wedged between the logbook and a roll of charts, he closed the shutters over the diamond panes of the stern lights, shutting out Mediterranean sun and bright water. *Let them see through planks of wood!*

Yet his conscience quailed a little at the result, for the cabin seemed smaller, softer, more intimate in the smoky amber light that remained, still air filling with the smell of beeswax candles. When the expected knock came at the door he pulled at his neck-cloth nervously, feeling stifled. "Come!"

The door opened and at once Donwell's presence filled the

dim light. Beams of sunlight, finding their way around the edges of the shutters, striped his healed face and blazed from the bayonets and the silver buttons of the marines on either side of him.

Feeling his own pulse thud hollow and heavy in his throat, John recalled the patient hours they had spent together while Alfie recovered. Music, some idle talk and some mere sitting, watching one another, as if they expected a revelation which never came. He remembered how easily he fell into the habit of reading aloud from whatever book was to hand, while they both made wry comments about the story, more amused by each other than by the author. *Did you have to make me become the tyrant?* thought John with resentment. *Why will you keep on pushing beyond what I can well ignore?*

"I don't think that will be necessary," he said to the marines, as they took up stations by the door. "You may go."

"But sir—"

Lifting his chin a little, he allowed some of his outrage to show. Did they dare question him? Did they think he could not defend himself from an invalid and a friend? "You may *go*, Sergeant O'Halloran."

"Yes, sir."

"And if you catch anyone listening, including yourselves, you are to take their names for punishment."

"Yes, sir."

The door closed behind O'Halloran with a firmness which made the flimsy wall shake. John breathed in and felt the muscles of his belly tremble. He had become quite used to the godlike position he now occupied, with all men jumping at his slightest command, but into that serene universe Donwell fitted like a blade into a bubble.

Stillness came over the cabin. Donwell stood as parade-ground straight as one of the marines, his hands clasped behind his back. The ship creaked, her planks working in the slow swells, her rigging humming with a low, pipe-organ note that

John felt in his feet and his breathless chest. It might have been years that he stood in the shared silence, watching his lieutenant's face; fascinated and perplexed.

"How long have you been in the Service, Mr. Donwell?" he said at last in a quiet tone suited for the atmosphere of smoky tranquility.

"Since I was thirteen, sir. That'd be a little under eleven years."

"You should know, then, that an officer does not brawl like a tar. You're fortunate he is not your superior, or you might even now be hanging for mutiny. What can possibly have come over you to establish such a precedent on my ship?"

Donwell breathed in, and from the sound of it John could hear the shake no longer concealed by his layers of coats, his firmly clasped hands. "You know what he said to me, don't you, sir?"

"I do not. I do know, however, that half of the money we had to pay to get you back came out of Mr. Hall's own pocket. I won't deny a certain amount of pressure was required to make him disgorge it, but still.... Your bizarre eccentricities towards me I can just about tolerate, but *this*? Damn it, man! What were you thinking?"

"He insulted me in a manner no man of spirit could abide," said Donwell, swaying a little. The sulky look made his face seem boyish; a child chided for not paying attention in lessons, and John bit down on the sudden desire to slap him across the downturned mouth and tell him to buck up his ideas.

"What did he say?"

"If it please you, I'd rather not repeat it."

"It does *not* please me, Mr. Donwell. *You* do not please me. Frankly I'm considering having you court-martialed for insubordination. Are you listening to me?"

Donwell looked up. His shoulders tightened and his mouth thinned; he caught John's gaze with eyes that in the dusk of the cabin looked tawny as a lion's. "Hall alluded to the use they made of me in Algiers," he said, brittle as a rain of glass. "He made certain implications...."

"Oh?" said John, not understanding at first, and then *"Oh!"* as the realization dawned and fear and shameful excitement swept across his body in a tide of hot blood. He looked away. "Oh. In that case I regard it in the light of inevitable consequences. If you wish to call him out, I offer my services to act as your second when we reach land. In the meantime, however, the minimum inevitable consequence of your brawling on board will be that you will have your grog ration stopped. If you will act as though you crawled up through the hawse hole, Mr. Donwell, you will be treated accordingly. I expected better from you. Do you understand me?"

"I do, sir," Donwell bowed, hiding his angry eyes, and yet managed to make even this sound ominously suggestive. "Thank you, sir."

A pain stabbed like a needle into John's cheek as he realized he was grinding his teeth again. "That will be all." He turned his back, the gesture less convincing when he faced a blank wall of shutters rather than the majesty of the sea. "Dismissed."

By nightfall they had turned back towards Gibraltar, sailing into the straits normally patrolled by the Dey's rapacious fleet. *Sailing back towards the slave markets and the pens....* When John crawled into the warm salt damp of his sheets he fell asleep with his imagination full of chains.

He dreamed red dreams. Frustrated fury flowed through his limbs, making him snarl into his pillow, thinking of Donwell's mocking smirk and hot temper; dreaming of the smack of his fists into that smile. *He could feel the breath on his fingers, the mouth splitting like fruit, and in his dream he lunged forward, caught the little wound between his teeth and bit. Blood on his tongue, hard hands grappling him, tearing his clothes, the buck and press of that big body crushing him into the wall, and he could half feel the pain of the cane on his own belly as he dug his nails into Donwell's open wound....*

Biting, blood in his mouth, hair tangled between his clutching fingers, he fought to teach the cocky bastard who was in charge here, teach him a lesson he would not soon forget, a lesson marked into his flesh like the mark of the lash. He'd chain the bastard down if he could, spread him across the desk, cane him like a midshipman with the stick on his bare arse, breeches round his feet, see if he'd be so very...insubordinate then.

But in his imagination Alfie was smiling—still smiling that sphinx-like secret smile. John hit harder, his arm aching, close to tears with fury and frustration, but could not wipe the smile away; he needed more, needed to get closer, stronger, needed more....

He woke, heart pounding and skin itchy with anger, grinding against the hard board of the mattress. *So close...so close, damn it!* His hand closed over his shaft, rough, half asleep, and for a moment he dreamed it was a bigger hand, burnt, the fingernails missing. He came in a rush like the gout of blood from a cut throat, lay half awake, panting. The dream came apart as he tried to recall it, fading into nebulous wisps of yearning and denial. By the time he fell back into sleep he could not remember it at all.

◖⟡ CHAPTER 6 ⟡◗

"Sail two points off the port bow!" the lookout shouted just as they rounded the cape of Bon, the sun coming up behind them, throwing their shadow before them onto the grey sea. "She's a big xebec, sir, under a full spread."

Alfie cursed the sudden weakness that dissolved his bones within him and hauled himself laboriously up to the main top, aware that everyone on deck was watching him for signs of fear. Once there, he took his own glass and focused it where the boy indicated. He could see only mist for a moment, peach and pink, curling into the sky in the level beams of the rising sun. Shaking the dew from his coat, he rubbed the glass, tried again and saw it; a brighter white smudge against the cloud. Something coming out from Tunis, with the lean, triangular profile of a xebec; the Barbary corsair's warship of choice. With her narrow hull, built for speed, and her oars which allowed her to beat directly into the wind, she was by far the handier ship. *And to be seen at this distance her size must be....* His heart seemed to freeze into a lead ball and choke him—she must carry at least three hundred men to the *Meteor*'s eighty.

"Set boommainsail and trysail!" he shouted, thoughtlessly grabbing the backstay of the mast and sliding down it, arriving on deck with his newly healed hands torn open once more. "Put her before the wind. Kelly, rouse the captain!"

"No need." Cavendish was on deck, in his nightshirt, barefoot, with his steward trailing behind him indignantly carrying slippers and a banyan. The captain put them on absently, listening to Alfie's account, and frowned. "Well, we'll run," he said after some thought, "but you may clear for action regardless. I'm not persuaded it is such very bad news, after all. The Admiral did direct me to return with prizes."

Alfie wondered if he had had such confidence, before Algiers, and looking at Cavendish's highly strung eagerness, the light of battle which had already transformed his face from classical elegance to something sharper, he wished he might have it back. But then he thought of the Dey's men dealing with the captain as they had done with him, and a heat began just beneath his breastbone, spreading into his trembling limbs and overcoming the weight of his heart. He would not allow that. Some things were sacred, and John, unshaven, with his hair flattened at one side, holding his hideous floral banyan closed about his threadbare shirt in the early morning chill, he was one of them. *They should not touch him....*

Almost as though he had sensed that flash of protectiveness, John turned and gave Alfie a sudden fierce smile. "May I?"

He held out his hand and Alfie passed him his telescope, indicating the direction. John watched the distant cloud of sail for a moment, "She's definitely turned to intercept us. Whether she recognizes us or not, I won't attempt to speculate, but I don't think we can afford to be caught." Collapsing the instrument, he handed it back. "Come to breakfast," he said. "No point in dying hungry. The men may eat too. Then we'll see."

He ducked back into his cabin, and Alfie saw to it that both watches were fed before knocking on the flimsy door himself and hearing a muffled "come."

The scent of coffee welcomed him, and Cavendish, dressed and drying his newly shaved face, emerged out of the night cabin just as Alfie handed his hat and greatcoat to the steward. Alfie thought he caught a flash of something other than professional interest through John's quicksilver eyes, just for a moment, but it disappeared before he had time to speculate on what it meant.

Having sat at table with his previous captain, Farrant, Alfie was far from impressed by the pewter plates and stoneware jugs of Cavendish's tableware. The food too hardly improved on the men's rations, though a good black pudding, and a Cheshire cheese, salty and crumbly, went down well. Alfie drank coffee gratefully, feeling the chill of the dawn watch, when the world stopped and the cold seemed to pierce the marrow of his bones, slowly ease its grip. He thawed into flesh and blood once more.

"If we can keep sufficiently ahead of her through the channel," John produced a roll of charts which he flicked open and pinned to the tablecloth with salt cellar and milk jug, "I think we can lose her in among the isles of Sardinia. When we have the weather gage on her, we come up behind, shoot out rudder and a few sails—see if the Ordnance Corps can't heat us some shot to possibly set her on fire—and then take her by boarding."

"You make it sound easy." Alfie could not help but smile, though the contempt of the Janissary officer who had captured him in Algiers had made a deep impression on his soul. *We too are a proud maritime nation. We were a proud maritime nation when you British were painting yourselves blue and hunting heads like savages.'* "They do know what they're about, you know, sir. They're not like the Spanish, who can build fine ships but cannot sail them."

"I understand that." John's certainty made something lurch in his chest, like a piece of buried shrapnel trying to work its way out. "But we are better."

"God, I hope so, sir."

"Mr. Donwell." John's voice softened a hair, but the captain's look of disappointment and sympathy was harder still to bear. "Once you would not have doubted. You must not doubt now. The men need you to be bold, fearless. You know that."

"I do. Some wounds take longer than others to heal, that's all. But I can swear to you that none of the men will have cause to suspect anything wrong from my conduct."

He was absolutely sure there was nothing but friendship behind the impulse which made John reach out and press his hand where it lay, palm up, on the table. The salt of John's fingertips made the rope burn smart, and Alfie withdrew it and let it rest in his lap, treasuring the sting. "Maybe if we asked them they'd take Hall away for us, though I can't imagine he'd fetch the price of a goat on the open market."

John laughed. "Don't tempt me."

By mid-morning the xebec's sails were visible, even from the deck, as a shining white tree on the horizon. To port, Sardinia loomed in craggy cliffs and inlets of white rock, scrubbed over with dark pines. The water beneath the keel, glass-clear, showed the sandy bottom fathoms below and even the little crabs that lived in the dragging skirt of weed choking the *Meteor*'s hull.

The *Meteor* rounded Capo Ferro and sailed cautiously on into the Strait of Bonifacio. Immediately she seemed alone. The shadow of Sardinia's cliffs swept over her, and all the sailors aboard could feel the shallowness of the seas, the loom of land to their lee. Here the ketch's small size and excellent maneuverability were an advantage, allowing her to pass above or between submerged boulders that would puncture the hull of its pursuer. Alfie stood by the lead and listened to them call the depth of the water beneath them; "by the mark, five, sand and soft shale," "by the mark three...." On the bow sprit the lookout lay gazing through the clear seas as they felt their way forward.

The decks had been swept clear from fore to aft; John's cabin had been disassembled and the pieces taken down to the hold, stacked next to the chickens and the goat. Slow match smoldered in tubs along the deck, and at a sound of whispered cursing Alfie strode swiftly down from the quarterdeck to find Captain Richardson of the Ordnance Corps berating the lever he was using to remount the mortar.

"All ready?" asked Alfie, ignoring Richardson's purpling face and strangled cries of pain. "Just nod."

At the companionway, the head of one of the boys he had sent to help the doctor popped up, giving an excited signal to say all was ready below. Alfie passed him with a pat on the back and went down to the gun deck, where the rest of the Ordnance Corps were huddled around the fire-box of the galley range with sweating, intent faces and a red glow in their eyes.

"All prepared?" Alfie swept a professional eye over the lines of cannon, run out and with their crews standing by, then peered with more curiosity at the cherry red metal of the galley, more customarily used for boiling stew than for heating cannon balls. He took note of the buckets of water and sand standing ready to throw over any accidental blaze, the long tongs poised in the ordnance officer's hand, and the silent, awestruck sailors who attended on the corps' attempt to heat the shot. "This isn't going to set us aflame, is it?"

"I can't promise you that," said the soldier in charge. "This operation is not designed to take place on ship. I could promise you perfect safety—within reason—if we were ashore on a stationary rock built fort, and we had the correct furnace for the job. As it is, well, we'll have to take our chances."

"Understood." Alfie cast a jaundiced eye over the men, who saw through his pose at once and grinned at him, already looking more like pirates than like Britons, with their scarves tied around their heads to soak up the sweat, and their shirts off. "Hear that? The teams I've picked to work the hot shot will be responsible for *not* setting the ship on fire—if you do, it comes out of your pay. Regular gun teams, you are responsible for getting the hell out of their way while they work.

"Everyone remembers how we left Algiers, yes? So you don't need me to tell you what they'll do to us if they capture us. Suffice it to say, it won't be pretty. If you don't want to end your life being force fed your own balls for the Dey's amusement, then there's nothing for it but to fight until we beat the bastards. That's all."

The thought of making himself an example almost closed his throat. Remembering Algiers was a roil of nausea in his belly. But every man aboard had seen him brought back broken; what better to play on their fear and their desire for vengeance? And he... he propped himself briefly on a knee of the deck above and breathed away the tremble of fury. He would show them that their pity was neither needed nor welcome, because he was fully fit again and perfectly capable of command.

Going out into the light again, Alfie saw that the helmsmen had taken the ketch between a rocky island and the shore. The sails had been furled and the sweeps put out, oarsmen gently, silently keeping the *Meteor* in her place, hiding behind a rock. As he watched, two of the topmen swarmed up the cliff and lay down among the colony of gannets on top of the island, glasses fixed on the bright sea beyond the headland. An overpowering scent of guano drifted down from the rock, and it was cold in its eternal shadow. Snails crawled up the walls all around them.

"Everything's in readiness, sir." Alfie returned to the quarterdeck almost on tiptoe, and gave his report in a low voice, conscious of cold and silence.

"Good." John—who had such a nervous look about him in every day life—seemed now as calm as the desert sands; empty of emotion, but scorching hot, burning like lime. Even Alfie found the man a little frightening at times like this.

"Good luck, Mr. Donwell." John put out his hand, and Alfie took it, holding it for a moment, conscious of the beat of blood through it, living and warm. The devil in his own blood woke then, making him squeeze tighter, turning his smile of thanks into a warmer grin. John snatched his hand back, looking ruffled, just as the lookout on the peak waved his red kerchief to say their pursuer, now their prey, had rounded the cape.

The xebec swept majestically past their little inlet, so close that the lookouts might have dropped stones onto her deck. The designs on the turbans of the men who worked the sails could easily be seen, and their voices heard, ringing out over the spray.

They passed as an eagle passes by the nest of a sparrow, and all the men of the *Meteor*, like a sparrow on its eggs, made themselves small and silent until they could see the lanterns of its stern, retreating. Then "out sweeps," said John. "Stand by to make sail."

"Make sail." Danger concentrating their minds, the topmen poured up the rigging, making ready without the usual sequence of commands, pausing occasionally to look at Alfie. Like a conductor with a well-trained orchestra he kept the sequence going with eye contact and small nods, manning the halyards and sheets, hauling taut, letting fall and sheeting home, all in silence. As the oarsmen took her out of the lee of the cliff and the wind filled her sails, Alfie was proud of them all. For a bunch of reject drunkards unfit for any better ship, they had done well.

She filled. Water began to whisper along the sides, then to thrum as their speed increased. With a slice like a knife they drove out of the shadow into the sunlight, and the ensigns streaming forwards on both masts glowed white and red against the deep blue Mediterranean sky. Light glittered on John's gold braid and made his buttons glint like sovereigns, and Alfie let go of everything except the joy of being alive in this one perfect moment. "Ready, Mr. Richardson?"

"Ready, sir!"

In place of their explosive shells, Richardson's mortars had been armed with makeshift containers of grape shot. One of his men stood by the helm, squinting out at the xebec, making minute adjustments—for the mortars could be aimed only by turning the whole ship. This too, like the heated shot down in the galley, was absolute folly, for the mortars were designed to be fired from a stationary vessel, winched from side to side by spring anchors. She had been built to take the recoil from a standstill, not while the frame of the ship was already strained by the enormous forward force of a stiff wind in the sails. It would double the forces acting on her; be like sailing at twelve knots straight into a wall. But Alfie didn't care about folly. Neither drowning nor blowing himself up had terrors for him—the only thing he would not abide was to be a slave again.

"Fire!"

In a cracking boom of gunpowder, the mortars spoke with tongues of flame. The *Meteor* lurched under Alfie's feet, lifting out of the sea and slamming back down, almost hurling him to his knees. He clutched at the rail as the masts bent with the recoil and ropes burst, snapping about his head. The whole ship came to a sudden catastrophic standstill, even the wind blasted out of the sails. She groaned and shrieked in protest, but the reinforced hull stood the shock. As the cloud of sulfurous yellow smoke rolled slowly over the *Meteor*'s deck, the sails began to fill again and she moved achingly forward, out of the smoke.

White-faced topmen raced to splice the broken cables, just as the lookout's cheer came shrill down the wind onto deck. Far beyond the range of cannon, the xebec's mizzen lateen flew in the wind, shredded, and her deck crew lay in piles, the murderous hail of shot having done its work. Their stern chasers boomed out, but the balls kicked up white spray five hundred feet before the *Meteor*'s head, and as new crewmembers boiled out of her hull to wrestle with the flying sail or stand, shouting defiance, Richardson cried, "Clear away! Fire in the hole!" and the mortars let fly again.

The xebec was turning to meet them, every sail manned. Even Alfie, no stranger to fleet actions, felt a little squeamish as he watched the bodies burst apart, the blood fountain out to stain the white sails red. Blood poured from her scuppers, and a red sea foamed beneath her sprinter's hull. The chains on the *Meteor*'s foremast gave a convulsive snap, then tightened with a noise like a dragon's wing-beat in the recoil, and Richardson came striding to the quarterdeck looking singed but smug.

"That's it, sir. With her closing on us, that's all we can do. She's inside our range."

"Very well, Mr. Richardson." John moved aside as a cannon ball came screaming up the deck. Alfie could feel its passing like a kick in the chest. "We'll try the heated shot now, if you please." John might have been at a garden party, nonchalantly ordering a glass of punch. Alfie's heart rose into his throat at the glory of it, making him grin into the freshening wind.

The *Meteor*—reinforced to take the strain of the mortars— had a hull twice as strong as needed in a ship of her size. The xebec turned, firing her larboard broadside in a raking fire across the *Meteor*'s bow, but at this extreme range her shot bounced off the ketch's hull and fell into the sea with disconsolate splashes.

"Helm hard a starboard!" shouted John, as the *Meteor* too turned, presenting her broadside. Alfie dived down into the comparative darkness of the gun deck to shout, "Fire!" and "Fire at will!" to the men of the Ordnance Corps, in charge of the heated shot. It might have been amusing to see them walk with such slow gingerness, each new ball held in tongs, heat pouring off it and making the air shimmer above it, if the infernal things had not been so dangerous that even one might suffice to set the whole ship alight. The gun crew nervously rammed home what looked like three times too much wadding, and rolled the burning iron down the barrel, touching the slow match to the hole with a gesture that looked like relief—overjoyed to get the deadly shot far away from themselves.

The cannon leapt into the air, its restraining chains twanging with a high metallic shriek. The deck beneath them shuddered with the impact as it crashed back down. Leaning down to look through the port, Alfie saw the ball pierce the lightly built xebec—a burst of splinters and a faint wham of impact almost inaudible to his shot deafened ears—and then a wisp of smoke.

Days upon endless days of desiccating heat welled out of his memory and made his heart smolder with the joy of revenge. "Good!" he said, even as a ball from the xebec burst the hull asunder on his left. Splinters flew. In a sudden rush of daylight one of the gun crew crumpled to the ground with a length of sharp oak through his throat, but his mates ran the cannon out again without a moment's pause.

"Dion! George!" Alfie signaled to the men at the end of the deck, standing by the companionway with a stretcher, helped them to get the man onto it and turned back to the guns, all without any real thought. "Let's have as many of the hot shot as we can."

The xebec crowded closer. Above, Alfie could hear the sinister thud and clang of the xebec's grappling irons hitting the *Meteor*'s side, just before—with a burst of flame and din that almost stupefied him—her final broadside came hurtling almost direct through the *Meteor*'s gun-ports. The deck now seethed so full of smoke he could barely see his feet. When he trod on the severed arm of one of his gun crew he kicked it dispassionately out through the port, reached down, and found the body it had been attached to getting in the way of the gun carriage wheels. *Nikolaos Gkranias*, a part of his mind noticed, calmly; a dab hand with portraits and carving the scrimshaw trinkets the other men liked to send home to their wives.

Knowing the ship's safety depended on its officers' ability to keep a level head in battle, Alfie shoved aside grief and guilt and nausea—every emotion that might hamper him from doing his job—kept them to feel later, in safety. He cleared the tracks of the cannon and heaved the body too into the sea. Above the screaming of the injured came the dull trundle that told him the guns were being run out for one last time.

Pools of red in the fog moved like ghost-lights towards him, and the faces of the ordnance men, lit from below by fire, swam like visions of hell into his gaze.

"Gunners report!"

Three of the four gun captains replied. Alfie sent the final round of hot shot to each working cannon, and stretcher bearers to those who did not answer. The cacophony of the guns going off was like being drunk—gloriously, fearlessly drunk, and yardarm to yardarm as they were, every shot went home.

"Close gun-ports! All hands to repel boarders!" he shouted,

remembering the sound of grappling irons a moment earlier. Leaving the dead and the dying behind, he drew his sword and raced up the companionway into battle.

On deck, the fog of smoke was lighter, but the marines in the rigging plugged away at the xebec's men with rifles, and as the wind blew away the cannon smoke, whiter plumes above the masts remained. Boarders armed with scimitars leaped down from the platforms at either end of the xebec onto the *Meteor*'s deck. As fast as the *Meteor*'s sailors could cut the cables, more hooks came flying out of the mist to catch against wood or bodies and drag the two ships together.

The quarterdeck seethed with fury, John only visible by the braid on his hat. As Alfie forced his way up the steps, ramming into men, using his sword more as a battering ram than a blade, a scimitar blow knocked the hat off. A glimpse of brown hair was swallowed up by a scrum of backs and elbows, and the brief but deadly glitter of steel. For a moment Alfie's spirit deserted him as he watched the captain fall, then something wild and hot touched off in him as if the fuse had finally reached the magazine of his soul.

He yelled at the top of his voice as he charged into the knot of men, mad and invulnerable. Sword through a spine here, blood on his face, kicking the legs out from beneath another man there and hewing his throat as he fell, Alfie carved his way through the press to John's side.

John, on his hands and knees, struggled to get up. A boarding axe embedded in his side dangled, pulling the wound's lips open into a mouth of surprise. As Alfie turned to confront the press of men closing in once more, John took a handful of Alfie's coat hem and hauled himself upright by it, leaving bloody prints. He swayed, white-faced beneath the splatters of gore, then wrenched the axe out of his flank, turned back-to-back with Alfie, and fought on, sword in one hand, axe in the other.

There are so many of them! Alfie hacked and slashed with a savagery and total lack of finesse that would have appalled his fencing master. But his heart was light and his body felt new again, reacting faster than his mind, strong and sure and utterly without doubt. It was bliss to share this with John; to feel the flex of the other man's back against his own, to fight as one and breathe as one, alone together in this moment poised just on the cusp of death.

His arms had only just begun to tremble and the air to burn his throat as it went down when he felt the swarm of attackers waver. A voice called over the deck like the muezzin calling the people to prayer, and as obediently they faltered, began pulling away. Joy drove Alfie forward; joy like the mounting ecstasy of sex, unstoppable, undeniable, pushing them back until they turned and ran—their vulnerable spines exposed to him. He cut them down as they fled, and saw over their heads the cause of their sudden retreat—flames licking out of the xebec's ports, snaking up her ropes, gnawing voraciously on the edges of her huge sails.

Even as he watched, something cracked deep in the body of the other ship, she jerked like a man who had been shot, and the water around her boiled. The contents of her hold began surfacing in great bubbles smelling of bilge water and human waste. She buckled in the middle. Masts swayed towards each other, stays parting, and fell into the increasing inferno on deck. Men were hurling themselves off her into the sea now, some tearing off their clothes to swim better, some—unable to swim—crossing their hands on their breasts as they sank, horrifyingly dignified. On the deck of the *Meteor*, her sailors took advantage of their enemies' dismay and distraction to stab them in the back or herd them towards the rail where they would share their comrades' fate.

"Stop them, Alfie…. No massacres on…my ship." The flame of battle had ebbed from John's face, his skin transparent and blue with shock. He staggered to the capstan and leaned on it in a vain attempt to disguise the fact that he could barely stand.

"Aye, aye, sir!" Not what he wanted to do at all, but Alfie ran from one struggling knot of combatants to another—offering the

Dey's men the chance to surrender. Uncertain whether he was being a fool, he ordered the boats put out and the swimming men rescued, taken down to the hold to be clapped in irons fastened to the keel. All this with a dread gnawing at him that was more than justified when he returned to the quarterdeck to find John slumped at the foot of the capstan, a pool of blood beneath him an inch deep.

"You idiot," he whispered as he lifted the limp body in his arms and carried it down to the doctor's station on the orlop. "You *bastard!* Don't die!"

"No way…to speak…your commanding officer." John opened an eye like a slit of mercury.

"You'd better get well again, sir, so you can punish me," said Alfie, and found resilience enough to raise an eyebrow at the innuendo.

John grinned at him, like the grin of a skull.

CHAPTER 7

A month later, Gibraltar

"I feel...I am such a burden to you," said John, watching Alfie open the shutters of their lodging house on Castle Street and stand for a moment outlined against the fragrant sky. He could tell from the set of Alfie's back that the man was sighing; whether in relief at the end of another anxious night, or in pleasure at the view and the fresh early morning air, John wasn't sure.

He hadn't been able to see the view himself—carried ashore in the grip of high fever, the axe wound badly infected and wrongly treated by a terribly apologetic Dr. Harper. Alfie had made the arrangements, banned Harper and brought one of the local physicians, applied the salves, changed his bandages, held him tight as he shook and raved, soothing his fever with cool cloths. Somehow he had also managed to make sure the *Meteor's* men were fed and housed, given such shore leave as they could be trusted with, and the ship herself careened and scraped.

He was owed more than a moment of standing and admiring the harbor; more than John could very well say. Yet though he knew he was being selfish by speaking, cutting short Alfie's moment of contemplation, John still felt weak and prone to tears, and he wanted the familiar presence back by his side, not all the way over there across the room, inaccessible.

"Not a burden but a joy." Alfie returned, just as he'd hoped, to draw up the room's single, black Spanish chair beside him and take his hand. At the touch, John closed his eyes and smiled, comforted.

"You are…" he said, for the lemon sharp sunlight touched only the end of the bed, illuminating bare plastered walls, ancient floorboards and the faded red coverlet, leaving the further end of the room, where he lay, in deeper darkness by contrast. A warm, private darkness in which things could be said which could never be said in daylight. "You are the best man I have ever met."

The morning crept over Alfie's face and made his eyes glisten, softened his slightly coarse features until his face seemed as fair and oval as one of Joshua Reynold's idealized portraits. When he licked his full lips they glistened too, turned up and inwards, in a self-deprecatory smile of great sweetness. "You can't have met many then, sir."

His warm hand held John's, reassuringly, and if a part of John wondered whether hand-holding was still in order, now he was getting better, he was not willing to give it up just yet. In fact, watching Alfie sitting there between light and shadow, elbows planted on his knees, with his coat off and his cravat undone— shirt gaping to reveal the strong column of his throat, the dip and ridge of his collarbone—he felt almost as though he witnessed something holy. As though he saw through flesh to glimpse God's work in its pristine, unfallen condition. He wanted to reach out and touch it; to explore it with his fingertips, to properly appreciate the artistry of it.

"You awe me," he said, trying to express something of this. "I never yet met a man so tempestuous and yet so…" but he couldn't say "tender", not even in this animal-smelling little world they had shared together for so many days. "Loyal," he finished, instead.

Alfie's smile untucked, his lips parting to show his fine white teeth. "You don't ask me what I see when I see you." He raised his free hand and unstuck the limp hair that stuck to John's forehead, pushing it away from his face. "It might surprise you."

John, who hadn't noticed the tickle of hair loose on his face before, nevertheless sighed with relief to have it gone. But the gesture reminded him once again of the musty sickroom smell of the place, and his own smell, having lain a fortnight abed, sweating through the hot Spanish days. "Well, your hours of nursing should soon be over," he said. "I mean to sit up today, by the window, perhaps. Can you see if our landlady will draw me a bath and change the bed? The stink of me is enough to drop the local pigeons out of the sky."

"It's true." Alfie grinned. "I was watching them plummet past the window when you woke. I'll do it now, if you'll eat first."

Closing his eyes, John let the bed enfold him once more. There seemed to be a little more to him now than mere insatiable desire for sleep—a space for him to become again a rational being. The itchy wrongness of all his limbs subsided, and he probably could eat something undemanding, if he tried. He touched the bandage that swathed him from one side of the body to the other, and it was dry. If he pressed, his hand no longer felt as though it would sink in up to the wrist. "Mmm…" he said, drifting into a warm, umber colored mist, on a boat made of eiderdown, and only woke up again when the servants banged the bathtub against the walls as they were trying to get it through the door.

He watched drowsily as the girls scurried up and down stairs with pitchers of water, filling it. White bloused and dark haired, their skin glowed golden from the sun, and their liquid eyes were knowing, amused. Their skirts brushed across the floor, the whisper mixing with pouring water into a sound soothing as rain. The open door let in the aroma of *cadereta de langosta* cooking, and an acrid rubbish tip smell beyond the back door of the kitchen, where piles of parings were fought over by poor children and mangy dogs.

Closer to him, he could smell the lavender they added to the water. John watched as they set out soap and towels. Alfie brought out his shaving kit from the chest at the foot of the bed, and thoughtfully stropped the razor as he watched this activity with the demanding eye of a good First Lieutenant. John smiled at the thought, for there was a flavor of the military about the whole operation. A flavor he found more reassuring than the fact that when the bath was full, a fire lit in the grate and two kettles of water reserved for rinsing, only one of the girls went away. The chambermaid—a burly creature with very fine eyes, but the beginnings of a black moustache, and the prettiest one, whose wavy hair was bright hennaed red at the ends—remained.

John did not like this so much, nor that when Alfie helped him to sit up, get the nightshirt over his head, the two of them looked at one another and smiled.

"I help you," said the redhead, with arched, suggestive eye-brows, "on bath. Adoncia, she help your friend."

A distaste for all things corporeal washed over John then; for loose women and—because he was fair-minded—for the loose men who encouraged them. He was always getting these offers and it tired him. Was it so hard for them to believe there might be one man in this world with some modesty and self control, who didn't wish to swive the first piece of skirt to throw herself into his lap? He pulled the coverlet tight over himself and leaned into the arm Alfie had put around him, to help him stand, feeling more dirtied than ever.

"Come on now, girls." Alfie gave her a roguish grin and a re-gretful look. "Give the man a chance! Can you…?" this to John, as he encouraged him to get to his feet. John had no desire to get up and stand naked before the women's measuring eyes, but he tried, for Alfie's sake.

Not even pride could keep him on his feet. He would have slithered gracelessly to the floor and lain there, gasping and help-less as a fry dropped on deck by a passing gull, had it not been for Alfie's strength. There was something deeply comforting, in fact, in being held so, like a child in its father's arms. Sighing, he let his head rest against his friend's cheek and closed his eyes.

"You see?" Alfie said wryly. "Nothing standing at present. You'd be wasting your time. Just change the bed today, and come back in a day or so."

Dimly, John felt he should be insulted by this, but he was too grateful to be lifted over to the bath and gently sat down in clean warm water. The rest of the world went away while he breathed in scented steam, his vision going as misty as the surface of the water.

"I soap—"

"I don't think so. Listen…."

He could hear Alfie spinning some implausible tale about religious vows and penances, and wondered why he couldn't just tell the truth. *Doesn't everyone in this room believe that fornication is a sin? Why then is it so difficult to understand that the thought of it fills me with unease?*

"There," said Alfie's warm brown voice at his back, after a moment of blankness when he must have fallen asleep again. The sounds of bed-making and scornful Spanish conversation behind him only threw into relief how much John wanted them all to go away. He looked up and found Alfie giving him a sideways look, lopsided and wry, ancient as the oldest profession. "But are you sure you won't? She's a pretty, plump little thing, you don't fancy her soaping you down, with her arms too short to reach around you without her pressing her fine bosom to your back—the water making the white blouse on her transparent as a veil?"

Suiting his actions to his words, Alfie had unwound the bandage and set it aside, and was now soaping John's shoulders, big hands firm and warm, slippery, but ever so slightly rough against John's skin. His insides tightened and his belly fluttered with a sudden wash of lust, thin and pitiful in his weakness, like overwatered grog. "Don't," he said. "Don't talk like that!"

"I don't know many men who would say no."

"Shame on them!" John hissed. *Why, chastity is simple.* He didn't understand why everyone seemed to find it so difficult.

Alfie did not reply to his anger, only bent his head and smiled that damnable knowing smile. He had taken off his waistcoat and rolled up his sleeves, and his own linen was soaked, molding itself to a lithe but powerful chest. Pressing down on John's head he tipped it forwards, and John found himself sluiced with water which trailed in skeins of silver off his newly shaggy hair into the bath. He closed his eyes against the soap, but an animal sense seemed to radiate from his flushed skin, allowing him to feel the man bending over him as though they were pressed together. Encircled by Alfie's presence, his body seemed to pull towards the other man's as one pole of a magnet to the other— and that was before Alfie's fingers were in his hair, soothing and slippery and very warm. Alfie's voice was all but inaudible, a velvet touch against the side of his face. "I know few women who would say no to you."

He couldn't find the anger this time, floating as if on opium clouds. "Shame on them too."

"You're very beautiful, John. Inside and out."

There was something about being whispered to in that smoky dark voice that made him shift beneath the ministering fingers, discomforted. What did the man think he was doing? Had he made some agreement with the girls that required John to join in? He…didn't know if something like that would come as a relief. Surely it was better that Alfie be a pander than a…. "I don't think you should say that to me."

"Permission to say a thousand other things, very much along the same lines, Sir?"

"No." John's conscience, never very quiescent, raised its head like a gazelle scenting a lion on the wind. "Permission denied."

There was a silence, and then Alfie laughed, ruefully. "You're a hard man to please," he said, and rinsed off the soap. They had put vinegar in the rinsing water, to counteract the soap, and the smell of it was sharp as a rebuke. It brought tears to John's eyes. *I really am very ill still,* he thought, for that small tone of disappointment in Alfie's voice to bring him so low. *But what else was I supposed to do?* There were things men did not say to other men, no matter how strong their friendship.

"What is 'Alfie' short for?" he said instead, steering them back into safer water as the lieutenant squeezed the water from his hair and pulled him to his feet to be toweled dry. "You can't have been given that name as a child, surely?"

Alfie knelt to dry his feet, and looking down at that bent back, at the top of his round head and the tendrils of sunny bright hair in springy damp curls about his face, John wished with a panic that he had another cloth to wrap about his hips. He was not normally a particularly modest man, but at this moment he felt excruciatingly self-conscious and exposed, particularly when Alfie looked up, cheek so close to John's thigh he could feel the heat of it like a minor sun.

But Alfie, thank God, after looking in his eyes and perhaps seeing the terror there, for once refrained from saying anything suggestive. "'Aelfstan,'" he said, with a sigh. "My parents were antiquarians. I believe they met over some fossil or fascinating bone somewhere. 'Aelfstan Petyt Donwell,' to make it worse— 'Petyt' after the author of *Jus Parliamentarium*, you know. A book which I may proudly say I have never opened."

He maneuvered John back across the floor to the newly made bed, and after examining the wound and declaring it would do well for a bit of fresh air, he helped him on with a clean night-shirt and lowered him gently back down to the pillow. "And so you have your revenge for my embarrassing you," Alfie said. His eyes as he looked down were full of warmth, though John thought he saw lingering sadness also. It dismayed him.

"I should have known better than to try. Go back to sleep, sir. Soon you'll be well, and I won't have the chance again."

Embarrassment? Was that what it was? John closed his eyes, ashamed of his recent thoughts. A little gentle ribbing at his "holier than thou" behavior? A mild and friendly dig at John's prudishness? *Oh dear Lord, I almost…almost suspected him of something unthinkable.* Ungrateful wretch that he was! What kind of a reward was that for the man's days of patient care? Well, he would not entertain such thoughts ever again.

He wanted to find some way to apologize without actually admitting to his suspicions. Wanted to say, *"Never have the chance to embarrass me again? No, please do. Your needling enlivens my rather dull life,"* but the effort of the bath had been too much for him. His determination to do battle against the shadow of regret in Alfie's eyes slithered away like an unhitched cable into the depths of the sea, and he fell asleep at once.

The following week, John felt recovered enough to take short walks about town, and they sat at a table outside a cafe, soaking up the reviving sunlight, the hot wind blowing the scent of olives and oranges down on them from the hills. Coffee steamed in a tall pot before them, and fresh fruit attempted to vie with the plate of custard-filled *ensaimades* for their attention. Vainly, as it proved, because they were too busy looking down at the waterfront and the harbor beyond to care about either.

Alfie leaned forward and tapped John on the arm, then pointed to the mouth of the bay, into which a Second Rate was sweeping like a stately queen. "I wonder who that is?"

Cicadas droned unnoticed. John took a sip of his coffee then brought his eyeglass out of his pocket, unfolding it. He watched in admiration as the ship drew closer. The prompt and even stylish way she handled her sails, the exactness of her slowing and furling, and the way she anchored with barely a splash formed a large part of his appreciation of her beauty. Though that was fine enough—her sails white, her hull red and canary yellow, her gingerbread work and cannons glittering in the sun. It was a joy to see so fine a ship handled with a smartness that befitted her.

He watched as the sailors lowered a gilded barge into the sea, and poured aboard it like a rush of white foam down the side. The oars raised like wings as the last man came aboard and sat down in singular glory—a king—in the stern. Only when the oarsmen began their stroke did John notice that they too must have been picked for their beauty. Golden light gleamed on tight white trousers and glistening muscles, on faces shaved to beardless perfection, and long hair curled loose on broad shoulders.

John's admiration altered to a kind of horrified glee. He passed the telescope to Alfie, wanting to share the joke. "Whoever he is, he must be an excellent backgammon player."

Alfie gave him a quizzical smile, as though he either had not understood the cant term for a sodomite, or simply did not believe John capable of making such a joke. Dusting icing sugar from his fingertips, he took the glass and looked.

Only a month ago, John might have missed the change that came over Alfie as he focused on the brightly braided gentleman John had pointed out. The lieutenant covered both the wince and the sudden drain of color from his face by ducking his head into the shadow of his hat. But after this past week, John could read Alfie's expression from the turn of his tensed back, the white knuckles of fists he had never seen so tightly clenched.

"What is it?" he asked, taken aback. Reaching out, he curled his hand protectively about the other man's wrist, and yes, it was trembling.

"Nothing at all, sir," Alfie looked up, in what was clearly supposed to be a gesture of reassurance. It revealed his suddenly terrified look to John's waiting gaze. Not quite meeting John's eyes, Alfie wiped sweat from his upper lip, scrubbing both hands over it, one after another. This having given him no apparent relief, he launched himself to his feet, his back held as rigid as if it had been lashed. "I think it must be time for you to get back inside. You don't want to overstrain yourself."

"Nonsense! I feel better than I have for months. I could climb the rigging, even."

"Well…." The terrace was ringed with planters full of trailing flowers. Alfie fled to the nearest one, and returned, in a pointless dance of agitation that made John's stomach clench. "Well…I've had enough of the sun. It gives me a headache. Wish you good day, sir, but I must…I want to go inside."

Returning to their rooms, John watched with concern as Alfie faded before his eyes; from a vibrant presence with a luscious, deep

brown voice—a sharp witted, sharp tongued, fiercely intense presence—to something not far from nothingness. He fell into the seat
in front of all John's paperwork; the chitties and reports, logbooks
and lists that made up a captain's day to day work, on ship or off.
The table had been placed close to the window, to have the light
for longest, but after a moment's sitting with his head bent, Alfie
moved it back into the shadows, complaining about the heat.

"Alfie," John began, a hollowness inside him worse than the
axe wound, "what's wrong? Tell me!"

"Is that a command, sir?" Terrified guilt met his gaze as Alfie
looked up.

"No. No, of course it isn't—"

"Then please leave me be."

A knot of rage drove John out of the room, leaving Alfie alone
in their shared quarters with the shutters closed. Returning to
the café to settle the account, John glared down at the Second
Rate. The captain's barge now nodded against the dock. The
man himself stood on the wharf like a beau at a ball, ready to be
admired. From the diamond cockade of his hat light lanced out
in a shameless star.

John clenched his fists and turned away, setting off downhill
towards the Admiralty offices, determined to discover the truth
at once.

"We're friends, Mr. Donwell, aren't we?" John asked. Returning to
their lodgings with the twilight, after an afternoon of discreet enquiry brought him the kind of news that made his blood curdle in
his veins, he found Alfie watching the door, with a book lying
closed on his lap and his hand on his small-sword.

Under that threatened, tense regard, John wondered if it was
true. This...whatever it was...they'd been engaged in over the past
few months, so intimate, so skirting the bounds of propriety—
was it really friendship? *But if not, what then?*

"I'm not asking as your captain, but as your friend. Alfie,
what's wrong?"

Alfie raised his head and gave a quick, defensive smile; a ridge of white teeth in the dimness, and his smoky eyes unfathomable. "How can I tell the friend without the captain finding out?"

"I may have already guessed," John murmured, heavily. "You were on his ship, weren't you? Did he...?"

John's breath came hard as he primed himself to fight even the horrible suspicion. He had sworn never to think this again. If he could just keep it at bay—a formless dark monster on the edge of his mind—he could challenge it, defeat it, and neither of them would ever have to think about it again.

"No, I don't need to know," he answered himself quickly. "No one has to know." Throwing open his sea chest, he delved inside for the box at the bottom. Laying it on the bed, he opened the clasp and lifted out one of the brace of pistols; long, heavy and comfortable in his hand. He couldn't afford enemies, particularly not this one—a Post Captain and a nobleman of a most distinguished family—but the monstrous suspicion combined with something bright and fearless in his heart, and for a moment he wanted blood more than he had ever desired anything in his life.

He stood on the edge of a razor, above a hell in which that man abused the boy who was to grow up to be his friend, and he would take steel and fire to that vision and make it go away, for Alfie's sake and his own. *I understand you wouldn't be able to face him. Let alone bear being dragged before a court of inquiry. But it doesn't have to come to that. I can find another excuse to call him out. I can kill him. If you want me to, Alfie, I'll kill him, for you.*

How bitter—Alfie put down book and sword, rising to throw open the window—to see all that deadly beauty arrayed in anger for his sake. Twilight touched John's face with shades of silver, and if by day he looked like Octavian Caesar, by the light of the moon he was an elfin knight, delicate as a crystal of arsenic.

This should not be happening! Alfie had fled in panic from Charles Farrant—Captain Lord Lisburn, first son of the Duke of Alderley—in order to stop this from happening. But it seemed his impulsive action had betrayed him. If he had only kept his head and stayed where he was! The flight itself had alerted John to the fact that something was wrong, and now, unless he wished John to become a murderer on his behalf, he had to speak. It was too early to speak—the ground unprepared, still arid with winter chill. Any seed sown there would rot before it saw the sun. That was clear enough from John's panicked rejection of his careful advance during the bath. If there ever could have come a time when it was safe to make everything plain, that time was not now. But speak he must, because nothing else would stop the blind, holy fool from charging to a rescue he didn't need, and Farrant had not deserved that of him.

"I'm touched," he said, surprised he could still sound so casual. Would John denounce him, accuse him, see him pilloried and driven from the service? He was almost certain that John would not see him hang, though the man was pious enough, devoted to his duty enough, to force himself even that far if he believed it was required of him. But hanging aside, this was the end of it. Alfie had gambled and lost; hoped to win John's heart and thereby to bring the rest of the body along later. Now he dreaded to speak; dreaded John's virtue as if it was a thousand stinging spines.

"But you have it wrong, sir." He forced the words out in short, painful bursts. "Lord Lisburn was my first captain. I adored him with all the ardor of my romantic little childish soul." As with stepping off a precipice, the first move proved the hardest. Once made, it was almost a relief to fall.

"I did everything I could to make him notice me, sir. Everything I've done with you. I used to treasure every word, and lie in wait for him in corridors, just to hear him say 'out of my way, Mr. Donwell.' He…anyone can tell his tastes run to men, so I thought it certain that one day he would notice my devotion and reward it. My hopes were high."

Looking back, Alfie recalled his younger self's tender, undefended heart opening in the flower of first love, still remembered what it had all felt like. No wonder it had taken him years to find the nerve to try again.

"One night—after I had been particularly obvious about this, the captain called me to his cabin. I was overjoyed! I spent what seemed hours in front of my glass, in equal parts nerves and lust, trying to make myself look pretty for him. But he didn't even invite me to sit down. He just gave me a pitying smile and said; 'I know what you're doing, son, but you're wasting your time. I require a certain standard, and you don't reach it.'"

Alfie laughed, because even now—especially now—it hurt too much to do otherwise. "I was crushed."

The past had given him many lessons; or perhaps the same one, over and over, which he had simply refused to learn. Looking at John's face now, he remembered his family. Even he had had a family once, until his father caught him kissing the stableboy under the hawthorn hedge. It had only been a bet—exploration, a bit of fun—he hadn't expected it to be the end of the world. But long after the beating healed, the snick of the door closing in his face remained in his nightmares, desolate and terrifying. He still dreamed of standing outside his home, beating on the wood and demanding, cursing, pleading to be let back in, while the night deepened around him and the rain fell.

After that, the Royal Navy became his family for a while—best of all the options of a homeless boy. Recognizing John's shock, the slow dawning of righteous disgust, he knew what was going to happen now. He bowed his head and studied the floorboards, to avoid watching the fondness and friendship in John's face be wiped away. Of course he was no longer the man who had fought at John's side, and nursed him back from death; no longer a shipmate, a flute player, an interesting conversationalist, a welcome defender at one's back. Now, all he was was a pervert.

He had no desire to see any of that reflected in the silver grey mirrors of John's eyes. Having been through the slave pens and survived the bastinado, he still believed there was no form of torture worse than what those you love can inflict.

"John…?" Whether he asked for forgiveness or just for mercy he didn't know. Possibly just for an end to the silence.

"No!" John's out-flung hand cut into his small field of vision. Looking up, he found exactly the look he expected on the carved face; the look of a man who has only just realized he has stepped in dog-shit. "I…" John withdrew the hand that had commanded Alfie to silence. It balled by his side into a fist, and for a moment Alfie hoped wildly that John would hit him. That, he could still see working—he would hit back, and they would fight, knocking over washstand and table and books. There would be blood and bruises and biting, and sooner or later John's animal nature would rise up in him and demand that ruthless rutting he so badly needed.

But John's temper held. "No," he said again. "I don't want to hear it." Snatching up his coat he turned his back, slammed the door behind him and was gone.

Alfie looked at the door. *Shut in, shut out, it amounts to the same thing.* He stood for a while quite still, then smoothed the coverlet of the bed and sat, looking out the window. Out there he could see the sea, the great shimmer of it, salty and wet as tears.

He should never have spoken, never have dared hope; should have tried to remain content with being a friend, valued for his skills and not his heart. Now even that was over. There were philanderers and adulterers aplenty in the officer's mess, but no sods. *God forbid!*

I thought I knew the man, and all this time we were strangers. John strode up the steep hill to the silence of the distant *maquis*, his lungs laboring at the unaccustomed exercise, his side throbbing with red fire as he ignored fatigue and wound alike, borne up on fury. The paved path gave way to a thread of white limestone through tangles of rosemary and rue, lizards soaking up the last of the day's heat on tumbled stones. Further on, under the mass of olive and laurel trees, night had already fallen, but here in the open the sky still shone pale silver-blue. Out of the town's enclosing walls, with nothing between himself and God but that luminous evening, he stopped, the driving anger draining away. Dizziness swept over him and he reeled to the nearest boulder to sit upon, looking back.

The town lay like a spill of sugar cubes below, and the harbor retained the day's sun, shining against the dark indigo sea like an aquamarine dropped into a cask full of sapphire. Gasping and faint, John shut his eyes and waited while the pain subsided. A warm breeze, full of the scent of thyme and lavender, stirred the pigtail of his wig and made his damp shirt feel cool. Behind him a small troop of Gibraltar's apes contentedly scratched one another, huddling close. But the evening's tranquility could not penetrate beyond the surface of John's skin.

I thought I knew the man! I thought we were friends! And all this time he played me for a fool. God damned liar! Alfie had lied—lied by omission, keeping this...*thing* that he was to himself. Playing games only he understood. *Gulling me; gaining my affection under false colors. All of it a lie!*

Now every sweet memory—every note he'd ever sung, which seemed at the time so blessed—was tainted; the tenderness he'd felt when Alfie turned to him for protection at Algiers; the glory of fighting together, like one soul in two bodies, invulnerable; the month of pain in which Alfie's presence had been his loadstar—*all of them* were tainted with this new knowledge. *The bath! Oh God, the bath!*

His skin crawled. He tried to get up and walk away from the complex of hurt and betrayal, from the touch. It seared, indelibly marked into his skin. Surely it must show; through layers of shirt and waistcoat and coat, it must show. People must be able to see it on him, like a stain. But even if they did not, he felt it himself—the pleasure, the lust—*oh God!* But he would never...he would *never*...if he had known. He had tried so hard not to know. *Damn Alfie Donwell! Damn him to hell for lying, for being a lying fucking bastard and invert!* John had treasured his friendship so much, and now it seemed clear there had never been any friendship at all. Just a plot. It had all been just a plot to lure him into sin.

Far below, in the harbor, a twinkle of gold winked at him, where the gilt-work of the First Rate caught the final rays of the sun. Slumping back onto the wall, John frowned at it. *How dare it look so splendid! How dare it look like the epitome of glory, the embodiment of all that made the Royal Navy great?* This was all the fault of its captain. Only half aware that his jaw ached and threads of pain had begun to run up from his tight clenched teeth to his temples, John made a valiant attempt to shift all the blame onto Lord Lisburn. *What message must an impressionable child get, after all, when his captain surrounded himself with Ganymedes?*

John himself had been lucky enough to have had a captain who molded him with a firm but kind hand, encouraging his excellence with praise and rebuking his faults with understanding. That was what a captain should be; a steadying influence on the boys and an example of personal morality. *Not a blatant sod!* Was it Alfie's fault he turned out wrong, with such a pattern to follow?

Night drew in; the gold drained from the light and by slow degrees the landscape turned from green to blue. John's thoughts darkened in sympathy. For there were other children to protect. In addition to the midshipman, Mr. Armitage, whom John could not see inspiring passion in *anyone*, there were three powder monkeys and two boys under fourteen serving as topmen on the *Meteor*. Someone had to think of them. As captain, that responsibility fell to him.

Whatever shaped Alfie into what he was, however much John might have come to appreciate the irreverent wit, the spark, the fire bright intensity Alfie brought into a room with his mere presence, if he was a threat to the safety of the boys he would have to be stopped. *Stopped before his affliction spreads, before he ruins other young lives....*

John wondered how to interrogate the ship's boys without letting them know why. He frowned at his hands, were shaking like new leaves in a spring squall.

Could he really do it? Suppose he found out that the children had been interfered with—could he really go to the magistrate and turn Alfie over? He *had to*, didn't he? Just because the man was personable, and John had liked him, did not mean he was not a threat to the fabric of society. In truth it made no difference if he had not forced himself on the boys. *If he had been…* John's thoughts faltered as he approached the impossibility of this idea…if he had been stalking John himself, as he implied, it did not alter the fact that his mere existence was a blot on the world that could only be erased with death.

The light dimmed further and early stars pierced the graying sky. The wind at John's back, cooler now, made his fever-weakened muscles tighten and ache. But he could not face going back to their shared room; could not conceive of talking, or being silent, or even breathing the same air as Alfie while these thoughts were in his head. So he gingerly levered himself down from the stone and sat among the chickweed and campion in the warm windbreak, rock radiating the day's heat in a comforting glow across his shoulders.

Despite the turmoil of his thoughts, his convalescing body demanded its due. Half lying on the springy herbs, with the heat soothing his aches, penetrating through his skin to relax over strained and trembling muscles, he drowsed. In the twilight state between sleep and waking, his cravat seemed to become a noose; *he could feel its harsh fibers scratching his throat, and the knot pressing against his spine; darkness outside his eyelids and within, waiting for him to sink, waiting to choke him….*

He clawed his way back to consciousness, gasping, the imaginary noose tight about his throat. No, he couldn't give up the man who had nursed him through this last month to be jeered at by an angry crowd, spat at by prostitutes, to become the target of every curse and flung stone and then to die by the rope. He couldn't do that to Alfie. It must surely be more merciful to challenge him. They could take the pistols to some private place and let God decide between them. A crack shot, John knew he could best any man in a duel. He could make it instantaneous and clean. A death with honor, a little private sacrament for the two of them.

Sleep claimed him again as he was thinking of it, and he dreamed....

Early morning mist, a shadowed cove, as they met on the shore. The smell of the sea. Everything falling away but for the two of them; Alfie's face eager and bright as it was in battle, all his formidable concentration leveled at John as he brought up his pistol. The weight of his own gun in his hand and the little sensory shock as the hammer pulled back, clicked into position. They fired together, and John felt his own heart stop even as a rose of blood opened on Alfie's chest. Somehow there was no distance between them—they were holding on to one another for support, watching each other's faces as the pangs of death pierced through them, sinking together into oblivion, lying tangled together, Alfie's head on John's shoulder, blood mingling warm between their sprawled bodies....

John shuddered, crying out, enchanted and appalled, and woke once more to find himself lying in a thin rain, thoroughly soaked, chilled to the bone, and bitterly weary. Slowly and laboriously—fighting a myriad of pains—he pulled himself to his feet and looked out to the East, where the sky was already turning a spiritless grey. He felt wretched. The thought that he had to question the boys on this unsavory subject seemed more than he could face, and his desire for any kind of death or vengeance—for having been so thoroughly taken in—waned to ashes after the climax of that dream.

Death had lost its enchantment that morning. Everything had lost its enchantment. Dawn's light grudged broadening, and the path back down the hill, perversely, tried to trip him with every step. The houses he passed, with their washing hanging out of the windows, and bleary-eyed sleepers emerging half dressed to feed the chickens before breakfast, seemed disheveled, unwelcoming. He was acutely conscious of the stares as he passed, sure the sordid state of his soul must be visible to all.

When at last he found his weary way back to Castle Street and unlatched the door of their shared room he still had no idea what to do, what to say. His thoughts would come together when he saw Alfie again, he believed. He hoped he would know how to act then.

So it was a different kind of death to open the door and find the room empty; the floorboards bare, all Alfie's stuff gone, his mattress unmade and rolled beneath John's bed. Cleared away so thoroughly there was no sign left that he had ever been there at all. John stood, swaying, amid the emptiness, feeling stabbed to the heart.

CHAPTER 8

Great Cabin, HMS Britannia

His fingers still pressing the pulse in Farrant's wrist, Dr. Bentley looked up from his pocket-watch. "Your spirits are disturbed."

"You are the only man on this ship who needs to count my heartbeats to come to that conclusion." Farrant pulled his arm away from the cool grip with a sense of revulsion. Turning slightly, to put the doctor at his shoulder, rather than directly in front of him, he folded his arms, looked out at the bustle of the harbor beyond the *Britannia's* stern gallery, and fumed.

"I am the only one," Bentley said, closing his watch to tuck it back into his waistcoat pocket, "who goes beyond animal instinct into science." His black enameled watch-chain hung, gleaming slightly, over his super-fine black wool waistcoat, beneath his super-fine black wool frock-coat. His linen and stockings, by contrast, were an arctic white. Gibraltar's sunshine turned the lenses of his glasses into circles of gold.

"Pedantic penguin," said Farrant. "*You'd* be disturbed if you'd been cut. Snubbed! *Me!* Before the whole gaggle of Admiralty sycophants and hangers on." He relived the smug blandness on the face of the flunkey: *"The Port Admiral is not taking visitors at present, sir,"* as the door closed in his face. *The carefully averted gazes and smirks unsuccessfully hidden behind newspapers, as he stormed back out of the waiting room. The overheard conversation and laughter that had greeted him out-side—some jumped-up nobody of a commander having been round earlier, stirring up the gossip.* "I'll break them all! I'll have them all cashiered. It's about time the Duke did something to warrant my filial obedience."

Pushing his distance glasses down, Bentley fumbled in his waistcoat pocket for the set of reading glasses that had been crushed beneath falling boxes in the recent storm. Coming up empty-handed, he blinked at Farrant with soft, unfocused eyes, dark as ink, impersonal as his touch. Bending down, so close to the book that nose and pen touched the page together, he made a note in his journal. "Your mode of life should have accustomed you to insults, my Lord."

Scratch, scratch went the pen, like the claws of rats scrabbling against the hull. "Even dampened by the laudanum," Bentley talked on, "your libidinous disorder displays itself in visible symptoms. You should transfer Bert Driver at the very least. The man spends your money ashore in ways that expose you to infection." Tucking the book away, he walked over to the long, polished mahogany dining table which filled the center of the great cabin. With a hand steady as the harbor wall, he measured out twenty drops of colorless liquid into a tiny cup. "Your father can do nothing if you continue to behave with flagrant indiscretion. Sometimes, indeed, I believe you make a deliberate show of it. If you reap the results of that now, well...."

Anger, and the walk to and from the Port Admiral's office, had lifted the gray fog this morning's dose of laudanum had smeared over Farrant's world. When he looked out now, he saw beauty everywhere—that stevedore's jaunty walk, that sailor's long pigtail, the end of it flicking enticingly just above the rise of his buttocks. The men's raw beauty seemed to spill out of them, to add meaning to the sails of the ships departing, to fuel his awe and wonder at the Rock of Gibrlatar itself; breathtaking on a wholly different level. Did lust truly underlie his whole world, so that his eyes could see nothing to admire when it was taken away? Or was it just that in cutting out this vice, so central to his existence, he cut out the greater part of his soul with it?

"We had success with the tincture of opium at first." Bentley offered the little glass. "No incidents for almost a year. Your recent relapse suggests that you have become habituated. I have doubled the dose, and we'll see what that achieves."

"It takes away from me everything but a kind of dull resentment." Accepting it, Farrant looked down on the poisoned chalice with distaste. "It fills my head with soiled rags, and the dreams...my God!"

"*Dreams*, sir," Bentley took off his glasses, straightened up. He was, Farrant thought, younger than his manner always led one to believe; attractive in a chilly way. Though making love to a marble figure would surely be more rewarding. "Dreams do not place your life in danger, nor contribute to the ruin of your career, nor the misery of your wife and children. You have a disease and, until I can affect a cure, I must address the symptoms. I hope you do not propose to be recalcitrant?"

Snubbed, turned upon by his brothers in arms, Farrant had returned to the *Britannia* as to his own kingdom. But here Bentley stood, their spy in the camp, their jailer. Farrant wondered for a moment what the doctor would do if he ordered two of his tars to deposit the man ashore. *Write to wife and father, no doubt,* suggesting Farrant be consigned—for his own good—to Bethlem Hospital for the Incurably Morally Disordered.

As if the thought of letters had summoned him, Lt. Nyman chose that moment to knock discreetly at the door. "The Packet Ship from Jamaica is in, sir. Shall I leave your post outside the cabin?"

Farrant put the laudanum down next to the carafe of drinking water and strode across the checkerboard floor with a sense of reprieve, throwing open the door with such vigor that the frame trembled. "I'll have them now, please."

"Yes, sir."

As he returned to the table, breaking open the wax-paper

wrapped parcel of mail, pulling out the bundle of sealed letters, where Isabella had continued to write, and to cross, even the outermost sheet, Bentley reached out and gently touched the letters with his long paper-white fingers, as though they were holy. "Letters from your wife?"

"Indeed." Farrant smiled, avenged, just a little. "That will be all, doctor."

Almost human for a moment, Bentley turned away in confusion, laid his hand on the door knob, then paused. "I will wait to see you take your dose."

My beloved husband, said the first letter—Farrant had broken open the seal with a thumb, scattering wax, and sunk down on a hard mahogany seat to read—

> *I hope we will see you soon. There is illness in Spanish Town, and the first cases have been reported here only this week. James insists on visiting friends, or so he calls it, in the old capital, and I fear for him. He pursues his studies like a madman, and all the estate staff speak highly of his management. But he is pale, and has become thin. I fear... I know not what I fear. Either he is wearing himself down in revelry, damaging his constitution and making himself susceptible to the yellow fever, or he has some unsuitable love. I'm sure it must be unsuitable, for I know of no eligible girls in our entire acquaintance.*

> *Frances and George continue well, and desire me to write to you of their achievements; Frances on the harpsichord and George on his first pony. But I wish instead to urge you to come home; to see your children's small triumphs for yourself. They do not miss their father, and that seems to me to be a terrible thing.*

I, however, miss him very much. Do come. Take us all away from here. To England, perhaps, where James can find more wholesome recreations, and where the specter of the yellow jack will not cloud my eyes every time I look on his face. But if not England, we could live aboard ship with you, until the outbreak is over. I am not afraid at all of the perils of the sea so long as you are with me. It is the perils of the land I fear.

Pushing the letter away, Farrant looked down into his own eyes, reflected with a russet sheen in the polish of the dining table. *But that...no*, he looked away, planting his elbows and bowing his head into his hands. *"The children do not miss their father."* He heard a rustle as Bentley picked the letter up and walked to the stern windows, holding it to his face, as though he was sniffing it.

"I will take your drugs." Farrant closed his eyes and in the darkness fought that part of himself that screamed protest. "For her, for them, for you. If you will tell me one thing. *Is there* any chance of a cure? Must I stay half-dead forever?"

Bentley placed the letter on the table and sat down opposite him. When Farrant looked up, it was to see the smooth white face looking almost kind. "I'm sure of it, Sir. This talk of vice is superstition. Lapses not withstanding, I have seen you struggle with it too long and hard for that. Do you remember Fryett, haunted by a ghost I was able to cut away with a scalpel? Or Pattemore, whose aggression I cured by trepanning? If I had more test subjects, I could make a more rapid progress, but I am confident that in time I will locate the source of your affliction and excise it." A shy smile. "If you could try and avoid getting yourself hanged in the meantime, that would be very helpful."

Bentley rose, pushed his glasses up and glided as if on gimbals back to the door, opening it just as Nyman, on the other side, raised his fist to knock again. Nyman, well trained, did not flinch; merely allowing his raised hand to divert to the scar beneath his eye, as if it ached. "Beg pardon, sir. There's a young man asking permission to come aboard. Says you'll know him. Lieutenant Donwell, sir."

As he stood in the entry port of HMS *Britannia*, watching her First Lieutenant report his presence to the captain, Alfie tried to reconcile himself with the idea of a new beginning. This pain was only the kind of pain—brief, fleeting, soon forgotten—that starts a new life. He had always loved beginnings—early mornings, first smiles, first kisses—mistakes left behind and the certainty that it was still too soon for everything to turn sour. Why should he not now feel that fresh hope again? He should. He *would*, when the deed was properly done and the cord cut.

Casually, *Britannia's* deck-crew thinned as the men not required on the upper deck sauntered innocently below. Those unable to disappear evaded his eye, "accidentally" turned their backs to him. Without any insubordination whatsoever, he received the strong impression that he was not welcome.

Something of the same hostility, closing up around a guilty secret, flavored the sour-faced disapproving look on the First Lieutenant's nightmarish face when he returned. Though Alfie had been on the inside of the clannish defensiveness of a crew before, it was unexpectedly daunting to feel himself its target. "Come with me. The captain will see you."

Seven risers in the quarterdeck stair—Alfie counted them, his heart thrumming more urgently with each step. Trying not to remember; not to be thrown back to the pudding-faced ungainly child he had once been, he took off his hat and bowed with what felt like an audible crackle of nerves. He still hadn't looked, his gaze on the tips of the captain's shoes, but as he straightened to salute he had to—had to drag his focus upwards and meet Farrant's eyes.

A rushing, disorientated moment, as a force reached out of the past to pull him back into an earlier, unformed life. He breathed in sharply, just managing to suppress a gasp. For, though the world had altered around him, it had not touched Captain Lord Lisburn. It was as though he had reached maturity and simply frozen there, the square, strong face no more lined now than it had been ten years ago. Farrant's blue eyes were authoritative as ever, as blue as ever—a forgotten, speedwell blue whose vividness astonished.

Alfie swallowed, bit the inside of his cheek, and said, "Alfie Donwell, sir. I served with you on the *Mercury*. Recently passed for lieutenant. I wondered if you might have a place available."

"I remember you well, Mr. Donwell," Farrant's smile was too cynical to be called friendly. He shared a sidelong look with his first lieutenant, who was hovering by Alfie's elbow as if providing the captain moral support. "You had no tact as a child either. Running in where angels fear to tread."

It was strangely, bitterly amusing; how well Farrant knew him, how little he'd changed from that impulsive boy. Alfie smiled back. "An unexpected attack may carry the day, sir, before your opponent knows what you're about." He bowed his head. "But I must admit I've had no real success with the strategy." Studying the grain of the deck planks, he wound the topmost button of his coat round and round until it would move no more. "I would do anything to be taken aboard, sir. I hope you can imagine why I would wish to serve with you again."

Farrant dug his hands into his pockets. "I can think of several reasons. You made something of a nuisance of yourself on the *Mercury*, if I recall, Mr. Donwell. One of the least promising little squeakers it's ever been my displeasure to know."

"Sir…" Alfie cursed himself for the note of distress that shook his voice, but it had not occurred to him until this moment that Farrant might say "no." Though the captain might dislike the sight of him, he'd expected some fellow-feeling, some recognition that they were on the same side against the rest of the world. But suppose he did say "no", and Alfie was left behind to face Cavendish? The very best that could happen would be him being turned off the *Meteor* with no character and no real prospects of ever getting another berth. The worst was hanging. But more than that—worse than that—he could not face the look on John's face again. He couldn't.

Raising his head in a spray of light from the diamond cockade of his hat, Farrant looked at him keenly. "Are you bringing me trouble?"

But Alfie knew, for all his power, for all his influential relations, and for all his apparent carelessness over what others might think of him, Farrant too must need to be cautious. Suppose Alfie brought John's condemnation with him. Did John have the zeal in him to go to the Admiralty office and say, "That man runs a floating Molly house, he's just given refuge to the most despicable man of my ship"?

He couldn't see it. John had a powerful temper—a temper you hardly suspected at first, so meek he seemed, until it burst out like a volcano erupting—but he was not malicious. Having solved his own problem, Alfie did not think he would go out of his way to destroy anyone else.

"I'm running from it, sir. But I don't believe it will follow me here."

Farrant strolled slowly forward and began to pace in a small, pondering circle around Alfie. A rush of self-awareness lifted goosebumps on the skin of Alfie's arms, as he remembered that running for protection to his first love might make sense to him, but to Farrant it would look very different. Risking his own reputation by sheltering the sub-standard, annoying brat he had to forcibly brush off last time? Why on earth should he?

Standing so straight that his back cramped with the effort, he tried to wordlessly convey the message that he would be no trouble at all, that he knew his place, that he would be ever so grateful.

"Mr. Nyman?" Completing his circuit, Farrant turned to his first lieutenant. "I understand our fourth has been expressing reservations about the culture of the ship. Tell him that if he gets up here packed and ready to leave in the next five minutes he may have a transfer to the…?"

He raised an eyebrow at Alfie, who said *"Meteor*, sir!" in an embarrassingly fervent voice.

"Oh…" A tone of realization, and then the captain said dismissively, "I'm sure our Mr. Teach will find a ship captained by an Aminadab more to his liking. Sour faced, canting capons, the both of them."

Alfie broke attention to look straight at Farrant, startled. "Do you know Captain Cavendish, sir?" He shouldn't care. Fascination, hope, a painful lifting of the heart should form no part of his sucking whirlpool of betrayal and hurt. He should not feel, in the slightest, jealous at finding out that Farrant knew as much about John as he did. He should not need—want—to know any more.

Farrant gave him a slow, suggestive smile and said, "Dine with me tomorrow night. You can ask me all about it then." He turned away to shout, "Bring Mr. Donwell's dunnage aboard," to the tars loitering on the gangplank, leaving Alfie so confused he almost missed the breath of relief that went through the watching crew.

Britannia's wardroom table, spread with a white cloth, glittering with glass and cheerful with blue and white stoneware dishes, would not have disgraced a gentleman's country cottage. The roll and pitch of the ship—now underway to the West Indies—slid the gravy clockwise around Alfie's plate. The servant assigned to him kept his glass filled with red wine, which gently rotated in his glass, tasting of vinegar and lead. After he had cut his meat into smaller and smaller pieces for the better part of half an hour, listlessly acknowledging his mess-mates' introductions, the Gunner's wife, Mrs. Shaw, cleared her throat deliberately and asked, "You're eating with the Cap'n tomorrow?"

Looking up, he was struck by the distaste on every face, making all the separate physiognomies match, like a set of tableware. *Oh, so it is* that *kind of dinner, is it?*

"Yes," he said into the tense silence.

"The captain is…" First Lieutenant Nyman leaned forward. He should have been a ferocious looking man, with the cutlass scar across his cheek and jaw, the empty socket of his left eye. But the anxiety in his remaining eye made him seem only fragile; a discarded paper of news that begs not to be torn any further. "He has…"

"He has his little ways," Mrs. Shaw went on. A well-fleshed, jolly looking woman with chapped red hands and an impeccably starched bonnet, she seemed a great deal more robust than the lieutenant. "Which those of us what sails with him has to put up with, eh? He's a toff, ain't he, and they ain't like the rest of us."

"I took from your conversation that you were a boy when you sailed with him before?" Nyman asked, not quite meeting Alfie's eye as he poured himself a drink.

"I was, sir." Alfie had caught the drift of this conversation already, and managed a slight, cynical amusement despite the feeling of emptiness. It did nothing to work this barbed hook out from beneath his ribs; to help him find the half of himself that John seemed to have taken away with him. But it distracted from the pain, at least. "I served aboard the *Mercury* from thirteen years of age. Transferred to the *Swiftsure* as acting lieutenant three years later. I recall the *Mercury* as a happy ship. Well run, efficient, fought several smart actions off the Gold Coast. I thought her captain lucky, and fair, a good patron. Though I own he is a vain man—dresses like a macaroni."

"Yes, well…" The second lieutenant, Mr. Carver, had an awful squint, so at first Alfie could not tell who he was addressing. "You do well to use that word. Damn it all! There's no delicate way to say this, but I believe we would all like to remind you that if you expose the captain, you expose us all to a great deal of ridicule and shame."

"It's a bloody disgrace!" burst out the marine sergeant, trembling with indignation. His pipeclayed white belts squeaked against his coat buttons as he leaned forward. "If I was that bloody doctor of his, I'd put him out of his misery soon enough!"

"Sergeant!" Nyman's knife clattered against his plate. "You forget yourself. Four years aboard, you are no longer in any position to criticize. Besides, Mrs. Shaw is correct, it is not our place to pass judgments on the future Duke of Alderley."

Alfie looked around at the nervous, indignant faces, and was half tempted to be honest with them. *I offered him* anything *to be taken aboard. He's quite right to assume that includes sex on demand.* He nudged the little weighted roll of cloth that kept his plate from sliding to and fro with each wave, and took as deep a breath as he could force into his aching chest. *Maybe I want something uncomplicated. If Farrant's changed his mind and thinks I'm good enough now, I won't be the one to say no.* But honesty had not worked out so well with John, and it was easier to slip back into the old, well worn pretence. "I'm sorry? I don't seem to be following…."

Mrs. Shaw patted Alfie's hand, then leaned back and passed him the plate of chops. "No more you should. But just in the course of things, remember; more'n one reputation's at stake, eh? You do what's right by the ship 'n we'll do what's right by you."

If he had felt better, he might have found it hard not to laugh. But as it was, he was evidently miserable enough to convince them of his innocent dread. They smiled at him encouragingly and urged him to eat.

ᓚᓬ Chapter 9 ᓬᓬ

"Captain Cavendish, sir. Message for you from the Admiral."

John, cravat untied, waistcoat lying over the end of the bed, wet clothes kicked into a soiled little heap in the corner, opened the door. The courier, a young man with a case of acne so severe his entire head looked like a boil, sniffed disapprovingly at the mess and said "Port Admiral wants to see you, sir. At your earliest convenience."

"Very well." Long practice allowed John to tie a perfect bow, shrug on a new waistcoat and resume his wet coat—it being his best—in less than ten seconds. Regretting the absence of Higgins, who would have done a better job of it, he doused his wig in white powder, shook off the excess and settled the wig over his damp hair. Buckling on his sword, impeccably dressed, he closed the door behind him moments later, looking imperturbable. But, as he followed the man down to Government House, he half expected each footstep to break him into a thousand splinters; within, he felt fragile as Venetian glass.

Sitting in the Admiral's waiting room, in a patch of sunlight that made his shoulders steam, he watched the flies bash themselves repeatedly against the closed sash window. *Poor creatures!* He knew well how they felt, his own thoughts trying to escape into the light, being constantly thrown back by some obstacle he could not see.

What did I miss? Yes, he had liked Donwell, but no, that

made no difference. Was he not morally obliged to condemn such an unmanly, unnatural vice, wherever he found it? *Yet don't I also have some obligation of friendship?* Didn't these past months when he had thought Alfie to be the best man on God's earth…didn't they count? But *what* did they count for?

The man clearly had self control enough to avoid assaulting me, but…. The bath returned to his mind, along with a loathsome wash of pleasure that had him angry again, launched him to his feet and made him pace. But Alfie hadn't—hadn't gone any further than suggestion. In his condition at the time John could hardly have stopped him had Alfie decided to press his suit by force, but on finding it unwelcome he had stopped himself, to his own regret.

He lied! He lied to me!

And was that really so surprising, considering John's reaction now?

"Come through, please."

Port Admiral Turner looked as uncomfortable as John felt, but the young man with him—the young man in the pristine new uniform, whose sword-hilt was covered with sapphires—smiled urbanely, with the easy charm of someone who is used to life delivering its sweets on demand to his palm.

"Commander Cavendish, this is Lieutenant Sir Eustace Foulkes." Admiral Turner nodded in the youth's direction, a slight inflection of weariness in his battle-roughened voice.

"I'm honored, sir."

"I hear you've had a transfer of lieutenants," the Admiral continued. "At least, an ex-*Britannia* has been through my office already this morning, explaining he's to replace your Mr. Donwell."

John's already unsettled nerves jumped at the name. So Alfie had run to his old captain for protection, not merely deserted. And he had seen to it that the *Meteor* was not left undermanned in the process. There was something horribly touching about that. So very efficient, so very much like the man, even in fear of his life.

Here was John's opening to explain why. He could not now claim to have been too busy to find an opportunity to speak. He could not claim ignorance. He must now tell all or forever know that he too had concealed the truth; the truth that would get Alfie hanged. "I…yes," he said, and swallowed, trying to clear his suddenly constricted throat. "I…." He could not do it. For all his repugnance, he could not really bring himself to think the man deserved death. *Let him go and be among his own kind, and good riddance.* "Lt. Donwell had served under Captain Lord Lisburn before, sir, and desired to return to his patron. I could not see any harm in it."

"Very well." Turner too cleared his throat, shuffling the papers in front of him. Behind him, a pair of amber and black bee-eaters squabbled on a tree-branch, a wing brushing the window, their chatter loud in the moment of silence. "We're not here to discuss that. The war is drawing to a conclusion, and Foulkes here is eager to be in at the kill. I have been directed to find him a ship as soon as may be."

John linked his hands behind his back in an effort to stop them balling into fists.

"I assume you know what I am about to say."

"Sir." After last night's shock, this was like the withdrawal of the bullet—the surgeon cutting open the hole and rummaging about inside for the shot. Grief compressed John's chest until he could barely force the air in. The *Meteor*…his ship…. She had become so dear to him. She had done so well against such impossible odds. *Such* odds! "But why, sir?"

"Why?" Turner sprang to his feet, the quarreling birds behind him whirring away in a flash of white barred wings. "'*Why!*' Goddamnit man! What do you mean 'why'? In the middle of a war, you take it into your head to firebomb the major port of a neutral nation? Consider yourself lucky you're not being hanged!"

"But sir!" *Piracy…slavery…kidnapped children….* "I was under Admiral Saunders' orders, sir!"

"Were you?" Turner held out a hand, its palm grey in the creases with accumulated tar. "Let me see them."

Closing his eyes, John struggled with the spun-glass pieces
of his composure. They would hold. They would hold at least
until he got out of this room. He would not have thought it of
Saunders—this duplicity, this behind-hand politicking. "My orders were verbal, sir."

"How convenient." Turner looked away, flipped open the top
of his inkwell and flipped it shut again, his gaze never quite meeting John's. John straightened, choking back the furious cry of "*Are
you calling me a liar?*" But it must have shown in his face. Foulkes
turned away, ostensibly to examine the books on the bookshelf,
and Turner's tanned cheeks flushed dark. "I am taking your ship,
Mr. Cavendish, and giving it to Sir Eustace. You are to consider
yourself officially reprimanded and punished. You will remain
here on half pay until we can find another situation for you. Understood?"

"Yes, sir."

"Very well then. Dismissed."

"Thank you sir." John's thoughts felt like a tangle of razor
sharp wire; he bloodied himself trying to hold them in. But hold
them in he did, and bowed again. "Sir Eustace." Holding very
still against the ruin, trying to become steel throughout, he
turned, walking away.

His footsteps took him as a matter of habit to the café, where he
sat at a table amid the tubs of flowers, in a scent of thyme, and drank
strong coffee until he was all but vibrating in place. But it was too
heartbreaking to sit here alone, at the same table he shared yesterday with Alfie. So he threw down a shilling on the tablecloth and attempted to calm his overstrung fibers with another long walk down
to the harbor. Better to spend the morning knocking on the doors
of squalid lodging houses until he found Higgins, still abed, with a
square-faced, Rubinesque young woman, who squeezed her ample
figure into stays, scraped her lead-blackened hair beneath a cap and
cooked eggs and bacon for breakfast, cheerfully unflappable.

"Didn't expect to see an officer in my humble abode, captain." Higgins pulled on a pair of trousers while this was going

forward and rolled the bedding away into a kitchen cupboard, his ginger hair standing up like tongues of fire. "Good to see you on your feet again, sir."

"I'm come to tell you I've been turned ashore, Higgins." John nodded gratefully as a plate was lowered to the table in front of him. Tempted to fix his eyes on the fork, he distained the cowardice of such an action and looked up at his steward's leathery and confused face.

"Turned ashore?"

"Indeed." John stabbed the bacon with unnecessary fervor, feeling his face heat with humiliation. "And my finances are not such as would allow me to keep a servant."

"But for why, sir? We damn well showed them—begging your pardon. They sent us in like a dog against a bear and we brought him down good and proper! Never was such a piece of glory, and us living to tell the tale. You should get a medal! We should all get a reward…." His flow of indignation faltered in horror. "What about our prize money? Thirty or forty ships we sunk! Are we going to get paid for them?"

"I understand the Admiralty's position is that it was a regrettable misunderstanding." John worked it out himself as he spoke. The men would know soon enough, when their money did not arrive; they were owed at least an explanation. "As such, they cannot pay prize money for any vessels destroyed. I don't know if they intend to recoup the costs from me. Admiral Turner made no mention of it.

"But that aside, it seems to me that—now the tide is turning against the French—we were sent to provide an excuse for war with Algiers. Parliament is concerned at the extent of Barbary raids on England. I believe the Admiralty thought we would be sunk; a shipful of martyrs to rally public support. Our survival must have been inconvenient. And our triumph…our triumph is politically disastrous, for it gives the pirates the moral high-ground—makes us seem the aggressors." *And Saunders has probably already denied any responsibility or even knowledge of it. I would never have thought him capable of such duplicity.*

Higgins' face was purple as a bruise. He pushed his food away untouched. John folded his hands around his pint of small ale, and cursed himself. Everything he seemed to do this week was ruinous. He had been thinking aloud, and forgotten his company, the possibilities of mutiny and desertion. Fortunately Higgins, sturdy as an oak, also had all the thinking capacity of an oak. "Me and the boys, we sat down and worked it out, three hundred and forty-eight pounds, five shillings and sixpence each, we reckoned. 'Fiddler's green,' I thought. Me and Evie here was going to buy a pub, settle down."

Evie gave an eloquent shrug of one rounded shoulder and snagged the last slice of bacon for herself. John sighed. "I'm sorry, Higgins."

"And they turned you ashore?"

"Turner did say I should consider myself lucky not to be hanged." John smiled, struck by the thought that this morning he and Alfie could both be swinging gently in the breeze from either end of the mainmast yard. It was, after all, something to be still alive. He caught Higgins' eye, and the amusement leapt across the connection like a spark.

"'Alf of the crew ain't been sober since we dropped anchor. Lor' they ain't going to be happy!"

"Poor Sir Eustace!"

Higgins snorted beer out of his nose, and for a moment everything went away as they laughed until their eyes streamed.

"Who?"

"Your new captain. Seemed an open, cheerful sort. I don't think I'm leaving you in the hands of a tyrant, at least."

Falling silent, Higgins drew a clove hitch on his plate with the yolk of his egg. John ate a piece of bacon in the increasingly embarrassed pause, conscious that he should say something; some thanks for all those years of nurture. Some acknowledgement of regret. "Still, we wiped the Dey's eye," he said at last. "He won't forget us in a hurry."

Standing up, John offered his hand, and after a moment's surprise Higgins rose and took it. "I wish you well then, Higgins, and hope we serve together again in kinder circumstances."

"You need me sir, you just ask."

A melancholy morning of saying farewell to the other *Meteor*'s segued into a melancholy afternoon of going through the ship's books with Sir Eustace. But when—after they had shared a meal too fine for him to eat—he left the new captain in possession and returned to his lodgings in the evening, he found that the business of the day had been a blessed distraction from his real thoughts. They mobbed him anew as he shut the door, saw again the bareness of a room that until now had been so comfortably, comradely cluttered.

Retrieving tinderbox and candle—the light draining out of a cold gray sky—he wondered, *Is it truly only one short day since yesterday? How quickly the world could be destroyed.* He set the candle in its carved wooden stick on the desk, took journal and writing slope from his chest, and trimmed a quill. As the night darkened, black behind the window, he could see his own reflection in the glass. He closed the curtains, dipped his pen.

> *I ask myself; am I being punished? Was I wrong to deal with Mr. Donwell as I did? I cannot resolve which way I should have acted; whether I was unjust in using too much mercy, or too little. Should I have removed the threat to society? Or should I have removed the plank in mine own eye before daring to pay attention to the speck in my brother's?*
>
> *I have seen many answers to prayer. I have seen men speak the words of God, His Spirit bursting from their mouths in fierce and fearless delight.*

*But today I can perceive no presence to guide me
at all. I remain lost in the labyrinth of my
thoughts.*

*Perhaps indeed I could have….But no, I could not
have asked for my orders in writing! I disdain to
be that kind of grass-combing sea-lawyer. The service runs on trust; zeal and trust. Confidence in
those above, loyalty to those below. And perhaps
that is that what I transgressed; my loyalty towards Lt. Donwell? If so, it is an elegant punishment. But my thoughts return again in horror to
the fact that he was a sod, an abomination. I wonder if it was my loyalty to the Lord which failed;
because I did not denounce him, because I kept
quiet when I should have condemned?*

*My mind will not be still; will not settle on any one
answer. God knows how I am to sleep. I pray constantly for understanding; to be shown of what exactly I should repent. But no answer comes.*

• • •

"You have improved, Mr. Donwell."

Alfie sipped his wine and watched the lantern light slide gently from one side of the highly polished table to the other, and
back. He felt…he didn't know what he felt. Resentment, perhaps? Misery, certainly.

The light picked itself up and ran honey-slow over the palm
of Farrant's hand, which lay open on the table. Alfie's gaze traveled up the blue-clad arm and was caught by Farrant's knowing
smile.

"Thank you," he said. "I hope I am better in all things. Including my taste in men."

Farrant laughed and topped up his glass. The wine was very

good, its sweetness not yet shaken out of it by the sea. "Lord, how bitter! And is mockery enough to content you?"

"No, sir," Alfie admitted, drinking deep. "Far too little. But far too little seems to be all I can manage at present."

"God's teeth! If we're going to be maudlin we need to be more drunk."

"Yes." Yet there was some comfort in this; being with a man before whom he didn't have to hide what he was. To be able to talk without deceit. To be able to shed for an hour that suffocating blanket of lies. Alfie knocked back the new wine and was about to ask for something stronger when Farrant unstoppered the brandy and filled his glass again. "You said something about Captain Cavendish being a Quaker? Is that public knowledge, or are you acquainted with him, sir?"

Farrant took off his wig and put it on its stand, hung his coat beneath it, and returned not to the head of the table, but to pull out a chair next to Alfie, dropping an assured, possessive hand on his knee. "I would prefer it if you were thinking about me."

"I'm sorry, sir. I…but do you know him?"

"I know his type." Farrant bent his head to watch as he slid both hands up Alfie's thighs until they rested at his hips, thumbs just touching Alfie's balls. He made a slow, gentle circle with them, and Alfie gasped and licked his lips after, tasting the rush of desire like copper in his mouth. His thoughts stopped sharp, like a horse refusing a jump, leaving him with the sickening feeling of falling.

"He was sneaking about the Admiralty yesterday." Farrant unbuttoned the flap of Alfie's breeches, one warm hand sliding down to cup his balls and gently knead them, while the other pulled up his shirt to expose his suddenly eager cock. "Asking questions about me. I had one of my men return the favor. He's a nobody, a little shit. I don't want to hear anything about him from you again, understand?"

"Nnh!" said Alfie, months of yearning and self-restraint coalescing into angry need. *Oh, that was good!* God, it was good to know that *someone* wanted him, even if that someone couldn't be John. Even if that someone was the cynical, heartbreaking bastard who'd rejected him a lifetime ago. Maybe even because of that. Let one mistake wipe out—just for a moment—the memory of the other.

His prick throbbed, painfully full, and fire gathered at the base of his spine. He rocked his hips up in offering, closing his eyes. "Why…?" he managed as Farrant changed hands—his left hand slightly less adept, rougher. Wonderfully, amazingly rough. "You, I'm not—you said…. Why?"

His answer was a rustle of cloth. Farrant laughed again, in a murmur hardly louder than that of the water against the hull. Alfie jerked as a rush of delight transfixed him like a spear, as Farrant's hand, slick with butter, closed over the head of his prick and stroked firmly down. His eyes flew open as his thighs were trapped between Farrant's and the captain lowered himself down onto Alfie's prick, taking it in with one long, firm push.

"You arrived like an omen, just when I was sick and tired of being told what I can and cannot do." Farrant's eyes were unfocused and his face fierce. He took Alfie by the shoulders and pulled himself up, almost off, before he rammed them back together again, back arching and breath hissing between his teeth. The hot, tight slide was fantastic, unbelievable, maddening as hell. "And I can't…can't get this from a man who doesn't want it."

"I want it." Alfie grabbed Farrant's bare arse, fingers digging in hard, pulled him down as he thrust up, and for a moment it was all sweat and flesh and demand. "I want it."

Farrant muffled his cries by biting down hard on Alfie's neck, and Alfie came explosively within the older man's body, transfixed by anguish and relief.

He sat for a while with Farrant in his lap, arms about his neck, Farrant's face tucked into his throat as he trembled into stillness. Then Alfie's leg cramped, and in the struggle to soothe the stabbing pain Farrant pulled himself off and stood, picking up his fallen breeches from the floor.

"Well, that's taken the edge off," he said, gesturing with graceful, patrician courtesy towards his sleeping cabin, "but I daresay you want your turn. Shall we?"

Alfie went in, without question. Brandy and sex; it was hard to say which was better at taking his mind off John. Neither was having very much success. It seemed such a shame that Farrant couldn't have turned to him earlier, when he would eagerly have died for the man's love. In those days this would have felt like a triumph, with trumpets and angels singing. Now it seemed only a temporary solace for the pain, like downing a pint of rum and passing out.

In the small sleeping cabin, the line of white wake behind them threw back a watery, dappled starlight over the hands that were slowly unwinding the cravat from about his throat. Farrant's short hair was also silver, unearthly and beautiful, and Alfie felt as though he had stepped in a fairy ring, been taken away to another world whose rules did not make sense.

A sixth sense told him that somewhere in the world, John was thinking of him, and he wondered if, one day, he would ever be forgiven. Did that matter? It was all over now. A different dream was coming true.

With his eyes closed, Alfie could smell the smoke of the Great Cabin's many lanterns; beeswax and turpentine on the polished table; the warm, red smell of port wine. In here—against the hull of the ship—was the scent of oak, and tallow from a bedside candle; the ever-present mildew of a life at sea. The partition wall smelt of paint, and the captain smelt of pomade, and ambergris, and the faint, hot scent of desire. Alfie's mind returned to John, summoning his scent of tar and ink, and the honey he spread on biscuits when he couldn't get toast. These were John's hands on him, John's slender body covering him, John's cock for which he spread his legs and begged. It was dream-John into whom he nestled, afterwards, and slept. But it was Farrant beside him whom he awoke.

"You called me 'John.'" Farrant, reclining on his elbow beside Alfie, smiled down at him in obvious amusement. "And after

I forbade you to mention him again! I hope you will not disobey all my commands so readily."

They lay together companionably in the little bunk. Its edge dug into Alfie's arse, making him squirm closer to Farrant. But it was the ever present pain that made him put an arm around the older man's waist and turn his cheek to rest against the sparse silver hairs of his chest. There *was* a mute, visceral comfort in this; hearing a firm heartbeat beneath his ear, being damp and warm, shirts tangled around their waists, glued together by drying semen.

"I loved him," Alfie murmured, soothed too by being able to speak to someone who understood every nuance—understood even the words he did not say. "He despised me for it."

Farrant's hand curved around his jaw, turning Alfie's face up to look at him. The captain's expression was exasperated, but kind. "Let me give you some sound advice," he said, as his other hand toyed idly with Alfie's hair. "Stop this. Stop chasing love. Love is not for men like us. We share a deviancy we must pay for with lives of exemplary duty. That's all. You will get yourself hanged if you try to think otherwise."

Alfie smiled, and for a moment all the unhappiness left him, as he felt how ridiculous it was for Farrant to lecture him about avoiding suspicion. The man flaunted his vice in the face of the whole world. As a boy it had been one of the things Alfie most admired. He traced the collarbone beneath the man's skin, touched scars and freckles and the wrinkles around the thin, salt-chapped mouth. As he did so, it came to him that Farrant was not the powerful god he had once thought. Just a man, like himself, made of fallible flesh and breakable spirit, like his own. Sometimes mistaken. Perversely lovable in his rebarbative way. And like Alfie himself, very, very alone.

Whether he had wanted to or not, Farrant had rescued Alfie from the intolerable position his mistake with John had put him in. Farrant had distracted and soothed him when he most needed relief from the heartache. Surely it was only fair now to offer whatever he could to make Farrant's life better?

"Yet I could love you, I think. If you gave me a little time to forget." Alfie pulled Farrant to himself, kissed him, letting him feel the promise of affection, of intimacy beyond the mere sharing of lust. Farrant was hesitant at first, but for just a moment he melted and in the darkness beneath their closed eyes they seemed to touch, closer and more intimate than any embrace of flesh. Then his hands tightened painfully on Alfie's hair, pulling them apart. He wrenched himself away.

"My poor boy!" he said coldly. "So eager to give your heart? Yet no one wants it."

An echo of the rejection ten years ago. But Alfie wasn't a child anymore—he knew from the inside the bitterness that aimed such barbs. For so many years he too had been afraid to reach out to anyone. He too had slaked desire wherever he could find a willing body, and not hoped for anything better. It was almost a relief to think that Farrant's dismissive sarcasm had been, all along, just a defense against heartbreak.

Farrant's face was turned away from him now, making him guess at the expression, but it seemed there was a glimmer beneath his shut eyelids. A shadow of silver stubble gleamed over a curving line on his jaw. Surprising himself, Alfie leaned in and kissed the half-moon a blade had left on that aquiline face. He understood what it was to be scarred.

◖◖◖ Chapter 10 ◗◗◗

October 1762, Portsmouth

There was no sight, John thought, better than that of HMS *Albion* coming down the slipway with the rush and splash and sudden majestic lift of a descending swan. Sir Eustace Foulkes, ashamed perhaps of the way things turned out, had put in a good word for him, and when John, tail between his legs, had stepped off the returning merchant ship, onto the docks at Portsmouth, he had discovered the *Albion* waiting for him. A newly commissioned fifth rate, he was to serve only as the third lieutenant, but after four months of existing on half pay, it was deliverance.

Gibraltar had been purgatory. Friends, met on the docks, had to be told that he had blown his chance at captaincy and had his ship taken away. He had gone hoarse regaling horrified listeners with the tale of his dealings with the Dey. Though each time the listener nodded sagely at the end and said, "in your position, old boy, I'd have done exactly the same," he could not avoid the thought that he was now marked down in the Admiralty's books as an over-emotional fanatic, not to be left in charge of the big guns.

The charge of fanaticism occupied his nights also. When another day of lingering fruitlessly in the white paneled reception rooms of the Embassy was over and his meager supper eaten, he would retire to his room to pray. His worn copy of the Bible had become something of a scourge, and he returned to it in morbid compulsion, his thoughts see-sawing between self rebuke and craving.

Frightening Alfie away had not helped. He just haunted John's nights, filling his dreams with the explicit lust and jealousy he fought off during the day. Finally Admiral Turner, tripping over John's ankle as he came in to the waiting room in the early dawn, had looked him in the face and said, "The climate here doesn't suit you, boy. You might have more luck at home."

So John closed the door on the room he had shared with Alfie; closed the weeks of fruitless prayer inside it, and returned to England. Throwing himself into balls and masquerades, he did his best to charm the ladies; an aim he succeeded in rather too well for his own liking. Now he had several of them chasing him, and he had begun to understand that what he had thought his inherent virtue was in fact a lack of capacity.

"You must be so proud!" exclaimed his escort, Mrs. Lavinia Deane, clutching his arm tightly and "accidentally" brushing it with her overflowing bosom.

"I am," he said, smiling as he supposed he ought to smile; inwardly quailing at the realization that his slight discomfort was not normal. Not virtuous at all—quite the opposite, in fact. If he were a normal man he should feel a little spark of desire at the contact. He should be courteously controlling it, not simply lacking in the feeling at all.

He turned his gaze back to the *Albion*, and at once all his doubts fled, enthusiasm dragging him forward a step. "She is beautiful! But really this is Captain Gillingham's day. He oversaw her building from the plans upwards and brooded over her like a chicken on an egg. In a way, she's his child. I'm just a hired servant."

"You're not 'just' anything." Mrs. Deane pressed his arm again, leading him to have uncharitable thoughts about the notorious lustfulness of widows. But it was hardly her fault that he had used her to prove something to himself. Smiling again, he felt grimy with guilt when she beamed back.

A beautiful woman, with her glossy black hair curled to the height of fashion and her robin's egg blue eyes startling in their frame of black lashes. Her complexion was all milk and roses and her figure upright but full. He knew from the reactions of other men that she was infinitely desirable, that he was infinitely to be envied. But it was becoming increasingly clear to him that he couldn't do this. He couldn't flatter, or wonder, or worship her as she deserved. He hated himself for it, but she spoke to nothing in him at all—and the weary, persistent gallantry prevented him from even becoming her friend.

Dishonesty, all of it. Yet another unavoidable sin.

"Let me take you on board," he said, eager to explore the new ship—to get to know her; wander through her curved recesses, stand alone in the great cavern of her empty hold and breathe in. Never yet inhabited, she was sweet-smelling still, scented of pitch and oak, sharp and clean and bracing as a strong cup of tea.

"Most of my gentlemen would prefer to spend their time on other sports," said Mrs. Deane, and laughed aloud at the expression on his face. Letting go of his arm, she tapped him sharply with her closed fan. "Oh, Lieutenant, you think yourself so inscrutable! But I assure you I have your measure."

"You do?" Confounded, he looked at her properly, perhaps for the first time, seeing the wisdom in her experienced eyes. "If so, madam, you have the advantage of me."

"You are so sweet." Her smile brought out dimples in both cheeks. "I do believe you're speaking the truth. Come, then, let me crawl around this damp hulk for your amusement and we'll talk."

Unsettled, John escorted her down into one of the small jolly-boats which plied to and fro across the harbor. She sat composedly in its bows, though she grew pale by the time he had rowed her across the turbulence of the *Albion*'s launch and to her side. There were, fortunately, carpenters and sailors aboard who could lower a rope for him to tie about her to haul her aboard, for she would never have got up the side in all those petticoats.

"As you were," he said to the men. "We're just sightseeing." And he noted with a lurch of regret how much more respect they seemed to have for him after seeing him with such a fine woman.

Mrs. Deane tore him strangely between two worlds. The sea, the ship, the tars and the ropes about him, they were his reality. She was something different, and it seemed she herself was not unconscious of the fact.

"Well, it is spacious, at least," she said, going straight to the captain's cabin and sitting down on a locker beneath the stern window. He wondered if she had deliberately chosen the place for effect, because the watery sunlight outside surrounded her in a tissue of fine gold, rubbing out such lines on her face as her careful make-up had failed to conceal. "Sit down here by me."

He perched beside her, feeling like a wild bird she brought to her hand with seed, poised to fly. Had he been completely underestimating her all this time? Missing out on a sharp mind because he was too closely concerned with his own concerns? "Have I been a very great idiot?"

She smiled again—the one with the dimples. "Only a small one. You see, I know your father."

John straightened as if he'd been kicked. "You didn't mention that."

"No need to pull that acid face with me!" Mrs. Deane opened her fan slowly with her left hand and gazed at him over the top. "I didn't like him at all!"

"It possibly shows an ungrateful spirit in me," John laughed, "but I'm glad to hear it. I should have been very embarrassed indeed if I knew you were one of his set."

"Dreadful people," she agreed. "They think one enjoys oneself by an endless procession of new vices. For myself I prefer to have one or two vices, properly matured." Raising an impeccably curved eyebrow, she challenged him to react to that. But beyond smirking in amusement and dropping his head in an attempt to hide it, he couldn't think of anything to say.

"Your father attempted to add me to his collection of trophies. This was at the time I was married to dear Deane, of course. Though I wouldn't have considered the man even if I had been free."

"You…have been taking your revenge?" John hazarded, still all at sea. It seemed that while he had been trying to prove something with her, she had been having her own game with him. It made him feel, truth be told, a great deal happier.

She laughed. "Oh, you *can* be sharp? I wondered if you were simply a little dense. But true, it's a pleasant thought to know that rumor of my bearing you company—voluntarily—will be a well deserved thorn in Cavendish's pride. But also, you know, I was curious. He painted you as such a prude!"

"I think…" John opened one of the windows in an effort to cool a conversation which had suddenly become very warm. It was telling, he supposed, that he had never enjoyed her company more than he was doing now, when all pretence of attraction had been dropped. "I think that certainly I have been a prude, in the past. What I am now, I don't…I don't really know. I haven't finished becoming it."

"Lord! A philosopher!" she mocked, not unkindly. "Well, I own myself defeated. What you were to me was a curiosity and a challenge. Only the second challenge, I may say, at which I have ever failed. And the first…" She dropped her fan, and when he handed it back put her fingers on his and gave him a mischievous look. "Well, his desires ran in an entirely different channel."

"You are the wickedest woman I've ever met!" he exclaimed, laughing. Half shocked and half delighted by the outrageous innuendo, he was at first simply diverted. A heartbeat later, however, the irreverence made him think of Alfie. Her joy in life made him think of Alfie, and his smile faltered as he thought that her laughing tolerance was so much more generous, so much more like the loving kindness of God, than his own condemnation. "But

I wish we had spoken like this earlier. We could have been such friends!"

She patted his hand in a motherly fashion—though John's mother would have been horrified to be seen in such a low-cut dress, or with her face painted like a Jezebel. "We were both playing for higher stakes, I believe," she said. "But in the end one or both of us had to acknowledge that the game was not worth the candle. You are a delightful boy—considering your family—and a pretty one. This interlude has been most productive for me. Do you know you've garnered me a set of pearls, a Wedgewood tea-service, two new carriage horses and a liveried page to go with them? Not to mention the highly satisfactory insecurity engendered in my other suitors. I set it down to your good nature that you did not try this experiment with a girl who could have been truly hurt by it."

John had not deliberately thought of it like that, but it was true that of all the young girls who had been smitten by his personal beauty, he had taken care not to encourage those for whom it obviously meant a great deal. "I know what it is for a man's... self exploration, to ruin a woman's happiness. If you know my parents then I need say no more. I hope that whatever I am I shall never be so deliberately cruel."

"Only inadvertently cruel," she said, smiling.

"Inadvertently cruel, yes. Of that, I admit, I am more than capable."

Mrs. Deane looked at him. For a moment the life left her eyes and she seemed all of her forty-five years—a woman who had buried one life, seen her grown children move away, and been left to fill her remaining years in whatever way she pleased. Less free than merely superfluous. Then she smiled, and by effort of will the desert was once more full of flowers. She drew her fan across her eyes as if to wipe away melancholy. "But we still can be friends," she said. "I presume you know how to write, yes? Just because you're sailing next week doesn't mean you can't write me long, passionate letters about your next *inamorato*. I am not above living through other people's interesting lives, you know."

Setting her hand in his, she rose to her feet. Impulsively, he kissed her fingers, and she gave him a sidelong look of reproach, as if to say it was a bit late for that now. "But if you write me sermons, they will go straight on the fire."

Taking her back to the dock, they parted with more fondness than he had thought possible. She stood on tiptoe to kiss his cheek and then envelop his face between her two silk gloved hands, looking at it carefully. "Such a waste!"

"You have a woman's heart," he said, a little stung. "There are other things in life than love."

"But none so important." Clutching her bonnet against the evening breeze she looked at him warningly. "Say you won't try to be some sort of saint of the wilderness. I'd hate to think of you withering away, untasted."

"Madam." Relief though it was to talk to a woman who seemed to understand, he felt her tolerance went too far. "There is no other choice I can make with honor."

"Forget honor."

Honesty, it seemed, did not solve all problems, even if it clarified what the problems were. "I hope I shall never do that."

"Then do write, John. Write to me. You will need a friend."

He stood watching as she got into her waiting carriage, waved, and waited until she was gone. Then he returned to the *Albion* and, taking a lantern, descended to the hold. Deep down, in the darkness by her keel, he walked the length of her, surrounded by ribs. It was like being in the belly of the whale. He wondered if he would ever be vomited up again, as Jonah had been; returned to the bright world and to life. But it was of no real account, was it? Because Mrs Deane saw things through a woman's eyes, and love *wasn't* everything. He *could* live life celibate and dutiful, like one of the old saints. It had not done them any harm.

Three weeks out from Portsmouth, and again descending into the hold with a lantern, John remembered his determination with a kind of despairing hilarity. It had seemed so simple. It had, after all, always been so simple before to curb his thoughts, to lose himself in mathematics or music, and emerge feeling purified. The mere knowledge of his desires should not make them ungovernable. Yet now it was as if his eyes had been opened. Blind, he hadn't seen the beauty that surrounded him, but Alfie had given him sight.

On the first day afloat he had come out on deck and stopped dead, ravished by the turn of Lt. Oxford's throat. Looking away, flushing, he saw the men of the lower deck with their shirts off in this mild weather, hauling on the ropes, their muscles limned in gleaming sweat.

Oh God no! he'd thought. *God, no, please!* But God, if he was watching, must have been laughing up his sleeve, because the sudden awareness had only grown.

For his new captain and his mess mates, he managed to go through all the familiar routine of the navy, performing his duties exactly as he used, as though nothing had changed. The naval routine around him was familiar as the rhythm of his breathing. But he began to dimly discern another world within it; jealousies too sharp for friendship, smiles too radiant.

Now, setting foot on the latticework of the cable tier, his ear picked up the sound of men arguing, the new sense in him hearing too deep a bitterness. He drew closer—it was his duty to do so, after all—and listened.

"Don't you dare touch him, he's *mine!*"

"Calm down! I was just—"

"I know what you were 'just,' you slut! I'm gonna…"

John didn't want anything to do with it. Wanted, in fact, to turn and walk away, to not have been there in the first place; not to have to make yet another decision to ignore his plain duty. But what could he do? He raised his lantern and edged around the coiled anchor cable.

"Sweet Christ, Billy, shut up! The Lieutenant—"

Who was more appalled—the love triangle or himself—it would be hard to say. He could imagine how he seemed to them, all innocent curiosity and gold braid in the dark. Authority coming upon them, unexpected and terrible, aglimmer, like the scythe of death. The third man, quicker than they, or smaller, squirmed through a loop of cable and was gone. He heard the fleeing footsteps bound up the companionway beyond. But Billy Wier and his tie-mate shrank together, clutching at each other for reassurance, and turned to face him. Even as he recoiled in understanding, the terror in their eyes struck him. Their linked hands sheltered one other, as though they huddled together over a candle-flame his breath might put out.

For a long moment he stood undecided, while the dark of the hold became his room at evening, their eyes on him like Alfie's—crushed, betrayed. He had done the right thing, expressed a correct repugnance for this mockery of love; he had hurt and condemned. Perhaps it was an appropriate punishment that he now found himself envying them.

Billy drew breath to plead, and John screwed his eyes shut against the memories. "I don't know what you men are up to down here, but get back to work."

When he opened them again, both sailors were transformed with relief, reprieved. "Yes sir. Thank you, sir."

"Don't let me catch you again."

"I won't, sir. Thank you, sir."

As he watched them run up to the upper deck, he had the feeling he had acquired at least one devoted follower. But it was little comfort. His shoulders tensed and ached everywhere that Alfie had touched them, and he was overcome with yearning as he understood that it would never happen again. Never again to be touched with loving hands. Never, even once, to be kissed.

Mrs. Deane had been right. Who should know better than a widow what it was like to have once known the comfort of a beloved body, once to have been enfolded, flesh and soul alike in intimate affection, and to have lost it. He could wish fervently that his appetites had not been woken, that he could return to the innocent, childish world from which Alfie had prized him, but it seemed it was not going to happen.

Carrying on with his inspection, he tried to ignore the pulse of blood in his veins. Tried to distract himself from the pictures of Billy Wier and his friend lying down among the tangled ropes and fucking slowly, but his mind was full of perversity and his prick was hard, and his chest seemed as full of darkness as the belly of the ship. He didn't know what to do; how much he was supposed to endure before God intervened and made it all go away. Why was the Lord not doing so already? Why was John left to hold on with bleeding hands to this thin cable of determination, feeling it unraveling and parting between his fingertips, dropping him into the pit?

If you want me to stop, help me to stop. I don't want to disobey you, but please! You know what I need, what I can endure. You made me what I am. Help me. Give me the strength to resist this.

But he knew that tonight, like last night, like almost every night for the past three months, he would sin in his imagination, and in flesh avoid the sin of Sodom only by committing the sin of Onan.

CHAPTER 11

December 1762, Jamaica

John tugged at his neckcloth, feeling sweat make its itchy way down his back to soak into the waistband of his breeches. With his head down and his large hat overshadowing his face, clad in his only suit of civilian clothes—an old fustian coat and dingy breeches—he hoped he was not recognizable as a naval officer as he leaned, falsely casual, against the broken fountain. Bright Jamaican birds hopped and squawked among the enclosed gardens which fenced this end of Kingston. He watched the men come down the street, towards the open door; watched them balk when they saw him, and either turn away or straighten up with a bright, fake innocence and pass him, talking loudly about trivialities.

For a while he thought that they were fighting their own consciences, as he was fighting his, but it gradually dawned on him that no, he was frightening them away.

Putting his hand in his pocket, he touched the little scrap of paper on which an untutored hand had scrawled this address. An end of voyage present from Billy, who had stopped him in the street as he was emerging from his newly rented lodgings. "What it is, sir, is that Simeon says you might like this. I says you's a gent, you don't need no invitation from the likes of us. Also you ain't interested. But Sim, 'e says 'give it him anyway'. So 'ere. Right exclusive club it is, nice and clean, you get me? Don't take it wrong, like. It was Sim what said you might want to know."

Though he had only a suspicion of what Billy had been talking about, the scrap of paper burned his hand. He felt its presence in his pocket as he went about the town, learning the layout of the place, tasting the humid air with its strange scents, marveling at the great houses and the markets that seemed to sell a thousand necessaries he had never seen before. The address itched more infernally than the many bites he discovered on himself next morning—wages of being haphazard with the mosquito netting.

The door was unprepossessing, a brown, dowdy thing with traces of green mold. No better nor worse than any other door in the street. Except that it opened on a regular basis and men came out, or—when they could nerve themselves to walk past John's lurking presence—went in.

A man emerged now; a big man, burly as a blacksmith, with a fist-flattened nose and shoulders that strained the seams of his frock-coat. He came towards John, tapping a gnarled club against his gnarled palm. John took a firmer grip on his own cane and stood up to meet the threat.

"What d'you want, Mister? You gonna stand there all day?" The accent was straight from Grub Street, London. It seemed Billy had given him the name of a place reserved for the most vulgar sort of displaced working man, and indentured servants scraped straight off the streets of the capital.

"I can stand where I please," replied John, annoyed.

"Nah, you see, that's where you're wrong. 'Cos this is private property, right. You come along in, or you move on."

Resentful though he was of being given orders by some riff-raff of the street, John had to acknowledge that the man was right. He couldn't stay forever poised between inside and out, between yes and no. Sooner or later he would have to make a decision.

"I have… an introduction," he said, handing the scrap of writing to the man. "What…what is the place?"

"Oh ho, it's like that, eh?" The brutish, threatening look on the big man's face transformed into a smile. On another man it might have been appropriate to say it "melted" into a smile, but the scars, the broken nose, and the missing teeth of this one made a smile almost worse than the frown. Shifting the club into his left hand, the man picked off John's hat, leaving him exposed. He snatched it back, only to find that big hand coming to curve around his cheek, turning his face into the light.

A palm, rough as rawhide, scraped against his skin. John was appalled. It was like being caressed by a rhinoceros, he was sure. Repulsive! He wanted to run as far away as possible from the place; to follow his namesake's voyages to the end of the earth. He wanted to find a mountain of ice and burrow into it. He did. So why he found himself moving his head slightly to better feel the pull of warm calluses against his chin, he couldn't say. The devil in him, maybe.

"First time, eh? Not to fret. Come on inside, princess. I'll look after ye. You just call me Bess, eh? Sweet Bess."

This was a good moment for him to turn and walk away. He did not want to get involved with the kind of world where a man like this could call himself "Sweet Bess" and not vomit at the thought. He was not the kind of man, himself, who could live with being called "princess." It defied reason, honor, every scrap of dignity.

"I don't want—"

"Course you don't," said Bess, and despite everything there was a kind of sweetness to his eyes now—the gentleness of a big man who can afford it. "None of us wants it, do we? But we has to make the best of it. Tell you what, you come in an 'ave a drink, see 'ow the land lies. Don't 'ave to do nothing less'n you want it. No crime in havin' a drink now, is there?"

That was true enough. He could go in and see what kind of club Billy had invited him to. There was no harm in drinking, and finding things out. *And maybe watching.* His conscience stabbed

him in tune with the flare of lust, but he was tired. He was so tired
of the sleepless nights and the ache of miserable arousal and his
damn torture implement of a body. He was tired of fruitless
prayer, tired of failing and of half measures, and it was beginning
to dawn on him that this was a fight he was not capable of winning.

"Just a drink then," he said, and went in.

At first glance it was quite a disappointment. He wasn't sure
what he'd expected—some oriental palace of decadence, like
the bath house he had once run from in shock and shame. But
this was only a large room, arranged like any parlor, with a table
at one end stacked with tankards and jugs of beer. Dazzled as
he was going into the dark from the Jamaican brilliance of the
street outside, he did not initially see the people.

They saw him though. He found himself surrounded by dim
shapes, touched by scores of unseen hands, and though his mind
and spirit quailed at the experience, his prick had quite a different opinion. The rank, tropical smell drenched him—too
many sweating men confined together in one room, with smoke
and beer and a hot undercurrent of sex. John's heart hammered
so fast he staggered, dizzy with it. He could have lain down right
there and let everyone in the room have him, and the thought
terrified him almost as it aroused.

"Bit of air, gents, please."

As the darkness eased, "Bess" returned with two tankards of
beer, his presence parting the crowd like Moses with the Red
Sea. *Except,* John thought, full of hysterical laughter, *not* very
like. He let himself be steered to a table, and when he could sit,
with the board a welcome shield between him and the rest of
the room, he felt a little more human. Clasping his hands around
his drink, he watched circles of waves speed across its surface,
betraying the trembling of his hands.

"Which the princess here is new," Bess was saying. "Right? I
promised him a quiet drink, so he don't get bothered unless he
asks. Understand? Or I'll want to know why not."

Bess sat next to him, and dropped a large, proprietary hand

on his knee, the fingertips working their way beneath the cuff of his breeches, snagging on the silk of his stockings. With almost equal hilarity, John thought that in one respect his mother would approve. Her principles maintained that all men were equal. She might point out the salutary lesson here, where he—a gentleman—found himself under the protection of such a brute. He doubted if she would approve of anything else, of course. "You are very kind," he said, imagining how dreadful it might have been had he walked in unannounced.

"Nah." Sweet Bess shook his prize-fighter's shorn head and grinned. His hand worked its way up to John's thigh, dug into the trembling muscle there with a grip so strong it promised pain. Involuntarily, John gasped, closing his eyes and moistening his lips with the tip of his tongue. If asked, ten minutes ago, whether he would ever find a coarse blacksmith arousing he would have laughed. Now, however, he felt he would die if that ruthless hardness did not press itself against his prick and ease the devouring need, just a little. "One good turn deserves another, eh?"

Bess's arm snaked across his shoulders, his hand curving about John's neck, fingertips like dried, roughened leather catching on the small hairs of his nape. *This is,* he thought, dazedly, *the point where I should struggle,* and for a moment he was overwhelmed by the picture of himself fighting to get away, by the thought of this huge, rough man shoving him back against the wall, overwhelming him by force, crushing his resistance and just taking him, whether he would or no.

His skin flushed all over, he could feel the tickle of his woolen waistcoat against his chest, the rough plaster wall against his back. His prick, confined in the coarse linen breeches, nudged at the soaked waistband, and he hated it for turning him into this. He hated it, but he said, "Yes."

Bess's arms tightened, bringing John into the bigger man's body, his hand slid up and cupped John's aching yard, and the burst of need and bliss and sheer relief made him cry out sharply as if in pain. He pushed against the exploring fingers, closed his eyes, shutting the sordid reality out and surrendered to the darkness within and without. One armed, Bess lifted him out of his seat until he was draped across the bigger man's lap, and the hard pressure of thighs beneath his, the mound of a straining prick against his arse, two layers of fabric notwithstanding, made him whimper with need. He didn't wait to be asked but spread his legs and rearranged himself so he was riding the man's lap as if it was a horse. Bess stroked him hard and pulled him further on, his own hips rising in little jerks that lifted John's feet off the floor. With his eyes closed, John was not expecting the kiss, chapped lips and stubble, the taste of smoke and beer and a rotting tooth. He cried out again, but the noise was swallowed in the other man's mouth, and what came out sounded piteous, pathetic.

"Fuck!" said Bess, pulling his stinking mouth away so that he could bite down the length of John's neck. "Ain't you never?...*ooh*...fuck!" He fumbled with John's buttons, and then with his own, before getting his hand inside the flap of John's breeches. John found himself grinding into the hot, moving pressure of a palm separated from his skin only by the thinnest linen shirt. Bess's hand was so rough the friction was like being licked by a cat's tongue, the scouring pull of little hooks, maddeningly intense, almost unendurable. His whole frame seemed to be drawing itself together, tensing, balls drawing up hard against his body, aching. Bess reached beneath him to stroke his own yard, his knuckles moving in the crease of John's arse. When he tried to kiss John again John bit his lip hard and sucked the blood out. It occurred to him suddenly that there were a score of men in the room with him, watching him, and at that he abandoned his last shreds of shame and thrust into the encircling hand, fierce and wanton and completely debased.

"Ah! Aaah!" As though he had purged the devil in his come, darkness and dismay closed over him. He clung on to Bess's neck, teeth gritted, his skin crawling as the big man thrust up against him, one hand clamped around his hips, pulling them for more contact, rough fingers still rolling John's spent member painfully between them as aftershocks of pleasure turned into horror. John began to struggle in earnest just as his partner pushed up brutally one final time, almost unseating him, then clung on, shuddering. Hot dampness spread beneath him, soaking into his breeches, wicking up the material like another indecent caress between his thighs, meeting his own slick wetness.

The hand slid through the come on his belly, and he imagined it leaving trails of dirt. It probed backwards, beneath his balls, slid on, and he yelped in shock and revulsion as it touched the pucker of his arsehole. Stiffening in fear and horror, ignoring for the moment that his spent prick nevertheless twitched with interest and a new wave of nauseated need went over him, he grabbed Bess's wrist. A febrile strength he didn't know he had in him enabled him to force the hand away, though the bigger man resisted. Bess's hand grabbed on hard to his cravat, half choking him.

"If you do not let me go at once, I swear I will rip out your balls and make you eat them," John hissed, rage—never very far away—coming to his rescue now. He could see his own white face, drawn with murderous certainty in Bess's widening eyes, then the man blinked, and he saw only the war of prudence and desire, and the slow trail of blood over the grimy jaw from the wound John had made on his lip.

"Alright, princess, no call for that." Bess let go of his neck, took a covering swig of his beer and watched as John scrambled off, tidying himself away with shaking, clumsy hands. His coat covered the stains, thank God. "Weren't gonna do nothing you didn't want. Maybe next time, eh? You come back to Sweet Bess next time an' we'll try it then."

"There will be no next time."

Bess laughed and leaned back, spreading his legs; fully clothed but with the flap of his breeches down and his yard ex-

posed for everyone to see. It was, John couldn't help but notice, really quite substantial. "O'course, mate. Ain't that what
they all say."

John fumbled the key in the lock, dropped it, and as he was trying
to pick it up again, his landlady opened the door and looked down
on his flaming face with what seemed to him to be a very knowing
look. The moon was shining like a great open eye in the sky above
him, watching, and as he bowed and stuttered out a nervous
thanks, pushed past her and fled up the stairs to his room, he wondered if the skirts of his coat properly concealed the damp patch.
He wondered if she could smell it on him, as he could smell it on
himself. He wanted—badly wanted—a bath, but would not have
the slaves awoken just because he was unclean. *Besides,* he
thought, closing the door and leaning back against it, barricading
the prying eyes outside, *at this hour it would advertise my shame
to the whole house.*

He dragged his sea-chest in front of the door, took off his
coat and looked down at himself. *Oh God! He was a damn pervert!* He was stained.

Panting and moving frantically, he stripped off his shirt,
damp breeches, shoes and stockings and stood naked in the
moonlight. In the barren light he examined his hands, his body,
and hardly knew them. Whey-colored in the light from the window, his skin gleamed, bleached and ghost-like. There was silver in the palm of his hands, like Judas' ten pieces of silver, and
he felt equally appalled at himself. If he could have flung it
away he would have done so, but it was only his own guilty
sweat, glistening with a lunatic light.

A jug of cold water stood by his bedside. He dumped his cravat into it, then washed himself down as well as he could, imagining the soot from Bess' hands burrowing into his pores,
scrubbing everywhere he had been touched, and breathing
raggedly, on the edge of tears. After, he set kindling in the grate,

slowly ripped up his soiled clothes, and burned them.

The ritual calmed him. Halfway through he found his jumbled thoughts had begun to resolve themselves into prayer; to slow and become something coherent.

Forgive me, Lord. Forgive me. I know that you take away sin. I know that you can make this as though it never happened. Cleanse me Lord and I shall be clean....

For he was not, after all, the only man who had ever sinned, and if he was abject and unable to resist the demands of his fallen nature, well, that was the very reason God had intervened in history. *Grace is enough. Your grace is enough for me.*

It was a strange lesson nevertheless. One he probably deserved for being so damn proud of his own chastity. *A fine thing to congratulate yourself for not lusting after women, when you are made without the attraction.* The moment his attention was called to a sex he did desire, he had proved himself no worthier, no stronger than any other man. What a self-righteous little bastard he had been!

With the linen burnt and the room full of the acrid reek, he got up from his knees and put on his nightshirt, sighing as it covered up his guilty flesh. How he wished he had known what he knew now, when Alfie needed him to know it. It was a sobering lesson, but if only it could have come at the right time. He should not then have been so merciless.

Stirring himself to light a taper, thinking that perhaps he should write to Lavinia Deane, who would at least find this amusing, he caught the gleam of golden buttons on his lieutenant's uniform coat, folded in his open sea-chest. Lighting a candle, he picked the coat up. It lay heavy, scratchy and unchanged in his hands, and he thought that, after all, she was still wrong. He had sinned, and he would never, never want to repeat such an experience. He knew now what he was missing, and it was nothing. He still had king and country.

And the sea.

◖ CHAPTER 12 ◗

January 1763, Farrant's Plantation, Jamaica

"He's looking better," Isabella said, pressing the cane of her parasol against her cheek as she watched her husband run beside George's rotund pony. The pony, a shaggy little creature made lazy by the heat, trotted across the landscaped lawn at a pace Farrant could easily match, and they were laughing, father and son, as they passed into the shade of the beeches on the drive. "Less like a man who has awakened out of a heavy sleep, and drags it around in a cloud over him all day long."

She smiled as the two burst from shade back into sunlight; George with a look of ferocious determination, bouncing in the saddle in an effort to go faster, Farrant keeping pace with an easy lope. Not a tall man, but so well put together that he made all others seem overgrown. How she loved the vigor in his gestures, the sturdy strength in his limbs, the vivid, masculine grace. "I hated to see him so…dazed."

"I cannot think it an improvement, my lady." Bentley's flat, parson-like hat cast an even shadow over his face, so that on a cursory glimpse he looked headless, a ghost of some quiet, formal young man who had never quite dared to live. "This rise in animal spirits…he says he is taking his dose, but I note he has become very furtive about it." He raised his chin, and the sun flashed from his glasses like the unexpected fervor in his voice.

"I am not his nursemaid, ma'am. I cannot tip the drug down his throat and hold his mouth shut until he swallows."

On the terrace a small table had been set out. She let Bentley pull out the chair and sat, a breeze from the sea fluttering the ribbons of her hat, cooling her sticky, flushed face. After a moment of whispered debate in the shade of the house over who should go first, the housekeeper appeared at the head of a procession of servants, bearing tea and cakes, arrack, lemon shrub and barley water for the children. A plucked arpeggio floated silvery sweet from the drawing room where Frances was practicing her party piece, and from a bedroom above came an indignant skirling shriek in the Irish language as one of the indentured servants cursed at the chimneys.

"I did not…" said Isabella, feeling ungrateful—she had so much, why was it she could only think of what she lacked? "You promised me a cure. I did not agree to keep my husband perpetually half dead."

"There is some purpose to a stallion which will stand to a mare," Bentley commented as he sat down beside her. He took off his hat revealing the long, dark tail of his hair, silken as the blue ribbon which carefully tied it back. "But if it refuses, then it is of more use to society as a gelding."

"Farrant is not a horse. Nor am I, for that matter."

Bentley choked on his tea, his eyes watering. His cup clattered against the saucer as he gasped in a roughened, regretful voice, "I did not mean…." He gave her an imploring look, eyes huge beneath their lenses.

She sighed. *Poor Bentley, poor boy.* "So your cure is as far off as ever?"

"He is recalcitrant." The doctor fingered the enameled black fob of his watch, his soft round face heavy as dough. "He finds excuses not to see me, not to give me the information I need. He has become increasingly private, and I must say there are…." Fixing his gaze on the cut steel buckle of his shoe, he fell silent.

"There are?" she prompted, both wanting and not wanting

to know. Was she not beautiful? Bentley liked her well enough, in his quiet, puppyish way. Farrant had courted her; danced, flattered, laughed at her timid witticisms, bore her parents' fawning thanks with grace. He loved his children—doted on them, even, with none of the stiff unease she noticed in her friends' husbands. And he came to her, when he had to, with his eyes closed, trying hard not to look as though he'd rather be doing his accounts.

"Bad influences aboard," Bentley said reluctantly. "Perhaps if you could speak to him; recall him to his obligations?"

She closed her gloved hands over her face abruptly, so he would not see the ugly twist of her brows, the wobble of her lip as grief erupted from her pretense of calm. "I am *not* an *obligation!*"

A cool butterfly touch alighted on the inch of skin between the lace of her sleeve and the silk of her glove. She looked up and found her own grief mirrored, amplified, in Bentley's worried eyes. "There is some cognitive defect in him if he cannot see how fortunate he is in you. But I will…I will find some way to make him see."

Isabella thought for a moment that he might go down on one knee and pledge it, like a knight of old. Then she could give him her handkerchief as a token. Giving a shaky laugh she poured another cup of tea. *A more unlikely knight errant I have never seen.* But she herself, lined about the face with age, and about the belly with the marks of three children, was no fairytale queen.

"There are many women who would envy me," she said instead. "I will be Duchess of Alderley; rich, powerful. I have only to name a thing and he will buy it for me. I just…I…What is that noise?"

Running feet rapped a tattoo on the marble of the passageway. Farrant tossed George into the air, caught him and landed him gently on the grass, turning towards the door with bright, alert eyes. Isabella gasped, as Myers, the butler, burst from the archway, straightened his wig and said, with his most poisonous precision, "My Lord and Lady; Lieutenant Nyman of the *Britannia,* and Prince Tamane of Tobago."

Lieutenant Nyman she knew already. She saw with aching resignation that he had brought a parcel of orders. The Admiralty was sending her husband away again, and he had barely been home a week. But the familiar distress was overwhelmed by the sight of Prince Tamane. A red-skinned youth, in breeches and frock coat, a plug of what looked like bone through the septum of his nose, and white streaks of paint on his face like the whiskers of an enormous cat.

She stood up. He smiled, and she felt morally certain that his teeth would be filed to sharp points; was faintly disappointed to find out they were not. Farrant, though striding rapidly forwards, was still yards away, so she swallowed nervously, glad to see that one of the Irish maids was blocking the door and keeping Frances inside. Holding out her hand, curtseying, she forced a smile. "Welcome to our house, your highness. Will you take a dish of tea?"

HMS Britannia *in the Caribbean Sea, off Isla Blanquilla*

Two days later, Farrant sat at his dinner table in the *Britannia*'s great cabin, with his orders unsealed and spread out on the polished wood about him. But there was nothing in the orders to demand his attention—a simple request to aid one native ruler against another and thereby strengthen the position of Britain against that of France. Tamane had told him more in the first hour: the prince had escaped a French invasion of Tobago in a canoe, and had made his way to Jamaica to ask for intervention from the British. He had been sent back with the *Britannia* as translator, liaison, and native guide. Since then a relentless swell had confined the poor prince to his cabin with a bucket. Still, Farrant had already a provisional plan which could not be improved without more information, and he was filling in the extra time with brooding.

Next to him, his hat swung dangling from the shoulder of one of the chairs. Meadows would have a thing or two to say about him bending the crown out of shape, so he picked it off. The diamond cockade glimmered coldly at him. Idly distracted, he moved the spray through the rain gray light of the great gallery, watching reflections and fleeting colors slide shyly through the centre of the stones. They looked so clear, they shone so beautifully, and yet they were hard and cold. Sometimes he wondered whether he too had folded in, folded up, bent and buckled and made himself small under pressure, until in the darkness and the oppression he had turned to stone.

The cabin door opened and damp blew in, bringing with it a shape cloaked in a long black boat-cloak, cold, graceful, and silent as the Grim Reaper. Farrant's melancholy invested the sight with a dark cloud of horror. Superstitious as any sailor, he rose and backed slowly away. Even when Bentley put down his hood—revealing himself as a very genteel Death—something of the unearthly lingered about him.

"Get out!"

Bentley paused in the act of extracting his new close-vision glasses from his pocket and blinked at Farrant in confusion. "I must take your vitals." His notebook, placed on the table, fell open on a long list of measurements: heartbeat, temperature, bowel movements, frequency of congress; attempts at graphs, correlations of factors, snatches of private conversations. Life reduced to ink and paper, to mathematics.

"Taking my vitals," Farrant repeated, nauseous. "What a good description of your activities, Dr. Bentley. I am minded of a leech, or one of those Prussian vampires. Who gave you permission to come into my cabin without knocking?"

Naked without his glasses, Bentley's soft, unfocussed eyes narrowed. "This anger…. You are not taking your dose, are you? It is a purely chemical anger, I assure you, occasioned by withdrawal from the drug. You do not mean—"

"Do not presume to tell me what I mean, sir!"

"Your grace—"

"Not yet. And if you wish to ever become Doctor to the Duke, so you can top it the nob with your scientific friends in London, as I've no doubt has been your ambition since we met—"

"You wrong me, my Lord." Carefully putting down his bag on top of the journal, Bentley hooked his glasses around his ears and brought out a pamphlet from the asafetida-scented depths. He held it out, his hand untrembling, but his mouth thin. "A man of ambition would have left you long since."

Farrant took the little yellow booklet, its coarse paper rough as the straw from which it was undoubtedly made. A glance at the cover showed him enough—himself drawn ridiculously thin, mincing and effeminate, with a simpering expression and in a wig two feet tall, along with the words "Duke of Al—y" and "in-famous practices".

"As you see, it is not a great recommendation to be in your service. There is a limit to how long the tide of public opinion can be held back. There is a limit even to your father's tolerance for this filthy moral disease of yours. While your openly sodomi-tial behavior attracts satire like this from Grub Street hacks, making you a laughing stock of the rabble and an embarrass-ment to your family, my practice and reputation suffer daily by continuing in your service. But if we can effect a cure, then—even then—all may be rectified. You must allow me to examine you, my Lord. More than your own life depends on it."

Returning to his seat, Farrant thumbed open the pamphlet, a cheap little gossip-mongering paper, designed to be bought by all those who delight in scandal. Its salacious outrage seemed somehow all the more sordid in its smug, heavy, black lead type. There were a great many exclamation marks. Opening the front of the nearest lit candle-lantern, without reading any more, he burned the thing entirely.

Never an unwilling partner, he swore to himself once, a long time ago. *Never a child, never a man who couldn't knock me down if he so wished. Why then this hatred?*

Thoughtfully, he took a pinch of snuff from its golden box, laid it on the back of his hand and sniffed it up, the burst of citrus and cinnamon like the sparkle of a diamond, but the later burn of the tobacco a more substantial warmth. Ingrained politeness led him to offer it to Bentley, who waved it off as he always did.

Was it possible that the Duke's power might be forfeited, Farrant wondered, watching the pamphlet burn. Might his father withdraw his protection—throw him to the dogs of the street? The old devil had as much as told him that he didn't care where Farrant found his diversions, as long as he married well and sired the next generation. As long as he kept out of his father's sight—in another country, preferably—so that the family need not actually associate with him. A career at sea had been Farrant's own choice, despite Article Twenty Eight of the Navy's law code, the Articles of War that said in no uncertain terms: *If any person in the fleet shall commit the unnatural and detestable sin of buggery and sodomy with man or beast, he shall be punished with death by the sentence of a court martial.* At least at sea he could do something useful with a life so evidently regretted by those who had given it to him.

And at sea, Captain of his own ship—given, under those same articles *absolute* authority—he was the undisputed king of his own small country, whose rules were dictated by himself. He was, he hoped, a benevolent dictator. Those who could not bend their necks to his easy yoke were not encouraged to remain. Those who seemed vinegar enough, zealous enough, fanatic enough to cause him trouble were not accepted aboard in the first place.

Yet still they made their demands.

Pulling open the draw in the center of the table, he took up the miniature that lay there, its sweet, powdery colors as fresh as when they'd had it painted, he and Isabella. It brought back Venice; the clear English-spring sunlight of winter in Venice.

Rosalba Carriera in her studio, painting tiny brush-strokes on ivory, while outside the waters lapped at the walls and boats full of oranges cried their wares to the overhanging windows.

In those days he really had hoped it would work; Isabella and he. Love! He had tried to give it to her. Fond of her, liking her, he had been faithful in his way—taking no man to his bed for whom he cared more than he cared for Isabella. If he could not love her, he had determined that he would not, at least, love anyone else better.

But it had been a cold decision, even when he had hope that it was temporary. *These days….*

Closing the portrait back in the drawer, he swept the ashes out of the lantern, rubbed the smuts from his fingers with a handkerchief and looked up. "I don't believe in your cure."

"You must!" Bentley cried, groping in his pocket for his watch, as he did when he approached a strong emotion. "You *must*. What else is there?"

"This affection in me, this attraction towards my own sex? I cannot separate it from my deepest nature. It appears to me that it is a part of my soul I cannot do without. You ask me to believe you can cure it—that you can make me desire Isabella as a man should desire his wife, but the thought of it…." He wanted to knock the lantern over, settled for clamping his fingers tight around the hot metal lid, relishing the scorch as something real in this world of shadows. "I don't believe I truly *want* to be changed. Can you cure a man of his own soul? The thought of it feels to me exactly like despair."

"No sir!" Bentley reached out, closed his hand around Farrant's wrist, practiced fingertips digging for the pulse. "Please, calm yourself! This is nothing but an acute attack of the disorder. It will pass and you will remember that it is hope—it is hope I offer you. Hope of being well again; of no longer having to be ashamed. You must understand that."

"Must I?" All he felt at the thought was a weariness he could not distinguish from defeat. Surely it would be better to accept himself for what he was—to build a new life around the truth, whatever the cost? *Oh, but the cost would be so high!* "Go away, Bentley. I despise the sight of you."

Not waiting for obedience, driven by the deep volcanic pressure of the world's disapproval, the need for an ally, Farrant picked up the *London Chronical* from the dispatches and strolled out on deck.

There, a thin drizzle beaded the front of his coat with droplets. Fog and grey spray rolled gently over the starboard watch—sullenly huddled into their oilskins, awaiting the next order. As they ran well before the wind, he felt it drive the damp into his right cheek. Water trickled beneath his collar as he turned to see Alfie Donwell jump down from his seat on the capstan and stiffen to attention.

"Captain on the Quarterdeck!" shouted Midshipman Hervy, belatedly, making Alfie unsuccessfully struggle to swallow a smile. Only a small smile perhaps, but progress. And the man was made for smiling. Farrant wouldn't have looked twice at him, sober-faced, but with that little grin he became a point of light and warmth in an otherwise dingy universe. A man who did not want him to be anything other than what he was.

"As you were," Farrant said. "Mr. Hervy, have Meadows bring us some tea, would you? You'll take tea, Mr. Donwell?"

"Thank you, sir," Alfie took his hands out of his pockets and blew on them. "It's deceptive—the weather—it seems too fine to trouble you, and then before you know it you're soaked to the skin."

For a little while after he had come on board, despite invitations to the Great Cabin that inevitably led to vigorous and— Farrant hoped—mutually satisfying couplings, Alfie had remained taciturn and professional outside the bedroom. Farrant imagined that John Cavendish must run the kind of ship where everyone was afraid to speak, where chit-chat and idle human contact was frowned upon, and enjoyment of any sort strictly rationed and preceded by prayer. He was glad to see the boy relax into the more informal style of his own command. It wasn't that he was competing with a pious little nobody like

Cavendish—frankly the man was beneath his notice—but Farrant was human enough to be glad his lover smiled.

Lover? *Oh Christ!* He shook himself sternly, almost dropping the paper in shock at his own thoughts. *No, not that. Never that.*

"Are you well, sir?"

At the solicitude, the delicate, melancholy care on Alfie's expressive face, Farrant's exasperated rage came snarling once more out of the shadows where it was chained. Trapped, trapped like a bear in a pit and beset on all sides by the little yapping forms of other people's needs—needs it was impossible for him to meet. A million open mouths he could not feed. Why would they not shut up and let him be?

How dare the boy assume his concern was needed? How dare he assume he could contribute anything to Farrant's carefully, rationally compartmentalized life? How dare he try to become yet another person in Farrant's life whom he would have to disappoint?

"Are you my doctor, Lieutenant? When I wish to discuss my health I generally do it with him."

"Yes, sir," Alfie said, bending his head. Behind him, Farrant saw Bert Driver watching, smiling with malice. *God's teeth!* A jealous malcontent tar; that was all he needed. Why had he come out here at all, to stand in the seeping rain next to a man who—though improved—had still become no beauty? Why had he sought out a mere lieutenant? And worse, why for a moment had he felt better simply for standing next to him?

A thrill of interest and dismay transfixed him at the thought. Love? Could it have crept up on him unawares, while he was hunting it elsewhere? Well, he didn't want it. He was too old for it. Too old to disturb his life, his wife, his aged parents and dependent children by developing a ridiculous infatuation with a penniless plebian of no particular talents or birth. But there was a perilous sweetness to the thought nevertheless.

"Set a course for Tobago," he said. "It seems the French have captured King Cardinal, in an effort to make his people give up their lands. His Queen is organizing a resistance, and we are directed to help." Catching Bert's eye he beckoned him over with a jerk of the chin. "My cabin, Bert. If you please."

"Aye aye, sir." Bert gave Alfie a poisonous look of triumph and deliberately loosened his neckcloth before walking over to the door. He opened it with a cocky tilt to his head and an assumption of ownership that did not sit well with Farrant at all. Alfie blanched, saying nothing. Feeling a complete heel, but certain that this was necessary to re-establish the delicate balance of indifference on board, Farrant re-folded the newspaper and handed it over, in lieu of his heart.

"Three months old but still the latest edition to reach Jamaica. It might interest you, Mr. Donwell. Enjoy the tea."

But he wondered, as he ducked back inside and looked at Bert, who was—despite his commonplace name—the most perfect Adonis, why he felt so little enthusiasm for the beauty, so much regret over the sacrifice of that one lopsided wry little smile. Closing the door behind him and shrugging out of his own coat, annoyed rather than aroused by Bert's eager help, he found himself facing this as though it were a chore. *Too old indeed!* It was laughable, but if he had known that things would become so complicated, he would never have allowed the boy back on board.

Alfie spread the newspaper out over the damp barrel of the capstan, accepted a cup of tea from Farrant's steward, the ancient and imperturbable Meadows, and curving his hands about it, he hid his face in the steam. He had been put in his place, and he felt it, like a prone soldier feeling the boot that drives him into the mud. Farrant was right—he was not wanted. He persisted in trying to find someone for whom he could care, and that, rather than his vice, was what blighted his life. God knew he could find willing bodies enough if he chose to frequent the molly houses and the cruising grounds. He could pick up a guardsman or soldier or anonymous young tradesman for a quick fuck in the bog-houses of London and the colonies—and with a modicum of caution and luck he could get away with it. But it wouldn't…it wouldn't fill the emptiness he carried in his breast like a winter night.

It hurt to look at Farrant and see the strain in his face; to see him isolated and lonely by his own choice. But it *was* his choice—it must be. For he had only to ask and Alfie would gladly lavish him with care, hoping that the act would help him seal up the wounds in his own heart. He wanted more than just sex; he wanted to find someone in whose arms he could fall asleep without fear. Someone who would comfort him and laugh with him; someone who would share his thoughts as well as his bed. But Farrant—well, he could not accuse the captain of ever having misguided him into thinking it could be him. The captain had been quite firm from the very beginning that he wanted none of those things.

If only he looked more happy about it.

Sighing at his own foolishness, Alfie looked up blankly at his replacement on watch, took the tea and the paper down the companionway to the center of the gun deck, where the galley was throwing out a welcome heat. He stood next to the red coals in the roasting racks for awhile, drying out the soggy sheets of the *Chronical*.

Mrs. Shaw, bent over a tub of steaming water, gave him an encouraging smile. "Easy sailing, long rainy afternoon, and you down here, Mr. Donwell?" she said, thrashing the clothes in the tub with a heavy, bleached dolly, big as a stool on the end of a stick. Her dress lay over a chair, to spare its sleeves, and her brawny arms were bare almost to the shoulder, though in her stays and many layers of petticoats she was decent enough. "Is the captain unwell?"

"He has…company." Alfie turned over another page of the paper, busying himself with laying it flat, and hoping the flush would be set down to the influence of the fire.

"Oh well, that's good, ain't it?" she said. "One less unpleasant duty, eh? That'll please Sgt. Peterson. It weren't right anyway, asking a well-bred young gentleman like yourself to do something more fit for the tars."

"Could we at least pretend ignorance!" he burst out. "It is not something of which I have any desire to speak." It needed embarrassment.

Mrs. Shaw patted him on the hand with a fist full of soap bubbles, put her homely face on one side and said, "Don't take it to heart, sir. If you don't mind me saying so, there's not many stains as don't wash straight off."

"I'm sure you're right." Having finished toasting the paper, Alfie folded it, watching the steam rise from his sleeves. "I only wish the rest of the world were of the same opinion."

"Oh, *them!*" Mrs. Shaw wrung the water out of a shirt and hung it up on a cord to dry by the galley. "What do they know, anyways? Us *Britannias*, well, it's not like we wouldn't all suffer if anyone was to find out. Don't you worry about that."

Alfie wondered how far her sympathy went—if she would still reassure and comfort him if she knew he mourned the loss of the captain's affection, rather than the shame of possessing it at all. But though he would have liked to talk to someone, he did not dare speak openly to her. He had been to enough hangings, seen enough mollies stand in the pillory to know that it was in general the women who cursed them loudest and threw the sharpest stones.

Slightly warmed in flesh if not in spirit, he retired to his own cabin to change into dry clothes. It was as he was tying a new neck-cloth, head tilted to one side as he struggled with an uneven knot, that the name caught his eye. He had thrown the *London Chronical*, haphazardly folded, onto his cot. Now he reached out for it warily as if it was a snake. The name struck out at him again, piercing him through the eye with a pain as sharp and vivid as a serpent's tooth. It lanced out from a jumble of war news; a small paragraph on the launching of a new frigate, fresh off the blocks in Portsmouth and on her maiden voyage.

HMS Albion, *to be posted to the West India station. Officers include…*a long list of strangers…*and Lt. John Cavendish.*

Fingers shaking, Alfie tore the paragraph out of the paper.

After standing reading and re-reading it, he stuffed it into his pocket where he might continue to feel its crinkle between his fingers. *The West India station. John was on his way to Jamaica. Might even have already arrived. God above!* They might…on some street in Kingston, by chance, under a heavy saturated sky and a sun like a branding iron…they might meet.

He returned from somewhere terribly distant to find he had crushed the paper between his hands, was hugging it to himself like a long lost friend. Backing away from it, he sat down on his sea chest before he could fall.

Was it possible that Farrant, who must have read this first, was—in his harsh way—being kind? That he had meant for Alfie to see it and suspected he would react like this? Frankly, did it matter what Farrant did or expected?

No, it didn't very much matter because, for the first time since coming on board, the fog about Alfie opened. A stab of winter sunlight, icy cold but bright, shuddered through him, intense as pain. As he put his hand protectively over the name in his pocket, over the talisman, he felt it again, like the slap on a baby's back that shocks it into breathing. He did not know whether he hoped or feared, only that he felt suddenly alive again, and it hurt.

⟪⟨ CHAPTER 13 ⟩⟫

New Years Eve 1762, Jamaica

Captain Gillingham eased his bandaged foot on the stool and gave a theatrical wince of pain. Beside him, Mr. O'Connor, First Lieutenant of the *Albion*, raised a hand to his forehead, accidentally displaying the hand of cards concealed in his cuff.

"I am far too ill to go," said the captain, holding out a gilt edged invitation to John. "And as you've been humming the same tune all the way from Portsmouth—driving your mess mates insane, so I've heard—I am sending you in my place."

John took the invitation with as much care as its pristine whiteness, the beauty of its calligraphy, and its eighteen-carat-gold embellishment seemed to warrant.

"It comes from a fellow called Hibbert, I understand," Gillingham went on, pouring himself a glass of port from the decanter that stood glittering by his elbow. With the stopper out, the scent, reeling sweet and over-warm, rolled stickily through the room, almost overwhelming the smell of cigars, boiled wool waistcoats, and the sweat that stood out on O'Connor's brow.

If Gillingham was too robust for a man with an attack of gout, O'Connor's blood red cheeks and over-bright eyes were too stark for a man in health. "A merchant of some kind. I believe someone did tell me, but I find I have forgotten. At any rate, he owns that big house on Parade Square. You are desired and requested to attend an opera evening in his gardens in celebration of the season. I've no doubt the Admiral and all the other captains have been equally desired. Wear your number one coat, I think, and best not to venture any opinions, not even if you're asked. You mustn't disgrace the ship."

John wondered if he could say, "Surely, sir, if you're too ill your Premier should go in your place," but a second glance at O'Connor's hectic flush stopped him. "I will attempt not to, sir," he said doubtfully.

"I can't bear the opera myself. Such screeching and wailing! Not to mention the machinery: painted waves ten feet high, gods descending in fluttering streamers out of the sky; explosions, fireworks and alarums. I always emerge with my poor head ready to split. But I understand it's quite the thing…." Gillingham felt underneath the skirts of his coat and brought out his own cards, examining the spread with an intent eye. "Very well. Dismissed."

So John found himself in his best coat, with O'Connor's best Irish linen shirt beneath it, his wig re-curled and powdered a shining glacial white, and the purser's gold laced hat—ever so slightly too small—precariously balanced atop it, walking across Parade Square in the fleeting tropical dusk.

In the center of the square a gibbet cut a sinister line across the sky, and as John clutched his hat to his head, the wind blew a maggot onto the cobbles in front of his shoe. Drawing back his foot from the writhing thing he looked up at the body that hung, decomposing, in its iron cage. One of its arms chose that moment to separate from its shoulder, falling with a sticky, tearing plop onto the grill beneath it.

Impossible to know whether this was a white man or a black, now, reduced as it was to bones and matter. Above it a yellowing notice proclaimed its crime in ink so streaked as to be illegible. Pressing his handkerchief to his nose, breathing in the sharply reviving scent of bergamot cologne, John took a step forward, standing on tiptoes to peer at the letters. It said "sodomite" surely? Death…the wages of sin…and it came to him that this could easily be him, putrefying for the public's entertainment, giving the young children nightmares and the older something to laugh at.

"A pirate."

John started, guiltily, half turning, hand dropping to the hilt of his dress sword. A glimpse of blue resolved itself into a rotund, middle-aged man in the uniform of a captain, whose absurdly cupid-bow lips primmed up in an attempt to hide a smile. "Did I startle you?"

"Lord, yes sir! My thoughts were all on death and then...."

"I am no phantom of the night, I assure you. Captain Smith of the *Otter*."

"Lieutenant Cavendish of the *Albion*, sir." John made a leg, and in straightening tucked his ill-fitting hat under his arm. They turned by common accord to look back at the spectacle of His Majesty's justice. It shivered in the wind, the rope creaking. "I thought piracy long stamped out in these parts," said John at last, encouraged by something comfortable, approachable about the other man. "Fifty years ago, perhaps, but now?"

"This war is responsible for many lesser misfortunes." Smith looked down to the harbor, whose waters held a phosphorescent light. In its unearthly glow, the topmasts of the fleet nodded gently back, lit from below against a dark sky. "We press men away from their homes to risk their lives at sea, will they or nil they, and if they desert we brand them traitors, outlaws, so that they have little choice but to turn to piracy to support themselves...." He shrugged apologetically. "At the same time we are so preoccupied by the war that we will not spare naval ships to patrol and defend the islands. In those circumstances it seems surprising to me that there hasn't been more piracy than we have seen. It is a weed that grows up when the patch is untended. But forgive me, I am tedious to you in anticipation of being tedious to Admiral Rodney."

To their right, light shone from the many windows of Hibbert house; golden sails cross braced by black sashes. Its brick colonnade had an almost monastic look, as shadowed figures hurried between its pink columns. The narrow front garden and the palm trees that edged the path glittered with a thousand lanterns in pierced work covers, as though the stars had fallen at Thomas Hibbert's feet. As John watched, two of them detached themselves and spiraled upwards on a gust of air—fireflies, he realized, anticipating the evening's dancing.

"Are you...?" Captain Smith indicated the blazing arch of the front gates, where a rank of servants stood, taking in the invitations, giving out glasses of rum punch. A long queue of carriages, coming down from Jamaica's plantations, had formed outside the gates. Teams of horses snorted, sidling as they were pinched into the narrowest space possible. Black grooms, in a rainbow of liveries, held the horses' heads, wiped the footplates of the carriages, held open the door for the peacock-gorgeous civilians and their bejeweled ladies to descend. At the door the guests, relieved of their invitations and cloaks, were plied with arrack and pastries.

The night bustled with raised voices, wheels, hooves, and feet. Within, however, a string quartet played Purcell, and the music spilled into the street, breathing calm reason, measure, and beauty, as a counterpoint to the clamor.

"I am, sir. Captain Gillingham is indisposed and directed me to come in his stead."

Smith gave a smile too good-humored to be called cynical. "He is a martyr to his ailments, poor man. Shall we go in together, then? I confess I have no liking for these affairs, and to cruise with a consort would be reassuring."

John wondered if his face showed the discomfort he felt at the laughter, the noise, the lights and music. Could Smith see beneath his over-groomed exterior to the child beneath; attracted and repelled, guilty, frightened? But circumstances had changed—the party was innocent enough, it was he who was stained. He shook himself and managed to smile. "I believe I would find it strengthening in equal measure myself, sir."

Inside, they joined the knot of other officers. Jamaica's naval establishment, grouped three deep around the punchbowl, made a wall of dark blue and gold that seemed to breathe solidity and tradition. The ballroom was otherwise a delicate creamy white, with jonquil panels, and flowers hand-painted beneath the cornice. Fresh and clean in Kingston's scouring light, no doubt, to John's English trained eyes it looked bare, fragile as the inside of an egg.

Once John had elbowed through the scrimmage to secure his glass of punch, he emerged to a dance floor where many of Jamaica's fine young things were dancing "All in a Garden Green." A faint restraint about the way they leaned in for the kisses indicated how very early in the evening it was; inhibitions not yet dissolved by rapid-beating hearts and too much to drink.

Through a door to the end of the ballroom hurried a steady flow of musicians. As John watched two men negotiating a kettle-drum through the arch, an eddy in the crowd brought him face to face with Admiral Rodney, conqueror of Martinique.

A slender, refined man with a thin face and ferocious, hawk-like eyes, Rodney nodded slightly as they made their bows. But when Smith introduced John, the Admiral gave a wintery smile. "Lieutenant Cavendish. Or should I do as my men do, and call you 'Bomber Cavendish'?"

John winced, turned the flinch into a sickly smile, and buried his nose in his glass, where various nameless fruits were turning to pulp.

"No need to be coy, Mr. Cavendish. Though circumstances render it impolitic to say so openly, you are owed the Navy's thanks."

Choking on a lurking grape, fighting down the involuntary cough and the watering of his eyes, John looked up, perplexed. Was he not supposed to be feeling guilty? How many reversals of interpretation would his actions withstand before he ceased to understand them himself? "I'm sorry, sir?"

Rodney rubbed at a speck which had had the temerity to

settle on his gold braid. He frowned. It was like watching a blade being half drawn, slid back into the scabbard—a moment's sharpness and threat, sheathed. "Mr. Cavendish, pray do not be so slow. It was necessary to put down the Barbary Corsairs and to halt—if only for a short time—the ravages of our coastal towns, the abhorrent trade in our captured countrymen. This you achieved admirably. It was also necessary to do it in such a way that the men in Whitehall could plausibly throw up their hands in horror and deny all responsibility. This too you achieved. Dear me, lieutenant, did you imagine that we would have confined ourselves to demoting you, had we been truly displeased?"

The orchestra—a true Italian orchestra, imported for the occasion—belted out "A Health to Betty" at a volume suitable to be heard over the sound of the top couple galloping down the set as fast as high heels and hoops would permit. As he watched the interweaving couples reversing, reversing, traversing down the line and finally—to great applause—returning to their places, John couldn't help but give a small, rueful laugh. What a fine illustration of the state of his life; enough to make a man dizzy.

"Forgive me, sir. Do I understand correctly that I was deliberately used, then punished for it? I did not realize His Majesty's Navy was so much a statesmen's tool. It smacks of dishonesty. Whether or not I can approve of the ultimate ends of the mission, the fact remains that my people were sent into the valley of the shadow of death and deprived of their prize money when they unexpectedly returned. If this is a moment for plain speaking, I should like to petition you for justice on their behalf."

Rodney's stare grew even more eagle-like, intent, inhuman. To John's right, Smith lowered his head and coughed politely into a closed hand.

"You take your heretical principles too far, Mr. Cavendish," said the Admiral at last, quite gently. "Pray do not forget that I am not to be questioned or rebuked by the likes of you." He pivoted neatly—with the grace an aristocratic dancing master must have beaten into him as a child—to catch Smith's eye. "You were saying something about pirates, Captain Smith?"

"Yes sir." Smith swallowed his smile, his round choirboy face assuming a serious expression. John kept his eyes fixed on the upturned tilt of the end of Smith's nose, as he breathed down his prickly, half apologetic, half defensive response to Rodney's rebuke. Rodney was right, of course. He *didn't* have the authority to speak to the commander-in-chief like that. He should not have dared it, insubordinate and undisciplined as it was.

"If you remember the *Queen Anne's Avenger*, captured last week?" Smith continued, giving a jerk of the head towards the open windows where the dim shapes of vendors and whores filled Parade Square, keeping the coachmen of the rich entertained. "The captain of which is hanging out there, looking somewhat worse for wear?"

"Of course," Rodney brought out a snuff box and sniffed away even the memory of the stench.

"While we were bringing him home, he told me—in exchange for gentler treatment—that he was part of a...*consortium*? A group, at least, which included two other vessels, their rendezvous being set for the third of next month at Pirate's Bay, Tobago."

"You want to bring off the hat trick? Get all three?"

"If you please, sir."

John had thought it was impossible for Smith to look less than good humored, but for a moment he caught a glimpse of boarlike ferocity on the heavy face. The cheerful hazel eyes had narrowed, darkened to bronze. "I thought you pitied them," he blurted out, astonished.

"I do." Smith's smile lay only lightly buried. It gleamed out once more, irrepressible. "As I pity anyone who falls so low. But a man who has become a wild beast must be treated as one, no matter the circumstances of his fall. I've seen what they do...." He emptied his glass in one swallow, then chewed on a slice of apple that had turned bright vermilion in the liquor, and looked up with sudden practicality. "But I'm under-manned; Purser, Coxswain, Master, both lieutenants, all down with this wicked ague. I can find volunteers enough to man the lower decks, but as for officers...."

A burst of applause from the garden punctuated his silence, and with one accord the crush inside the ballroom began to force its way out through the double doors. John found himself swept along, an ostrich feather in his eye, the panniers of two heavily brocaded skirts digging into his flank and buttocks as a lady and her chaperone tried to push their way past. With a half shrug of resignation, the outermost layer of naval officers allowed themselves to be scoured away and swept out into the relative cool and space of the garden. There, on a stage crammed full of minarets and miniature siege towers, Rinaldo, Goffredo, and Argante discussed in recitative song the siege of Jerusalem, Rinaldo's love for Goffredo's daughter Almirena, and the prospects of a truce.

The babble of conversation continued unbroken around the stage. Off left an idle-looking boy was already throwing walnuts. One smacked into Goffredo's calf, making him lose his place, and there was a roar of laughter from the crowd.

"I understand the *Albion* is being careened?" Rodney watched the musicians with the appreciative eye of a man who understood teamwork.

"Yes sir." John smiled, relieved to have been forgiven.

"Then I imagine Gillingham's officers are standing about with nothing better to do than attend the opera. Do you suppose any of them would volunteer for the task, or would I have to issue an order?"

John looked at Smith, who was now grinning openly, and at the Admiral's wry look of challenge, and laughed. "I would be very happy to volunteer, sir."

Behind him Rinaldo hit the first notes of an aria. Silence swept through the hall as the angelic voice soared into the heavy tropical night, bracing as a fall of cool water. John gasped as memory came flooding back on the castrato's voice: *Alfie looking at him as though he was the fixed point about which the stars moved, the answer to every riddle in the universe....*

The yearning notes should not leave him pierced through the heart with regret; should not make him want to learn poetic words of love and frustration and sing until he had made something sublime out of his pain. Instead he eased his nails out of the crescent-shaped wounds in his palms and said, rather more fervently than necessary, "I should be *very* happy to be employed, sir."

12 January 1763, Pirate's Bay, Tobago

Otter slipped silently around the rocky point. Sun beat on her decks and melting tar dripped in heavy splashes from the rigging. Captain Smith, agleam in his best uniform, stood on the quarterdeck with his spyglass under his arm. His cabin had been dismantled and cleared away, all his possessions moved down to the hold. The decks were swept bare, fore and aft, sprinkled with wet sand to douse any accidental fire. Splinter-netting hung overhead like the work of massive spiders, and around the quarterdeck, walls of rolled up hammocks gave an illusion of protection. Cannons run out, the silent crew stood waiting, watching for the first sign of sail.

John walked the length of the deck, checking each gun and crew, conferring with the midshipmen in charge of the divisions. Slow matches smoldered in their tubs, thin plumes of brimstone-scented smoke blowing away forward from each one. A sense of poise, the moment of peace before a duel, the knife edge between life and death, lay over the ship as the wind drove her steadily onward. To her weather side lay wild, rocky coves tipped with palms and purple hills beyond, swathed in impenetrable jungle. It could have been a hundred years ago, and himself part of Maynard's crew, tracking down the infamous Blackbeard. An unsettling thought; that time could mean so little—that enlightenment and modernity might be a fleeting thing in the face of these mountains, these coves. *All man's concerns and his philosophies ephemeral as the smoke....*

"Helm two points a larboard!"

"Aye aye, sir!"

The rudder answering, she turned in a long sweep about the point and began to sail into the island's great deep water bay, bracing round the sails to catch the wind. The distant breeze filled with the throb of drums and a thin high pipe of reedy music, disquietingly alien.

"Sail ho!" The lookout's voice quavered as he yelled. John felt the poised world plummet from waiting readiness into panic. "Sir! Sir! Fuck it! There's a fucking fleet! A cutter, four ketches, couple of brigs and a fucking two decker with French colors sir! It's a *trap!*"

The color drained from Captain Smith's ruddy cheeks. "All hands to tack ship! Ready about! Stations for stays!"

Dropping rammers and spongers on the deck, the gun crews raced to the rigging as the helmsmen spun the wheel hard to starboard. "Helm's a lee!"

Jib and flying jib fluttered, canvas snapped with a sound like immense wings beating. "Brace to! Rise tacks and sheets!" Flinging the fore sails aback, they came up into the wind, slowed, the way falling off her, edged inch by inch past the eye of the wind.

"Haul taut! Mainsail haul!" She began to fill again, a whisper of life, of forward motion, and as she struggled out of the tack the brigs, sailing large, surged out from the huge bay, hemming her between them.

Pirates jeered and laughed from the rigging. Tanned men weathered by the sea, in a motley of stolen clothes. Their voices rang metallic as they carried over the water, but their branded faces were bestial, grinning like hyenas.

There were officers among them. Officers clad in blue, red and gold, with the bold, self satisfied expressions of French nobility. "The French navy would never ally themselves with pirates!" John exclaimed, despite all the evidence, his indignation just keeping the top on fear. "They're honorable opponents, they wouldn't…."

"Not unless they were desperate." Smith's voice held something of the same tightness. "Britain is winning this war, after all. If the circumstances were reversed I too might do something this…*rash* in an attempt to turn the tide." He clasped his hands together in front of himself, his shoulders hunching as if with cold. "Still, at present the presence of the French is our best hope for humane treatment. They are gentlemen at least, and we must rely on them to keep their allies in order. I don't like our prospects otherwise."

The other craft had followed the brigs out from the bay now, and *Otter* was surrounded by bristling cannon. Smith nodded, and John called out "Lower our colors!" even as one of the brigs opened fire, shooting out *Otter*'s sails.

The air fell still, dampened by smoke. That, or John forgot how to breathe.

☙ CHAPTER 14 ❧

10 January 1763, King's Bay, Tobago

Britannia sailed into King's Bay cautiously, stripped for action, her three rows of gun-ports open and ready.

"D'you see anything?" shouted Farrant to the lookout, after the shadow of cliffs had lain on the water long enough for the man to become accustomed to the change of light. Like the ship, Farrant had stripped away his finery and dressed for the occasion. No one who knew the strutting popinjay ashore would have recognized him now.

The blue duck trousers and before-the-mast look suited him better, in Alfie's opinion, than the splendor of his normal uniform. He was not a tall man, and the effect of breeches and long skirted coat was to make him look shorter. Now clad for battle in a sailor's jacket and trousers, with his shorn silver hair uncovered, he looked formidable—small but fierce.

"There is a ship, sir, but she looks unmanned. No, wait, they're struggling to let down sail now."

Continuing her stately glide, primed for immediate battle, *Britannia's* shadow swept over white cliffs shaggy with peppery smelling flowers. A rank, acrid smell hovered over the jungle, and even here on the water the incessant chirping of small frogs filled the head with irritation. Alfie adjusted his sword and savored the privilege of being invited to stand by the captain on the quarterdeck, rather than banished to a gun-deck below, like Bert. It said something, he believed, that Farrant had arranged it so that Alfie would be at his back, would be the one who protected him; his right hand and shield.

As the moments went by he began to discern the shape of a hull ahead. Taking out his own glass, he saw it was a two decker, a little worse for wear, with her masts fished and several of her spars broken. She swung about, held by a single anchor, and he read her name, *Arc-en-Ciel* on her stern. Beyond her, on the sloping beach, were heavy tracks, broken trees and the scars of several fires. As he watched, several of her port lids went up with a rattle, and the guns ran out. Shots pocked the smooth surface of the bay a hundred feet in front of the *Britannia.*

"Give them a warning," Farrant called. "Upper deck only, aim at the rigging."

A bundled flag, on the main mast of the anchored vessel, reached the top of its transom and broke out into French colors, the defiant gesture bringing a smile to Alfie's face. Someone on the *Arc-en-Ciel* was having a very bad day, but handling it in style.

Britannia's broadside severed painters and stays, knocked splinters from the mainmast and burst the end of the mizzen boom into a firework of falling shrapnel. Farrant held out a hand, and Alfie handed him a speaking trumpet.

"*Arc-en-Ciel,* you are unprepared and outgunned. You have taken hostile action against a British ship in a British protectorate. Surrender now and you will be well treated. If you do not, we will blow you out of the water."

There was a lieutenant left in charge. Alfie could see him engaged in heated argument with one of the warrant officers. Soon afterwards another couple of men joined in, gesticulating and shouting, even the common sailors contributing their opinion. "I sometimes wonder how they sail them at all, sir," he said, watching Farrant's amusement at this with a swell of affection.

They were going into battle; it was no time to bear grudges.

"Indeed." The captain's mouth twitched with sympathy. "And yet they do, and they rule half of the world with it. A very civilized people, I've often thought."

On the decks of the *Arc-en-Ciel* the lieutenant won the argument, the colors lowered in jerky, resentful bursts of movement, and Farrant sent the boat crew out, with Lt. Nyman to take possession.

"Glad to be home?" Alfie asked the slight, half-naked man at his side. The *Britannias* had confined the French in their own hold and sailed the *Arc-en-Ciel* out into the deep water with a skeleton crew of British seamen aboard to prevent any attempt at escape. The rest of the men had built a rough stockade on the shore of King's Bay, and were enjoying the delights of fresh water, firm ground underfoot, and a profusion of greenstuff to eat. Now night came down on them like a flannel pressed over the face. The sky went from astonishing multicolored radiance to blackness like the blowing out of a candle.

"It is very strange," said Tamane. "I am gone so short a time, and I fear all is changed."

"You can find your own people though?"

Tamane smiled, the freshly painted streaks of white writhing over his face like adders. He gave Alfie the look an adult reserves for speaking with a curious child. "Oh yes."

Alfie looked and saw darkness, trees, tangled bushes and trailing lianas. Something gibbered in the air by his ear and he managed not to jump merely because Tamane was looking at him. An insect the size of a fingernail was crawling up his calf, and his polished buckled shoes were already clogged with mud to the ankle. Tamane had seemed merely annoyed by the crew's jokes about cannibals, but to Alfie, in this place anything seemed possible. "I'll look forward to it then," he said, and went back to sit next to Farrant.

Farrant was taking tea, polished as a diamond on this mud-heap, and Alfie felt a tug pulling him towards the man as to an anchor in a storm. When the captain touched his face he forgot all about onlookers and smiled.

"I'll need to discuss tomorrow's plans with you in my tent, Mr. Donwell."

"Yes sir, at once."

12 January, Pirate's Bay

"My apologies, gentlemen," said Captain Babineaux of the French two decker *Achille* as one of his crew hammered the spike of John's irons into a tree at the center of the camp. The short chain that joined the two manacles around his wrists passed through the hole in the pin, and as they nailed the pin up high his arms were raised almost straight above his head. If he pulled down on one wrist to ease that shoulder, the chain slid through the pin and dragged the other taut. John tried to sidle to one side, to give the similarly confined Captain Smith a little more breathing space, but was shoved back as Lt. Collins was nailed up next to him.

"But do not have any anxieties. Whatever our colleagues, *we* are not scum. You will be treated well, I assure you."

Behind his back, behind the two marines who flanked him, the cluster of *Otter*'s seamen huddled, bound, in a stockade of thick wooden stakes, deeply entrenched, their ends pointed and angled inwards. The men had been given no bedding, no food or water. John's shoulders already throbbed, and he would have been inclined to question the French captain's definition of "well treated", if it had not been for the expression on the faces of the watching pirates. At the word "scum" a lounging man in a red cap had looked up and sneered, revealing a mouth full of gold and brown teeth. Twists of fuse paper were wound into the man's beard, and he wore his hair long and curled like a sultan on a Persian frieze. Turning away, he joined his own knot of followers, speaking to some urgently before wandering away, apparently aimlessly, to join men at another fire. John watched, unhappily, as a few minutes later the men to whom he had spoken also got up, going each to a separate fire themselves, sitting down with intent looks and gestures that spoke of violence.

"Sir," he whispered, "something's afoot."

"I know." Smith gave an experimental tug at his irons, then planted his feet and tugged with all his might—to no effect. "Can you get your hands out?"

John had tried the experiment already, his wrists rubbed sore with the attempt, but the cuffs were snug. Even with blood making them slippery it was simply not possible to shift them. "No sir."

"Ne parle pas! Silence!"

"They might have let us sit down." Smith glared at the officious marine. John shifted from foot to foot and agreed. The short evening snuffed into darkness, but the heat did not abate, and sweat ran down his upraised arms, down his back. His hands crawled with pins and needles, his arms cramping, and if he tried to relieve his tired legs and feet by leaning on the bole of the tree, his weight pulled at aching shoulders, ribs, and his abraded wrists.

"It could be worse," he said, after a while.

Smith's wisps of receding gray hair clung to the sweat on his forehead. He had still not entirely lost the kindly, apple-faced look of a favorite grandfather, but his voice was bleak. "Oh, I'm afraid it will be."

"Do you think we should warn the French that their allies are planning something?"

The cane sliced out of darkness, smacking into John's face before he even registered the movement to his left. He jerked against his chains in shock, pain bright and all consuming as lightning for a flash.

"Silence!"

It kicked off at midnight.

Having fallen asleep on his feet, John jerked awake at the

sound of shots. The night still pressed, smothering as a blanket, over his face. He could barely see the white blur of Smith next to him. The cooking fires of earlier had died down, and in the sullen glow around the base of the trees he could guess at moving feet. Then a tent went up in flames and he caught a glimpse of pirates running full pelt towards the harbor. Sprawled bodies, leaking black fluid in the red light, showed that the French had quietly had their throats slit while they slept.

Flame from the tent crept across a liana into the branches of a nearby palm, smoldering up its trunk and roaring out in its umbrella of leaves. With surprise lost, the running shapes gave tongue, yelling curses and obscenities, hooting with laughter as they chased after the few remaining Frenchmen, who had escaped the massacre and fled for their ships.

The palm burnt like a torch. Fire spread, creeping down the cables towards the stockade in which *Otter*'s crew were imprisoned. Watching it, John pulled in panic against his chains, scanned the ground and saw—*there*—a dead French officer, face down.

God, please! He pulled himself away from the tree, stretched his leg out, bending back like a bow, and managed to hook the tip of his shoe into the dead man's belt. As he tried to pull the corpse towards him, the shoe fell off, but it was easier to get his stockinged foot back beneath the leather and drag the man towards them.

Flames caught eagerly in the brush inside the compound. Through the slats of the wall, he could see *Otter*'s crew—tied together with thin cables—trying to roll themselves on the conflagrations. Their dirty, frightened faces shone through the bars of their cage, sweat reflecting fire.

"If you can…" Smith got his own foot under the limp form and together they managed to raise him to waist height. The handle of a throwing knife protruded from his back. If they could only get the corpse high enough from the ground so that one of them could seize the knife, they could cut the irons out of the tree and…

The stockade blazed. Dooley, the boatswain, rolled himself deliberately into a fire, screaming as it ate away his bonds. With blackened, bleeding hands he tore at the ropes around his mates, freeing them, but even as he worked the flames spread. They reached the rum barrels stacked against the outside of the cage, crept over them like curious, nosing snakes, changing color to blue and purple. Then with a sound like an arm coming out of its joint, the barrels exploded. Flaming debris flung itself through the air like heated shot, spattering the men within the cage with blue-hot liquid.

John grabbed the body around the waist with his feet, held tight to his chains and lifted. Just for a heartbeat the knife hilt was within grasping distance of Smith's hand. He made a grab. The corpse's belt—supporting its weight—broke. It slid out of John's grip. *God damn! No!*

But Smith had dug his fingernails into the hilt. For a moment the whole weight of the dead man hung from them. Blood seeped out between nail and fingertip. Then, with a sucking noise, the corpse slipped off, Smith gathered the knife into his palm, and began to hack at his bonds.

◖ CHAPTER 15 ◗

12 January, King Cardinal's village, near King's Bay, Tobago

"They hold him in a fort here." The Queen brushed back leaf litter to expose the rich red earth, and drew a map of the French encampment with sticks and leaves. "There are many men. All those who came from the ship you saw…"

"The *Arc-en-Ciel.*"

"Yes. And some more, left behind from other ships, to keep us in order." The Queen favored Farrant with a sharp blaze of a smile. She had shown all the pleasure appropriate on seeing her son Tamane again, and he in return had abandoned his English dress, now standing by her side in feathers and fronds. Warmth, nevertheless, pervaded the camp, and outside the Queen's house the *Britannia*s were being very much welcomed by the women of the tribe, both sets of allies still in the happy stage of being enchanted with each other.

"On this side the sea," she said, "and here a tall wall of rock. They think no one can pass here, but we can come down on ropes. Lift him away."

"While the *Britannia* creates a diversion." Farrant nodded approvingly, crouching down himself to study the dirt map. Privately, Alfie thought that he and the Queen—whose name no one had dared to ask—were two of a kind. They had certainly recognized each other's talents the moment they began to talk strategy. "Two forces, I think, here and here." Farrant pointed, indicating the scratch which represented the coastal path, more suited for goats than Englishmen. The bay itself, however, was encircled by shoals, and the landing perilous enough if all else was peace. Defended, there was no possibility of assailing it from the sea.

"Mr. Donwell, you may take a company and two cannon. I will lead a second down this stream and come at the fort from the mouth of the river, creating a crossfire. In the ensuing firefight, her majesty's forces may come down the cliffs unobserved and free King Cardinal. After that, we may as well take the fort for ourselves."

"Yes sir." Farrant made everything sound so easy, as though he had never known doubt or loneliness in his life. For a moment Alfie understood why he and John seemed to think that duty was enough. A kind of martial glory shone about them both like the halo of light about the drawn blade of a sword. Trying to be worthy of them, he turned, gathered his men together and departed.

Farrant watched him go, bowed to the queen and called together his own followers. An hour later found him working his way down the river at the head of a procession of men disgruntled at being called away from their diversions. The soft mud of the river bed oozed around his feet with each step, sucking him down, making every movement a struggle. He fell back to watch the cannon, to make sure that the men carrying it held it out of the water—and to make sure they did not break themselves under the task. Pride, after all, was not confined to the upper classes.

At points the river silted up and they found themselves slogging through reeds. Thin, slimy things wriggled in his shoes. When the first sailor fell from exhaustion, he called a break, and burned the leeches from his legs with a cigarillo, passing his case around so that the men could follow suit. Then he chewed on a lump of last night's plum pudding, which his steward had put into his pocket this morning, wrapped in a handkerchief.

Clouds of biting insects, too numerous to swat, crawled into his shirt. The heat made him feel like a suet pudding being slowly boiled 'til tender. He put his head in his dirty hands. How nice it would be to be sitting at home with a cup of tea and the newspaper. *Am I getting too old for this? Should I do as Isabella asked; go back to England?* Shock his father into the apoplexy for which he was long overdue, reorganize the Admiralty, take up a seat in Parliament, and court scandal in the cruising grounds of the Inns of Court.

Or perhaps, now he'd tried Bentley's way—tried to exhaustion the idea that he would ever change—he could even allow himself to love. If he set up a certain young man in an establishment somewhere deep in the obscurity of the countryside, with a small pension, he could even, quietly, run a second household with him. The picture enraptured him briefly—*driving up the grassy lane to a hidden cottage, sheltered by beeches, his lover greeting him at the door with a charming, lopsided smile and obvious, genuine happiness….*

Shaking his head, he pulled himself to his feet; got the men moving again, slogging onwards. At the mouth of the river, coming out onto the bank, the men carrying the cannon slipped, and he was under the harness in an instant, saving the gun, hauling them up without thought. Fantasy aside, Farrant knew Alfie was hardly the sort of pampered Ganymede he could keep in a box for occasional use. Nor could he do that to his wife. So he couldn't give this up, not really. Not if it meant a life of false and frigid peace at her side.

On the other side of the fort, Alfie paused to breathe and eat a handful of biscuit crumbs. Even the hard tack had not been equal to withstanding the last climb, when they managed to winch the cannon vertically up a chimney of rock onto this perfect little concealed platform. From here, one or two good shots should take out the gun emplacements in the fort. Strenuous though the climb had been, he felt well satisfied with the morning's work. He settled down with a glass to observe the doings of the French in the fort.

Almost directly below him, Lt. Jameson, with the bulk of the *Britannias*, set up their own cannon in preparation for attacking the wall as soon as the signal came that Farrant's men, and the Queen's, were also in position.

Sucking the biscuit crumbs from his teeth, he took his coat off and allowed the fresher breeze up here to dry the sweat on his back. Then he saw to it that the cannon was secured and in working order, set up a system to lift the shot from the ground, and watched it stockpile with satisfaction. When the captain's party was in position to begin their attack, he was ready to make sure they faced only bullets, not cannon balls from the fort.

Hunkering down beside his resting men he looked out at the fort, trying to see the captive chief. Why did some men get everything—a kingdom, a wife who would fight a war for him—when some were lucky to be allowed to scrape up the leftovers? *And why can't everything in life be as cut and dried as siegecraft?* If only there were tactics for storming a heart, or at the very least, for subduing his own.

◖ CHAPTER 16 ◗

3 a.m., 13 January—Pirate's Bay, Tobago

Smith drove the throwing knife into the bark of the tree, gouging out a great notch to the side of the pin which held his irons. A flare of mad hope leaped up in John's heart like the fire that was spreading all across the clearing. Smoke veiled the red light, throwing into shadow the frantic faces inside the stockade. Darkness and fog turned the night into a vision of the pit, and somewhere in among the captive *Otters* the screaming had started.

Chopping a second time, Smith wrenched at the pin. It wiggled. Pulling it with all his weight, throwing himself from side to side, he wrenched it out of the wood, turning in triumph towards the roped up gates of the cage. Running forward, knife in hand, to cut the ropes and let the prisoners out of the burning pen, he did not see the pirate until the oar came whistling through the darkness and smashed into his forehead. Lifted off his feet, he flew backwards, landed in a crumpled heap at John's feet.

Involuntarily, John yelped, a sharp *"ah!"* of sympathetic pain and despair, and the pirate walked forward out of the smoke to look at him. It was the red-capped man from before, the fuses in his beard smoldering, lighting his face from beneath by their glow. Smoke curled around his eyes like the whiskers of a dragon.

Smiling, he placed the tip of the oar just below John's adam's apple, pushed until he had lifted John off his feet, the rounded wood driving all John's weight into his throat. Agony transfixing him, his heart racing and blood thundering in his ears, he grasped his chains, pulled himself up and away, coughing out blood. "Stop the fire! They're *dying!*"

"You don't say?"

The man's comrades came to his shoulder and jeered at John. French blood ran from their fingertips as though they'd washed in it.

"Please, the fire, you can't let—"

"You're right." The leader showed his rotting teeth in a broad, unfriendly smile. "I can't *let* them die. But, you know, they're not a lot of use to me live."

He shouted instructions in Jamaican patois. John sobbed with relief as the pirates stamped out the blazes in the clearing, and caught the breath again in horror when he realized they were wedging extra supports into the walls of the stockade. Flinging tinder in, they hacked the fingers off the hands that gripped the top, sending the climbing, frantic men tumbling back into the flames.

"No! No!" John shook his head, as if he could shake away the screams. The broadening light showed him pirates laughing, warming their hands at the blaze as though it were a Guy Fawkes-night bonfire. They passed great round-bellied bottles of rum from hand to hand while their captives burnt, watching the deaths like a seasoned audience at a play. Occasionally—for a particularly blood-curdling scream—they would cheer.

"Fucking animals," whispered Collins, forgotten on the other side of the tree from John. Still seeing phantom stars, his whole body shivering from the attack on his throat, John reached a hand around, and Collins brushed his fingertips in mute, terrified, fellow feeling. The air filled with the smell of roasted flesh.

Red-cap returned, still with his oar in his hand like the scepter of a king, but with his beard extinguished; a sooty, sweaty look about him, and a swagger. At his word, they picked up the fallen form of Captain Smith and poured seawater over him until he sputtered back to consciousness. Groggy as he was, a plump, eld-erly man, he tried to fight them with the chain of his irons as a weapon. It amused them for a while, until a Lascar smashed a bottle on Smith's head, felling him again.

Doubling his arms behind his back, they hung him up by them next to John. As his shoulders ground out of their sockets, he woke with a scream.

They tortured him for most of the night, until he had no voice left with which to cry out.

John leaned his cheek against the bole of the tree, closed his eyes, but could not stop his ears. Through his flank, pressed against the captain, he could feel the spasm of every agony, al-most as if it was his own, but do nothing to take it away. Clinging on to Collins' hand, he tried not to give them the satisfaction of seeing his fear. When it was his turn, he would not let them break him, he would not give them the satisfaction. *But God!* If only he wasn't so damn scared.

John's mouth filled up with blood, cloying copper sweet, as he lay still, pretending to have swooned. It flooded his nose and throat, gagging him, and he coughed, gasping, before he could drown in it. Mocking laughter beat at his ears, almost covering the sound of Collins weeping. Raising his head, blood and mucus hanging out of his mouth in red strings, John tried to see if Smith was dead, tried to avoid seeing what they were doing with the boys.

It was too dark. Dark as the pit that seemed to have opened in his soul. His wandering mind returned to Algiers and for a mo-ment he was the one stuffed into the tiny prison, clay so hot his skin melted off, sticking to the walls.

A hand under his chin dragged him upright, pressing on the bruises. Someone else took the chain of his manacles and ham-mered them back into a post. Drool and blood began to slide down over his naked chest, and he felt the lash wounds in his back bleed anew. He had long forgotten his initial shame over being stripped naked for the amusement and remarks of the crowd—it was now too much of an effort to breathe, to chase down human thought through the twisted corridors of his darkened mind. What had started as unbearable pain had become something quite different. A new world, blossoming behind his eyes like a black rose. But the slave pens were there, with their stench, and he could not remember if he was there or here, where *here* was, who he was....

"We shouldn't have dirtied this pretty face, mates, should we?" Red-cap spun the chain. John, dangling from his wrists like a side of beef, did not trouble to raise his head again. He could feel their gazes on him without looking. "You need a wash, mate."

Grabbing his blood-tangled hair, Red-cap pulled him upright, nodded, and his first mate emptied a bucket of piss over John's head. John had thought himself safely in his own inner world, gone to hiding in a darkness from which no one could hunt him out. But at the splash every nerve awoke as though doused in acid. His world went white, then red, and he found himself once more struggling against his chains, laying his wrists open to the bone, awake, blazing up with fury and humiliated by the filth.

"There." Red smiled, pleased. "Now how's about we kiss it better?"

The camp erupted in hooting and cat calls. John ground his teeth.

I'm going to kill you. I'm going to kill you. I'm going to fucking kill you all....

ᘃ Chapter 17 ᘂ

Sitting on woven mats in the chief's house, Alfie found himself plied with bowl after bowl of unidentifiable food. A second bowl, kept brimming, held liquor brewed from some herb the chief's daughters were chewing and spitting into a bowl. It tasted as appetizing as it looked, a thin, milky liquid still with the strings of bark hanging out of the bowl, but after a couple of swallows it left a tingling sensation in the mouth, and it became impossible to remember the pressing reasons for self restraint and self denial.

Huge basins of the stuff were circulating among the men of the tribe, who mixed it with plundered beer and brandy from the fort and pressed it on their new friends. Beyond the open sides of the pavilion—for one could hardly call it a house— someone had struck up a jig on the fiddle and several of the tars were demonstrating the dances of Britain to a laughing, appreciative audience. No one seemed to care if the dancers were too drunk to get their footwork right, as long as when they fell a friendly bosom waited to receive them.

The *Britannias* ate like men possessed, and sang. They showed the ladies of the tribe the hornpipe, and other dances less suitable for public performance. The more shy men, blushing beneath the ribald comments of the rest, allowed themselves to be led by their island maidens into the private shade of the trees. The bold simply coupled where they sat, then sat up to drink again. King Cardinal, wearing a French captain's coat, a number of bruises, and three severed heads on his belt tucked in to his dinner with a trencherman's determination, slowly and steadily eating course after course. The queen, giggling like a debutante, with her eyes sparkling and the flowers falling askew in her hair, gave a speech of thanks to which no one listened, but everybody cheered.

By the end of the evening they too had retired behind a palm screen, and Alfie, looking up over the firepit, was struck to the heart by the sight of Farrant laughing with his officers. The fire-light gilded him, but it was his own energy that added the brutal grace to his gestures; the king of a pride of lions, even in this happy mood. Thinking back, Alfie could not discover another memory of the man thus open, not even in the most intimate mo-ments of sex. Where had he hidden all this joy, this flame of life that lit his face now more wonderfully than the fire, making him young? *Why* had he hidden it, and grown to be so crabbed and calculating? Victory suited him.

Farrant looked up, saw Alfie watching him. The shape of his smile altered, taking on something of the heat and debauchery of the night. "Help me up, Alfie. I think I'll retire."

Alfie got his shoulder beneath Farrant's arm and half dragged, half supported him back to his tent. "Oh," Farrant sniggered as he lay down, "this wound is so severe, I believe you'll have to help me undress."

"I'm shocked, sir." Alfie chuckled, helping the man out of his coat and waistcoat, making a long, teasing business of unwinding the neck-cloth and unbuttoning his collar as he punctuated each movement with a kiss. "Could I not fetch your valet?"

Caught by his own stock, he found himself slammed into the floor, then pinned against the foot of the tent pole as the captain took control. "Damn my valet. Just get these trousers off and stop talking."

Surrendering gratefully Alfie went down under the exuber-ance with no more protest. It was indeed a long time before he spoke again—in coherent sentences, at least.

"You'll have to fuck me," Farrant said, when he was sprawled on the blankets naked but for nightshirt and the bandage about his thigh. "Bastard got me with a bayonet, and I daresay I ought not to jostle it for a while."

"I think I can manage that." Kneeling, Alfie pulled Farrant's arse off the blanket and into his lap, holding the wounded leg carefully over his shoulder, watching the expression on the captain's face as he fucked him; carefully, gently, but very, very thoroughly. When they lay together afterwards Farrant deigned to fit his face into Alfie's shoulder and sleep—an altogether new evidence of affection. Firmly telling himself it meant nothing, Alfie pulled another blanket over them both and held vigil.

The sounds of the party still going on, laughter and singing, faded by degrees into sodden sleepy silence. It was absolutely dark and private in the tent, and Alfie indulged a tenderness he was not normally permitted to show, pushing up the shirt, gently exploring Farrant's body with light fingertips. Tracing the old scars, rubbing over the small brown nipples that perked beneath his touch, he worked his way down to the flawless silk of the skin over the man's arse and thighs. And there his touch was balked by the rough linen of the bandage.

"Trying to sleep…." Farrant murmured. Yawning, he took Alfie's hand in his own, and though he knew it was only a way to still it, a ridiculous joy welled out of Alfie's heart at the touch.

"This bandage is someone's cravat," he pointed out, rather than confess any of the inappropriate, unwelcome things he wanted to say. "Did you tie this yourself? Have you been to the doctor at all?"

Farrant rolled himself onto his back and reached up to tangle his fingers in Alfie's sun-bleached hair. Reflected firelight gleamed from his half open eye, crinkled at the edge into an affectionate smile. "No more bloodsucking leeches—no more doctors. Never again. And you, don't fuss. Can't be coming home to fuss. Get enough of that with m'wife."

"I think I might love you," said Alfie, settling down with the top of his head beneath Farrant's arm and his nose pressed into the captain's ribs. They hitched slightly, he thought with laughter.

"God knows why," Farrant replied, but he stroked the top of Alfie's head.

Coming home, Alfie thought, with a catch of his breathing that almost felt like pain. "Maybe I have no sense of self-preservation," he said, truthfully enough. Laughing quietly, Farrant fell back to sleep with the suddenness of exhaustion. Floating on contentment and alcohol, Alfie let himself follow.

"Sir! Sir!"

Farrant, feeling thoroughly rumpled, with a thick and throbbing head, awoke to find Price-Milton, *Britannia's* youngest midshipman, shaking him by the shoulder. The boy held a candle-lantern so close to his ear it was a wonder his hair did not singe. In deference to the child's youth and delicate sensibilities Farrant reached down and drew the sheet up over Alfie's sleeping face. Price-Milton, too focused on his own news, didn't seem to register the movement. "What is it, Mr. Price-Milton?"

"The king says we'll want to know there's more French in Pirate's Bay, sir. He says it didn't occur to him before now, 'cos of seeing his wife again, he says. But if we was to go now, in the middle of the night, we could get there before they heard anything about this, and wasn't expecting us. Begging your pardon for disturbing you sir, but it was the King what said it."

"He'll give us guides?"

The boy gave a sudden smile, full of the resilience of youth and unencumbered by a hangover. "They're here already, sir."

"Give me a moment to dress. Then you may rouse the men."

"Aye-aye, sir!"

As soon as he had gone, taking the lantern with him, Alfie sat up and began rummaging about for his clothes, dressing rapidly, with a disgruntled air. He pulled up pegs and ducked through the back of the tent, maintaining the illusion of coming from somewhere else. Farrant found it faintly amusing, and yet faintly

sad. But he dismissed it from his mind almost at once as he concentrated on manning the *Britannia* and the *Arc-en-Ciel* with
every body who could haul on a rope; even some of the young
women. He sent Lt. Carver over land with the king's elite war-
riors and hurried to the attack.

Britannia reached Pirate Bay in the still, cold hour before dawn,
when the profound darkness and the silence teetered on the edge
of infinity. No sign of activity stirred on the decks of the numerous
ships at anchor on the placid water. If there were look outs they too
were asleep or occupied. Making up boarding parties of men experienced in cutting out expeditions, Farrant sent them one by one
by over the rails of the unwary ships. There, very quietly, they would
pad through the sleeping men slitting throats until the vessels
passed without a murmur into their control. In this slow, secretive
way two hours passed, and half the fleet let down their sails and
began to stand out to sea, British colors fluttering from their masts.

Then someone shrieked aboard the schooner. A shot echoed
over the dark water, a rush of feet boomed hollow over deck
planks and her bell pealed out the alarm.

Almost immediately, running figures burst onto the beach.
Scarcely pausing as they saw their ships abandoning them, they
heaved their longboats out into the white line of surf to give
chase. "Lower your elevation," cried Alfie to his gun crews, gaug-
ing the range and distance with a practiced eye. "Make ready to
fire."

With a series of thuds, *Britannia*'s cannons hunkered down.
Her gun captains took the wheels off the carriages in order to
aim low at the rowing men battling the surf. "Grape shot, Mr.
Gunner please," said Farrant grimly. "Fire as she bears."

Britannia's broadside filled the night with over a ton of
screaming iron shrapnel. The shore disappeared in a flume of
red-stained water and flying wreckage. The gun crews hastily
wormed and sponged, dropping uncombusted wadding in the
sea. Barrels steamed at the touch of the damp sponge. Smoke

parted on devastation. Five of the launches had burst into splinters and rags of flesh. Another three drifted, no movement aboard, the prone forms inside lapped over by crimson waves. But the last one limped back to shore. As *Britannia* fired a second time, Price-Milton raced up to the quarterdeck and hollered, "There's some in the trees, the lookout says, sir! Sheltering, like."

"Damn them!" cried Farrant, who by this time, Alfie thought with some concern, was looking unshaven and worn. He limped to the helm and back. "Launch the boats. You have the ship, Mr. Nyman. I'm going after them."

Dawn's cold light broke over the jungle as Alfie waded ashore in Farrant's wake; sloshing through water that smelled of blood and shit, musket and powder flask held up above his head to keep them dry. The *Britannias* hunted the pirates through their coverts with something of the enthusiasm most gentlemen reserved for big game hunting. It was a disturbingly cheerful party.

Following the tracks of their enthusiastic people, Alfie and Farrant came to a wide, open clearing where smuts were beginning to settle over a scene that might have come from the head of Hieronymus Bosch. The very grass beneath their feet bent black and greasy beneath a thick layer of ash. Alfie nudged a dimly lit form with his foot. The body turned over, but the head remained, detached, in a jelly of cold blood. Tarnished *fleur-de-lys* braid on the back of the corpse's uniform glimmered like its open eyes.

"God's teeth!" Farrant bent down and picked something off the ground; a shiny polished brass button, with the English rose in the centre that marked a British midshipman's uniform.

Looking up from the little flower, Alfie saw a scar of smoldering earth surrounded by stakes, where blackened bones and charred flesh heaped about the bases of a half burned wall. The stench was roast pork, but those were hands wrapped around the stakes, their finger bones white in the newly risen sun.

"We should have been here," said Farrant, all his urbanity gone in a moment of blistering rage.

"We didn't know." Alfie put a hand on his wrist, remembering that they had been making love while this happened. Celebrating, not ten miles away.

Farrant pulled his arm away as though it stung.

Cold. So cold. Ice seemed to have settled in the marrow of John's bones, and he wished he could tell his captors that his shivering was from shock, not cowardice. But his teeth chattered like dice and his throat was too raw, and they would only laugh and hurt him again.

Somewhere in his inner world, he was screaming. He could feel it; all his emotions held away like a fire behind a sheet of glass. It was better to concentrate on the cold, the crystals of frost in his blood with their sharp little edges, the desolate moony white of winter; deep under snow.

So why...why did he see marines' hot red coats and plumes of scarlet flame?

Smoke curled across the ground, heavy and blue. As the rays of the rising sun stabbed through it, it billowed about Alfie's feet like the Styx. Hell was too close. For a moment, seeing the bodies hanging from a stake in the centre of the clearing, he felt he had stepped out of the world, into the realm of his own nightmares. Horror drove through his chest like a thrown spear.

Later he would remember that all three men had been stripped, crimsoned with blood as if they had been painted with it. That the arms of the eldest were cuffed behind his back, and he hung from them, at an unnatural angle, the shoulders broken by his own weight. Later he would have time to remember and grow faint at the tar poured hot over the man's face, skin where it showed suppurating with burns.

But at the time his eyes barely registered these things. He scarcely saw the other two men, as a hook in the centre of his chest pulled him towards the third. A month's nursing, and every inch of that slender body was familiar to him; he could have told who it was just from the shackled ankles, without needing to look at the bent swan neck and drooping head. *John!*

Sailors with bloodied boarding axes began to wander back into the clearing, hands cupped around looted jewels. Alfie seized the nearest pair. "Get these men down!"

The axes made short work of the tree, digging out the pins of the chains. As more *Britannia*'s returned, sobered up enough to understand what they were seeing, the mood in the clearing hushed to a kind of awe. Careful and silent, they lowered the victims down to lie on the blanket of ash, picked through the debris left among the skeletons for tokens to send home, wrapped in one of the many letters of sympathy Farrant would have to write. Something for loved ones to remember them by. Though it was a vital and generous action, Alfie did not stir to help the men— couldn't. He couldn't move.

Coming up with Dr. Bentley beside him, Farrant looked down at the three crimson men, then up into Alfie's stricken face. "You know them," he said. Not a question—it was obvious enough.

"It's John." Alfie's throat closed as he shivered with nausea. He should say something—Farrant deserved that of him—but the gleam of bones at John's wrists, where he had pulled the cuffs deep into his own arms, made words superfluous. Pointless. Blowflies crawled over the ugly bruise on John's throat.

"Ah," said Farrant, meaningfully. His eyes and mouth thinned, briefly, his face gray in the dawn light. Then he swallowed, tilted up his chin and gave a rapid-fire volley of orders. "Stretcher bearers, get the living onto the ship. Doctor, I rely on you to separate corpse from casualty. Master, organize a party to get some kind of grave dug for the others. Mr. Carver, you may see to distributing prize crews…"

Alfie vaguely registered Farrant turning towards him, his mouth open. He was speaking. But then John opened his eyes. John's face could not have been more bloody had it been peeled off. His eyes were silver as swords, inhumanly cold. So must Mars Ultor have looked before unleashing the first war of vengeance across the world.

"You may go back to the ship, Mr. Donwell," said Farrant's voice, a long way away, also faintly cold. "Deal with this."

"Yes, sir."

Farrant was right to be angry, Alfie thought, as he sat in the launch supporting one end of the stretcher on his knee. He'd taken Alfie on board after the promise that Farrant would not end up being involved in Alfie's romantic disasters. Alfie had sworn he would not bring condemnation on board, and yet here it was in the very person of John Cavendish, cut up so badly he more resembled a side of beef than a man. John with his delicate conscience on board the *Britannia*—the most irregularly run ship in the kingdom. It didn't bear thinking about.

Deal with this, he thought unhappily. Deal with being in love with two men at once—both of them so very proud, so unsuitable, so stiff necked and intolerant, each in their separate ways. Deal with the lure and threat and heartbreak that John represented. Deal with it, and report back afterwards, when it was done.

A kind of morbid hilarity seized on the whole party. When Bill Drake on the tiller said, "Well, mates, I reckon from now on we'll call this the dead center of the Caribbean," Alfie joined in the general, somewhat hysteric laughter.

"John," he whispered. But John just looked at him with that reptilian look, with no sign of recognition or even humanity; no voice, no tears. They rolled off Alfie's chin instead, falling on to John's face, making tracks in the blood, while old Ezekial White handed him a handkerchief and said, "Friend of yours, is he?"

"Yes. A very good friend."

"He'll maybe come out of it," the seaman gave a reassuring grin. Scurvy had stripped all the teeth from his mouth, and the set he had now was wooden. Alfie found himself examining the grain as though memorizing every swirl was vitally important. "Those as don't go mad generally do. If I could have the wipe back when you finished with it? I only got the one, like."

"Naturally, Zeke. I thank you."

Alfie wondered what he had brought down on the ship; what he had done to Farrant. And he felt—now that it was too late— all the remorse appropriate for forgetting the man so completely the moment this other, more unsuitable love came back into his life. So much for his vows, so much for the second-rate affection he had had to spare for the captain. In a small corner of his heart he felt like a heel, but the rest was incapable of thinking of anything but grief for the ruin before him, and terror that it might never be rebuilt.

"Wake up John. Wake up. You're safe now. I'm with you."

໑໑ CHAPTER 18 ໑໑

Darkness filled John's dreams, full of agony and fire. For a time he had entertained thoughts of rescue. Indeed there had been a long period where he seemed to be lying on his back under the open sky, sun above him, and Alfie Donwell of all people weeping over him. He regarded the vision with the contempt it deserved. He didn't need the comfort of illusions. Above all he feared to believe, even for a moment, that he was saved. If he let himself hope, if he let go now, only to find himself picked up and drenched in piss again, he would break. He would break into such tiny pieces he might search for the rest of his life and not find them all. Best not to soften, even for a moment; best to face down the vision and stay braced for the next blow.

It wasn't long before the darkness returned, and fire with it, floating above him. Straps on his ruined wrists held him down, and slow, deliberate pains pricked him all over, like needles. He laughed aloud at the thought—they could hardly think that *needles* held any terror for him now—and saw a new man's face floating above him; a white face above a white cravat with a bloodied bow, floating disembodied. It seemed a very gentle face for a pirate, with soft round cheeks, round glasses and a disapproving expression, as though it felt laughter was not appropriate.

He dreamed of white boiled bandages slipping around his wrists, concealing the black blooded holes of them. And then someone said, "Drink this," and he was thirsty enough to do so, though he knew it too would be a cup of piss.

But it tasted like laudanum, and before he could be astonished at the thought, work out what it meant, there was an alter-
ation in the fabric of the world, as though someone had taken the
loose ends and tucked them back in. He worked out what it
was—the pain going away—just before he fell asleep.

When he woke he recognized the darkness as the close fug of
a ship's orlop deck. He swung in a hammock, the sea rocking him
from side to side, the wood of the deck only an arm's length above
him, and the "fire" a lantern swinging above the doctor's desk. He
tried to pull himself up, but discovered he was as limp as a wet rag.
The effort, however, alerted the doctor, who checked his watch,
made a notation in the margin of his book, and walked over.

"Got your body back," John observed, in an attempt at levity.
He could now see that the doctor's fine black suit had blended
into the darkness, giving the impression that the head was floating. It was too much of an effort to explain this, however, and he
received only a quizzical look in return. "I'm sorry...."

There was a pressure under his breastbone, quite unlike the
natural pain of the rest of his body—a pressure that seemed to
demand he apologize for the state of the world. He had been so
very angry, and now he was ashamed.

"Well, Mr. Cavendish," the doctor picked up his wrist to feel
the pulse, and John jerked it back out of his grasp before he finished closing his fingers. He found himself poised on the point of
hitting back, stopped only by the owl-like gleam of the man's
glasses. "I should recommend bathing in urine as a general cure,"
the doctor said, as though nothing had happened. "I have never
seen cleaner wounds." He cocked his head to one side and
pushed his glasses further up his nose. "I must take your pulse
now. So let us not have any prudery."

"Forgive me." John, back on the other side of the oscillation
again, allowed the touch though it made his skin want to creep
away. "Captain Smith, is he...?"

"Dead, I'm afraid."

It was hard to see the man's eyes. Lantern light caught in the spectacle lenses, and John scrambled to turn, seeing the reflection of darkness, fires, behind him. But there was nothing of the sort, only a handful of further hammocks, swaddling other invalids. Seeing them he was ashamed of his fear. He was being a trouble to his hosts. He should stop. "And Collins?"

"All dead." The doctor indicated the chrysalis forms of the other patients with a sweeping, possessive gesture. "These are all *Britannias*, injured in our own battles. Of your own ship, I do assure you, you are the only one left."

This was surely another dream, for God would not spare John, who was wrongly made and deserved execution, while allowing the innocent boys to die. But, when John turned his face into the side of the hammock to weep, the material scratched against his cuts as though it was real, and the tears soaked into his pillow and spread, stinging, beneath his face. *Why am I not dead too?* They had moved on to Collins when they finished with him; when they could wring no more anger or agony out of him. He should have held on, had more to give.

He should have endured longer.

"Move Mr. Cavendish up into the sun, will you? Some clean air and warmth will do him good."

John woke to the sound of a mocking, good-humored voice he recognized. For a moment he wasn't sure where he was, whether the whole year of doubt and failure had been a fever dream, and he woke now in a soft bed to the early morning sounds of Gibraltar; birdsong and street calls, pigeons in the dovecot of the nunnery a few streets below, and the whiskey and brown sugar of Alfie Donwell's voice. His mind tangled itself in turmoil and confusion, but deep inside something unfolded like a seed in the spring. His muscles, which had been clamped up tight against further pain, relaxed, as his body—wiser than his mind—told him he was saved.

On deck, the Caribbean heat pierced through his aches. He felt himself come together again, the sap rise through the barren husk. There was no lack of willing hands to secure his hammock in the rigging, tilting him up so that he could watch the activity on deck. When he slept he was left alone, but when he woke it was usually to find one of the tars, or Mrs. Shaw, or a beautiful youth from the launch crew, on hand to offer him cool drinks and undemanding conversation about the weather.

The weather which continued hot and bright. The same wind which had blown them so swiftly to Tobago continued to blow. Now, rather than run before it, *Britannia* had to work her way back against it, tacking and tacking again. The journey that had taken days on the way out from Jamaica took weeks returning, and John spent them soaking in the beauty of sky and sea, the white wings of the ship above him, the great clean expanse of the water, and the kindliness of *Britannia's* crew. Day by day he felt the treatment wash away stains, restore his bruised faith.

Britannia, he could not help noticing, was a happy ship. True, the tendency for even the officers to wander about without neck-cloths or coats, hands in pockets, chatting audibly even on duty, was informal to a point that made him wince. But he couldn't accuse the crew of being sloppy in their duties. And their kindness, the small gestures of goodwill he received, unearned, un-asked for, bespoke a humane influence he would never have believed.

The captain did not go out of his way to speak to John. But John felt he deserved that, for all the terrible things he had thought of the man. Besides, Captain Farrant did not look well. Under his tan he seemed flushed, and John—with nothing to do but watch—at times caught him limping when he thought no one was watching. The man had his own troubles, and though John would have liked to thank him for the rescue, he received the impression that his thanks were unwelcome.

Alfie too, after the first days, stayed away. John knew he had amply earned indifference, if not active shunning, and said nothing in complaint, but he felt the absence as a hurt worse than his wounds. So on the second week, after John had managed to hobble from his hammock to the heads and back, and was sitting watching the improbable string of prizes behind them, it was as if another broken bone had healed to find Alfie's shadow over him.

He looked up and smiled. The first smile since Tobago—it made his face feel odd. "How can you man them all?" he said, unable to face saying anything else. There was such a lot lying between them. *Such a gulf! How could words reach across it?*

"Once we were in possession, many of the pirates began sneaking back to give themselves up. Forced to join the pirate crews or die, they had never consented to the life, they said, and begged us for a chance to return to civilization."

Alfie's brow was scored with worry, and his eyes strayed to the captain, as to a problem he needed to solve. But he looked back in time to catch John's flinch of fear. "Don't fret. They're well spread out in ones and twos, and being watched. King Cardinal let us take as many of his men as we needed, and for all they're inveterate lubbers who don't understand English, they can haul on a line at need. It's only 'til Jamaica. And think of the money! We'll both be set up for life."

Pulling himself upright, John looked more intently at Alfie. It was a mistake. The climate clearly agreed with the man, for his unfashionable tan only succeeded in making him look radiantly healthy. The newly bronzed tone of his skin lightened his brown eyes to amber, and his hair too—worn uncovered on this informal ship—the sun had streaked with platinum. John found he had forgotten the presence of him, forgotten that merely being beside him felt as though there was a second sun shining a warm light on his skin. Alfie wore only breeches and shirt in the heat, and the width of his shoulders was apparent through the thin white linen, while the breeches hugged tight around his muscular legs and ass. It was the first time John had seen the man after that moment on the deck of HMS *Albion* when he had first become aware that he was surrounded by beauty. He felt as though Alfie's confession in Gibraltar had set him on a long, complex calculation. All his process of self-examination this last year had been working out the sums in the margins. But Alfie...Alfie was the answer.

Despite torture and revulsion, John was suddenly overcome with a picture of himself sitting on Alfie's lap as he had done with Bess; Alfie's hands on him, soaking up the feel of Alfie's skin as he had soaked in the reviving sunlight. *I wouldn't bite Alfie. I wouldn't stop Alfie from...*

He breathed in sharp. His heart fluttered in his throat and his mouth dried. Healing skin tingled as the blood rushed to his face and prick. It was jarring to find he was still alive, still faced with this same problem, still without any kind of idea what to do about it. *A second chance!* Dear God, he had a second chance to put things right, and no more idea what "right" was than at first.

"Both of us?" he said in a strangled voice and caught Alfie's quizzical look with shame.

"The captain means to share the prize money between the *Albion*'s and the *Otter*'s, and as you're the only *Otter* left..."

"Why?" John didn't want this; didn't want to feel indebted to Farrant. True, he already owed the man everything, but this extra generosity felt like a challenge, like the claim that the captain was a better man than he was. A magnanimous man. A capable man who did not need to rely on others to rescue him like some swooning maiden. A king, handing out largess to his subjects. "I want no pity or charity from him."

Alfie reeled back as if he'd been slapped. The wind, freshening, flattened the shirt to his chest and made his hair and its black silk ribbon stream. *Beautiful*, John thought unbidden. But his mobile face took on the expression of a man who smells something rank. "Christ almighty! Captain Farrant was right about you from the start." Alfie looked over to where Farrant stood on the quarterdeck. "You *are* a jumped-up little nobody who doesn't have the wit to understand him! If you can't recognize a great man when you are in his presence, then do us all a favor and *shut up.*"

There was a long pause. Long enough for John's instant flare of anger to turn into shame. He grasped about for words and could not find them. Alfie looked astonished at himself, and then mulishly obstinate as though he waited to receive an apology which he intended to spurn.

A sharp flapping broke the silence, as though a thousand swans were beating their wings above them. Sailors both, they turned to watch the sails; the wind had hauled forward and the sheets shivered at the edges with a clapping sound. John watched Lord Lisburn look up sharply, open his mouth to bellow "trim the main course," and stop, catching his breath on a high-pitched inward gasp of surprise. The heat in the man's face was now so crimson he too might have been painted with blood. He staggered, eyes rolling back in his head. Fighting to stand, he grabbed the helm for support. There was a choked noise by John's side, and Alfie sprinted across the quarterdeck in time to catch him as he fell.

It felt like the end of the world.

◖◎ CHAPTER 19 ◎◗

"And you tell me he had this all the time, and did not want to 'trouble me'?" Dr. Bentley's mild, civilian face was as awful as any Admiral's as he stripped off the makeshift bandage on Farrant's thigh to reveal the black, inflamed wound. Alfie tried not to breathe in, for the thing stank, moist and putrefying. Ribbons of black wormed their way under Farrant's skin from the wound down his leg and up into his vitals. Alfie had to look away to the man's sweating face, and then out of the window to the sea before he could speak.

"He said it was fine…" Alfie's voice was dry. "Just a scratch."

"And you noticed nothing when you and he had congress?"

Even in these circumstances, Alfie did not like the doctor's tone. Didn't like the clinical discussion of his private life as though he was a corpse to be anatomized for the benefit of students. He clenched his fists and said, mildly enough, "We did not…not at all. Since we rescued the *Otters*."

"No? And you didn't question that?"

"No, *sir*." Stung by grief and guilt, Alfie rounded on the man. He should know better than to poke at an open wound. "No, sir, I did not 'question that.' The captain is not a man who tolerates being questioned."

Bentley uncapped a jar of leeches and began to place them on Farrant's thigh, where they fastened with enthusiasm and began to suck. "Besides…" Alfie quailed afresh at the sight, "I thought…"

I thought that, knowing my feelings, he refrained from re-spect for me. I thought he took account of my distress over John; because my thoughts were full of John. If he had not—if John had not been here—perhaps we would have, and I would have noticed.

"Well, it is too late now for your thoughts and regrets to be of any moment." Bentley shook his head, and his stern professional look flicked briefly to something human, gone before it could be guessed. "I've no doubt it would be a comfort to him to know he brought it on himself, the stubborn fool. And perhaps that was his intent."

He measured out a variety of pills while Alfie stood dumb with shock. But when he placed the dish beside the captain's table, Alfie reached out and grasped him by the wrist. "What do you mean?"

"Let me go, Mr. Donwell. You will find your influence much declined now. You do not wish to offer me insult."

"I don't wish to offer you anything." Alfie did not let go. "What do you mean?"

Bentley drew himself up to his full five feet two. The light ran across his glasses like spilled water, and then away, and Alfie found himself looking into the eyes of a man who knew death and human weakness better than any of them. If he, John, and Farrant had fought their individual battles for survival, Bentley had fought, lost, and won many thousands of times. His gaze was chilly with eternity. "I mean, Mr. Donwell, that the captain had a…an un-fortunate condition. One, I may say, that you have exacerbated. This may be, for him, a solution to an intractable problem."

"You cold bastard!" Despite the warning, Alfie could not keep a rein on his temper. "Don't talk as if he's already dead! *Do* some-thing! You're a doctor, aren't you? *His* doctor. So cure him!"

Bentley twisted his wrist in Alfie's grip, with a look of disdain that made Alfie very aware that he—a six foot tall military killer—was menacing the civilian dishonorably. He dropped it, and Bent-ley coolly took out a handkerchief and polished his glasses. "I am

Captain Lord Lisburn's personal doctor," he agreed. "I owe him a great deal. I owe you nothing. But I will tell you this; the man is dead. Against an infection this severe there is nothing I could do but amputate. And the wound is too high for that. The corruption is already in his vitals. Even if I took his leg off at the socket—a procedure, I may say, I have never known a patient to survive—it would do no good.

"If you care for him—and I must suppose, from your behavior today, that in your diseased way you do—I suggest you prepare yourself. This cannot be a happy outcome for you in many ways."

Alfie floundered among miseries, unprepared to find such hostility in a man he to whom he had scarcely given a second thought, but above all unprepared to find Farrant ill. To find him mortal as any other man. It was an unnatural thought. "Are you threatening me?"

"Warning, rather." Bentley took a vial of laudanum from his bag and mixed a dose into wine. "You are new on board the ship, Mr. Donwell, and possibly not aware of the jealousies which surround you. Not that you have made any attempt to become aware of them; trailing the captain's favor as if it were your inalienable right. But…well, let us not argue over him as though he were already a corpse. Go. Go and do whatever it is that you do, and allow me to do my work here. We will all be feeling the chill soon enough."

Stumbling on deck, Alfie felt the many eyes on him, the curious gazes. After Bentley's enmity it was hard not to feel them as hostile. The ship, which had begun to feel like home, took on a strange unreality, and when the lookout shouted "land ho!" from the masthead there was a moment in which Alfie did not understand the words and could not make himself move. Then the needs of the sea returned to him and he checked helm and wind, and called out, "Port your helm, four points south south east." The ship responded, the crew moving out of their shocked stillness with relief, and a smattering of voices began to stitch the silence back into a more human garment.

They turned into Kingston Harbor four hours later, and with the salute to be fired, the bustle of mooring, the notes to the Admiral, the fuss of finding anchorage enough for the huge string of prizes, the paperwork to be completed, and the loading and unloading of seachests and men, fear and sorrow had no time to interrupt.

"I wanted to say," John had disentangled himself from the crowd piling into the boats and stood before Alfie, holding out his hand, "thank you. And I'm sorry." But Alfie was watching the infirmary's invalids being lowered in canvas slings into the barge as Bentley secured Farrant to the harness. Drugged with laudanum, Farrant had not woken, though slits of eyeball gleamed beneath his half-open lids. His head lolled out of the sling and Bentley had tied his wig on, with a handkerchief beneath his chin. Alfie's preoccupation dissolved like fog at the sight, leaving the land-scape of his heart revealed.

Farrant could not leave the ship looking like that—not ridiculous, anything but that—he would hate it. Every little vanity in his heart would revolt from being seen with his wig tied on like a country bumpkin at a hunt. Not so much ignoring John's outstretched hand as not even seeing it, he crossed the deck at a run, untied the wig, and stuffed it into Bentley's pocket. The doctor took a breath of outrage, then stopped, standing a moment in thought. Eventually he nodded then followed Farrant down into the boat, and Alfie watched them row away with the feeling that all the bolts holding him together had rotted beneath the water-line; the slightest breeze and his whole frame would peel apart, sink suddenly, irrevocably into the depths. For the moment though it held. It held, barely.

Alfie turned and found that John too had gone, taking his action as a dismissal. His hands trembling, he stared wildly about the deck, and met the one-eyed, worried gaze of Lt. Nyman.

"Is the captain—"

"Dying, Bentley says." Saying the words made a great black

bubble of grief well up through Alfie's tumultuous thoughts, pushing his ribs out with the pressure of it. His eyes prickled and filled, Nyman's face floating distorted through tears. *It cannot be true! It can* not. Farrant was an immortal, larger than life, like a Greek hero, Jason or Odysseus, a wanderer on the sea, blessed by strange gods. He couldn't die, *stupidly*, of an infected wound like an ordinary man. It wasn't possible.

Nyman's thoughts had gone in another direction. "I fear for the ship," he said, "in that case. He has built up, by his manner of living, such a fund of condemnation! I may hope that the hatred will follow him to his grave, but I fear it will turn out otherwise. More likely, with the protection of his rank and birth withdrawn, the admiralty will find some excuse to punish us for tolerating him so long."

"Certainly you cannot see him!"

Farrant's butler quivered with indignation, his eyes like two pins set point-upright in a sheet of leather. He raked them over Alfie once more as if to draw blood, and sneered.

At the end of a long graveled drive, Farrant's house nestled into the Jamaican hillside. Against the cool, tranquil shade the grey stone stood classical, elegant. Stables curved in a block behind an archway over which bougainvillea trailed like droplets of blood. An inner courtyard lit the hall beyond the butler with airy sunlight, and the music of a distant fountain.

"The Master does not wish to be bothered by business at present. And there can be no other reason for your presence."

"I…" Alfie looked at the man, standing like a mummified bog body in the midst of this picture of rational peace. Upstairs lace curtains billowed at the windows, and to Alfie's sea-adapted sense of balance the whole place lurched and heaved nauseatingly. A lie; a damn pretty, fine expensive lie. *I am the one who ought to be with him. I am the one he most nearly loves. I should be holding his hand, sitting by the bedside. His children may all be squabbling over who shall inherit what, and you be waiting im-*

patiently for the passing, so you can parade your self importance in your best black suit. But I…

He had been too numb, too distracted by things that needed to be done, and he had stood by and done nothing as Bentley stole the captain away from him to deliver him into this prison. He hadn't said the things he should have said. *I didn't tell Farrant…* And he wanted to be there, to soothe the fever and comfort the pain, and to let Farrant know that he was loved before he died. Not to let him die in an atmosphere of cold reproach.

"I wanted to say goodbye."

"This is a Christian household, Lieutenant." The imperfectly concealed disgust on the butler's face blazed out into a white fervor. He raised his chin so high he seemed to be looking at Alfie with his nostrils. "Your sort are not welcome here."

Stepping back, he clicked the door shut, firmly, pointedly, in Alfie's face. Instinctively, Alfie, caught between this and another nightmare, flung himself at it. Solid wood jarred his shoulder. Decorative nail-heads left a pattern of flower-shaped bruises on his arm as he took a couple of steps back and did it again, the door rattling in its frame at the impact. Gravel crunched behind him on the drive, but he ignored it, balled his fists, and punched the solid oak. His knuckles split, and the wave of pain blazed red in his darkness, urging him to do it again, and again, until someone finally let him in.

But he'd been through this before. He knew it wasn't going to happen. He could rage and scream until he exhausted himself, and the door would stay shut. Breathing hard and trembling all over, he stopped himself, leaned hands and forehead against the door for a moment, and then straightened up and turned.

Two black footmen in bright turquoise livery watched him warily from the drive. Sent, he supposed, out from the kitchen door to be sure he left. Well, if Lady Lisburn or her butler wanted to provoke him to violence, they would be disappointed. He hoped he had enough self control, at least, not to pick a fight with Farrant's servant outside the man's home while he lay dying.

Straightening his wig and pulling the creases out of his coat he gave them both a bow and walked away, feeling their eyes on his back all the way down the long tree shaded ride to the road. He would find the *Britannia's*. Some of them were sure to be mourning too; Bert at least, if not all of the young Adonises on the launch crew. He could surely find someone to have a drink with him, and laugh and curse the world, in honor of Charles Farrant.

◖◖ CHAPTER 20 ◗◗

March 1763, Kingston, Jamaica

John thought at first it was just the torrential, tropical rain thundering on the cobbles outside. His rooms were on the ground floor of Mrs. Milton's establishment, and his desk shoved up against the wall beneath the window, for the light. Only when a brick smashed against the window, bending the leads inwards and shattering two of the panes across his papers, did he realize that there were figures running out there, that some of the flashes were not lightning but pistols.

Old instincts threw him to his feet, had him scrambling in his sea-chest for his own gun. He slung the cartridges in a waxed waterproof bag around his neck, buckled on his officer's smallsword, picked his boat-cloak from its hook at the back of the door and stopped as if he had run into a wall. The door was shut, but behind it there were angry men and screaming and violence. In his unseeing eyes the firelight of two months ago glowed like a glimpse of hell, and he could hear the sobbing. His muscles spasmed, rigid, and pain cut across his back. *Pain—God!—the pain!*

He couldn't get past the doorway; found himself standing there, trembling, his bones like water.

Damn you! he thought, watching himself with contempt. *Damn you, you coward!* He would not submit to this—would not

be unmanned like this by something that was long over. If a boy
fell from the horse, one should put him back on at once, bleeding or no, or he would be afraid the rest of his life. This must be
no different. Forcing himself, step by tiny step, he put the boat
cloak around his shoulders, raised the hood. That feeling of con-
cealment helped a little. Now to open the door. He reached out,
laid his hand on the latch....

'Hows about we kiss it better?'

Fuck you!

And opened it. One foot forward, shift his weight, and then
the other. And again. He was outside. Shutting the door firmly on
the idea of retreat he stood and panted for a moment, while the
rain beat on his shoulders and poured in gray streams from his
hood. Then he took a deep breath and launched himself into the
street. Sword in hand, he followed the skirling, shouting figures
down to the docks, wet rats running about his ankles. The grip of
terror loosened as he recognized the rioting men as British
sailors, not pirates—though at times it was hard to tell the difference. Stepping over unconscious bodies, he worked his way
down into the thick of the scrum. Among the warehouses the
fighting was positively Homeric in its ferocity.

Crouching behind a barrel of dried peas John saw a boy he
knew—Ned Jupp of HMS *Albion*—his ginger hair still luminous
and distinctive despite the downpour. The tot was hurling half-
bricks into a fighting knot of men. "What's going on?" John demanded, seizing the boy by the collar.

There was a brief scuffle as he evaded the boy's snakelike
writhing and flying fists, before Ned finally looked at his face.
Then the boy straightened to attention comically. "Oh, it's you
sir!" He knuckled his forehead, leaving a streak of mud. "It's the
fucking *Britannias'* fault, sir, begging your pardon. We was all
'aving a drink up at the Royal Oak. Us *Albions* was just laughing
with them, friendly like, and they kicked off."

Lightning sliced the night in two, and in an instant of shock
and horror, the fighting men were picked out white against the

night. The picture of Alfie Donwell, blood spattered black down his white waistcoat, pale distorted face and bitter eyes, giving the boatswain of the *Albion* a good thrashing, imprinted itself on John's memory. Seared there by thunderbolt.

The crew of HMS *Britannia* cheered him on, clustered around the fight like children about a scrap on the schoolyard. Like the pirates in their leering circle around the stake. John didn't know what drove him through that circle of hatred. Indignation? Outrage? Sheer possessiveness? Whatever it was, it was stronger than his fear; he felt lit up from within as though the lightning had passed through his mouth and now inhabited him.

"Mr. Donwell!" he shouted over the roar of the rain, his voice ringing with command. He had been Alfie's captain once. He could again. "Control yourself! Control your people! For Christ's sake, man, you're an *officer!* You think *this* the epitaph your captain would want?"

Alfie's fist tightened in the boatswain's neck-cloth, holding him off the ground, shaking him, not seeming to register the limp man's lack of threat. "They have it coming."

John shivered. Alfie's eyes were not entirely sane as they looked at John, pleading for something. He had remembered Alfie wrong—he realized it with a start of fear and unwelcome lust. Somehow he had treasured a picture of litheness; a teasing, mischievous, lighthearted creature. It came as a surprise now to notice that Alfie's pleasant face could be brutish, that he towered over his companions, powerful and dangerous as a young bear.

"Farrant's not yet cold in his grave and *they* said—"

I bet they did, John thought, drawing breath to shout above the thunder. "I don't care *what* they said," he yelled. *And if they did, whose fault is it? The man flaunted his infamy.* "Get your men under control *now* or I will see you disrated for this!"

The storm flared in Alfie's eyes. A storm raged about the two of them. Lightning cracked overhead and the prickle of it made John's hair stand on end, stirring like a live thing. His skin tightened with shock and static, his heart thundering. He was a gal-

vanic rod, fully charged and set opposite its mate. Any moment
the spark would leap, and until then the tension mounted and
mounted. He felt alight with power and perhaps it showed, for
Alfie surrendered.

"Alright, lads, leave it now. That'll do."

They worked together, shoving at the fighting knots of men,
shouting at their respective crewmembers, bringing down the
lash of rank and arrogance against the mob. For all it was terrifying—being once more in the dark, the focus of all that violence—watching the rioting sailors fall back, daunted by his
command, lit the fuse of something wild in John. He found himself grinning, choking back laughter. See, he was not totally unmanned after all! Not useless, not laughable. Men obeyed him,
were daunted by him as they always had been. *Thank God! Oh,
thank God!*

The roar and crackle of lightning were in his bones and his
body felt so sensitized towards the other man he could feel Alfie's
movements as if they were his own.

On the cluttered front of an empty warehouse, its great doors
gaping wide, white flashes of lightning lighting up dangling
chains, the last group of men parted before them and ran. They
stood shoulder to shoulder in the rain, suddenly alone.

John turned, saw Alfie watching him; pale hair eerie in the
night, wide eyes gold. Rain trickled down Alfie's face, streaking
through the blood and dirt. He licked his lips, panting, his mouth
open slightly, gleaming with water. "John, I…."

The look of shock, vulnerability, was just the same as he had
worn that day John walked in on him when he was playing the
flute. Off balance, taken unawares, and he was so…oh so beautiful. *Why not? After all, why the hell shouldn't I?*

Seizing Alfie by the wrist, John hauled him into the warehouse's private darkness, shoved him up against the wall and
kissed him—desperate, demanding, furious. The storm crested
and broke in him as he forced his way into Alfie's mouth. Warmth,
and rain trickling off their hair onto his lips, and Alfie's solid body

trembling against him, and for a lightning flash he had no thought at all; abandoned to sensation like an animal. Only slowly did he recognize the shaking of Alfie's pinned arms, the shudder of his chest, and the low, irregular gasp of his breath for what it was. Head back against the wall, eyes closed, he was sobbing very quietly, stripped of his authority and broken at John's touch.

The spirit stove in John's rooms sighed and guttered, damnably slow. All the time it struggled to heat the water, Alfie sat at the table with his head in his hands, rain, blood, and mud dripping off him onto the clean floor. He took the teacup with numb fingers and did not drink, cradling it, bent over the steam.

There was so much John wanted to say. Principally, "I've been an ass. I'm so sorry. I don't dare ask for your forgiveness but tell me what I can do now, to mend you. Please. Please don't carry on like this. I can't bear it." But he couldn't force it out. "You'll catch your death," he said instead. "Come, let me lend you some dry clothes."

Alfie looked up, his gaze as bleak and bedraggled as his clothing. He made to speak, but as he did so, there came a sudden, shocking hammering noise. They both flinched. Then John put down the linen towel he had been using to dry his hair and opened the door. Light shone out across a self-important, down at heel, middle-class man and the two bruisers with cudgels who lurked behind him.

"Certain accusations have been made concerning the late Captain Lord Lisburn," the man said, unconsciously patting his own belly. Indeed, he looked almost pregnant with satisfaction.

"What is that to me?" said John coldly, trying inconspicuously to stand in the man's line of sight. It did no good, he merely stepped to one side and looked past John, straight at Alfie.

"Some very serious matters have come to light about the captain's...ahem...*relations* with one Lieutenant Aelfstan Donwell. I have been directed to take the gentleman in, for questioning. Enquiries at the harbor indicated he was last seen with you. So I came here. I presume this is him?"

John froze. So it had come to this after all; the death they had both been courting had found them here in his own rooms. He considered lying, considered drawing his sword and taking all three men down, hiding them somewhere. But as his soul revolted at the thought, Alfie slowly dragged himself to his feet. "Yes. Lieutenant Donwell at your service. What can I do for you?"

"Hand your sword to me and come with us."

"Alfie," John whispered, aghast. Alfie reached out and squeezed his wrist—he thought reassuringly, though it was hard to tell through the explosion of pain. His thin, new skin parted beneath the touch.

Alfie frowned at the blood on his fingertips as if he couldn't work out what it was. "Goodbye then, John. Pray for me."

◖Ϙ CHAPTER 21 Ϙ◗

"The man was notorious, a disgrace to the service." Admiral Rodney turned from gazing down at the harbor to fix John with that
penetrating look of his, eyes like blued steel, aquiline face as finely
drawn as a razor. "You are something of a celebrity at the moment,
Lieutenant, for your suffering, and your sudden acquisition of a
great fortune." He pushed the papers on his desk into a neat pile
and tapped the edges. Then he lined up the writing slope and scroll
of charts into a more parallel row.

Behind him his servants struggled with the heavy velvet curtains, hauling them down. The walls behind them, less faded by
sunlight, were stripes of emerald against the sage green of the
paneling. Rolling up the red and gold Turkey carpet behind the
desk, the servants worked with their heads turned away, making
a good pretense of not listening. Rodney's physician, Dr. Gilbert
Blane, however, watched John with professional interest from his
seat by the window.

If it could be allowed that so successful a hero looked frail,
Rodney did; over slender, and with a translucent complexion that
seemed half made up of cobwebs. But his eyes were extraordinary. "Yet your luck is as changeable as an Orkeney squall, Mr.
Cavendish. And in deference to that I feel it necessary to urge
you to leave this sordid matter be. You will spill your present good
fortune before you have begun to drink it."

"I wish with all my heart, sir, I could walk away from this."

John had begun to shiver so obviously that Blane motioned a servant to bring him a seat. Caught between gratitude and consciousness of the impropriety he looked inquiringly at Rodney who said, "For goodness sake sit. I have fought many a battle from a chair. I won't begrudge you it."

"Thank you, sir. I cannot walk away because…" After this kindness, so unexpected from an Admiral he had heretofore found fierce, John felt less able to speak than ever. He had to lie. A night spent sleepless, praying, and wandering about his rooms until his healing frame would bear it no longer, had lead him inexorably to the conclusion that he should lie—that Alfie deserved this sacrifice of his personal honor. More, that honesty might require execution but justice could not possibly do so. That it was therefore somehow morally right to lie.

But this conclusion was so foreign to John's nature that, despite the cause, guilt burned in every blood vessel like a course of mercury when he said, "Because I know Lieutenant Donwell to be innocent, sir."

Blane snorted, disbelieving, and Rodney put hands like eagle claws down on the desk and stared.

"I have no doubt Captain Lord Lisburn was guilty," John clarified. "But Lieutenant Donwell had served with him only as a child. He regarded the captain in the light of a father. I know Lisburn's behavior was…suspicious, but Donwell would hear nothing against him. Refused to believe it. Could not understand why his innocent admiration could be taken in such a way. Confessed himself utterly in the dark as to the captain's conduct with others. For God's sake, sir, if every man who'd ever shared a bed with another was to be suspected, you'd have to hang us all."

Rodney picked a tailor's bill from the top of his pile of papers, shuffled it to the bottom, leaving an innocent dispatch on view. "What do you want of me? I cannot let the man go. An accusation has been made, and a court martial is being convened. I can no more stop these things than I can stop the tides. And would not if I could. If your friend is as innocent as you say, it will be apparent then. If not…." Rodney still wouldn't meet John's gaze. He cleared his throat before continuing. "Well, as I say, you might discover it would have been better to distance yourself from the affair."

"I heard you were leaving, sir." John looked about at the half packed up office in confirmation. "And I…It's well known, sir, that with you gone, the presiding officer must be Captain Cordingly of the *Wasp*." He bent his head, toed a dropped pencil back under the desk, leaving a broad smudge of lead on the floorboards. Recollecting that Rodney, like Fortune, favored the brave, he looked up once more into that cold aristocratic gaze as he criticized a superior officer. "Captain Cordingly has been known to hang on rumor alone.

"You recall the case in '59, sir, when he hanged a married tar on the evidence of an accuser who later confessed to have dreamed the whole incident in a stupor of gin? Forgive me my presumption, but I cannot let my friend's life ride on the decision of a man like that. I say nothing of the captain's fitness to command, sir, but he is no proper judge in a court martial on this offense."

A snort from the corner diverted the Admiral's wrath. He glared at his physician, but Blane kept his head down, turning the pages of his newspaper with a decided, humorous crackle. Gratefully, John took another breath, plunged on. "You, on the other hand, sir, are a champion of the common man, not letting a fellow's birth or low state detract from his merits. Mr. Donwell is a plain man, without influence in the world, and I fear that Captain Cordingly would take his lack of family to be evidence of guilt. You, sir, would not. All I ask for him is a fair trial without pre-judgment, and that I believe only you can provide. Please stay, sir. You are a hero of England. No one could doubt your verdict one way or another."

Rodney's dark brows lifted in a skeptical flick at this eloquence, as though he had heard the like before from too many professional courtiers and toadies to be impressed. John waited out the practiced examination with patience, knowing that the Admiral would see nothing but sincerity in his gaze. He *was* sincere. His admiration for Rodney at least was no lie—the man had a genius for the sea; for turning the circumstances of any battle to his own advantage. His dash and enterprise were as sudden and awesome in action as the stoop of a hawk. Nor did he hesitate to recommend the lowliest for the best positions; and if his judgment was a little flawed in picking out his followers, it did not negate the principle.

Of course, Rodney's debts were also legendary, and his cupidity one of the few stains on a character otherwise entirely admirable. But John had cause to know, now, that no man was so entirely free from sin that he could afford to be too nice with his admiration. He held his head up beneath Rodney's cynical gaze, and at length the Admiral turned aside to lift his silver-topped sand shaker and set it gently back inside its baize lined box.

He capped the inkwell, slid it into place beside the sand, then rubbed his long fingers on a handkerchief, in a gesture John found disturbingly reminiscent of Pontius Pilate. "Lieutenant Cavendish, I believe I have told you that, in my opinion, the Navy owes you a debt of thanks?"

"You did, sir."

"And is it in consequence of that, that you are emboldened to make this application?"

"No, sir. I do not consider my own merits at all, trusting entirely to your regard for justice."

Blane huffed behind the sanctuary of his paper. John lifted his chair so that the servants could draw the carpet out from under its feet. Rodney took off his neat wig, revealing a head of sleek, dark brown hair that made him look full twenty years younger. He paced away to drape the wig over the bust of Emperor Hadrian that graced the window ledge.

"You're a man who appreciates honesty, yes?" He looked out of the window, down into the courtyard, until John said "yes." Then he turned and came back to lean a hand on the back of his chair, the other balanced on his sword hilt. "Then I will be honest and tell you that I have you down as my choice for captain of HMS *Boreas* in the unhappy event—which I am told is now inevitable—of her present captain's death from the fever."

The floor surged up beneath John as if it had crested a wave. Just for a moment he felt sunshine and a glory of bright silver spray against a clear washed sky. A fair wind on his cheek, blue water beneath his keel, and freedom. His own ship? *His own ship!* Poor *Meteor* flashed to mind. How much he had loved her! Handing her over to another man had been like handing over his first born child. The pain, even now, in memory, went close to choking him. On its heel came desire, ravenous, black desire like salt in his mouth. His own ship.... *To be captain again.*

"I should be more than happy." The uprush of glory tipped over the edge, went racing down into the hollow dark. Mountains of water cut off the wind and sun, and he shivered, becalmed, in the trough. It took no special talent to hear the "but" in the Admiral's cut-glass Harrow-educated tones.

"But the Navy, Mr. Cavendish, prefers not to have its ships captained by fools, and if you genuinely believe this young man to be innocent, then you are a fool. If you want him spared and you are no fool, then you are something worse. Something that must never be permitted to tread a British quarterdeck. Are you following me?"

John shut his eyes for a brief moment of self pity. When would the world stop hurting him? This was becoming more than he could very well endure. "Yes, sir."

"You are owed one favor, Mr. Cavendish. One. If you ask me, I will stay. But I strongly advise you—for your own sake—to take the ship and let this filthy business go."

Trudging out of the Admiral's office, John climbed up to the battlements and walked along the quarterdeck of the fort, passing the patrolling sentries with an unacknowledged nod. From here he could see out, over Port Royal's small white storehouses—the town a disheveled shadow of what it must have been a century ago—to the blue curve of the distant horizon and the white flecks of a crowd of sail against it. Pulling himself up to sit in an embrasure, hand on the metal of the cannon's stoppered mouth, he gazed out at the sea. A smell of warm brass polish and new red paint on the tompion surrounded the long gun. The ocean's lift and glisten, the dappled patterns and differences in shade which showed where currents slid beneath the surface, calmed him like an old friend sitting sympathetically beside him.

Half an hour later, he wrenched up a deep sigh, bent his head into his hands, and pressed his fingers into his eyes. Then, turning, he looked down into the courtyard of the fort, seeing the square tower like that of a church, and the sturdy brick arches of the walls. Beneath them, sheltered in the centre of masonry and cannons, the tall, whitewashed offices had their blue-painted shutters open to the breeze. Behind them, in the scant shade of a sapling oak, stood the windowless brick building of the jail.

John's spirit fluttered within him at the sight. He did not wish to go down and face confinement; darkness, chains. Just the thought had him breathing hard, leaning on the merlon behind as he fought off nausea. The reaction infuriated him more than his merely physical weakness, but he could not make it stop.

When he forced himself down, through the guarded door and into the gloom, however, he realized he was not the only one revisited by past torment. As an officer and a gentleman—and to keep him alive until trial—Alfie had been given the benefit of a cell of his own, away from the single great common room packed with malcontents and pirates. But as a result he was confined in a space in which he barely had enough room to lie down. He was separated from the common rout only by a hastily flung up grill of bars, through which they yelled and taunted, and pelted him with their filth.

Under the dirt Alfie looked healthy enough, but John could tell from the tilt of his head, from his gentle, ironic smile, that he was shattered inside. He had worn that same look those first weeks back from the slave pen—as though, dead within, he merely waited to decay.

"You shouldn't be here," he muttered in greeting. "A god-fearing man like yourself. Don't you know that if you touch pitch you too will be blackened?"

John dragged over a stool and sat, jammed tight to the bars. Alfie too dragged himself listlessly across the small space to be close enough to whisper a private conversation despite the eaves-dropping and jeering of the crowd.

Twitching a little at the nearness of the rabble, at their hateful coarse voices and the mockery—so like…so very like—John made an effort and laughed. "I'm afraid that's already happened, Mr. Donwell. Many things have changed since we parted. Tell me what I can do for you."

Alfie laughed in return, and a glint of tired amusement flickered like a rushlight behind his eyes. "So I woke you up for someone else's benefit? Story of my life." Then it snuffed out. He bowed his head into his hands and mumbled, "Before they hang me they'll let me speak. I'm almost looking forward to it. I've got a lifetime's silence to make up for; a hell of a lot to say. I'm going to tell them I could have been the philanderer they take me for. I could have fucked every pretty boy that came my way, but I didn't. I didn't. I'm going to be proud to tell the world I'm hanged because he loved me. To say I died for love."

"*Alfie!*" The words struck John like shot, lodged in him, but in this battle—as in all battles—he did not have time to stop and consider his wounds. He wanted to shake the man, but refrained. "Please tell me you will not blurt out the whole story to the court martial. Continue to protest your innocence and I will find some way to force them to see it."

"You can't see a thing that isn't there."

"There must be something I can do! For God's sake Alfie, this is not the time for you to play at martyrdom. There must be *someone* who can be bribed. Threatened…Tell me! *Think!*"

Alfie raised his head and looked at John quizzically, as if he did

not recognize what he saw—unsurprisingly, for John did not recognize this in himself either. But then, as if returning from a long
way away, Alfie said "You could speak to Mrs. Shaw, the gunner's
wife. She said...but I don't see..."

"I will find something," John insisted. "As long as you don't
confess. I know you have no cause to trust me but I will find a way
to save you. Storm the jail with pistols—as half *Britannia*'s crew
have stopped by my lodgings this morning to suggest—if I must.
I swear."

Rats scuffled in the straw as damp trickled down the bars between them. Even with the pirates' defiance and despairing gai-
ety in the cell beyond, the jail brooded over them, haunted with
phantoms of the past. Outside, the fort's clock struck noon with
an incongruous silver jingling of bells. Within, the air pressed too
close to breathe, hot and damp as the jungle and equally deadly.

"I can't believe he's gone," Alfie choked out at last, a glimmer
beneath his closed eyes as he leaned his head against the bars.
John hauled in his jealousy, though the lines creaked with strain.
This was not the moment to say "it was Farrant who brought you
to this" or "he never cared for you the way I do. Do you know
what I have given up for you?" There never would be a moment
to say that last, no matter how the loss ached and burned.

"Time brings healing," he tried instead, conscious of how
badly they both needed it.

Flakes of rust peeled from the bars and dusted Alfie's pale
hair. Their faces tilted so close together their breath mingled as
if in a kiss.

"Death brings it sooner," Alfie said.

⟪☾ CHAPTER 22 ☽⟫

With a grating clash and clatter, the jailer shot the bolts of the outer door and pushed it open. The shriek of rusty iron hinges on rusty iron pintles woke Alfie from his feverish doze. A stripe of sunlight fell across the floor like a spill of burning oil, scorching his eyes. His head throbbed and his tongue lay stiff and dry in a mouth choked with sand. As air billowed in from outside, it stirred the fetid air within, and scents of piss-buckets, puke, and ordure washed over his face.

The marines' cheerful crimson coats, stainless stockings, and the shining bayonets on the end of the rifles leveled at Alfie's chest, seemed glimpses into a heaven of cleanliness inaccessible to sinners like himself. He scrambled to his feet, backed into a corner, and stood passively as the jailer's servants unlocked his cell, took out the night-soil bucket, and locked it again.

"S'your lucky day, Mr. Donwell." The jailer passed bread and a mug of weak breakfast grog through the bars. "I seen men rot away in here for years, waiting for a court. Yours is set already. Day after tomorrer, you'll be out of here. One way or another, eh?"

While marines and lackies moved on to the communal cell, the man leaned his shoulder on the bars, buried his hand in his right hand waistcoat pocket and arranged his handkerchief to just peek out over the top.

Alfie received the sign with blankness, though it brought to mind some memorable occasions on park benches in the cruising grounds of London. That too was another world, shut away behind a closed door.

"'Tis the end of the war." The jailer rubbed a hand over his bald spot, undeterred by this lack of reaction. "All the captains back on station ready to go home. There weren't no problem finding five to make up a board for you. S'good, aint it? His Majesty's hospitality not being what you might call Fiddler's Green."

Alfie swallowed a gulp of the grog, worked his mouth until it felt capable of getting out speech. Why had he never noticed before what a complex procedure it was? "Yes…it's good."

Beaming with pleasure, the jailer tucked his pocket handkerchief away and hitched up his threadbare breeches. "So, is there anything I can get you? You made a packet, from what I hear, on the *Britannia*. May as well spend it while you got the chance. Oysters and champagne? Doxies? Nice new suit for the trial? You name a preference, I can provide it, for a little finder's fee."

What did Alfie want? He found it hard to think of anything, his mind stupefied. Looking up he caught a dozen pairs of eyes watching him from the adjacent cell as the whores, thieves, and dockyard gutter trash listened in. "Privacy?"

"Can't do that, sorry, sir. If you was to off yourself beforehand there'd be hell to pay."

Death. It seemed, all at once, a pleasant prospect. Farrant had found it a release from a problem, a life, he could not untangle though he tried. At the thought, Alfie breathed in sharp, bit his tongue until the blood flowed, coppery and warm.

"Water then, for washing. Clean clothes. I stink."

"Can't tell, in here." The jailer lifted a dismissive shoulder, but looked downcast. "That's all? How about a priest, maybe? Very comforting, a chaplain, in times of need."

"What do I have to say to a priest?" Alfie untied his moist cravat and wiped his face on it, leaving a rusty brown stain. *Would a priest listen if I tried to tell him that love was the fulcrum of my existence? That all I want is what any married man has; someone to share my life with. Someone into whose bed I can crawl at night. Someone to cherish and protect. He'd* nod in sympathy right up until I told him the man's name.

"Maybe you're right." The jailer sniffed, settled a little more solidly against the wall, squinting up with his colorless eyes. "You want to write a letter t' your family?"

"I have none."

"Cheery soul, ain't you?"

Alfie gave the ghost of a laugh. "But I should make a will. Paper, pen and ink, then. And whatever food is easiest. My servant, Jack Chisholm, on the *Britannia*, will pay."

The jailer's presence had been an irritation, but his absence left room for the endless round of recriminations, doubts, and self-examination to begin again. He had such dreams, and they did not seem particularly vile. He didn't want to corrupt anyone's children, ruin anyone's life with bribery or blackmail. He didn't want to make the whole human race like himself, only to find one other man of the same persuasion whom he could make happy.

Is it truly so terrible to set one's heart on finding love? John, with his Christian principles, should have an answer to that, but who knew *what* John thought, these days? Farrant had certainly tried to be what everyone had expected him to be; tried to be both the husband and the monster. But it had not seemed to give him a moment's satisfaction.

Alfie pinched his eyes shut and dug the heels of his hands into them until the darkness was full of sparkles, as the thought of Farrant's death broke over him again. Had he really meant to die, as Dr. Berkley implied? Had Alfie disturbed, somehow, the balance of his lusts and indifference, and brought the man to an impasse he could not solve in life? *Please no! Please say I did not.*

If that was the case, it was in its small way John's fault. If John had not flown out on him in such a rage that he feared for his life, he would never have brought his unwelcome presence back into Farrant's life. If John had not been such an idiot as to get himself captured, Alfie would have known the wound was not healing, would have insisted on its being professionally handled. They might have caught the infection in time, if not for John.

And now John thought he could make it better with a word. Unconsciously Alfie licked his lips, trying to taste the kiss. The kiss like a punch in the mouth, unwanted, unwelcome, the pain of it staggering. *Self-satisfied, merciless bastard!*

A prickle of tears wet the palms of Alfie's hands. His shoulders shook. He sniffed to clear a suddenly blocked nose, but as he was softening into the embrace of grief a dead rat hit him on the back of the neck. He snapped upright again, hearing the laughter.

They had no call, any of them, to treat him like this. He didn't deserve this. He'd done no one in the world any harm. *Except perhaps…*

Imagination stirred slowly, suggesting that—if this was, as John said, a sort of martyrdom—there was still one last sacrifice he could make. When writing equipment arrived, he squeezed into the corner of the cage where the jailer's lantern was most bright, steadied the folded paper on hat and knee, and performed the only act of penance he could feel was appropriate.

Lady Lisburn, he wrote, the ink spattering from the badly cut nib as his hand shook. *Forgive my impertinence and allow me to present my condolences to you in this unhappy hour.* He was sure he could not be in more agony if he wrote the letter in his blood, but this needed to be said. While he could not see what was so evil in wishing to love, the truth was he was still not entirely innocent. He had hoped, after all, to separate a man who was—in his own way—a loyal husband from his loving wife.

Please allow me to take this opportunity to tell you there was no one in your husband's heart but yourself. There never was any rival in his affections for you. All his thoughts and deeds were motivated by your welfare, and to my knowledge a more faithful husband never breathed.

For, if Alfie was determined on honesty, "he loved me" was also a lie.

ᵈᶜᵉ CHAPTER 23 ᵉⁿᵈ

"Millie! Millie, a beer for the lieutenant! And bring us some of that plum duff from last night. You'll take a glass of something, sir?"

John hesitated only for a moment in the doorway of Mrs. Shaw's house before surrendering to the inevitable and finding himself drawn in and forcibly sat down in a small parlor. He'd never seen a room so full of knickknacks and linens. A gallery of watercolors hung on the walls, and occasional tables littered every free space, cluttered with scrimshaw trinkets. Despite the heat outside, a fire burned in the hearth, with a crewel-work fire-screen before it which matched the heavy embroidery of the tablecloths. Curtains of lace hung limply at the window, and rag rugs completely covered the floorboards in shades of jonquil and heliotrope.

A pleasant, fussy, feminine room—the only indication of a man in the house was a pair of work boots by the door, and they mysteriously disappeared behind drapery while his back was turned. He kept an eye out and so caught the way Millie swept up the pipe and twist of tobacco from the mantle, to deposit it in a basket and draw a flowery cloth over it.

"Or will you have a cup o' tea? For I heard you was a religious gentleman, and maybe you doesn't drink anything proper?"

John perched on an overstuffed chair, feeling obscurely threatened by all the frippery, and said, "You are remarkably well informed, Mrs. Shaw. I wasn't aware my antecedents were so generally known."

"Oh lor' bless you, sir," Mrs. Shaw laughed, and encouraged Millie—a black girl who might have been slave or servant—into the kitchen with a glare. "All the *Britannias* knew everything about you in moments. We took a friendly interest in you, like. Finding you like that."

"I'm very glad you did. Find me that is." John relaxed a little. She had, after all, seen him at his worst, and despite the over-feminine surroundings, she was a shipmate and a potential ally. No need to stand on ceremony. "I'll have tea, if you please."

"What brings you 'ere then, Lieutenant, as if I don't already know?"

"Mr. Donwell."

"Aye, poor lad, it's a shame. Ain't it always the way, though. Them what has money and rank behind them gets away with it. The rest of us don't."

"Mrs. Shaw, I'll be honest with you, for I recently became aware that the observations of an intelligent woman are worth those of five men. I am not willing to allow Mr. Donwell to be hanged without a fight, and I believe you may know where I may find ammunition for that battle."

"Well, now…." Mrs. Shaw beamed until the ruddy light of the fire gleamed off her shiny cheeks. She waited for the tea tray and then poured him a dish, setting it in front of him with great satisfaction. By the time she had repeated the procedure with a cold slice of plum duff he was itching with impatience and unable to scratch. "I do have a couple of names for ou. Me and the rest of the *Britannias*, we don't want to be known for running no mollyship, and it ain't our Mr. Donwell what's bringing us into disrepute. You want to speak to that Dr. Berkeley and Bert Driver. Accuser and prime witness they are. Ginger them and the whole thing falls apart. I'll do the rest."

"In there, sir." Price-Milton gave a self-satisfied grin, jerking his head to the side to indicate the hovel from which emerged the roaring laughter of men at play. "Spending his money like water, and the clothes on his back too."

They watched the door together for a while until a louder howl and an outbreak of clapping was followed by the lurching exit of a disappointed sailor with a dead cockerel swinging from his hand. Price-Milton sucked in a thoughtful breath through the gap where his front teeth had been lost to scurvy and said, "It ain't true, what they're saying about the captain. Is it?"

John paused for a moment, looking the boy up and down, unsure whether this was naïveté or jest. He was a typical midshipman of His Majesty's navy, with the cheerful air of having already lived through more perils than a landsman might see in a lifetime. *And a slouching habit of standing that will instantly get him caned by any new captain,* John noted idly. "That's for the court martial to decide, Mr. Price-Milton," he said, with automatic oppressiveness. But he passed the boy a shilling nevertheless. "Take your hands out of your pockets and keep them out. Lord Lisburn may have tolerated such slovenliness, but the same cannot be said for the rest of the fleet."

"Aye, aye sir!" Price-Milton gave a huge gappy smile, knuckled his forehead in salute, and darted away, back up the coast road towards Kingston where he could spend his new bounty on rum, or creamed ice, depending on the depravity of his tastes. John spent five minutes screwing up his courage, then elbowed his way into the tiny room.

Bert Driver was indeed inside, sitting on the edge of the pit, with a red cockerel under his arm, examining the steel blades on the bird's legs. Bert's ridiculously handsome face was lined with suspicion and anger. His gentlemanly clothes—a dove-colored suit and yellow silk waistcoat—were spattered with blood, and his white stockings covered in a motley of stains, some distinctively foot-print shaped where he'd been kicked. In front of him, on a new handkerchief, his watch and fob lay, with a pile of loose change and a promissory note.

John wiped spilled kill-devil rum and blood from the side of the ring and sat down. "A word with you, Bert."

"Not now."

They did not belong to the same ship, so it could be taken for mere insolence, not mutiny, but still John slammed his hand down on the poor little fortune, leaned forward, letting the three uniform buttons on his coat sleeve make the point: *Do not force me to see you flogged, because I will do so without hesitation or regret.*

"I was told you gave yourself airs because of your…standing with Captain Lord Lisburn. I see it's true. I *will* speak with you, Bert. Here or in private. The choice is yours."

Bert flinched, his slate blue eyes almost contriving to look pitiable. "Sorry, sir. Didn't…didn't recognize you at first." Getting up, he passed the cockerel to a scrawny fellow in a long leather apron and gauntlets. "Nah, they was on right. He won fair and square. Take the watch and the coin, you'll get the rest later."

Wiping the blood from his fingers on to his handkerchief, Bert passed that over too, then walked out to the narrow, dusty street. The smell of sewage came up from the sea, but overhead the first stars poked out their glittering needle points.

Bert was a big shadow, silhouetted against the glimmer of the horizon, and John, his heart hammering, clenched his hand around the hilt of his sword for reassurance, the twisted wires of the grip pleasantly rough against his palm. "This is a strange way to honor the memory of your captain," he began softly, "by destroying his reputation. Do you not owe him your silence?"

"I don't owe him anything." Bert snorted through his nose, scornful, not quite loud enough for a laugh. "Fuckin' old sod. He got what he paid for."

"Your transactions were entirely monetary then, no affection involved?" It wasn't that John had no experience of this frame of thought, but that his opinion of whores had been fixed in his youth. He found the idea of selling something so intimate as one's own body frightening, and also perplexingly sad.

"*Affection?*" Bert did laugh this time, the sound echoing between the lines of poor cottages and warehouses. A dog half way down the street lifted its dripping muzzle from the gutter at the sound, its eyes gleaming gold for a moment before it returned to whatever it was eating. "Hoo! You sound like a preacher. Nah. I've expensive tastes, me, and—"

"Who's paying you now?"

The sidelong look Bert gave him almost made his head ache. The man was so handsome John found himself constantly assuming that he must also be good. It jarred him on a deep, irrational level, to see such a perfect face express such imperfect thoughts. "Dr. Bentley," Bert said. "But not enough. Why? You here to make a better offer?"

"I'm here to deliver a warning." John stepped back into the shade of the cock-pit's roof. It was easier to threaten and blackmail—even in a good cause—in the dark. "Your shipmates are not pleased at having *Britannia* made a laughingstock, and them with her. If you do not withdraw your evidence, they ask me to tell you that you will be next."

"What?"

"If you light the fuse, Bert, don't complain if the bomb goes off in your hands. If the *Britannias* can't hide their shame, they will be forced to expunge it, with zeal, by delivering up every other perpetrator to the noose." John locked his hands behind him to prevent himself from rubbing the stress from his forehead.

"But I ain't no sod! I done what I done for money."

It was John's turn to laugh, astonished. "I think you'll find the Admiralty does not make that distinction. And you were never particularly discreet about it. I will have a score of witnesses and a court martial board on hand. If Mr. Donwell dies, the crows will be feasting on your eyes before the month is out."

Bert growled, put his head down, and crouched in readiness to spring at John, but John slashed out his sword in an arc of starlight and pressed the tip beneath Bert's chin, proud that even the light on the blade did not tremble. Only he knew he was shaking, inside. Stilling, breathing hard, Bert eased away, his hands spread, clearly aware of how easily John could gut him and walk away, no one the wiser. Men dying of stab wounds in the gutter in this part of town was a nightly, expected occurrence.

"I'm only the messenger," said John, more gently than he had intended, seeing the other man's fear. "If you get rid of me, any one of *Britannia's* officers will bring the charge." He reached into his pocket, brought out the small pouch of doubloons his prize agent had offered as an advance against his new wealth. This was a touch of his own—Mrs. Shaw being all in favor of the neat threat, undiluted by reward. But John could not bring himself to be easy with that. He could not, in all conscience, see Bert tried for bringing false charges, no matter what he thought of the man. The charges were not false.

Letting the gold chime between his fingers for a moment he threw it into the road by Bert's feet. Bert's eyes flicked down and he wetted his lips, but his chin stayed raised, propped by the blade.

"The *Africane,* with a cargo of sugar and rum, sails with the tide to England. I suggest you be on her."

John sheathed his sword, and Bert picked up the bag, tipping out some of the coins. His face smoothed with a near angelic look of awe. "Sir," he whispered. "Yes, sir."

"You navy men, do you have no shame?"

Elated by his success with Bert, John had gone the next morning to call upon Dr. Bentley, and on being informed that the Doctor was at Lady Lisburn's side, he had swallowed his courtesy and walked up into the hills to try again there. Only to find himself pinned like a butterfly to a card by the glare of a formidable, leather-faced elderly Irish butler in a severe black suit.

"I have no intention of disturbing your Lady's mourning, but I *must* speak with Dr. Bentley. It is a matter of life or death."

"We have too much death of our own in this house." The butler began to push the door closed.

John fished in his pocket for his card case. "At least take—"

A woman's voice from within called, "Let him in, Healy. Inform Dr. Bentley and then you may bring tea to the garden."

So John found himself ensconced beneath a mahoe tree, shaded by vivid orange flowers, while Lady Lisburn pushed back the black sleeves of her gown to pour tea into black rimmed cups. Dr. Bentley, beside him, watched him with narrowed eyes that looked disconcertingly huge beneath their thick-lensed glasses. Bentley's wig was black, and his suit was black. John, in his naval blue and cream, felt vulgar, as if his mere existence was as impolite as his presence, unspeakable as his mission.

"Lady Lisburn," he began, "your husband saved my life. If you have need of anything that I can provide, call on me and it will be yours."

Her mouth thinned and she turned her face away for a moment, concealing tears. It lasted mere seconds before she recovered, smiled at him with an expression more melancholy than agonized. A grief that had already reached resignation, already come to the tempest's end, and sailed into calm water. "Bentley would have me avenge him."

John sipped his tea, frowned in confusion. "The pirate who stabbed him, he cut down with his own hand—so I heard. The man's long dead. I don't see how vengeance is possible."

"There was a…an *underlying condition,*" Bentley broke in. He picked up his napkin, smoothed it, folded it and smoothed it again, his face growing sourer all the while. "Oh, let me not mince words. I want to see Lt. Donwell hang. But for him the captain's placid life might have continued as it was. There was a trend, perhaps, but he exacerbated it."

Society had drilled John's first reaction into him. He turned to look at Lady Lisburn, concerned for her comfort at discussing such a subject. "Should we be…?"

She laughed a little bitter chuckle and raised her eyebrows at him. In mourning, she had left off powder, rouge and paint, the wrinkles and flaws of her skin cruelly evident. *She must be,* he thought, *about the same age as Lavinia Deane, but less fortunate in her life.* "Please don't, lieutenant," she said. "I have an estate to manage and an angry father-in-law to placate. Pray do not treat me like a fool merely because I am in petticoats."

John ate a couple of kickshaws of pastry and raspberries to fill the moment as he wondered how to proceed. This was far more complicated than dealing with the likes of Bert, and John knew himself not to be particularly subtle. *Honesty, then.* "It is about Lt. Donwell that I came to try and speak to Doctor Bentley. Donwell was my First on the *Meteor.* A good man, a fine sailor. I am come to beg for the prosecution to be withdrawn."

"You don't argue for his innocence?" Lady Lisburn filled up the tea cups again, the perfection of the bend of her arm, the music of poured liquid into translucent, fragile porcelain, and the little smile she produced at the end, all infinitely brave.

"I am not a fool either, madam. Nor a habitual liar. But I know Alfie—forgive me—Lt. Donwell well enough to say that whatever may have happened would have been as much your husband's doing as his."

Bentley stiffened with anger beside him, but Lady Lisburn smiled an oddly fond, doting smile. "Three quarters Farrant at least," she said. "He was, God forgive him, never very apt to restraint." She held up a hand, forestalling the doctor's indignation. "Well, he wasn't. Had he been a normal man he'd have had a string of mistresses and no one would have thought the worse of him. It isn't fair. It honestly isn't."

"It is not fair to you either," John said, seizing the tide. "If Mr. Donwell goes on trial, so by necessity does your husband. A mere rumor will become an attested fact, a scandal." He gave Bentley a milder look than he intended—it proving impossible to intimidate a man who had seen him raving. "Would you really bring the humiliation, the shame of a public trial on your lady, her children? I thought it was your place to heal wounds, not to inflict them."

Taking off his glasses, Bentley polished them with shaking hands, his face as white as his shirt.

"Yes," murmured Lady Lisburn, "why?" She reached out and

curled her hand around Bentley's wrist. He stilled at once. "I didn't think you loved him more than you loved me. But why else would you do this to avenge him, knowing it will ruin me?"

Pulling his hand away with an oath, Bentley shot to his feet and strode away, his glasses still on the table. A hundred feet away he stumbled on a molehill, caught his balance and stood, head down, mumbling angrily beneath his breath.

Rubbing his eyes, Bentley straightened his shoulders and returned to lean heavily on the back of his chair. "My work," he confessed. "My life's work. I was so close to understanding, to finding a cure. So close! And then *he* came along and ruined it. Wasted! All those years! All those years of biting my tongue and bearing with the man's intolerable rudeness. Of telling you to hope and watching you die a little more each day. Impatient years in which men were being hanged by the score, whom I could have saved had I just perfected my cure…."

As he sank into his seat, head in hands, the handle of John's cup fractured between his fingers. The cup fell, shattered on the ground, warm tea spraying over his ankle. *A cure!* "A cure?" He dragged his mind back to the present, stood aside while a servant picked up the pieces and wiped down the table. "You talk of cures as if this were a disease. But if that's so, how can you hang Mr. Donwell for merely being ill?"

Silence for a moment, while a footman in what seemed, now, heartless turquoise livery, placed the tea things on a tray, replaced the spattered cloth and John's broken cup, tidying the mess away. Bentley returned to creasing his napkin, eyes following the motions of his hands, with his mouth set. The sun had swung past the tree, and Lady Lisburn opened her parasol, the green silk covered with a layer of black crepe.

A cure! John tried to imagine what that would mean. The thought had dark roots. It crept out like a vine, grasped and pulled, threatening to choke him. It didn't feel like hope.

Out from the house ran a young boy, his white blond hair startling against his funereal clothes, and a girl who must be his sister, her face uncertain beneath its careful dressing of ringlets. Both stared at John with curiosity, before turning away to the ornamental garden to throw stones into the fishpond.

"The Duke," Lady Lisburn's hand tightened on the handle of her parasol, "their grandfather, gave very particular instructions to Farrant. 'No scandal,' he said, or the title would pass to Farrant's brother. The title is gone as it is, but I fear for my children's inheritance if you press this charge, Bentley. You would not do that to them, or to me, would you?"

Bentley's mouth pulled itself into a firmer line. He picked his hat from the ground beside his chair, screwed it firmly onto his head and, rising, bowed with formal, chilly precision. "Forgive me, Isabella, I promised to visit the hospital. They are overwhelmed."

Do something. Stop him. Make him understand! John gripped the edge of the table, half rose, and could not think of what to do. Neither threat nor bribery would help, nor could he offer either in front of the lady. And persuasion had failed. It was Lady Lisburn who breathed in deep, her black silk fichu tightening over her breasts, her eyes hurt and hopeless. "You will think on what I said?"

"I will, my Lady. Good day to you. Lieutenant."

They watched him depart together. John rubbed his forehead, his fingertips coming away pale with spilled wig powder and smelling of orange flower water. Lady Lisburn raised her fan to cover her face. "You see, I am on your side."

"Thank you, Madam."

"I will talk him round."

"I am very obliged."

"Is he your lover, this Mr. Donwell?"

John almost broke another cup, snapped out of despair into astonished embarrassment. "No, madam!" he exclaimed and found himself half smiling despite it all. "Just my friend. My very good friend."

"I had no idea Bentley could be so single-minded." She lowered her fan and smiled back, wearily, her eyes straying to the silhouettes of the children, who stood together with hanging heads, surrounded by the water's silver glitter. "But Farrant too loved nothing more than his work. It must be a man's peculiarity. A failing of the whole sex. He causes others to depend on him, desires it, enforces it, but chafes beneath the responsibility. For his own fame always takes first place in his heart."

The sting of this observation passed John by in its revelation. So Bentley mourned for his lost life's work, his fame, his fellow-ship of The Royal Society, all killed along with his captain. But if he could be distracted from his loss; given new hope? With un-expected fondness, John thought of Sweet Bess, whose mouth had been full of the taste of rotting tooth. Surely he, and any number of his regular clientele, would be happy to exchange in-formation for the care of a properly qualified doctor? "Give me a sheet of paper, if you please," he asked. "I will write down an ad-dress for Dr. Bentley where he may find as many new subjects to experiment upon as he could possibly wish for. He will be too busy for vengeance then."

Afterwards, John took a flask of brandy to the cliffs and sat with the sea hundreds of yards beneath his feet, picking once more at the skein of his tangled thoughts. A year ago he would have been hor-rified by his behavior today, the idea of tampering with the course of justice an anathema to him. Now he only wished he could be sure he had done enough.

Unearthing a pebble from the dirt by his hand he flung it out in a wide arc of flight, clean and mathematical against the sky. The surf closed over it. He might have said that it disappeared, but reason told him that it had not. It settled on the white sand and shell of the ocean bed, blending with its new surroundings. Time would tumble it in the tides, wear off its sharp corners and leave it indistinguishable from any rock of the sea. Change came, arbi-trary and yet inevitable. *A cure...* Suppose there could be a cure for his desires? Suppose he could be made normal. *What then?*

In his father's house, John had clung to Biblical certainty as to everything his father did not represent. He remembered a sweet childhood floating about the fens in his own little skiff, drifting on water so still he might have sailed in the heavens, reeds hissing, waterfowl paddling and peeping about him. The great churches of Ely and Sutton on their islands above his head like some fantastical cross between angel and gargoyle. Long days of loneliness and peace. Then he would come home and find his father's party arrived from London, actors, courtesans and fops in every room, laughing at his country ways; his mother shut in her study, weeping.

All the sensual world had seemed to him then only an excuse for cruelty. The cruelty of a man who loved his wife's money but not her person, who went out of his way to shock and humiliate her, moving his mistresses into her house, into her bedroom.

John, seeing her alone in the rout of contemptuous strangers, had always run to her, his sense of justice as well as his love outraged. His father would look wearyingly on them both, hugging one another for comfort against the invasion, call John a pious milksop, a disgrace to the name of manhood, and pass by, calling for his guns.

Alfie's grief in prison, that brief "I can't believe he's gone," reshaped the stone of John's soul like an ocean. How could anyone say that such love, such sorrow, was somehow less worthy than the hell on earth of his parents' marriage? How could anyone think such love required a cure?

Above the sea, bands of orange light streaked the sky, and the sun was a ruby. The brandy tasted like the sunset, and John weighed good and evil, love and lust on the scales of his understanding; lust such as his father's which only brought misery, love such as Alfie seemed to have felt for his unworthy captain.

Only one of these two things could be counted a sin. The other he must admire.

◖◗ Chapter 24 ◗◖

30 March 1763, HMS Britannia, *at anchor in Kingston Harbor*

The great cabin looked heartbreakingly familiar to Alfie as he stood in irons by the starboard door, flanked by two marines. He tried to keep his eyes fixed on the bustle of small craft outside the stern window, bum boats going out to newly arrived merchantmen and warships with everything from melons to whores on board. A party of them indeed, half clad, with their breasts hanging out of their stays, sailed close enough to throw rotten fruit at the *Britannia's* great gallery. Orange pulp dried into a small sunburst on one leaded light.

But the novelty of having things thrown at him had long passed. He was more moved by the green velvet cushions of the stern lockers, remembering how they had felt against his back that one time when…

The very table beneath the hands of the five judges must cry out against him. There was a black hilarity about the way that Post Captain Bentick, when he was annoyed, had a habit of rubbing his thumb across a certain flaw in the polish. Alfie could have given him some information about that stain which would cause him to go home and wash his hand until it bled, and there were times he could have laughed with despair.

Beyond the window a slave ship came in, trailing its reek of

death and human dung, and as he watched the cargo being dis-
embarked, too weak to move, he felt glad to be leaving this ugly
world behind.

"Mrs. Shaw," announced a marine by the door as the next witness arrived. Alfie drew back his attention with a start seeing her
come in, in a vulgar dress of pink tulle and a starched bonnet of
nun-like rigidity around a face like a side of ham. One could not
lose oneself in dreams while Mrs. Shaw was in the room. If New-
ton was to be believed, she exerted a gravity of her own.

Even Bentick seemed impressed. Rodney, at the center of the
table, took snuff to numb his nose to the smell of the slaver, and
looked imperturbable. Beyond the open doors of the cabin a
press of onlookers milled on the ship's upper deck, craning their
necks to see inside, the ruin of a man by sexual scandal being a
fine spectator sport.

The Judge-Advocate rustled his papers. "You are the Gunner's
wife on the *Britannia*, and serve as a laundress, I understand?
You washed the officers' linen?"

"Yes, sir, your honor." Mrs. Shaw curtseyed deeply, continuing
with some pride, "Had me own barrels and rigged up a trap for
rainwater, so as not to have to use salt. I'm not one of them young
women what raids the ships' drinking water to wash me smalls. I
shares your lordships' horror for such larks."

Bentick bowed his head to conceal his reaction, but the smirk
lay reflected on the tabletop for everyone to see. From a chair
pushed back against the curving wall came a flash of golden light
as Dr. Bentley took off his glasses, wiped them on his handkerchief. Alfie noticed him draw in his feet as if to stand, his mouth
opening, and then he balked. His adam's apple jerked as he swallowed, then he subsided. *Need to piss?* Alfie thought. *I hope you
choke on it.*

"That's as may be, Mrs. Shaw," the judge-advocate said, gathering himself. A colorless little man, no doubt accustomed to sift-
ing through filth, he was the only one in the cabin who didn't
wince when he asked, "What can you tell us about Captain Lord

Lisburn's sheets?"

Mrs. Shaw bristled like a boar. Alfie's amused detachment was squashed anew under another wave of revulsion for how sordid this all was. Though intellectually he did not believe he needed to be ashamed, it was hard not to be cowed with a courtroom of fine gentlemen picking over his stains.

"Nothing at all, sir, Lord love you."

In the embarrassed, disapproving silence Admiral Rodney leaned forward, gesturing with fingers like frost-covered twigs. "Mrs. Shaw, may I remind you that while you serve on a ship of the line, you are as answerable to His Majesty's courts martial as any man. Do not treat this tribunal with contempt."

"I wouldn't dream of it, your honor, sir." Mrs. Shaw raised her watery blue eyes to the heavens. "I know'd the captain had a reputation, but as God is my witness, sir, I ain't seen nothing of it on board. I can't swear to what he did on land, but the *Britannia* was a clean living ship, and you won't find a one of her crew willing to say otherwise."

"As we have been finding, indeed." Captain Bentick rolled his eyes. "And the complaint brought against Lieutenant Donwell…?"

"Malice, sir. Sheer malice. You'd be above knowing this kind of thing, I've no doubt, but there's men what'll make a good living from threatening to call an honest man a sod. Asking for money off of him to not go through with it. This is something of that sort, I've no doubt. And Mr. Donwell there, well, o'course he wouldn't stand for that. Knowin' 'imself innocent, like."

"You make a good case, Mrs. Shaw," said Bentick after a pause. "I presume you have no other information pertinent to the case?"

"No sir, except to say that if it was that Bert Driver what laid the charge, everyone knows the little shit—begging your pardon—has been cherishing a resentment against Mr. Donwell since that time Mr. Donwell had to take his name for unclean behavior in the hold. Icy it was that day, and Bert pissing in the ballast rather than go to the heads. And Bert never was one that liked to be taken down."

Alfie listened to this exchange with a creeping of the skin at the back of his neck as though a goose had walked over his grave. Such a plausible liar, she made! So forthright, so guileless. *By God, if I get through this, if I only live, Mrs. Shaw, I'm going to give you such a kiss!*

Sunlight poured in through the window and the air reeked of beeswax polish, damp woolen uniforms, sewerage and slaves. The judge-advocate cleared his throat with a dry scratching sound, having already raised a disapproving eyebrow at Bentick's tendency to take over the running of the court. He looked down at his list, mumbling into the paper, "Very well. I call Bert Driver."

The usual stir and head turning in the crowd. Alfie rolled his shoulders, trying to ease them down from around his ears. The thought of Bert Driver testifying against him was like a wasp sting between his shoulder blades: he could try to ignore it, but it would still burn. *Come on*, he thought, *come on, just get on with it!* Life or death—anything but this sweat-choked, disapproving silence. *Come on!*

"Not present, sir." The marine in charge of witnesses delivered this with a certain theatrical pleasure, a gleam in his eyes that only brightened when Alfie couldn't stop himself and lurched forward a half step, manacles clinking. Outside the door the audience fluttered, humming with rumors. Within, Dr. Bentley gave a gasp and clutched at his bob wig as if it had bitten him.

Time stopped again while the judge advocate's pen scratched over the surface of the record of the trial. Ink dripped into the inkwell. A petal fell from the vase of red flowers, so incongruously gay in the center of the long table. Alfie bit down on the urge to scream, to lay about himself with the chain of his irons, to just smack one of the self-satisfied bastards across the face before they shot him down. He clenched his hands in front of him, breathed in deep, trying to slow his racing heart.

The judge-advocate swept the cabin with a rheumy gaze, as if he half expected Bert to be crouched beneath one of the chairs. When it proved not to be so, he sniffed disapprovingly, made another note in the record, and said, "I call Dr. Theodore Bentley."

Bentley rose, the color in his face so drained he looked like a black and white print of a man. "I…might I ask for an adjournment, for a moment? I need to…I have something I would like to convey in private to the gentlemen of the court."

At that moment an unusually large wave lifted the anchored *Britannia,* and as the onlookers on the deck fell against each other, laughing, Bentley too lurched for the back of his chair. A burst of clannish smugness and superiority went through every sure-footed naval officer at the sight, Alfie included, drawing them together against the civilian world. There was more than a touch of condescension in Rodney's shrug. "As you wish. The Court will adjourn."

Taken out onto the quarterdeck, Alfie scoured the crowd, then craned his neck to look down onto the jetty, barely allowing himself to admit he was hoping to find one particular face. The absence of John Cavendish squashed that hope like a spider underfoot. All his fine words and what did they count for? Nothing at all. It would have been *something* to be able to look into that mob and see one face not baying for his blood, not lit with gleeful contempt. But John failed the test, yet again.

Marines took Alfie's arms and turned him in the direction of the companionway, taking him down to be kept watch on, in the cavernous cool of the hold. There, with the sea pressing on the timbers all about him; underwater, in the dark, he wrapped his arms around himself as far as the chain would allow, and shivered. He'd thought he was resigned to death—he'd almost been looking forward to it, as the end of all the struggling, all the pretence. But now he could feel his own heart beating beneath the hard knot of dread in his chest; he could see his breath come in clouds of gold against the dark, and feel blood move through his fingertips. Even the pinch of his best breeches at the knee felt precious, sharp against the void.

It was a flawed, impractical, ugly world, but it was better than the alternative. His mind filled with the picture of the last hanging he'd seen; *some poor little bastard with the rope around his neck winched up to the yardarm by the throat—too light to strangle quickly. In his struggles he had got the knot under his chin, so that the pressure meant to mercifully stun him ended up as one more torment....* At the memory, panic raced in a torrent through Alfie's body, shaking him. *No! No! I can't! I can't!*

"Up you come then." Some time during this attack of terror word had come down from the court. The marine on Alfie's left hauled at his arm to make him stand upright. The man's face was covered with gnarled pustules around the rotting mess of his nose—the pox having written its signature on him. "Don't look like that, son. There's worse things than dying fast, ain't there? I should know."

"You think..." Alfie tried, strengthening his trembling legs with what pride he could muster. "You think they'll find me guilty?"

"Let's go and see, eh?"

The spray of hot red hibiscus flowers on the courtroom table fell shriveled around its vase, dropping petals onto Alfie's sword, which lay in its scabbard in front of the judges, hostage to his fate. The great blaze of the stern gallery ran across the silver hilt and the gold braid tassel as if to make a point.

It stood for his life's work—the hard but worthwhile work of setting himself as a defense between his countrymen and their enemies. It stood for his status as an officer and a gentleman— the duty, the unwavering stoicism and willingness to kill, but also the educated refinement of his nature, the gentility and gentleness that should coexist with military prowess. It stood for the ideal he thought he had met in life in the shape of John Cavendish. The perfect, beautiful, and deadly symbol of what it was to be a man. And he wanted it back.

Guilt or innocence hardly seemed to matter beside the wish that they would at least treat him with the respect that—*damn it!*—he had earned. He stood to attention, and fixed his zealous gaze on Admiral Lord Rodney, daring him to object.

Rodney gave no reaction whatsoever, except to pat his forehead with a white silk handkerchief before the sweat ran into his eyes. He had on his full dress uniform, and the criss-crossing patterns of gold braid on coat and waistcoat would have looked overdone on other men. However—as slight and thin as he was—he wore them as the sword wore its tassel—effortlessly elegant.

"I do not know when I have presided over a more extraordinary case," he began, with a gleam of amusement about the corners of his mouth. "It appears from the evidence of the witnesses that the *Britannia* was an exemplary ship and her captain a model of decorum. I have rarely heard such universal praise as has been here poured upon the accused."

Looking up without warning, he returned Alfie's gaze. It felt like being skewered on icicles, and Alfie froze from the heart outwards. So it was to be death. The *Britannias* had overstated their defense. Whatever Bentley said in private had proved decisive, and the Admiral knew he was being lied to by everyone else. Alfie's throat closed for a moment, as though the noose was already around his neck, squeezing. But then he caught a snatch of song from a passing skiff. He noticed the fascinating patterns in each pane of window glass. The dying flowers were still giving out a round, fruity scent, and the deck beneath his feet heaved comfortably with each wave. If this was all he had, he wasn't going to waste an instant of it with panic.

He smiled. Rodney gave a chilly little smirk in return, straightened the edges of his papers, and said, "I hesitate to accuse an entire ship's company of deliberately conspiring to pervert the course of justice—a circumstance all the more unlikely when one considers the universal abhorrence of this particular crime. A crime *more pernicious* and more likely to lead to the unraveling of the bonds of society than any other. A vice, indeed, so *vile* it may not even be named in public. Since, as I say, all reasonable men detest this sin with a repugnance that does them credit, it seems unlikely that every witness in this trial is being willfully deaf and blind.

"That being the case, I am prepared to accept that Dr. Bentley, in bringing this charge, was taken in by the malice of one Bert Driver—now absconded—and to accept his plea for the charge to be withdrawn. Take back your sword, Lieutenant Donwell. It seems no one is accusing you of anything. My regrets for the inconvenience you've suffered, and my compliments on the extraordinary loyalty of your people."

Alfie, plunged from ice to fire, could scarcely tell for a moment which was which. It took the marines unbolting the shackles from his wrists to make him stir, and he stepped forward to receive his sword like a sleepwalker. But its hilt in his hand was real enough, so warm from lying in the patch of sunshine it was almost painful to hold. He buckled it on with clumsy fingers.

As marines cleared the decks of disappointed, disgruntled spectators, Captain Bentick rose, heading for the door. Then he paused and returned to shake Alfie's hand. "I won't treat you as a guilty man," Bentick smiled a rather anxious smile, as though he was not sure if he could afford to pay what this generous gesture would cost him, "since you are none. I hope you find the same treatment from others."

It was a noble act—an act that John Cavendish had not been capable of—to be seen by all the town's gossips being kind to a man accused of sodomy, the verdict of innocence notwithstanding. Alfie hoped the kindness would not put Bentick's own reputation at risk.

"I am...obliged, sir," Alfie managed, a wave of trembling beginning in the pit of his belly, trying to force its way up through the rest of his body. He had to get away before it became obvious; had to find somewhere to go to accept this, to reforge the links between body and spirit. Taken unawares by life, the necessary lies he had once been comfortable with felt like new chains. "But I am satisfied that my name is clear of dishonor. I know how to behave toward any man who wishes to challenge that."

Bentick nodded, beat a hasty retreat. Admiral Rodney, looking unheroically weary and gray, paused to murmur, "You are a fortunate young man, Mr. Donwell. But you will not work the same miracle twice. I should take this opportunity to amend your life, if I were you," before leaving, taking the other captains with him.

Alfie stood in the empty space, grasping the hilt of his sword for reassurance, until his friendly marine gave him a nudge. "This is where you goes home now, sir."

If a newborn child could have wandered through the streets of Kingston, it might have been in the same frame of mind as Alfie's as he left the ship; overwhelmed by the richness poured out before him. His head hurt with the day's colors and all the suppressed thought. The smell of bammies cooking over charcoal—hot, greasy, sweet—enraptured him. He bought a couple from a street vendor as he passed and filled his mouth with the taste of cassava and coconut. *Oh, that is good!* Life *is good.* But it would be better somewhere cool, somewhere he could wash away the stench and the memories together.

◖ CHAPTER 25 ◗

30 March 1763, Kingston Harbor, Jamaica

Captain Gillingham of the *Albion* shuddered minutely at the sight of the court martial flag. His feet ached from the walk down to the harbor, and he was sure that the smell of fish and sewage carried the effluvium of every tropical disease straight into his nostrils. How Cavendish could stand it, particularly given the severe blow the man's health had taken recently at the hands of those pirates, puzzled him. It seemed indelicate to enquire too closely as to what exactly they had done, but certainly Cavendish had left for Tobago like one of those angels from the last judgment—all pure, cutting beauty and righteous fury—and returned as frail as an eighty-year-old. Yet every day he did more, walked further, found some new task to undertake to make the ship run more efficiently.

It was rather exhausting, to be honest, and Gillingham felt it to be something of a veiled rebuke. However, having so diligent a lieutenant meant less work for Gillingham himself. And that— given that the *Albion* was finally re-stocking in preparation for a lengthy scientific voyage into the Arctic—could only be a good thing.

"What did you want to speak to me about, Lieutenant?" he asked the man beside him, therefore, genially enough. "And can it be done in the ale house? I don't wish to miss my dinner."

"Of course, sir." Cavendish turned from his unblinking

scrutiny of the *Britannia* and gave a small, depreciatory smile. "I've taken the liberty of ordering us a beefsteak at the St. George, if that is convenient to you."

It was. More than convenient. Gillingham did not like to be reminded of the excuses he had had to make in order to not sit on this particular tribunal. *Such a bore!* And besides, courts martial in their very essence made Gillingham nervous. He often dreamed of them; of some terrible, energetic Admiral taking his sword and banishing him to a life in which he should have to depend on the largess of his older brothers—neither of whom was known for generosity. Though he woke from these dreams determined to get stuck in and make a name for himself, and he tried, he did try, very hard, for weeks at a time, the wind always went from his sails before the destination was achieved.

As he sat down at the table and noted, approvingly, the cleanliness of the place—cobbled floor washed rosy pink, and the glassware sparkling—he reflected that it was useful to have officers who could provide the necessary impetus themselves. Even if it meant putting up with an uncomfortable level of zeal.

"This is very satisfactory." He tucked his napkin into his collar to protect the Belgian lace on his cravat. "I'm to gather you're feeling much recovered then, Lieutenant?"

"I am, sir." As always, Cavendish was spotlessly turned out. Though Gillingham was reliably informed that the man had no valet, he still managed to give the impression of starch. "Though I cannot, unfortunately, say the same of Lieutenants O'Connor and Giles."

Gillingham took a reviving sniff at his handkerchief, perfumed with orris root, and shuddered again. *What a place this was indeed! Pirates. And the French. And the Spanish.* And slaves everywhere, looking at one with justifiable but frightening resentment. Then, as if that wasn't enough, there were the plagues. Despite every effort to fumigate the ship with brimstone and vinegar, fully a quarter of his men were dead from the yellow jack. He was tempted to lock himself in his lodgings and not come out again until it was time to return to England. Indeed, had he been in politics, he would have been strongly behind the notion of letting the slaves have the entire Caribbean, and bringing all the poor settlers home. *They could not possibly wish to live here, could they?* Trade could supply what force now extorted.

"I am shocked, and grieved naturally, but I cannot say I am surprised," he said. "I only hope that we will leave these troubles behind in the cleaner air of the North."

"I'm sure we will, sir." Cavendish had a light, deferential, young man's voice, and Gillingham felt he used it to good effect in wheedling his superiors around to his own point of view. "But nevertheless, we are lacking in our complement. Lieutenant O'Connor is not expected to recover. So I wondered if you would consider taking on Lieutenant Donwell as a replacement."

"The *sod?* Surely not, Mr. Cavendish! We are not quite *that* desperate."

Cavendish gave another of those small smiles that stretched the skin over his cheekbones. He had lost a great deal of weight since the pirate incident, and had not been exactly heavy before that. If he was a skeleton, however, he was a very elegant one. "Sir, if he's found guilty he will be hanged. I am not suggesting you employ him after that. But if he is found innocent—"

"There is no smoke without fire, Lieutenant."

"And so the mere accusation is enough to lose an innocent man his livelihood? That's monstrous! I know you to be a kind man—and more, a man concerned with justice. Consider, sir, some malicious mind has laid this accusation against an officer of extraordinary zeal and talents. Is he to be shunned by all society now, simply because he had the misfortune to make an enemy? It is not *right*."

"John," Gillingham said, polishing off the last bite of mashed yam, and feeling pleasantly full and pleasantly patronizing, "you expect too much of human nature."

"But, sir," John replied, raising those strange gray eyes of his pleadingly, "Mr. Donwell is known to me as an exemplary offi-cer—you recall he was my first on the *Meteor*. If there was any-thing to the rumor, I would know about it. But I assure you, you will not find a better officer in the fleet. And if Admiral Rodney finds him innocent…"

"Then who are we to question?" Gillingham laughed, though the thought of arguing any more was tedious. Cavendish was quite capable of nagging him for hours and hours until he gave up from sheer ennui. "I will think about it."

After the over-large dinner, John paid the bill and sat on a while over the claret. On a good day he found Gillingham's indolence amusing and oddly touching; it aroused a desire to protect the man, as one would protect an unpromising child. On a bad day, however, he found it infuriating that merely because this helpless creature had a wife and seven children back in England he should be thought of as more manly than Alfie.

Or himself.

The ramifications of his nature had unfolded gradually like a leaf, emerging crumpled out of a hard bud into the sun. So many things he had taken for granted now needed thought. So many as-sumptions were proved unsound. Though this path had led him into needful lies, he still felt as though he more nearly ap-proached a true understanding of himself and the world. Unex-pectedly, he found himself thanking God in his daily prayers for leading him out of darkness into light….

Dread and anger stabbed through his musings. *Sitting here with the glass untouched for half an hour. What a coward!* But, once he went outside, he would have to look up at the flagship. And when he did so, he might see Alfie hanging there. Limp by now, not kicking and clawing the air with his face turning blue and his eyes and tongue protruding—John had carefully given them plenty of time so he did not have to watch that. But still dead, still hanging there dead—that would be calamity enough.

"You want more?" The barmaid appeared out of the darkness

like a banshee. Taken unawares, John scrambled to his feet, pressed his back into the corner and stood, shaking, while the candlelit room became a dark clearing, and the flames roared like bonfires in his ears.

An eternity later he emerged out of nightmares with a start, grasped for a chair and sat before he could fall. She, black angel that she was, had not retreated, nor had she made any move towards him, practiced in weathering the storms of a Jamaican alehouse. Now she whisked away, returning unasked with a tot of rum. "Thank you," he said, hoping that conveyed the feeling of rescue, his shame and gratitude. "I am…" *I am what? 'I am plagued by devils'? 'I am splintered to pieces within, and may not rebuild them, though I try'? 'I am not as insane as I seem'?* "I am very grateful."

Sitting down beside him, she leaned forward to put a hand on his knee, a gesture which brought an abundant cleavage more clearly to view. "I help you chase them dreams right away." And he reflected that some things at least had not changed. Now, however, he found the offer oddly reassuring. In the midst of death, life went stubbornly onwards as it always had.

"Can you tell me," he said, taking the offer on its face value, "if they hanged the young man being court-martialed this morning? If you would step to the door and look… I can not quite bring myself to it."

She gave a disappointed pout, flounced off to the door, then came straight back with a frown and an out held hand. "No one hangin' out there. That be a penny for the drink and another for the errand."

The news that the coast was clear enabled him to get out of the place. Bracing himself, he looked at the flagship, and indeed there was no body dangling from its yard arm, nor any sad little grouping of hangman and assistants tarring the body for display, or wrapping it in sackcloth for disposal.

He hardly dared allow himself to hope, in case the hope was brutally dashed, but perhaps, just perhaps, it had worked? *If that is so, now what?* Where would he find a man who had barely been long enough in Jamaica to acquire lodgings before he ended up with no need of them?

Hiring a horse outside the tavern, John rode up along the coast road. If he had been long in darkness and confinement, he would have sought out the sea as soon as he was released. The sea washed away all ills. Danger and death one might find out there, but dirt was confined to the land.

He found Alfie in a cove so steep-walled its water lay in eternal shade, cool and quiet, though opening out into the Caribbean's uncompromising light. Strange orchids, flowers like purple-winged bees, and white, hairy shaving brushes rooted in the nooks of the rock and hung down, scenting the air with peppery sweetness. In the middle, between day and night, Alfie stood waist deep in water, facing the sun.

John slid from his horse as gently as he could, recognizing that he had come as a trespasser into a sacred space. Looping the bridle around a rock, he left the horse grazing and began to scramble down the narrow path into the cove. Shale slithered beneath his leather soles, so he sat on a ledge half way down, startling a mass of black and yellow butterflies into wheeling flight, and took off his shoes and stockings. It seemed appropriate, and reminded him of Moses approaching the burning bush, until he began to pick his way down again, and he remembered that Moses did not have to walk on sliding shale with edges like razors.

But this was a good pain. Self-inflicted, self-chosen, and well within the possibility of even his broken spirit to endure. When he reached the softer beach beneath he felt both as though he had done a penance—cleansed—and as though he had proved something to himself. The sting, as he waded into water so clear he could hardly see it at all, was more like the soaring tingle of ecstasy, than like torment. He waded through healing.

Which might have had more to do with the man now turning to watch him, than the water. For such a long time he had looked at Alfie and seen only what he expected to see, reflected. Now, for the first time, he felt he saw the real man. Alfie was beautiful. Not with John's mere surface, accidental beauty, but beautiful in his youth and strength. Beautiful in the open honest way his soul seemed to show in his face. Tall and sturdy, he moved like a dancer, as though every step was a pavane. Arrested by the perfection of the angle between Alfie's shoulder and neck, John stood and looked, and found he had no words.

"John." Alfie laced his fingers together and brought them up so that the knuckles brushed his lips. "They didn't kill me, and I didn't say any of it."

"You said it to me." John reached out and closed his own hands around Alfie's. It was like finding a rope to save him when he was lost overboard in a storm, and he held on with something of the same desperation. "I heard you. You told me you loved him."

Jealousy provided a thousand bitter words. *You didn't give me a chance! You were gone before I had time to think. You knocked down the foundations of my world and then disappeared! What did you expect of me?* And more base than that—a petty cry of pain of which he was ashamed, but could not silence: *Do you know how much I've given up for you?* Swallowing, he pushed them back down into the darkness, concerned instead for the man before him. Alfie's every gesture spoke of endurance, empty of joy. He stood patient in the limpid light, quiet, placid as a horse well broken to the bit. Words died on John's tongue, inadequate.

There was no prudence in the way he worked his fingers into Alfie's fists. When they opened, obediently, he lifted them, one after the other, to kiss the palms. Pure folly, a risk to name and fame and life itself, but oh, it felt so right. He hauled down the false colors under which he had been sailing all his life, and exchanged them for true. "I wish I had not been such an infernal prig, that night in Gibraltar, and driven you straight back to him."

"Is that an apology?" Alfie's fleeting smile recalled the cockiness of his earlier, more rakish days. Standing this close, touching him, John was alive with sensation—the lap of the waves against his flanks, the small changes of cold and warmth in the water. Air moved the fabric of his shirt against his flushed skin. Soft-beaten linen fluttered maddeningly against nerves he had scarcely known he possessed ere now.

Water curled about his loins, gently stroking, and he recalled with sudden urgency how Alfie would, at one point, have been watching for this opportunity. He would have stepped forward, turned his hands in John's grasp and pulled the two of them together, and the cool embrace of the sea would have turned into honeyed heat.

John craved that touch; thirsted to make the first move, but after the disaster of the kiss at the warehouse he didn't trust himself to do so without inflicting more pain. He wanted to say *Alfie, now's your chance*, but settled for babbling. "It is. Yes. I was a coward, and did not understand a thing about myself. It came upon me like a lightning strike. Blinded for a moment, I reacted without thought. But since then I have turned the matter over and over, searched its meaning so diligently, and...."

Alfie's expression glazed over. He was not listening. In falling silence, the *sssssh* of the sea on the shingle spoke like a command. Alfie's pulse rocked against John's encircling fingers, the only thing about him to give evidence of life. A droplet, like an errant diamond, slid across the bunched muscles of his jaw and pooled in the hollow of his throat, making John want to lean in and lick the little "v" clean of its salty taste. His mouth watered at the thought and that discovery aroused as much as it alarmed him. Perhaps this was not the time to attempt an explanation of his moral and theological self-questioning after all. Something more basic was required. "Please forgive me?"

Pulling his hands away, Alfie turned them over, examined his palms as if for incriminating stains. "I don't know," he said at last, his voice muffled and thick. "I don't know if I can."

He raised his head, his tawny golden eyes cold and grim as a hunting lion's. "I have no idea what to make of you any more,

Cavendish. And until I've decided, I'd be obliged if you didn't assume I'm yours for the asking. You had your chance, and you chose to shut the door in my face. When I turned to you for help...*twice* I trusted you and you let me down. Farrant, God bless the bastard, never did. He never did!"

A surge of water clear as air rushed in as Alfie wrenched himself aside. Beneath the waves the bay's little coral fish whisked away, startled, into cover. Alfie covered his eyes with one hand, thumb and fingers digging into his temples. John had to speak, he *had to* speak, the need to justify himself came crawling up from prick and belly, joined with heartbreak, pushed itself out like a long splinter of oak up his throat. And honor stopped it there. No. Alfie owed him nothing. Never would.

"Maybe I've learned the lesson you chose to teach me, Mr. Cavendish, *sir*," Alfie went on quietly. "Maybe I'm going to 'amend my life,' so that *I* can look down on *you*. Now if you don't mind, I want to be alone."

◖◖ CHAPTER 26 ◗◗

April 1763, Kingston, Jamaica

"Sir! Lieutenant, sir!" The door shuddered in its frame as Alfie raised his aching head from the pillow. Something sharp dug into the side of his face as he moved. He brushed off hardened bread-crumbs and flung his feet out of bed. Panting fur sent a shock of revulsion through him as his toes landed on an enterprising rat. With an indignant squeal it wiggled out from beneath his sole and scuttled back to the refuge of the disintegrating mudbrick walls.

"Mmn?" he said, pulling his foot back and rubbing it to remove the sensation of damp rat. "What is it, Emmie? End of the world?"

"Might be for you if you don't get your sorry arse out of bed Mr. Lieutenant, sir. Hoo! When this captain see you in your state, him turn straight back round, walk out again."

Shooting to his feet, Alfie flung open the door. "Captain? There's a captain downstairs?"

Emmie—owner, housemaid, and kitchen girl of this fine establishment—looked him up and down with a wide smile. Her headscarf tormented his hangover with swirls of angry red and yellow, and her amusement made him conscious of his frowsy, unwashed state, bare legged, tousle-haired and abominably unshaven.

"Uh-huh." She rocked back on her heels, folded her arms,

and lifted her chin at him in the manner of exasperated women everywhere. "He's set down in the garden with a jug of beer. You got maybe three, four minutes—"

Alfie shut the door with one hand, and reached for the breeches slung over the bedpost with the other. As he hopped on one foot to get them on, tucking in his shirt and buttoning, trying to remember if he had a clean pair of stockings and if so where he had put them, she carried on, voice raised, unperturbed.

"...before he think to himself what a lazy good for nothing you are and go away. And maybe that be your last chance of a ship gone. Yes?"

"Yes!" He scraped his face with an unstropped razor in a basin of cold water, thankful that a lifetime's practice on tossing seas made the exercise swift and only marginally dangerous. "Please go and tell him I'll be down directly. All being well, I'll pay my bill at the end of today."

Emmie chortled. "I add extra for playing messenger." But as he was shrugging into his coat, he heard her red-heeled shoes go snapping down the rickety staircase. Straightening everything, he rubbed the sheet over his own shoes to give them polish, checked his reflection in his hand-mirror—a little red and sore around the cheeks but nothing to signify—and hurled himself down, two steps at a time, after her.

From the angle of the sun, which hit the wall of beans direct, making their orange flowers glow with an almost painful intensity, Alfie realized it must be almost four bells in the fore-noon watch. *Ten o'clock in the morning!* No wonder Emmie had seen fit to be so scathing.

Still, the eastern wall, climbed over by trained fruit trees, sliced off the solid weight of sunshine above their heads. In the shade beneath it, the day remained tolerably cool. There, on a bench made of biscuit barrels, sat a whey-faced man, whose waistcoat gaped at the buttons over a substantial paunch. His laced cocked hat sat on the bench beside him, revealing a foppish wig, the two long queues of which reached to his waist.

The super-fine wool of his coat, instead of falling in elegant folds, drawing attention to broad shoulders and a narrow waist—as intended—merely emphasized his bulges, combining vanity and extravagance to create a particularly undesirable result. *Farrant had worn such a coat,* Alfie remembered, swallowing hard. *But on him it had looked magnificent.*

Sweeping off his hat, remembering at the last moment to turn the crown towards his guest, Alfie made a leg. "Alfie Donwell, sir. Forgive me for causing you to wait, I…um…"

The captain's jowled face lifted, his expression softer than seemed possible for a man of his rank—like a scene blurred by an out of focus spy-glass. He picked nervously at the lace on his cuffs, their wide band of tarnish proclaiming this a constant habit. A reprimand would have reassured Alfie that he was in the hands of a man of some authority, but this captain half rose from his seat, reconsidered, and sank down again, thankfully.

"This terrible plague!" he said, apropos of nothing.

"I'm sorry sir?" Behind the captain something moved among the row of pumpkins. Alfie had the impression that one of the vegetables had stretched itself. Wedging his hat beneath his armpit, he clasped his hands behind his back, pinched the webbing of one finger between his nails, trying to look attentive and trustworthy as he did so. It seemed unlikely behavior even for foreign fruit.

The look of mild anxiety on the heavy face became a look of mild enquiry. "You seem taken aback, lieutenant? Am I to assume Cavendish has not informed you of our state? That seems very unlike him. I declare I am normally exhausted by his efficiency."

Alfie licked his lips, the bewildering rush of yearning and disappointment almost a physical taste in his mouth. If he could have bitten it, it would have been salty-sour like rancid stockfish. "Mr. Cavendish has proved himself no friend of mine. He could not have been quicker to distance himself at my trial. Not a peep from him did I hear and I saw neither hide nor hair, though I had hoped he at least would stand by me."

This must be Gillingham then, John's captain, of whom he had heard much—all of it accompanied by a mocking snigger. "He's full of fine words, Captain Gillingham, but test him and he rings hollow every time."

"Oh." Gillingham picked a damselfly out of the beer jug by the wings, and set it on the edge of the bench to dry off. "Do you think so?" He frowned down at the half-drowned creature's attempt to right itself, brought out a pencil from his pocket and separated its fragile, black-veined wings. It looked up at him with bulbous, blood colored eyes, and Alfie decided that next time he heard someone mock this captain, he would knock that man down.

"You see, he was very eloquent about your merits to me. Assured me you were a highly superior officer, and there was absolutely nothing in the charge. Urged me to take you on at once, what with this terrible—positive *epidemic*—of the yellow jack and good officers dropping like flies. Seemed to think I would steal a march on the opposition by the deed." He looked up and smiled like an absent-minded country vicar. "And are you now telling me that you feel you have fallen so far out of friendship that you could no longer work with Mr. Cavendish? That you must—in principle—decline the berth?"

Lost for months in fog and storm, unsure of his position, the sentence was a glimpse of land. Alfie dropped all other concerns at once and steered towards it. *"No sir!* No, sir. Not at all."

A ribbon of orange wound its way sinuously down from the pumpkin, sliding across the liana that connected the vegetable to the ground. In his current state, Alfie would have happily believed some part of the pumpkin itself migrated, but when he bent forward to see closer it proved to be a centipede. A centipede the size of his forearm, with red-tipped yellow legs and a mouth like a pair of tweezers.

"Oh good God!" he exclaimed without thought. "Anything to get away from this place, sir!"

Twisting round, Gillingham caught sight of the little monster, and, recoiling, struggled to his feet with a grunt of effort. But then a look of morbid curiosity came over his face. He leaned forward to peer at it, picking up a discarded pea-stick and motioning as if to nudge the beast into further movement. As the shadow fell on it, however, it lunged, and buried its mandibles in the stick. Gillingham dropped it and sprang back, hands clasped over his heart.

"It looks as though it could swallow a rat, don't you think? And *poisonous*, I have no doubt. I sometimes think the whole island is poisonous and resents our presence here. What a place!"

During the short conversation, the sunlight had slid off the wall and onto the ground. The shade shrank and warmed. Alfie's scalp prickled under his wig as sweat and horsehair mixed. The smell of leaves, bean flowers, sweet peppers hanging red and glossy like newly plucked-out ox-hearts on their bush, fought a losing battle against the stench of the latrine.

"I could bring my dunnage to the ship in less than fifteen minutes, sir. I'd be perfectly willing to sleep aboard."

Gillingham laughed, but he retreated to the house, waving Alfie before him and shutting the door behind them both on Jamaica's less attractive fauna. "I see we think alike. But is there no one you should inform first? Your old ship, for example?"

That was an interview he didn't wish to recall. *Britannia's* new captain had made certain things abundantly clear. *"If you had any shred of decency you would leave the navy of your own accord,"* not being the worst of them. *"You will never set foot on another deck."*

"The crew of the *Britannia*, including her officers, sir, has been broken up and dispersed among several ships. Her new captain does not wish me back on board." It had been an expected blow. Admiral Rodney, after all, was not stupid, and if he could not punish the sod, he could at least send the principle liars into other berths, where they would not have the comfort of their mutual support.

"No, well….the rumors…you understand."

"It is a bitter thing—" Alfie paused before opening the street door, the hall's gloom almost blinding him after the bright garden, "—to be thus dogged by a reputation I have not deserved. I was falsely accused, and yet they treat me as though—"

"So Mr. Cavendish said, in almost the same words." Gillingham laughed, though the sound trembled like a cable parting under stress. "Would you not now consider thinking better of him? As you see, he has not been entirely idle in your cause. If I may be permitted to say so, but for his persuasion, the rumors might have counted against you in my eyes also. It isn't enough?"

The taste of something sweet, gone bad. A piece of sublime music, played flat. Part of Alfie wanted to forgive—to at least try friendship again. Part, with the dumb loyalty of a dog who sits by his master's grave until he dies, felt any civility to John would be a betrayal of Farrant's memory. And a final, powerful part just wanted to hurt John as John had hurt him. If John, knowing the decision of the court, knowing there was no longer any danger to himself, had thrown him a sop, what of it? It was almost more of an insult than not acting at all.

"It isn't enough, sir. I counted on him and he failed me."

The double queues of Gillingham's wig swung out and tapped Alfie's arm as the captain turned to leave. It was the closest thing to a reprimand Alfie had received from him, despite being late, ill-shaven and over familiar.

"Just so." Gillingham inched up the corners of his mouth in a smile, then allowed them to fall again. He fixed an anxious, mildly stern gaze on the door frame just to the side of Alfie's shoulder and rubbed a thumb along the braid of his cuff. "Nevertheless, this will be a long voyage—the better part of a year—and I need you to assure me you will not bring any animosity on board. No challenges, no backbiting in the ward room, no forming little cliques and setting the ship at odds with itself. I don't feel that I can usefully demand friendship, but I do feel, quite strongly, that I must insist on courtesy."

"I can manage courtesy, Captain." The words left a lurch in their wake. Everything within him rattled and swung in a moment's inward seasickness. *Serving with John, on the same ship once more! This would be kill or cure!*

Screwing his hat down firmly on the wig, shaking off a little snow of orris-scented powder, Gillingham's face settled again into a look that might have graced a pet linnet in its cage as it confronted the house cat. "You haven't had yellow jack at all?"

"I did, sir, yes. In the year 'fifty-nine. A mild dose, I'm told, though I puked for four days straight. The inside of my nose might have been scraped off by a carpenter's file."

At this cheerful description, Gillingham brought a lozenge-shaped silver vinaigrette from his waistcoat pocket, snapped open the cover and sniffed. The scent of lavender-infused vinegar lit up the morning briefly before he closed it and tucked it away. "Then you won't mind coming with me to the hospital? I have two lieutenants and three score of my people on their death beds with the disease. Though I really have no desire to visit them, I feel I should. I feel I owe it to them."

"I'm willing to go wherever you most need me, sir. But does this mean…?"

"Yes, yes. Pathetic though it sounds, I don't like to go alone. All that misery. Cavendish will be there too. Afterwards, if I am content with how you conduct yourselves with one another, you may send a couple of the people to move your dunnage into the *Albion.* And we will get away from this ill-favored place, to somewhere more fitting for Englishmen."

"We're going home?" Alfie could have hugged the man, if he had not known how that would be taken.

"Not quite. To the Arctic."

◖◙ CHAPTER 27 ◙◗

The "hospital"—a warehouse emptied of its slaves and supplied, by the good will of the town, with straw mattresses and the occasional blanket—crouched among the fetor of the wharves. Men lay there in heaps, vomiting, lying in it, their skin yellow, blood trickling from nostrils and ears.

An orderly, with his cravat wound about his face like a mask, paced through the arched darkness swinging a burning thurifer of brimstone. Yellow smoke billowed about Alfie, biting at his eyes and scouring the inside of his throat. Taking his own cravat off, he wrapped it over his nose and mouth. It mellowed some of the burn.

Gillingham coughed protractedly, sweat standing out on his brow and his reddened eyes watering. Blinking back the tears, he bore it with more fortitude than Alfie would have expected; silent, staggering only when he tripped over the patients. Alfie took his elbow and clung on, pretending to offer comfort, but taking it in equal measure as they waded forwards through hell on earth.

The sharp snap and thud of a rope's end on flesh punctuated the moans of the sick. As they picked their way on through the stinging clouds, stepping over the dying, a gang of slaves parted for them. Dark gazes rested like weights on Alfie's back as they straightened from their brooms and buckets to watch him pass. The stench of lime and vinegar in the washing water almost made him gag, but their flesh peeled with it, hanging in strips from their legs.

"Sodding animals! Get back to work!" Encouraged by a driver with a heavy starter of rope, the slaves bent back to their toil, stopping only to hack up sputum and spit it in glistening gobs into the drainage channel of the floor.

Eternity had already passed by the time Alfie caught sight of John, a basin under his arm, crouched by the bedside of a dark-haired youth, whose pimples stood out purple against a skin waxy and yellow as a lemon. John was mopping sick from the boy's face with economical movements; distantly tender. Nodding a greeting, rather than breathe in this murk enough to speak, he indicated a large jug of beer and a cup that stood on a small table by the opened iron bars of the door. His demeanor revealed nothing—neither resentment nor pleasure, not even discomfort—upon meeting Alfie again. Perfectly polite. Perfectly meaningless.

A channel built into the center of the room—*cell, rather,* Alfie corrected himself—drained the swabbing water, blood, piss and vomit out into the corridor, where it joined a deeper runnel of filth, making him glad of the brimstone. Manacles, hanging from their hasps buried deep in the stone walls, fitted themselves into his memories of Algiers. As John poured the stinking water out of his bowl into the gutter on the floor, Alfie picked up the end of one of the chains, pulling it taut with a rattle and clash of metal. "This is fucking obscene!"

Gillingham flinched then applied himself to fiddling with his vinaigrette once more. John stilled, head bent over his jug as he dipped it in a barrel of fresh water. "Fresh" was something of a euphemism, for the liquid had the oily, greenish look of water which had lain in rotting barrels in a ship's hold as it traveled twice around the world. A man would have to be crawling the borders of death from thirst before drinking it would become appealing, but for cleaning the clogged blood from the noses of patients, and the sick from around the edges of their mouths, it was well enough.

Stirring once more, John refilled the basin. The quiet, musical lilt of pouring water threaded through the sounds of hell. Then he looked up. As their eyes met, a shock seized Alfie from his balls to his throat. He swallowed, leaning back as he fought an almost physical tug forward. With a shock of recognition, he saw again the incandescent *something* for which he had left his ship and his career, lifetimes ago in the Bay of Biscay. After betrayal and heartbreak, here it still was, pulling on him like a magnetic pole to a needle. At times it seemed this thing between them was the only fixed point of Alfie's compass, whether he steered away or towards.

John's face, hollowed by shadows, looked gaunt as the faces of the dying. He had unbuttoned his cuffs and rolled up his sleeves, and each wrist bore livid scars that might have fitted the cuffs of the manacles exactly. Still holding Alfie's gaze, he nodded, politely. But the expression said *I know. We know, the two of us. But this is not the time. Stand down, lieutenant.*

Almost involuntarily, Alfie's lips twitched. He stepped forward, responding at a level beneath thought to the urge to challenge—to crowd John against the wall, test his authority and see how deep it went. A rush of thick heat in his stomach...and then away in the darkness someone screamed like a stuck pig. The incantation, holding the ugly world away from Alfie, popped like a bubble. He flung the manacles against the wall—where they knocked a further splinter from the deep furrow they had already gouged there—and glowered, disappointed now not only with John, but also with himself. *How can I fall for this a second time?*

John's silver gaze slid away. He turned his face aside, his shoulders drooping. Then he braced them up once more, motioned with his chin, and Alfie followed him through one holding cell after another. Sulfur and brimstone settled like wig-powder over them all, making them gleam yellow as their patients.

They soon established a wordless rhythm. Alfie waited until John had washed each man's face. Then he took each one by the soiled linen over their bony shoulders, hauled them up, and helped them drink. Gillingham followed behind, the vinaigrette pressed beneath his nose by one gloved hand, the other clenched in the fastenings of his waistcoat, like a child holding tight to a protective blanket. Speaking halting words of painfully sincere encouragement and comfort, he passed down the line of diseased sufferers without touching, suffering ravings, accusations, and sometimes pitifully grateful tears.

It wasn't much to give; one symbolic gesture per man. But the *Albion's* people were far from home and did not deserve to die unknown and nameless, in the harried and over-busy hands of strangers.

Burning powder settled on the sick men. Torches flared greasily in the long central corridor, and their smoke hit the ceiling above them, spilled down in darker arabesques through the smog. Moving through their fitful light, Alfie looked back at the room from which they'd emerged and it seemed to him a field of shallow graves. *A corpse jerked, scrabbled convulsively upright, and lurched towards him. "Help me! Help me! Take me with you!" it cried. He froze up. Nightmare images of the thing falling to pieces as it touched him, screaming from a tongueless mouth, its eyes gone, made his stomach twist like a cold eel….*

He lurched away from the creature just as John stepped in front of him, took it by the arms, and leaned close to calmly speak to it. It sagged into his support, turning—to Alfie's shamefaced gaze—from a revenant to a frightened boy whose nightshirt was embroidered at the shoulder with his initials. As John lowered the youth back to his bed, Alfie punched the wall. The sting across his knuckles felt clean, as nothing else in this place could, no matter how hard John swabbed.

Kneeling down by the next sufferer, Alfie got an arm beneath his shoulders, lifted him slightly from the floor, and set the cup to his mouth. The man retched over Alfie's fingers. Blood and sputum curled into the beer, dripped from Alfie's hand, burned like acid in the new grazes, running beneath his cuff, up his arm to the elbow. He cursed, dropped the cup in the patient's lap, and watched the wet stain spread with hopeless fury as he scrubbed and scrubbed at his hands, plunging them deep into the jug of beer. A chuckle sounded behind him. He spun, ready to lash out, and saw that it was Dr. Bentley, thin-lipped and smiling. "No rest for the wicked, eh, Lieutenant? Yet it will get easier once they begin to die."

Alfie shook his head. The man had become his own personal demi-urge. Should Death ever visit him, take down its cowl before the final swing of its scythe, he swore it would look like Bentley. The same gentle, remorseless chill. Eyes pinched closed as if, unseen, the doctor would vanish like a fever dream, he pressed his hands over his nose and mouth, and did not notice John's approach until he felt a firm touch on his arm.

"Go home, Mr. Donwell. Take the captain with you. I'll deal with what needs to be done here."

"I…" Alfie wanted to be angry. Surely he should want revenge for what Bentley had done to him? He should not feel this mere hollow desire to be out, out, away, where he need never see another doctor's face. Most of all, he did not wish to need protection; to have his endurance called into question, or his pride insulted yet again. But whatever his wishes, he wasn't sure he could bear this another moment.

He looked from John to Gillingham, carefully not watching Bentley turn away with a smirk. The captain was all but transparent now with distress, having to hold a thumb beneath his chin between each bed to keep his teeth from chattering.

Seeing the wavering look, John pressed on quietly. "This is too much for him. He means well, but he is weakening himself with every breath. If he carries on like this he will catch it himself. Please. Take him away."

Someone had clutched at John's wig—the palm print was clearly visible in smudges of dirt and blood—pulling it out of its stiff binding on one side. The ribbon sagged, unraveling. Yellow dust coated John's bottom lip. His sinewy arms were gloved in a layer of dried blood. Obedient to Alfie's will, they had not spoken since the incident in the cove, and all those unsaid words swirled about them both like heavy falling snow.

Alfie thought, again, how terribly thin John was; a dry reed, waiting to be snapped. Of the three of them, he, barely recovered from torture, must be most at risk. "Come too," he said, moved by an empathy deeper than his resentment. "These men, they don't know we're here. You're risking your life for nothing."

"If so, it's mine to risk," John bared his teeth in a gesture that was either smile or defiance. At times it did not seem possible for him to be so much himself, and still to be the wretch Alfie thought him. He was a dissonance that made Alfie's head ache.

"But you impute me too much goodness. If anything, I am being selfish. This work—I'm finding it healing."

Alfie nudged the dropped cup with his foot. On the other side of the brick wall from the cells a woman's voice screamed on a high pitched note. A chorus of piercing howls rose to meet the sound, as one lamentation set off another like wolves following their chief into song. The hair on Alfie's arms and over the back of his neck rippled and stood up as he realized that, in the cells adjacent, this same scene repeated among the women of Kingston. Reluctant as he was to accept John's pity or his help, horror infested him like weevils in hard tack—one tap and he would crumble to dust.

"I'll do as you ask, then, and take Captain Gillingham away. But Cavendish…." A "thank you" was stuck in Alfie's throat. *Thank you for allowing me to escape from this place. Thank you for speaking to your captain and finding me a berth.* No amount of careful breathing could dislodge it. Weighed in the balance against John's sins, this little mercy was no more than a grain of sand.

"Don't forget we sail with the tide."

◖ CHAPTER 28 ◗

September 1763, Lancaster Sound (off Baffin Island)

Snowflakes settled on the deck of the *Albion*. Her rigging stood taut and grey with ice. Each footstep crunched with a squeak into a layer of pristine pallor. White as her name, as she ghosted through the night she seemed another cloudbank, another eddy of the thin, interminable snow.

The final handful of sand gathered above the waist of the hour-glass, tumbling towards the end of the middle watch. Almost four o'clock in the morning. Alfie crouched down, slipped his hands inside his shoes and warmed his numb toes back to aching life. No one was watching, after all.

Captain Gillingham lay in his cabin with all the gaps in windows and doors plugged with rags. Since the Davis Strait he had been so securely swaddled in every layer of clothing he owned or could borrow, that Alfie couldn't help but wonder if he relieved himself at all, or if he was holding it all in for extra warmth.

A week ago Boatswain Creevy had harpooned one of the white bears that paced along the ice-locked shores of Bylot Island and handed out teeth as souvenirs to the ship's boys. With only minimal reluctance he gave the ill-cured, crackling, frozen skin to the captain, who had worn it ever since, flesh side outermost, looking—when he came on deck at all—like the massive grey larva of a particularly unappetizing moth.

Standing up once more, Alfie minced gingerly down the shining quarter-deck steps. Clinging with one hand to the manropes as he went, he paced the length of the ship, hoping to force some warmth back into his feet. His shoes pinched, stuffed with caulking, and bitter frost pierced the hand on the rail through glove and two layers of turned down cuff.

The main course creaked. A sparkling, crackling rain of crystal fell tinkling from the yards. The wind on Alfie's cheek bit so deep he could scarcely tell if it froze or burned. Coming up to the bow, checking each of the lines, belayed around their wooden pins, he looked over. *Albion* drifted forward under enough sail for steerage way and no more, barely rippling the milk white sea.

Cold in his hand became pain, sung up his arm, caught in his chest, settled deep in the marrow of his bones. He set his back to the mizzen mast, tugged off his gloves and curled his fingers about the dying warmth of the brass hand-warmer he had borrowed from the Master. The puffs of his breath made smudges of snow in the black sky.

In the waist of the ship the enterprising midshipmen had built a small hut of rolled up hammocks. A changing pattern of gold and red light stabbed through the cracks, and a plume of steam blew forward from it. Inside, the deck crew huddled around their brazier, smoking. Heather-and-tannin-scented pipe-smoke gusted over him. Out in the darkness where veil of snow met sea, something grumbled with a chill, inorganic voice. Trembling as he was in every limb with cold, Alfie laughed for the first time since prison—laughed for mere joy, intoxicated.

"Masthead!" he shouted. "I hear ice. What d'you see?" As he pulled himself forward across the deck, his shoes slithered in the powder of snow. He tugged off the wicker-and-blanket door of the hut with a flourish and a special arrogant officer's smile. The damp warmth within washed luxuriously over him.

"Gentlemen, you're not being paid to take Turkish baths on his Majesty's time. Prepare for handing over the watch. Mr. Midshipmen Wilson and Sturridge, I want the log thrown. The rest of you, that deck needs sweeping clean, we don't have enough skates to go around."

He squinted up into the flurry of flakes towards the platform on top of the main mast, from which the lookout should have replied seconds ago. "Masthead there! Did you hear me!"

Silence.

"That's his third time fallen asleep on duty this trip, sir." William Barry grinned at Alfie. "He won't last long in a net over the bows in this weather."

"You're a top-man, Barry, aren't you? Get up there and check on him," Alfie said, discouraging the familiarity. Barry was one of the *Albions* he had laid flat with a left hook in the riot at the harbor in Kingston, and the man seemed to feel it had established a special bond between them since.

Alfie peered up at the fighting top where the lookout crouched, tucked into a loose-stuffed mattress of straw. He still couldn't make out the dim grey shape for falling snow.

Icicles thrummed into the deck like a flight of arrows as Barry climbed the shrouds, and again there came that booming crunch and growl across the waves.

Sailors all, the men straightened up from their brooms to listen for the direction of the sound, but Alfie saw nothing more definite there than his own conviction that it was entirely too close for comfort. The wind whistled thin through the rigging. A sheet of ice the size of a dinner table came knocking down the side.

"He's stone dead, sir!" called Barry at last. "Frozen solid, poor bugger, and his hand so tight around the puddening, I'm gonna have to break his fingers t'get him down."

"Do that," Alfie shouted. Sucking in a breath that numbed his teeth and skewered a stiletto of pain through his nose, his attention was caught by the darkness on the lee bow. He snapped out his own glass, squinting through the eyepiece. It showed him darkness and white snowfall. But as he moved his head it struck him anew—a sense that there was something wrong about the billowing flakes. The curl of wind, the round, antic dance of them, as though…as though they fell not *down* but *around* an invisible bulk—an invisible something that surged closer even as he watched. It lay dead ahead, whatever it was, they had to slow, to turn! Alfie's shout tore his frozen throat, making his lips bleed. "Main course aback! *Helm hard a larboard!*"

"God's bloody wounds—!" Barry's high pitched shriek tailed off into a falling scream as the *Albion* rammed into solid darkness. The foremast bent beneath the impact. A cracking noise and a split ran up the great trunk of it from foot to collar. Its backstay snapped and lashed across the deck like the tail of a dragon, knocking the midshipmen into the captain's launch and sweeping one of the luckless idlers into the sea. The split gaped, writhing like a mouth trying to speak, as the mast sagged forward and stilled without falling, held by the royal mast and preventer stays.

The bowsprit splintered against a white wall. Beneath the bursting, tearing sound of tortured wood, a deep reverberation like a struck cathedral bell trembled through its socket, into the *Albion*'s keel. It resonated in harmony, and the rigging squealed as though *Albion* herself cried out in shock and pain. The mass before them surged towards them, driving *Albion* backwards. Seas breaking over her poop, she heaved her head up aboard the floating island, turning her icy deck into a steep hill. Alfie dropped his spyglass and lunged for the manrope with both hands, as his feet were swept out from beneath him by the impact.

The hut of hammocks tumbled across the deck. Burning embers from the brazier scattered into a new celestial map of gold sparks across the darkness. A hand clamped around Alfie's ankle as a skidding shape careened into him. Barry's body slid past on the other side, rammed itself against the quarterdeck and lay in a spreading pool of black.

Another lurch. *Albion* rolled to starboard. Men's shouts and the screaming of the animals in the hold echoed a tormented groan deep in the superstructure of the hull. A moment of stasis, in which she hung, motionless. Alfie loosened one hand, reached down to grab a handful of tarpaulin jacket. Blood seeped from beneath the nails of his other hand—distractingly hot—as he clung tight, supporting not only his own weight but that of the bosun. He hauled the man up so that Creevy could grab the line for himself. Panting, they stared at one another, recognizing the sick, wordless certainty that *Albion's* movement had merely paused, not stopped. Creevy's petrified grin mirrored his own.

A thunder-clap, and then another, escalating to a single ripping tear. Out there in the darkness a part of the berg split off and fell away. The sea surging beneath her, the ship raised again, rolling further starboard. Men hung from the line like flags as she slipped sideways down the white shore, back into the white sea. A wall of freezing water, rough with chunks of ice, smashed across the deck, stopped Alfie's heart as the chill hit him. His hands hung on of themselves, immovable for a long moment of unnaturally stretched time. He had time to wonder if he should scream, decide against it as being too unmanly, as the pounding water sucked back past him, pummeling his frozen fingers. Brittle as twigs, they still held.

Albion righted herself. Alfie's feet touched the deck and he collapsed onto his knees, gasping, curling around the flickering core of heat deep in his chest. Panic swarmed in his lungs like a hive of wasps. *Breathe! Breathe, damn it!* Beneath him, *Albion* moved with the heavy, sluggish wallow of a ship filling with tons of seawater. Somewhere behind the reluctant spasm of his heart he could hear it, pouring in. *Move! Breathe! Sodding hell!*

He heard running feet and shouts. Absurdly brave—bringing tears to his eyes—he even heard the tattoo of a marine drummer, beating out "all hands on deck." Then more shouting and the pumps throbbed into life about the main mast. As he tried to gasp with relief, mouth open wide, a thick wooden bar smacked him across the back with enough force to break ribs. The hot, slicing pain jerked the breath out of his lungs and shocked his heart into hammering. He whooped in air, scrabbled to his feet, found

John—the wooden bar in hand—pulling him up by the elbow. John was all diamond; sharp and brilliant as he had been in Algiers, and Alfie stood trembling in front of him, feeling rescued all over again.

"You're perished with the cold. Go below and stand to the pumps for a watch."

"I can…." The arctic wind blasted his soaked clothes. They grayed over with hoar-frost even as he dithered, but his toes and fingers felt warm as they hadn't been for weeks. *"Help,"* he was going to say, but John had already run past and jammed the bar into the capstan, shouting as he worked.

"Launch and pinnace crew! Row out the small anchors. Find a crevice on the iceberg and get them jammed in hard. Everyone who isn't on the pumps to the capstans! We'll winch her up onto the ice until we can float her again. Look lively! She's sinking beneath your feet!"

Alfie tried to turn to run below, but found his limbs heavy. As he stood, frozen to the spot, a white mass, impossibly warm, settled about his shoulders. He pulled it close with clumsy fingers.

"I think we are ever so slightly superfluous," said Gillingham, shivering without his fur. "But a turn on the pumps will free up more able hands. Shall we?"

They stumbled down into the relative warmth of the gundeck. A lantern's light picked out the group of twelve men left to man the pumps, all of them anonymously swaddled in layers of blankets and hats. Alfie could not stop the chattering of his teeth long enough to speak, but laid a hand on the shoulder of the man turning the handle in its round casing. He moved inwards to make room and Alfie set his hands to the pole, picked up the rhythm without a break. The chain rattled up its long wooden casing, sucked the water up with it, out of the hold in great gouts like blood through a vein until it burst gushing over the sides at a rate of a ton a minute.

Despite the triumphant spewing of the pumps, a knocking came from directly beneath Alfie's feet. He could feel the impact through his soles, as the contents of the orlop deck, barrels from the hold, even bodies no doubt, rose with the flood to drive themselves against the planks of the deck below him. Flaws in the caulking began to well with freezing water. They had started pumping in the dry. Now it was damp underfoot.

As Alfie pumped his heartbeat thinned, strained, and then steadied. His petrified muscles ached and tore, burning like branding irons. Trying not to whimper, he drove himself on by willpower alone. Gasping for breath, he threw off the fur. Two of the men waiting in line to take over snatched it and huddled inside. Gillingham reeled away, clutching at his chest, and collapsed on one of the cannons. Wordlessly, Alfie gestured for the next man in line to take his place.

A bubbling noise came from the stairwell and a wash of icy water lifted over the ridge of it and splashed against their shoes.

"It's still rising!" wept the cook. Despite his wooden leg, he clambered nimbly enough onto the galley table, and thence to the top of the coppers, which still retained a faint heat from yesterday's supper. "It's coming up! Pouring in twice as fast as we're flushing it out. The pumps ain't good enough! God preserve us, we've got maybe ten minutes to live, lads. Maybe five!"

"None of that!" Alfie bellowed, feeling the panic as if it was his own. He'd started out his naval career on the lower decks and felt its clannish comfort still, deeper in his blood than the cold honor and duty of an officer. But if he gave into the group now, they would all die in screaming, irrational terror. "Let's have a third man here to replace me. Alright, Jack Grady, you clap onto this, and we'll see if we can do better. We're not sunk yet!"

It was bravado, pure and simple. He could feel the rising water around his toes as well as the rest of them, but *damn it!* Five more minutes and John's hair-brained solution might be in place. Five minutes more and they might not have to die at all. He pumped harder, watching Grady leaning in, preparing to hand over the plunging bar to a new man. As he did so, the cook's mate—a Chinaman the crew had affectionately named Sung

Flat—darted forward, grabbed Alfie's pistol from his belt and leveled it, trembling, at Alfie's face. Grady crowded away, jostling his neighbor, and the pump's rhythm slackened as they flinched from the barrel of the gun.

Gillingham, still clutching the cannon and wheezing, raised his head. "Now, now, um…Sung. You—"

"You open spirit room now! Dying men, we have right to last drink. We have right to go out happy! Custom of the sea, neh?"

Alfie straightened up and curtly gestured to the next man to take his turn at the pump. The man rubbed his hand across a bald head, replaced his knitted cap and said "Yeah, but he's right. Custom of the service, ain't it? I'd pump if there was some kind of point to it, but there ain't. We're all gonna die. Now or ten minutes later, what's it matter? We wants the rum, sir. You ain't gonna make us go sober, is you?"

Terror and fury mixed like ice and fire in Alfie's head, so intense they overwhelmed his ability to feel anything, left him in a kind of ruthless, focused calm. Tilting his head to one side, Alfie crossed his arms. "Go ahead and pull the trigger, Sung. And you, Bill Murray, you'll look fine hanging on the end of a noose as a mutineer. The rest of you, pump or drown."

"Who are you t'give us orders anyways, Alfie Donwell? You ain't no gentleman and you's only an officer cos you sucked the—"

Never had it felt better to punch a man straight on the nose—to feel the cartilage burst and flatten beneath the blow. Murray slipped and fell backwards into the inch of water that now covered the gundeck. In the splash, the momentary distraction, Alfie slammed the heel of his hand into Sung's extended elbow, caught his pistol as it fell from the man's slackened grip, and cocked it, turning back to watch his audience. The men at the pump labored on, unaware of anything but the next push. Gillingham pushed himself upright, his face clotted purple, his eyes half shut. The group waiting their turn at the pump regarded Alfie with wary eyes.

"I reckon that powder's soused as a hog's face," muttered

someone from the back. "An anyroad he's only got one shot. If we was all to rush him…."

As certain as the shadowed speaker that the pistol's powder was wet enough to be useless, Alfie dropped it to the flooded floor. He drew his sword. Water sloshed about his ankles as he eased *en garde* trying, desperately, to retain that balance of calm; not to snap and lash out for no better reason than that he was seething. *This is such madness!* "You've all seen me fight, lads. If you rush me, you *will* die, carved up into bite-sized pieces. Pump and you may yet live. Work hard enough, and I may forget this conversation ever happened at all."

The men on the pump had not been relieved since this stand-off developed. Now they had begun to reach the limits of their strength. Jack Grady's neighbor faltered, fainted, slid to the floor. As the chain slowed, the uprush of water surged perceptibly higher. Alfie hit the next man in line with the flat of his sword. "Get to work!" he ordered, just as the mutterer at the back—one Ephraim Gross—leaned down to pick up the handspike by his cannon.

The air stank of bilge-water and terror. "You'll doom us all, Gross." Alfie kept his voice calm despite the raging frustration, thought about how John would handle this, and lowered his sword. "Didn't you hear Mr. Cavendish? We need only pump until we are anchored to the island. That is going forward *now*. God knows I share the need for a drink. Any man that can pace me on the pumps I'll buy a double round when we get back to Kingston, but I don't drink with mutineers."

"What's the point? We're gonna die!"

"We are *not*—"

Albion lurched sideways, her timbers creaking. As Alfie caught his balance and slid his sword into its scabbard, the clashing twang of the anchor chains pulling taut rang down from above. The men on the pumps faltered, and in the sudden hush he caught the sound of stamping feet, and a lone fiddle playing "Row Well Ye Mariners"above the rumbling creak of the capstan.

With a thud, the ship's hull touched something solid to starboard. The pumps stood silent, but the water no longer rose. *It's working! By God,* Alfie thought, incredulous, *it really is working!*

"*Now* we can stop pumping. Everyone to the capstan, if you please."

Outside, dawn had begun to break over a colorless world. The floating mountain showed as a mass of lighter grey in a pewter sea. Great storm anchor cables stretched between *Albion* and the berg in perfectly straight lines, and as Alfie and his crew added their weight to the capstan bars, turning it one more pace, and then another, the ship gave a shivering groan and, heeling to one side, lifted a foot further out of the sea. Water trickled, then plumed from the jagged gash beneath her bow, taking ballast and bodies with it, but they rode the iceberg like a louse anchored to a man's head, saved by the very force that had tried to crush them.

⸜⸝ CHAPTER 29 ⸜⸝

"You look like a marble statue," said a light, polished voice by Alfie's elbow. "Frosted over, all white."

Alfie made a final hitch on his line, securing the heavy, slush-greased canvas tight against the scarred flank of the figurehead, and turned. John stood there, in a long boat-cloak whose hood hung far enough over his face only to show sharp cheekbones and pools of darkness for eyes. John's full, almost feminine mouth smiled, veiled in steam. "I brought you a coffee."

Alfie hesitated before taking it. Though indolent and ineffectual, Gillingham was no fool. He had assigned Alfie and John to opposing shifts at sea so that they were scarcely ever awake at the same time. On land, John had been in charge of the survey-ing expeditions, being gone for months drawing maps of the coast of Newfoundland and Baffin Island. Alfie, in charge of provi-sioning, had spent the same months fishing and hunting seals. They had scarcely had to say more than "good morning" or "good night" to one another for the whole voyage, and Alfie had been half expecting that this stalemate would continue forever.

Last night's work, and the morning's, had only increased his respect for John. Knowing himself safe, Gillingham was now back in bed, and if the *Albion's* captain had been chosen by merit, the honor would have been John's. John's quick thinking had saved them all. But Alfie wondered if the man thought he was owed something in return. Why break the silence now? "Is this some manner of metaphor?" he asked. Every muscle in Alfie's body stood out marked in lines of pain, over a skeleton made of frost, but still there was room for a new ache, somewhere deeper than flesh. "An obligation? I stand by my words earlier. The laws of God and man are my constant companions now, you know. I won't take it if it's—"

"Alfie, it's a cup of coffee." John put down his hood, letting his white wig be powdered with snowflakes. There was color in his face now—the pink of chapped cheeks. His smile opened little wounds along his mouth where the skin had cracked in the cold. "To celebrate the fact that the water has gone down far enough for the galley fires to be lit. Drink it, or let it turn to ice, but do get the cup back to the wardroom steward afterwards. He values the set."

Under the force of that smile, Alfie thawed. It might after all, just be a friendly gesture from a shipmate. And besides, could he really turn down a hot drink? He drank the coffee and its smoky, bitter taste was heaven on earth. Warmth bloomed in his belly, spread outwards, making his hands and feet tingle. He closed his eyes and groaned with bliss. "I'm sorry. I needed that. Am I being a cad?"

"No more than I have been in the past."

He handed back the Derby coffee-cup and saucer with their pretty sprig of roses, and brushed in passing fingertips that felt almost equally delicate. "Oh, that would be a great deal, then! I had not realized I was so monstrous."

John laughed on a note of strain, and a heartbeat later Alfie joined him, choosing to allow him to take it as a joke. The little falsehood rang like a cracked bell between them for a long, uncomfortable moment. Then John, squinting against the flakes in his eyes, drew up his hood again. "How goes it?"

Alfie walked down the line of hitches, across the bow, to where the waterproofed sail had been passed under the keel and drawn up tight on the other side, a bandage over the great gash in the ship's hull. "Salem Joe lost a couple of toes from swimming down to get it fixed beneath the keel, but we've passed a second sheet over the lower hole and we're ready to start pumping again."

"Good." John motioned with his head, and Alfie followed him down into the gundeck's squalor. Half the remaining crew hung from the deck above like bats folded in their wings. They had slung their hammocks as close together as possible, blankets and coats piled high above them. Here and there two sleepers rocked in one sling, the second hammock drawn for extra warmth about the first. The invalids and the boys, by common consent, were slung above the galley and lay steaming faintly in a stench of mold, wet lanolin, and sweat.

Though the deck, and the galley in it, lay at forty-five degrees to the horizon, the lids of the great copper cauldrons were screwed tight shut. Lumps of gristle drummed cheerfully against them as they boiled for a future meal. Salem Joe, an ancient black man whose true name no one dared try to pronounce, raised a drying head, hair white and curly as sheep's fleece, from his pile of blankets, and nodded to Alfie as they passed.

He nodded back, picked out the six men from the starboard watch who looked most rested, and set them to the pumps. The rattle and whoosh made the rookery of sleeping men above him stir a little. But the stretching and muttering died down in seconds as exhaustion did its work. Shivering with remembered chill, Alfie hugged himself, dropping his hands guiltily as he saw John watching. They moved on to the companionway, sidling carefully from rope to pillar to line like spiders on a wall, to keep from plummeting down the inclined deck.

Alfie held tight to the table winched up by its ropes to lie snug against the underside of the deck above his head and wedged his feet into the raised lip of the stairway. John, hooking his lantern to the handle of a rammer above him, took up station beside him. Their hands lay almost touching on the same rope, their feet nudged together. At the touch, Alfie's imagination—never entirely still where John was concerned—suggested that he could put out an arm and pull John into his side. They could wrap that big black cloak around both of them. *Just stand, touching, a layer of thin, soaked linen between the icy chill of each other's skin. Warmth would kindle like a dropped spark, well up and flood between them. Or perhaps they could lie down, doubled up in the same hammock as the men were doing, and he could sleep, warmed through with John's warmth….*

It had been a long night. He swayed, caught himself before he fell and looked at the square of mirror-black water that drowned the stairwell.

"It *is* going down," John murmured. Alfie smiled to himself, hearing the same soft exhaustion in John's voice. If he offered sleep—sleep in his bed, sleep, tangled together in a warm nest of flesh and heat, like badgers curled in their sett, would John really refuse?

Their reflections hung side by side, white and weary in the surface of the water. Then it shivered and they broke into wavering ribbons. A tread showed pale beneath the surface for a moment, then emerged, dripping, just as a lower step became traceable against the dim. The process fascinated him. *If only I might empty myself of darkness so easily. Suck it up from the depths of me, spew it out and be rid of it. Go back to how I was when I would have died for him; when I hoped he'd want to die for me.*

He looked up to study John's face in the light of the lantern. No condemnation there now, only the weary, patient look of a man too tired to rail against his pain. But Alfie remembered it; remembered the recoil at Gibraltar. From "you're the best man I know" to shit John would have gladly scraped from his shoe, in the time it took to comprehend a single sentence.

"Once the pumps have emptied the orlop and hold," John said, quietly, as if he too was aware they spoke of deeper things behind their words. "I'll organize the carpenters to concentrate on repairing the hull. I'll also need an inventory of—"

"Supplies."

A shy flash of a smile. "Yes, and usable storage vessels. The livestock must be drowned and the dry stuffs ruined, but they may be used for bait. Fresh water should not be a problem so long as we have barrels to put the snow in. But if the rum is spoiled we may yet have a mutiny on board before we get home."

"You'll keep them together."

John's startled, sidelong look grazed Alfie's face like a bird's wing, soft and warm. Then John ducked his head in an effort to hide his pleasure. "I will," he agreed, both of them so sure of it that the statement could scarcely be called a boast. "The *Meteor* was good practice for that."

You ought to be a captain. Alfie looked down, watching the water suck away down the stairs. The top of the gunroom's scuffed table was visible now, on its side, with the pewter dishes gleaming beneath it on the floor. He lowered himself carefully down the slanted steps and fished up a floating ditty-box. Inside, amid needles and buttons, laid a lock of brown hair tied in a pink silk ribbon. At the sight he snapped the lid closed again, clutched the little thing tightly, its carved decorations of frigates digging into his fingers.

No. The love token was a warning, an omen of what might happen if he carried on down that path. He couldn't afford to soften toward John, to say anything that might be mistaken as encouragement. John's damned competence! It hurt. It hurt to know that John had been more than capable of doing something for him while he lay in jail awaiting his court martial, but had not done so. *If only*… If only John could have been more like Gillingham. Then Alfie could have put his inaction down to mere weakness—human, excusable weakness. *But he was not. He could have done something to help. He chose not to.* He chose not to be involved in the sordid details of Alfie's life. *What kind of a friend is that?*

"It taught us both a great deal, I think," he said coldly, "about who to trust, and how far. I'm thankful for the lesson." Turning away from John's flinch, with a mixture of triumph and shame, he made a crablike, undignified exit. "By your leave, I'll just go above while the water recedes. I left the marines fishing the sprung foremast, and you know what they're like, if unobserved."

"Lt. Donwell, you're a sight for sore eyes!" Major Pascoe of the marines nudged the fish on the deck with a fastidiously polished shoe, and smiled widely. A handsome dark haired man, with a ruddy face, his unselfconscious beam—which revealed an unquiet graveyard of rotting teeth—never ceased to be startling. "The crack runs through the whole of the lower mast, and I'm in some perplexity as to where the bandage should be applied."

Alfie rocked back on his heels and considered the sprung mast. "Heave it up and let me see it in place," he said, folding his arms and settling companionably into place next to the major. The marine company divided into two parts, the larger hauled on their apparatus of blocks and line, raising the fish up until it dangled against the mast. The smaller company swarmed into the rigging to guide it into place.

Like a splint for a broken leg, the fish was a shaped, hollowed piece of wood designed to be attached to a split mast to strengthen it. Undoubtedly, there were rules of mathematics involved in calculating where it should best be positioned, but Alfie didn't know them. He watched with narrowed eyes and said, "A little up. Up. No, above that knot. Maybe a handsbreadth to starboard. Yes, there! No, stop. There!" with a kind of instinct for where *Albion* would feel least pain. When it was done, hammered into place, wedged tight and reinforced by the blacksmith with iron bands, Pascoe sent his men up to repair the rigging and offered Alfie brandy from a small, silver hip flask.

"So, Lieutenant. You think the carpenters can plug the hole before we perish of thirst? Starvation?"

"I'm sure of it, sir." Alfie cherished the burn of the liquor down his throat and licked his lips to be sure no trace of flavor escaped him. "As soon as the men are rested and fed, I mean to send them out in the boats to fish for herring. Maybe a small whale. We've no lack of brine for storage. As for the water, we can carve ourselves as much as we care to take of the berg. Pack it into barrels and we're done."

"It's sweet?" Pascoe clambered up to the rail, took out his pocket knife and chipped a flake of ice from the berg. He shivered dramatically as it melted in his mouth and smiled again. "Good lord! I was worrying all night long, and for no reason. You chaps make such a career of not looking concerned. I'm ashamed to say I can't tell when it's genuine and when it isn't."

Alfie laughed, touched the snow himself then licked the white line of it from his finger before it melted. The cold set his teeth on edge, but the taste burst brighter than white wine on the back of his tongue. "We must sometimes appear to be what we're not," he began, frowning as the double meaning sank in, "in order to keep the company together. But it's just a show. Inside we're as scared as the next man. Moreso, maybe, for the inability to show it."

"I have no idea whether I should be reassured or not!" Pascoe admitted, squinting up at the men who were splicing the foremast backstay.

"Well," Alfie shook off the clouds of half-meanings and clapped the major on the shoulder, delighted to receive a tolerant smile in return. "You may be certain that when it comes to casting off from here, our complaisance will be a little strained. Get that wrong and we could be blown back on. But, until then, with only a score of men lost, I think we have cause to be cheerful. It could have been a lot worse."

He moved to the tangle of broken wood and limp lines where the bowsprit lay crushed. The pile of wood and pulverized ice should be sifted for both water and fuel. But he paused before giving the orders, thinking about Pascoe and what—unconsciously—the man represented. An offer to forget his past and welcome him back into polite Society. A door, held open, just a crack, through which the light of forgiveness shone.

If he pleased he could pull that door wider and go in. He could do what Farrant had tried to do—but he could do it better. Slake his body's needs with his own right hand instead of casual encounters. Stop looking for love. After prison, and Rodney's warning, how could he dare continue to chase that phantom any further? So far it had led him only to one precipice after another, then disappeared, leaving him to fall.

A league to larboard the watery sun peeked briefly through thinning cloud. Coming up to greet it, out beyond their strange harbor, the humped backs of five whales lifted glistening from the waves. With a great huff and hiss they breathed out fountains, and for a second the sun in the spray made pale rainbows.

They swam together, slow and graceful, keeping pace with one another, the flukes of their tails at times touching, their long square jaws occasionally bumping. Perhaps they only tried to scrape off irritating barnacles, but to Alfie those movements looked like caresses. He wondered what they were to one another. *Father, Mother, and children? Lovers and friends?*

They slipped beneath the waves as the cloud drew back in, leaving the ocean grey, unbroken, empty. The outer world mirrored his inner, as light dimmed and snow fell once more. Head bowed, he went below.

Cold water dripped in a steady patter of drops from the orlop deck above and trickled down the stinking, filth-daubed bulkheads. A faint light shone through the two layers of canvas wrapped about the bow, drawing him to the hole in the hull. The greasy sails bowed inwards there, held in place against the gap by sheer pressure of water. Runnels, squeezed through the fabric, slid in the shifting light down into the ballast—it sucked marshlike beneath his feet. Flickering light, and the deep, underwater silence, made him think of the stories of Davy Jones' locker; of the cities beneath the waves, where mermaids dragged their captive souls to live damp and fishy lives far away from human love. But then a clatter and a face leaning over the edge of the cable tier above to shout, "Ahoy down there, have you seen my hammer…oh, sorry, 'tis you, Lieutenant! Never mind, I'll get it me-self," broke the spell.

He opened spilled barrels, found flour and suet, peas and raisins soaked into salty puddings. Behind the light wicker fences of the animal pens the captain's cow, the two goats shared by the wardroom, and the midshipmen's pig lay swollen and cold. By the chicken coop, a bird under his arm, his foot caught in a twist of rope, lay the corpse of one of the powder monkeys—a boy nine years old.

Alfie knelt down in the sludge of ballast, hearing footsteps suck and crunch towards him, took off the boy's shoe and worried the soaked knot over his heel—no stockings to tear—before slip-ping the loose felt shoe back on.

"Samuel Jenkins," John whispered above his head. "The bird was his pet."

"Oh, God!" Alfie hitched a breath, covered his eyes with his hand and shuddered. The boy had come to rescue his pet and been trapped as the water rose. Tears poured scalding hot down his hand. "God, *I can't…!*"

John sighed, the exhale shaking with his own emotion, but he bent down and took the little body into his arms, carrying it up into the light. Three brothers on board ship, two sisters and a fa-ther working in the dockyard in Portsmouth. *It can't be! It can't be allowed.*

Alfie silently wept, for Samuel Jenkins at first and then with-out pause or halt for Farrant. For Charles Farrant, who would—if he were here—undoubtedly say something cruel. He wept as he had not been able to weep in prison; hiding behind his hands, shivering. Emptying himself out until he felt as besmeared and tossed about as the hold.

Such a bastard, Farrant had been! Covering up his misery with harsh words and extravagant habits. Why had it taken them all by surprise when he finally let the pain kill him? *He had prob-ably been looking for an excuse for years*, Alfie realized.

And why was Alfie now thinking of following his example? Of

forbidding himself love, of making his own life so unendurable to him that he would do nothing to save it? Death had come to the boy and the man alike, regardless of merit or sin. Was that any good reason to reject the happiness he could attain? Young Samuel, who died trying to save his friend, knew better than that. Caution was one thing, cowardice quite another.

Sniffing back his tears, he picked up the abandoned bundle of feathers and stumbled up the companionway onto the gun-deck just as the bells rang for the first dog watch. The ship rumbled with shouting and laughter as the starboard watch tried to take down their tables for dinner, while the larboard were being roused from their sleep, hopping about, half clothed.

Jenkins' brothers knelt in an island of silence around his still form, but they took a look at Alfie's tear-streaked face and allowed him to place the dead bird gently back in the crook of the boy's arm. He stood up, watched them put the cannon balls by the boy's feet, stroke back the drying curl of fringe from the cold forehead, and begin to sew him into his hammock for burial.

"Did ought to eat that chicken," said the eldest, his hand trembling as he pushed the needle through the nose of the corpse.

"Nah. The little beggar'd only come back and haunt us."

"I...." Alfie choked up again, and the brothers looked up at him with strange and terrible sympathy.

"D'you mind leaving us alone with him a moment, Lieutenant. T'say goodbye, like."

"Of course. I'm sorry, I.... Of course."

As the sun went down, seabirds settled on top of the ice mountain and roosted all over the *Albion*'s rigging, to the delight of the midshipmen and the purser alike. The boys combined skylarking with stalking, creeping up the shrouds and along the yards, crowing with laughter as they pounced and grabbed in an explosion of swirling, scolding birds. Their shouts made Alfie smile, as did the thought of barrels of pickled seagull. Oily and fishy though the meat was, it was better than nothing.

They rigged church immediately afterwards, lining up in divisions so far as that was possible on the slope. The sun lowering in the west threw the ship's shadow, spiky and black, over cliffs of ice that seemed to glow like polished amber in a cloth of gold sea.

In the absence of a chaplain, Gillingham read the funeral service. The small body went over the side, splashed into the water, and the glory of sunset closed over it, the crew standing with their heads uncovered to the chill, tears freezing on their eyelashes. In a steady voice, Gillingham read out the names of those others found missing, now also presumed dead.

"'I am the resurrection and the life,' saith the Lord; 'he that believeth in me, though he were dead, yet shall he live: and whosoever liveth and believeth in me shall never die.'"

The parting guns boomed out, muffled with only half a charge, and the noise echoed and re-echoed from the crags. Easterly, the sea was choked with ice. A dozen bergs drifted amongst smaller boulders and flat sheets of it, snow covered, all gold and peach and fire in the sunset. Grumbling and booming muttered on around them even as the light faded. They clapped on their hats, grateful for the cover, and ran below.

Off duty, Alfie wormed his way into the center of the straw and blanket nest he had created in his cot. Pulling all his coverlets tight around him, he thought of finding his servant and sending the man off for hot toddies and warmed stones to set at his feet. But the galley fires had been doused for the night, and his personal stores had never contained more than three bottles of brandy—all now smashed.

Cold moved through him. His skin warmed, but his flesh felt brittle as glass. Exhaustion brought him close to the point of sleep again and again, only for panic to jerk him awake as he felt his blood slow.

Only a wall of canvas and battens separated him from John's cabin. There he could hear the restless rustle and the creak of rope as John's sleepless movements set his cot swinging. *What keeps him awake? A guilty conscience?*

Alfie turned over, drawing the blanket, his boat cloak, tarpaulin jacket, and best dress breeches up over his head, then shivered at the blast to his kidneys. *Oh, for a down comforter!* Oh, for any excuse to take his bedding with him and go crawl in with John....

"What would you have to say for yourself, eh?" he murmured under his breath, the words pleasantly warm as they passed his lips. "Gibraltar I can understand. If anything, I knew what you'd do. I blame myself for coming out with it too early. Bad timing...."

A frustrated exhale of breath in the dark, almost a groan, and for a moment Alfie thought John had heard him. But no, the noise came from the other side—where the ship's surgeon rested in his dispensary. A couple of grunts and a cut off, incomprehensible word of deep Scots Gaelic, and the breathing settled back into sleep.

Alfie lowered his voice until he could barely hear it himself, the warm mist of ghost words a strange sensory pleasure in his mouth. "But why aren't you more guilty? You promised me aid, in prison. You promised, and then you disappeared. I thought you were more honest. Less of a coward."

Perhaps he would put the question to John if ever they touched at England and found themselves in more private surroundings than these? It would be a day much like today. Cold. Silent snowfall outside the windows. The two of them would sit together in a room in John's house, wherever that was, with fire glowing in the grate, brandy and gingerbread on little tables beside their deep armchairs. The servants would be bickering and laughing in the kitchen below, their voices forming a pleasant drone with the crackle and murmur of the flames.

They would talk, John and he, all through the short day, safe together away from the prying world. And then perhaps go upstairs together and make love all the long night. He could imagine that too. John's bed would have crisp white sheets, and a heavy bed-rug covered in the same garish flowers as his banyan. *Something his mother had embroidered for him.*...And it would smell of John—that faint cream, salt, and citrus smell that made Alfie think of royal creamed ice.

But at the thought of ice cream his surroundings returned to him in a trickle of shivers down the back. He could hear ice thickening on the water outside, grinding down the hull like a saw. Love and lust and disappointment were all nothing to it. If the wind picked up and the seas rose he could find all his ponderings cut short by the indifference of nature. Perhaps it would be better to reach out and snatch what was offered than to freeze into a block while mourning over lost illusions....

The thought had a bitter taste, lodging in his throat like a bite of half-cooked seagull. It gave him resentful dreams.

◖ CHAPTER 30 ◗

"Make ready to cast her loose!" cried Alfie. The drums rolled, their staccato tapping echoed back from distant caves as a deep, inhuman roar, as though the *Albion* rested in the land of the ice giants and—unwisely—kept shaking them awake.

Sailors poured up the companionways, the topmen running on, unpausing, up the shrouds, ice falling fractured from the ropes beneath their rag-bound bare feet. Teams of four men on each anchor cable stood waiting with axes to cut the cables simultaneously on his signal. All had been prepared for above a week now, but for the wind that had blown relentlessly on to the ice for day upon day. This morning, however, it had wheeled directly astern. There was a chance, now, that once the *Albion* was back in the water she might get clear.

"All hands lashed aboard?" Alfie tightened the rope about his own waist that held him to the binnacle, watched impatiently while the men on the yards secured themselves. Any moment the wind could wheel again, trapping them for another month with fuel for the galley running out and winter tightening its grip.

"Aye aye, sir!" the midshipmen of their divisions reported, passing a final line about themselves as they huddled about the main mast.

"Make fore and main topsail, mizzen topsail and mizzen staysail!"

As the topsails sheeted home, the sprung foremast creaked

with a strange high pitched whine. The masts bent forward, rigging pulling taut as iron. The anchor cables strained. Alfie's breath came fast and shallow.

"On my mark, loose the anchors. Three, two, one. Mark!"

The axes flashed like mercury through the air. The aft cable parted a sickening moment earlier than the fore and *Albion's* stern began its slide an instant before her bow. Then the bow rope twanged apart and the whole ship went sliding sideways into the sea. With a great flume of bitter spray she plummeted into the waves and the sea surged aboard. Deep in her belly the pumps throbbed back into life. The yards twanged like longbows and the men tied to them yelled, clinging on with both hands. Alfie's feet left the deck. The line around him drove up under his ribs as it caught him. He coughed and gasped out, "Let fall fore and main sail!"

Wind snapped in the wet sailcloth. *Albion's* speed picked up and she began to move forward, driving herself through a sharp-edged spume of floating ice. Blocks tipped up beneath her head and shattered on either side of her bow, drawing back together beneath her stern, fouling the rudder. Still she ploughed on, thrust onwards by the gale, the berg so close the men on the starboard studdingsail yards might have reached out and grabbed a handful of snow.

With a sick feeling of inevitability, Alfie saw the sails shiver at the edge and felt the wind behind him veer a point. Nothing significant at all if out at sea, but here it placed the berg to leeward. As they moved forward, he saw, they would drift sideways back into its facets, to inevitable grounding on sheet ice, hull split open like a fruit beneath the knife, bleeding warmth until she seized in place and snow covered all.

"We must claw off, sir!" Alfie yelled, throwing off the lifeline so that he could move again.

Gillingham, all his blankets clutched about him, nodded. "Yes, we must. Make all sail! Helm hard a larboard."

The whole ship's company hauled on their lines as if possessed by devils. The sails thundered out and drew taut, the water by her bow foaming up as her speed increased. The hole in the foremast twisted, gaping, but the mast endured even under the full spread of canvas. *Albion* began to turn slowly to port, even as the wind was still blowing her leewardly towards the ice mountain. Snow skirled away from the thing in plumes, leaving it bare to the sunlight. It glowed like a single huge sapphire in Alfie's vision. Shadows moved in its heart—indigo and midnight surrounded by secret, nameless colors. Its cliffs and cleaver-sharp precipices shimmered emerald and aquamarine.

Helm hard about, all the sails set, they could do no more but wait. Wait and hope for the course to take them past before the ship's leeway drove them onto the facets of the enormous gem. Alfie knew the silence aboard was awe mixed with fatalistic terror in the face of this deadly beauty, their own helplessness.

"Have everyone not on the braces stand on the center line," Gillingham said to Alfie, quietly. "That will stiffen her a little. And then I think we may pray." He smiled weakly at John, who had come silently to Alfie's shoulder. "Something simple for the occasion, Mr. Cavendish, if you please."

"Me, sir?"

"You and He are on more regular speaking terms than the rest of us. Isn't that so?"

John glanced nervously at the ice, now cutting out the sun above them. Ghost lights shone around its edges, and from it there came a sharp cracking noise, like repeated lightning. Swallowing hard, his lips white, John closed his eyes. Alfie watched his face smooth out as he tried to forget death and disaster, concentrating on whatever still, small voice he heard. "Oh Lord, please bring us from darkness into light, from death into life. Amen."

Like a candle coming out from behind its encircling hand, a beam of sun lanced past the far edge of the berg, then another. Soon after they could see sea ahead, a strip of it, the same strange milky blue as the ice. The crew leaned over the side, fending off the mountain's skirt of floating boulders with oars and boathooks, and slowly *Albion* ground past and away. Too close for comfort, not quite close enough for disaster. As she sailed east towards the deeper water of Baffin Bay, the carpenters raced to plug the new holes in the hull, and the larboard watch replaced the starboard at the pumps.

Alfie, highly doubtful whether the Lord had anything to do with it—the course having already been set, and only inevitable mathematics in play from then on—nevertheless watched the ice dwindle behind him with a feeling of revelation.

From death to life? Perhaps I have *mourned long enough.*

He returned to the binnacle in time to see the final grains of sand slip from the top bulb of the glass to the lower. The Master bounded up the quarterdeck steps, ready to take his watch. The youngest midshipman skidded to a halt beside the bell and grasped for the hammer as eagerly as if it were a sugar plum. "Turn the glass and strike the bell," Alfie said firmly, conscious of the symbolism. The sweet eightfold chime punctuated his life like a full stop, closing one day, opening the next.

Handing over to his relief, Alfie joined the rush of off-watch men pouring below. The wardroom's damp heat billowed around him as he stripped off coats and mufflers, shaking off the ice into the pools of snowmelt on the painted floor. A brazier stood, surrounded by a tray of damp sand, in the center of the table, with a weary circle of officers around it, their faces stained red by the coals. Joining them, Alfie held out his hands to the heat, felt wires of pain draw themselves through his numb fingers; a blaze, an ache, and then an unbearable tingle as they returned to life.

Within, his heart unfroze with something of the same agony, as he thought about John. So John had proved disappointing? So John was not the paragon Alfie had hoped for? Well then, might this not be an opportunity for Alfie to be generous? He had willingly born so much ill usage from Farrant without more than a moment's resentment. He could surely endure John's faults in the same way, regarding him as a man injured by his own nature, worthy of pity.

Though he preferred to worship at the shrine of his lover, it might be interesting to try being worshipped instead. Suppose he went to John and said, "I forgive you. I forgive you for making me promises in jail that you could not keep. I know what it is to be frightened—I don't hold it against you. Feel free to thank me now, if you wish." *Would it not be splendid to be the target of so much inevitable gratitude?*

Rubbing the last prickle from his fingertips, Alfie left the wardroom, brushed past the drying clothes in the corridor and scratched at the sliding door of John's cabin. *He would say, 'How about it?' and John's face would light up with thankfulness. Perhaps they could even squeeze into the corner between door and frame and he would let John bring him off with those narrow, delicate hands of his, John's face tucked into the side of Alfie's neck, his heaving breath, deliciously hot over the sore, chapped skin of Alfie's throat….*

The sliding door opened with a rattle. "Yes?" John backed up with a look of confusion as Alfie crowded into the narrow space between cot and wall, then slid the partition shut behind him. "Alfie, what is it?"

His diary was in his hand. He turned to place the book face down on his bed, and the quick, lithe movement made Alfie catch his breath, a yearning indistinguishable from anger heating his blood. *Oh yes, or he could pin John up against the wall and just rub himself against that back, that perfect curve of arse. Too cold and too dangerous to take any clothes off, and besides, it was all John deserved.*

"I…." he tried, and found he had no idea what he wanted to say. It was all too much of a mess. He lifted a hand instead, drew two fingers up the line of John's jaw; felt the rush of blood scalding against his fingertips as John blushed, the thunder of the pulse in his throat.

John gasped, moving closer. "This is not…." The words left his mouth half open. Looking both shocked and vulnerable, he gazed at Alfie with a mixture of hope and terror. The skirts of his coat swung forwards, grazing Alfie's thighs as he leaned in. John's warmth soaked slowly through Alfie's breeches, a fugitive touch against Alfie's stiffening yard, and Alfie gritted his teeth, wanting—not wanting—not sure…. "Alfie, this is…."

God, will he ever shut up? Alfie lunged forward, slid that exploring hand behind John's head, knotting it into his short, salt-stiffened hair, and pulled John to him with all his strength. John stumbled, caught by surprise, and for a moment his hands came up to ward Alfie off, but Alfie just crushed John's smart mouth to his and forced the clamped lips open with his tongue. He shoved John backwards against his desk. It clattered against the wall, stilled, then held tight as Alfie pressed himself full length against John, free hand slipping down to cup John's arse, tug him ever closer. *Oh, the heat of him, and the way he trembles!*

John's fists, twisted in Alfie's shirt, loosened, slid around behind his back, and clung there. His head tilted back, his mouth opening more fully to the plundering kisses. As his muscles softened in sweet, unconditional surrender, John's body molded itself to Alfie's trustingly. Alfie broke the kiss to look at John's expression—the closed eyes, lashes trembling on his cheeks, the faint smile that drew up the ends of the full, bruised lips. John's long throat tipped back, exposing itself to Alfie's teeth and rippling as he swallowed.

For a moment Alfie forgot all the complications in sheer bliss, as he hitched John up until the man's arse was on his desk, nudged his knees apart and ground himself against the one part of John that did not yield.

John's arms went about his neck. He opened eyes full of amusement even as he gasped. "What? Why…?"

Amusement? The little bastard was finding this funny? Shoulders heaving with the labor of drawing breath, his cock painful and his heart painful too, angrily aroused—aroused and angry— Alfie reached between them, wrenching at the buttons that held the flap of John's breeches closed. *If only John would keep his mouth shut, just for three seconds!* Everything was perfect when

John forgot how to speak. He was not here for *conversation*. "I thought…It's a…it's a new year coming. Make a new start."

John smiled and touched the back of his hand, affectionately. Alfie slipped his hand inside the placket of the breeches and grasped John's member through his shirt. The heat of it felt as though it could burn his palm, as John shivered all over with a sound half chuckle, half protest. "Cold hands!"

Alfie's own yard ached at the touch. His heaving breaths filled his lungs with frost and his stomach roiled with a kind of nausea. Where was that gratitude he had promised himself? Why was John still not acting like a guilty man being given something he did not deserve? Leaning forward he pressed John down, licked beneath his ear, bit his neck and, with something very like contempt, watched him writhe. Perhaps it was the ghost of Farrant, making one last parting shot. Perhaps he had merely bequeathed Alfie some of his cynicism. As he nuzzled his nose into the warm, cologne-smelling thickness of John's dark hair, as John arched up, wanton under him, he whispered in John's ear, "And where are your fine principles now?"

Albion rolled slowly to larboard. From forward, muffled by the cabin walls, came the snatch of a reel on a well-played fiddle. The uncapped ink bottle lay by John's splayed right hand on the desk. Spilled ink trickled down his little finger to the floor.

Alfie found himself listening for the uproar of condemnation he deserved. Surely the whole ship must have heard what he'd said? Surely the whole world had heard it? He was so appalled the hard shove in his chest didn't register at first as a blow. John— rumpled, debauched, and white in the face with fury—had to draw back his hand and slam the open palm into Alfie's ear before Alfie reeled away. A marlin-spike of pain sliced through his skull, leaving pressure and darkness, a ringing noise. He shook his head, speechless.

"Get. *Out*." John tidied himself with swift, precise movements, then splayed his ink-stained hand on Alfie's chest and pushed him towards the door. "You did this to *put me to shame?*

To prove a point? You piss-drinking cunt! If you knew…if you had *any idea* how far I'd come. For *you!* And you…"

"What?" Shame snapped aback into defensive anger. Alfie got his hands around John's shoulders, shoved him, hard as he could, sending the lighter man crashing into the cot. The jolt and clatter—John's little grunt at the impact—made up for so many things, so many separate moments of anguish. If he couldn't have sex, bloody hell, taking John apart with his bare hands would probably scratch the itch just as· well. "What *have* you done? Given me insults! False promises. Acting like I *owe* you something. Letting me down at every fucking turn! I should—"

"What? You should *what,* Alfie? Strike a superior officer? Get yourself hanged? You seem to have quite the talent for it." John, back to the wall, bristled like a cat. Though Alfie's fists ached to lash out, to blacken John's eye, he couldn't. He needed to strike—to purge this raging confusion, the disappointment, the misery, to get past it all and clean for a new start—but he couldn't, because damn the bastard, John was right.

If Alfie hit a senior officer he would lose this berth. His last chance. He would be dragged back to prison, and stand in front of the disdainful scrutiny of another court martial. *No, God no, not that!* He would hang for mutiny, his tarred body strung up to provide an example to the fleet.

Worse than that, though, John—a gentleman through and through—would never, ever forgive a man who struck him. Angry as he was, Alfie could not bring himself, even now, to do something John would not forgive.

Instead he wrenched the door open, forced himself through it as though walking through a hurricane, and leaned against the jamb, biting his lips and breathing hard until he could stalk stiffly away.

He fumed all the way back to Jamaica.

◖◖ CHAPTER 31 ◗◗

December 1763, Kingston, Jamaica

Once the *Albion* made landfall—the week before Christmas—Alfie found a room above O'Flaherty's shebeen and retired there to lick his wounds. An unlicensed pub run by an indentured servant who had worked off his contract ten years ago and decided not to go home, the sheebeen made a strange haven. Its normal clientele were rough working men only a notch above slaves. But if O'Flaherty liked the cachet of having a gentleman in residence, Alfie liked the freedom to come down stairs when he couldn't sleep, sit in the corner of the one dark room, unshaved, unwigged, his shirt collar open, and listen to the music, where no one had the faintest idea who he was.

Half way through the first evening he went upstairs, returned with his flute and played Sainte-Colombe's *Tombeau les Regrets* for the packed crowd of hard drinking men. In the hush afterwards O'Flaherty handed him a mug of porter. "D'you know this one, then?" said a sandy-haired youngster with a set of pipes, and before he knew it, he was installed as a resident musician. The relief of being able to have one too many, end the evening slumped against a cool, mudbrick wall grumbling, "thinks he's better than me…" or, "not going to apologize, he can come to me," in an environment where such outpourings were greeted without suspicion was soothing as ointment over a burn.

Orange rushlights burned smokily in the dark. Fiddle and pipes interlaced a yearning melody through the babble of voices. They spoke in Irish, most of them, but he could communicate easily enough in music. On particularly bad nights, when the music and his despair struck the same chords, he would sometimes find a free drink left quietly by his elbow, look up to a sympathetic nod. They were, most of them, a thousand miles from their own homes, and knew well what it was like to be unwillingly parted from friends and brothers and sons.

Spending Christmas Day with a raging hangover and half a chop he discovered under the bed, however, brought it home to him that even he had to eat. So when the market re-opened on the twenty-seventh, he shaved, brushed his coat, powdered his wig, levered up the floorboard under which he had nailed his purse, and walked into Kingston to buy food.

As he stood on the curb of North Parade with a bag of bread and a jar of cold Jamaican sorrel in his arms, a coach and four burst from an oncoming dustcloud in a rattle of wheels and hooves. Leather squeaked, and the four matched horses snorted, sitting back on their haunches as it drew up to a sudden halt in front of him. A woman's voice from inside the closed carriage called, "That's him! That's the man! Tell him to get in."

Alfie groaned. Had there been no scandals since his, to occupy the imaginations of the town? He had already received a hundred more sidelong glances than he could well tolerate, let alone the conspiratorial, "amusing" jokes. He could find no appeal in the thought of brazening it out one more time here.

A footman, in somber black livery more appropriate for a priest, hopped down from his high seat. The chestnut mare in the right rear trace snuffed at Alfie's bag of apples. Warm horse breath huffed over his knuckles as the ever-present Jamaican wind blew the coach's raised dust in a gritty fog against Alfie's side, leaving pale streaks along the creases of his coat. "Lieutenant Donwell? Her ladyship wishes to speak to you."

"You can inform your lady," Alfie held on to his hat, "that I am not a public curiosity. I do not wish to relate my recent unfortunate experience with His Majesty's justice at any of her dinner parties, and I would be obliged if she would drive on."

A white hand in a black ruffled sleeve unlatched the door and pushed it open. As the footman folded out the steps, sunlight caught the dull black side of the coach and revealed the outline of a coat of arms, painted over. Alfie stepped back as if shoved, then he put down his packages and traced the barely raised ducal crown on the lion's shaggy head, with reverent, gentle fingertips. Tears prickled at the back of his eyes. He gasped "oh!" and looked up just as a woman's head in a heavy black veil leaned out. "Please get in, Lieutenant Donwell. Just for a moment."

Outside, the crowded cobbled streets and even the wind had seemed full of disapproving eyes. But as he grasped the edge of the wooden doorway and felt the carriage sway beneath his weight as he hauled himself aboard, the inner world lurked more terrifying yet. He sat, green leather seat creaking beneath him, as the footman shut him in. Gold lacquered walls curved around him like the shell of an egg. Embroidered cushions bore the same crest as the door—red, blue and gold, a lion rampant, a spotted stag.

Taking off his dusty hat, he placed it on the seat beside him. The woman lifted her veil, smoothing it over her hair, away from her face. Alfie's gaze slid from the cushions to the floor. He struggled to raise his eyes from the hem of Lady Lisburn's dress and the two small feet, in black satin slippers, poking out beneath it.

"How old are you?" she asked, after a long silence. "You look about the age of my eldest son. *Our* son. Farrant's and mine."

Pulse roaring in his ears Alfie glanced up sharply, his shame not quite enough to allow him to bear scorn. Her slate blue eyes widened, an artful blonde ringlet trembling beside the angle of her jaw as she too braced herself against the urge to recoil. Almost as surprised, as appalled as he. *My lover's wife!*

"You're not what I was expecting," she said, just as he was thinking the same. Strongly made and wide mouthed, she had a masculine, roguish look. It occurred to Alfie that, in her bean-pole slender youth, she must have looked like a midshipman, poised on the cusp of manhood's strength. If she could have stopped time, found some way never to ripen, to stay bony and boyish for all time, would Farrant have been able to love her then?

Alfie pressed a knuckle to his lips, pushing down nausea and terrible, unwelcome sympathy. "I don't know what to say."

She laughed, a little tremor of tears shaking the sound, and tapped at the ceiling. The coach rolled forward at a gentle walk, the interior swaying slightly on its springs. "No more do I."

They drove slowly through the midst of a group of maroons, who scattered to each side. A woman in a brightly colored head-scarf called out something scornful in her own language, as the covered pot on her head emitted a smell of goat curry.

Lady Lisburn rummaged deep in one of her pockets and brought out a scrap of paper which she passed to Alfie. "You sent me this."

His own writing confronted him—shaky with emotion, in wa-tery-brown prison ink, on coarse-laid prison paper.

Please allow me to take this opportunity to tell you there was no one in your husband's heart but yourself. There never was any rival in his affections for you. All his thoughts and deeds were motivated by your welfare, and to my knowledge, a more faith-ful husband never breathed.

"Was it some form of mockery?" she asked sharply. "I've puz-zled at it ever since. Can a man, going to his death, have so little opinion of his immortal fate as to make fun? I cannot make it out."

He could not force his first attempt at speech through the ob-struction in his throat. The hot, bright cell in which they trav-elled filled up with the scent of Lady Lisburn's jasmine perfume, manure on Alfie's shoe adding its own blend of horse and straw. The hollow between Alfie's brows ached with frowning, and he felt his chin crumple as he pressed lips and eyes firmly together, resisting the urge to weep. "It…it was no lie. I meant every word."

A moment spent looking out at the road down to the harbor, the sea bisected by the long causeway that lead to what remained of Port Royal, helped him gather himself to carry on more strongly. "Your husband regarded what he did as a vice; like playing for high stakes at cards, like whoring. It meant no more to him than whoring—the slaking of a physical thirst. You were his reality. You…there was no one he loved but for you."

"A cold love," she observed.

"Perhaps." Alfie bared his teeth—it was as close as he could come to a smile. "But, Christ, at times I could have died for envying you."

Lady Lisburn sobbed with laughter, brought out a lace-edged handkerchief, and bent her face into it, her shoulders shaking. They rolled on a little while before she composed herself, wiped her face, sniffed and wiped again. Pressing the handkerchief to her nose, her blue eyes still shining with unshed tears, she said, "Does it help to know I too would gladly have exchanged places?"

The absurdity of it took him by surprise. He sniggered, tried to repress it behind his hand, looking up apologetically as he did so. But her mouth twitched at the edge as well, drawn up in jerks against her will. His snigger turned into a chuckle at the sight, and then she tittered too, and before long they both were laughing in great guffaws, sides heaving, bent over the mirth as if it was a stomach pain.

When that too passed, Alfie bit his cheek to sober himself up again. "Will you be well? If there's anything I can do…?"

She tucked the handkerchief away inside her skirts, locked her hands together in her lap, and gave a more genuine smile. "Between you and your friend Lt. Cavendish, I am inundated with offers of help from handsome young men. But no, with Farrant gone, my exile no longer serves a purpose. I will sell the plantation, take my children home to England, and live modestly on the proceeds. I am ashamed to say it is a kind of liberation."

She turned to smile out the window, her speech less for his benefit than for her own. Which was just as well, because Alfie, arrested by the name, had not listened further. "Forgive me, Lady. You spoke to Cavendish?"

"He didn't tell you?" To her left, the sea stretched out to the ends of the world, and its light beat on her cheek, washing out all the flaws. By contrast, the other half of her face lay in shadow, barely to be seen.

He registered only the lift of one skeptical eyebrow, but it was enough. An oppression he had not been aware of eased its grip on his heart. Hope reeled over him like the dizziness from one too many pints of rum.

"The lieutenant came to speak to Bentley. To urge him to withdraw his accusation. I believe he arranged for the departure of that odious catamite too. I cannot see any other reason why Bert Driver should flee when Bentley was paying him to remain. Truly, you had no idea?"

Shutting his mouth—how long it had hung open, Alfie had no idea—he reached out and brushed the dust from his hat with jerky movements. Anything to conceal the way the world had stopped with a sickening lurch then started up again a completely different shape.

"Yet I suppose it is very much the part of a friend to do such a thing in secret…." Lady Lisburn went on, filling the silence with nervous speech. "To avoid giving rise to any burdensome obligation. And he did say you were his very good friend."

"I didn't give him a chance to speak of it." Alfie's turn now to fill the rocking, confessional box of the coach with his own private thoughts. *I expected the worst. I assumed the worst. Yet all that time he was working to save my life.* Gillingham's invitation to join the *Albion's* crew took on a new significance: John had not been at the court martial because he already knew the outcome. Because he was too busy arranging a berth for Alfie, making sure he would not be tried and condemned by public opinion, even when exonerated by the law.

And I could not have been more vile to him.

Alfie's spirits expanded like a hot air balloon around a flame of happiness, filling his mind until there was no room for guilt, making him lighter than air. *Not a false friend at all! Not the wretch I have believed him recently, but the paragon I thought at first!*

He had to think. He'd been a fool—no surprises there—but now, when he had wrestled back this glee, got out of this stuffy, creaking box of a carriage, he must some way, some excuse to seek John out and finally put this right.

"Forgive me, madam. Could we go back? I have suddenly remembered something I must do."

❦ CHAPTER 32 ❧

Naval Officer's Club, Kingston, Jamaica

John looked up as the street door slammed. Footsteps rapped smartly on the club's pretentious marble entrance hall, softer on the teak sweep of stairs. Nausea rose under his breastbone, his fingers prickled with sudden cold, and he looked down at his cards abruptly, before he started to tremble. A few seconds later, the cocked hat of an officer of the marines rose into view, gold loop gleaming.

"I…I'll stick," said John to Captain Gillingham, as he folded up his hand of cards. The new arrival was not Alfie. No new arrival for the past fortnight had been Alfie. He tried not to loathe the marine, from his death's head buttons to his boots, for the fact, but it was more of a struggle than he would have wished. Where Alfie was staying these days, he had no idea. The club had seemed the most likely place they might meet by chance. But enduring the close quarters, the din, the smoke, and the crowding presence of far too many strangers was proving…difficult. And he still had no idea what he meant to say to Alfie if he should arrive.

"I do believe your mind's not on your play." Gillingham dealt himself another card and smiled. Placing the cards face down on the scuffed, cheaply made table, he fished an ivory snuffbox from his pocket and offered it to John.

From further in the room, deep within the cloud of pipe smoke, a roar of laughter rolled over them both. The sound of crockery breaking into shards made John think of knives. The tremble in his fingers spread to his cards. He slapped them down quickly and clenched his hands together in fists, restraining their treachery. But his legs weakened and shook—the buckle on his shoe squeaking as if deliberately to alert every onlooker to his cowardice. He bit the side of his cheek, grinding it between his teeth as he fought not to do this. *Not again!* But when three dark figures lurched from the billowing fug, knocked into the card table by his side, and turned to laugh, arms raised in drunken, expansive gestures, John scrabbled back further into his chair, cringing.

"The little girl's scared!" hooted the man at the back, a horse-marine by his coat, and his two friends chortled. John's terror transmuted instantly into incandescent rage. He leapt up, shouldered aside the other two, and grabbed the marine by his stock. The man's eyes widened, and he swayed drunkenly in John's grip. As he did so there came the rustle and soft thud of Gillingham struggling to his feet behind John. Past the marine, Captain Davis of the *Leopard* and his first lieutenant, Hawkins—who had been sitting together pouring over paperwork by the window—also stood, took three indignant steps closer.

"John," said Gillingham, gently, "the man's blind drunk and doesn't know what he's saying."

"Nevertheless," Davis fixed all three marines with a look of contempt, "if you insist on satisfaction, I would be honored to be your second."

Their kindness astonished him. He pulled slightly against the knotted fabric, and when the fellow braced to pull back, he let go suddenly. The mocker measured his length on the floor, falling with a splash into the widening puddle of piss and wine, where guests, Christmas-merry, had missed the chamberpots. John pulled out a handkerchief and wiped his hands, thankful it would be taken as a gesture of defiance, and not as evidence of his cold sweats.

"I don't think he's gentleman enough to deserve a challenge." Hawkins smirked, nudging the fallen man with a foot. At his arched, mildly inquisitive look, the other two drunkards shook themselves and made a break for the door. "Your servant, sir," he said to John, watching them go.

Absurdly, at this gallantry, the feeling of being rescued, John wanted to cry. He managed to smile instead, though it felt watery. "I can't say…I am very obliged to you, Captain. Lieutenant." A jerk of the arm successfully indicated seats. "Will you take a glass of wine with us?"

"Not today, thank you." Davis' courtesy would have graced any royal court. "Need a clear head to do the books. We'll bid you good night."

Resuming his seat, John found the pack of cards scattered on the floor. As he leaned down to pick them up, Gillingham said quietly, "I own I am relieved. A wound doesn't heal without it suppurates first. After your treatment on Tobago I expected this earlier."

John bent his head over tidying the pack, easing all the edges into order. "I have…had distractions." The driven energy pulled from him by the needs of Alfie's court martial, terrifying though it had been, seemed almost attractive now that it had waned. The comfort of shipboard routine too had now been lost, and his ghosts risen up to take its place. "My friend's…trouble. And then the voyage. But now I have nothing to do but think."

"Well, the *Otter* at least made you a rich man. You could wager me some of that scarcely touched prize money." Gillingham topped up his own glass, then John's, from the bottle of Margaux that stood by his chair. "If *vingt-et-un* is insufficiently absorbing, I can ask Davis and his premier to take us on at whist. Let go that penitential rigor of yours a while and celebrate. It *is* Christmas, after all."

Cupping the glass between his hands, John watched the room, paneled walls and candelabra, regimental crests and paintings of nude nymphs, float—in reflection—upside down over the blood-colored wine. The laughter had not ceased, and now a cracked, off-key voice sang;

> *"It was pleasant and delightful on a bright sum-*
> *mer's morn*
> *When the green fields and the meadows were*
> *covered with corn*
> *And the blackbirds and thrushes sitting on*
> *every green spray*
> *And the larks they sang melodious at the dawn-*
> *ing of the day."*

"And the larks they sang melodious..." Gillingham joined in, his voice reedy and unpracticed. "And the larks they sang melodious.... Come on Lieutenant, a little jollity won't kill you. And the larks they sang melodious at the dawning of the day."

Summoning up a wan smile, John drained his glass. After being called a little girl, nothing in this world would entice him to sing ever again. His skin crept at the thought. But still, unwelcome, unwilling, bringing with it a yet deeper twist of misery, came the memory of himself in Alfie's cabin, soaring unselfconsciously on the music of Telemann. *"By God, you'd be a sensation in Italy, sir. The girls'd be running after you down the street."*

"I think I'll go home," he said. "I find I'm in no temper for more company at the moment. I have bought a little house near to the harbor, and I must provision it against the shops shutting."

Outside, he dared the markets, and walked from shop to shop ordering food he had no real mind to eat; chicken, pies, plum cake and gingerbread, a basket of oranges and a pineapple that would have cost him a month's wages back home in England.

A brief flurry of delivery boys filled his house with the thunder of boots and the pipe of their voices, riotous and cheerful as the midshipmen's berth at sea, but it ended before the sun set, leaving him marooned. The thought of finding an employment agency and interviewing servants—*at this time of year!*—was more than he could face. So he ate a cold dinner, lit his solitary candle, and brooded over the problem of Alfie Donwell.

Would it have killed Alfie to think well of him? Perhaps Alfie did not know to what lengths John had gone to save him and could not therefore be expected to be grateful for them. Indeed, ensuring he didn't have to be grateful was the whole purpose of not telling him. But still, who would have thought he could be so resentful, could play a low, vile, *cruel* trick as to raise John's hopes in order to deliberately humiliate him? Had he now added malice to his scarcely repressed violence? *Barbaric, intolerable, infuriating man! Why could he not give me a chance to explain?*

Yet that was unfair. Alfie had every reason to believe himself ill used, and had dealt with it for the most part with dignified avoidance. What if that vehement, glorious, intolerable encounter aboard ship had not been cruelty at all? What if it had been a chance for them to begin again—one of Alfie's blind charges into the unknown that went wrong as they so often did? What had he said?

"The new year is coming. How about a new start?"

John rubbed at the headache that twisted like goat's horns across his brow, Alfie's voice, dark and rich as chocolate, more real than the bare walls around him. Perhaps that was the key? Perhaps the man—in some freak of antic superstition—had meant it literally?

He took his candle upstairs and went to bed. Perhaps it was worth enduring until the new year before he gave up hope entirely.

The week passed in austerity. John struggled with a thousand domestic chores he had scarcely conceived existed before. They passed the days, making it possible for him to deny that he was just marking time as he waited to be forgiven.

New Year's Eve dawned like every day in Jamaica—sunny, breezy, hot. John slept till noon, pulled on breeches, and breakfasted in his shirt sleeves, on bread gone hard as ship's biscuit. Time had become a thin wire, puncturing his chest, passing through his lungs and out through his backbone. He moved along it by slow inches. By tomorrow he would know if Alfie had been speaking of a literal new start in a new year. But tomorrow lay inaccessible at the end of this interminable day.

At three o'clock, disgusted with sitting in the kitchen, bare feet on warm tiles, door open on the weedy courtyard of back garden, where tendrils of pumpkin were even now choking the life out of a stand of English roses, he finished dressing and repaired to his writing desk. Drawing up the chair, he took out paper, pen, and ink, and began writing.

> *My dear Higgins,*
>
> *This is late in coming to you for this Christmas, but I hope it will find you before the next. I am enclosing your prize money, which I am in the fortunate position to be able to pay out of my own funds. Please do not mention it to the other* Meteors *as I cannot do the same for all, but I hope this will enable the new year to find you and Evie settled in your own establishment.*
>
> *If, for any reason, the thought of an innkeeper's life no longer appeals, I am also in need of a reliable servant, or two. Livery could be arranged.*
>
> > *Yours,*
> > *Cavendish*

Sealing the letter, he walked down to the officer's club and confided it to a lieutenant due to sail for Gibraltar in a week. He refused drinks, smiled wanly over jokes about his tea-total and killjoy Methodism, and returned home, buying a copy of *The Life of Sir Thomas More, By His Great Grandson* on the way.

Alone in his front room, John opened the book and read the

first paragraph before drawing out his watch and sitting, fascinated by the white face, the slowly moving hands, the tick. How slow midnight was to arrive! How obvious it was to him now that he had been deluding himself. This evening was no different from any other. By half past eleven he knew no one was coming, and it only remained to try and be glad of it. *One more day of not giving in to sin.* One more day of the virtue that used to come so easily, and now was like being slowly eaten away from within.

The truth was, simply, that John was not *lovable* as, with all his faults, Farrant had been lovable.

He got up to close all the curtains, pour himself a drink. His father's contempt floated on top of the brandy. *Who could love such a cold fanatic as myself?* His own parent had not managed it.

Lighting a candle, John returned to his desk and brought out his faithful diary. His ears hurt from listening too hard for a knock on the door, so instead he repaired his quill and filled the silence with the scratching of thought.

> *It occurs to me now, when I contemplate sin, that perhaps my father had something of the right of it after all. If the Lord came that we might have life, and have it more abundantly, does it not follow that whatever kills that life, whatever constrains, dries and desiccates that life is a sin?*
>
> *It must have been a chill household for a man to rejoin, who was used to roaring parties, mirth and splendor. I can imagine, now, how hard it must have been for a sensualist to depart from the theatres and concerts of the capital to our cheerless disapproval.*

He dipped his pen and found his gaze caught by the candle flame as all the lost chances of his life ran together in his mind.

*I wonder, when it is too late for the realization to do
me any good, whether my father might perhaps
have desired my affection. Was he such an unnatural father as to have taken no pride in his son, had
the son only allowed it?*

Too late, as usual, he saw again the outpouring of noisy life, light,
and color as his father burst into the tall white hall of their country
home with his entourage of actresses and hangers-on. Even now
he could not excuse the whores and mistresses, but found it hard to
praise his own recoil—the clenched fists and look of scouring contempt with which he had greeted his father every time.

*Might he have been less cruel, if I had looked down
upon him less? My virtue does not show in so white
a light as I had once supposed. Critical, offensive,
sanctimonious. No wonder….*

John's watch chimed the hour with a sweet little silvery voice.
John stilled, the sound piercing him like a fountain of pins. Bowing his head into his hands, he swallowed, rubbing his eyes. Damp
under his fingertips seeped through his eyelashes. He sniffed to
clear a nose that had unaccountably become blocked. His breath
caught in his throat with a soft "ah," and at the sound he dipped
his pen again, angrily, drew it back to hover over the page.

*No wonder I have also finally disgusted Alfie. He is
a man of the same sort; impulsive, at ease with the
things of the flesh. Luxurious. I might have let him
teach me some of his joy in life. Instead I have repeated in small my mother's mistake; withholding
forgiveness, comforting myself with my own piety.*

I have only myself to blame.

CHAPTER 33

The "e" of blame faded into the paper. He put down the dry pen and picked up his watch. It was now five minutes past the hour. A new year had arrived, and Alfie had not come.

Indeed, why should he have come? He meant nothing of the sort. He was speaking generally. That I have twisted it into some sort of promise says more of my own powers of self-deception than his intent. The incident in my cabin must have been mere revenge, after all, and not an invitation to begin again.

A damp wind tugged at the windows, rattling them against the frames, as the scent of sugar cane and furnaces, the sewers of the streets, filtered in through the cracks. John stood, stretching out knots of tension, wincing as pain lanced from his stiff neck to the small of his back. *Yet, if I told him…?*

He stooped to the fire. If he was admitting defeat—going to bed alone—it should be raked apart, allowed to gently die. But he couldn't, he couldn't, not yet. Something fierce moved through him, made his hand shake as he scooped up a shovel of coal and poured it on.

What, I should tell him he owes me his life? I should force him to come to me out of debt. Out of obligation? No! The petty, whining creature in his secret heart—the infant demon responsible for his devouring jealousy, his outbreak of martyred anger—whispered that it made no difference how he conquered the prize, so long as he won. But honor revolted.

The shovel must have been half full of dust and clinker—the fire smoked and sputtered. His shadow reeled drunkenly over the walls, inconstant, almost alarming in the brown dusk of the single candle. As the coal settled, it fizzed and clicked. He jumped away just as a lump burst apart, hurling glowing cinders out onto the wooden floor in a smoldering fan of embers. As he stamped them out, he thought of Algiers, for here in miniature was the firebombing of the harbor. He could just taste the wind on his face, imagining the glorious chase after. Back when he still thought he could achieve anything to which he set his hand.

Yet had he not done just that? Sent to take on the pirate fleet of Algiers in a single elderly ketch, had he not snatched victory from inevitable defeat? Warned not to interfere in the course of justice by no lesser a person than Admiral Rodney himself, had he not rescued Alfie's life whole out of the noose? If he had wrought his will on the might of the Barbary corsairs, and foiled the authority of King George's courts, why was this last task beyond him? Was he now to be defeated by the mere memory of a rabble of pirate scum? Despite their best efforts, he was alive, and they dead. Their ghosts could not now make a coward of him unless he allowed them to, and he would not. *Damn them! I will not!*

Shaking the reverie away, he raked the coals together, covered them with the stoneware curfew, and walked into the hall, taking his wig from its stand on the sideboard.

Tomorrow, perhaps, he would write to his father and attempt some sort of reconciliation. *But now....* Why was he sitting, brooding and waiting for a lover to call, like a polite country miss after her first ball? So Alfie had not come to him? Very well. Then he would go to Alfie. If there was one night of the year on which Alfie *must* be in one of Kingston's numerous ale-houses, this surely was it. John would check every one until he found the man, and he would not leave him until they had had this out one way or another. He would not blackmail, but surely he could woo?

With the wig jammed on securely, he pulled his stockings up, tightened the garters and buckled the knees of his breeches over them. Winding a light muffler about his face to keep out the unhealthy night air, he opened the door just as someone pealed on the doorbell as though the French were invading. Dark shapes in the porch sang something Gaelic in not quite harmony. As they lurched towards him, he suppressed the desire to flinch.

Jamaica's tropical moon sailed out from behind the clouds and showed him a riot of Irishmen, unstable, bright eyed and grinning. Even as he watched, a shape just outside the porch raised his arm in a toast—the elbow angular and black against the pewter sky—tossed back a dram, and fell straight backwards into the struggling box-hedge.

Everyone laughed, John too, some of the inebriation passing to him by sympathy.

"Can't take the strain, the poor wee man."

"We hate to leave him t'ye sir. But sure he can't lay out here in the street for the thieves to pick over 'til dawn."

"No, no." Joy rose to John's head like champagne. He had to fight not to clap both hands over his mouth to keep his giddy spirit in. "That is perfectly fine. Bring him inside and lay him on the chaise. I'll sober him up and send him home. I'm afraid I have no whiskey, but will you have rum?"

For what seemed hours, his hall seethed with men. He tensed at first against the laughter and the crowd, and the stench—hot unwashed bodies, smoke and liquor—but the rough voices and camaraderie were so like the lower deck of a well-run ship that he soon found himself at ease. Passing out tots of rum and pieces of gingerbread all round, he received a lump of coal in return, and a thousand blessings.

"Please," he offered happily, after emptying out the round-bellied bottle and running down to the cellar for two more, stopping off in the kitchen on the way back. "Take the bottles, and this cake. May the new year be a good one for you all!"

By the time he had separated himself from the protestations of eternal devotion which greeted this generosity, shepherded the more drunk into the arms of the lesser, and shut the door on them all, his face ached from smiling. For a moment, in the silence they left behind, he felt their boisterous, animal joy still glowing in the walls, rivaling the pale moonlight which slanted through the fan window of the door.

Stripping off his coat and muffler, he placed hat and wig back in their accustomed spots, almost afraid to turn around in case all this happiness was proved only an illusion caused by darkness and too much desire. But, when he turned, the limp body was sprawled on his floor, still dead drunk and never more welcome—Alfie Donwell, the lightweight, who couldn't stand the pace.

In the important task of hospitality, John had overlooked the fact that they hadn't dragged Alfie any further than the hall. He lay now on the cocoanut matting, with the side of his face pressed against the skirting board, hat trapped in the door and wig askew to reveal his shaggy mop of curly hair.

Hanging up his coat, John returned to kneel next to the unconscious man. The effervescent sparkle of his spirits quieted, mellowed. The desire to stride about the room to walk off the dangerous pressure dwindled, as he allowed himself the rare luxury of a moment just to look. What an absurd thing a sleeping human being was! How vulnerable, how infinitely to be treasured.

Without the vivid life pulling it into strange shapes, Alfie's face was surprisingly handsome; oval and regular, with strong brows and a generous mouth. His eyes turned slightly downwards at the corners, which should have made him seem permanently sad, but did not, adding instead a faint exoticism. The fan of his pale eyelashes against bronzed cheeks looked boyishly innocent, but a tiny mole just above his top lip on the right seemed an invitation to kiss here first. Altogether it was a quirky, unique face which John could not imagine himself ever growing tired of watching, fascinated and charmed.

"But I had other things in mind for this evening than holding the bowl while you vomit," he said at last. "Come on then." Picking up the sadly flattened hat and wig, he placed them with his own. After considering angles and leverage for a while, he took Alfie's wrists and hauled the man into a sitting position, got his shoulder into Alfie's belly and staggered to his feet. "Let's get you to bed."

Lifting an unconscious drunkard, solidly made as he was, lying heavy and limp over John's aching shoulder, should not have been an erotic experience. But perhaps it had been a mistake to allow the ideas of Alfie and bed to coexist in his mind. No amount of stern inward admonishment could stop him from finding the hip pressed against his face distracting. He closed his eyes, shifted a little so he could feel the hollow and the swell of buttock against his cheek. The coarse linen of Alfie's breeches rubbed the wrong way through John's midnight stubble and the tickling scratch made the hair stand up along his arms as his body prickled all over with delight.

Would it really be terrible to slide his hands up the thighs around which they were currently clamped? *Not with any evil intent, obviously, just…just to feel the shape of them.* His thumbs moved by themselves, sweeping in restless, needy circles as if they could burrow through to skin beneath the coarse linen. He checked them, sternly, frowning at himself. *Yes, it* would *be terrible.* He was no pirate, not to give a fig for consent.

He pulled his cheek away, took in a deep, strengthening breath, and almost choked on it when the belly pressed against his neck trembled with laughter. Alfie's dangling hands came alive, stroked up John's thighs, leaving a riot of pleasure in their wake, and cupped, shameless and wanton around John's arse, kneading.

"I thought you'd never ask." Upside down and gleeful, Alfie giggled like a schoolboy.

Under this onslaught and indignity, the surprise and the lust, not to mention Alfie's not inconsiderable weight, John's knees gave out. He lurched into the wall, his waistcoat buttons scoring white scars in the peeling paint as they slid down it together, both laughing, scrabbling for purchase to stop the slide from becoming a fall. Too distracted by the bump and slide of each other's bodies to break apart, they end up tangled in a sprawl of limbs on the dusty matting of the hall corridor. The chaise in the withdrawing room might have been a hundred miles away. John could not bear the thought of unwinding himself from Alfie long enough to walk there.

They lay on their sides, facing one another, shoes scattered across the hall, John's leg trapped between Alfie's, his calf and ankle—*his ankle, for God's sake!*—lighting up his every vein with molten heat as Alfie stroked him with silk-stockinged toes.

"You're drunk," John gasped, even his own voice strange to him, gone thick as pouring cream. Alfie's careless, smug look made him seem again the wicked, predatory presence he had been so long ago on the *Meteor*. So much pain it had taken to teach John what he wanted! It had been too long since Alfie had looked so very pleased with himself.

"I must confess I am." Mouth half open, tongue pressed in the corner, Alfie concentrated on undoing John's buttons. "After I was such a coxcomb to you on the voyage home, my courage, if not my other parts, needed a little stiffening."

John wanted to say, "No, no, I understand. God knows, my own actions have not been particularly consistent. I'm sorry, Alfie. Sorry I was such a prig. Sorry above everything that we could have spent this year together, but I condemned us both to go through hell. Is this…are you…do you forgive me?"

He wanted to say this, but he was too busy pulling up Alfie's shirt. Acres and acres of shirt, warm from body heat. He thought of the words and then there were buttons, his fingers fumbling with the buttons of Alfie's breeches, and—*ooh, God*—Alfie's hand beneath his own shirt, on his skin, hot, slightly rough, not enough!

There were words, there were—the little noise of encouragement and pleading that was all he seemed to be able to make stood in for so many more eloquent phrases. He might have found them, if all his being was not poured into his exploring hands. Alfie raked fingernails gently across one of his nipples, his other hand pushing aside John's neckcloth so that he could pepper John's throat with little bites.

"*Nnh!*" John managed. His trapped cock hurt, bent and straining against the heavy, harsh fabric of his breeches. Wriggling, he tried to push them off, his fingers too clumsy to undo the buttons. "Damn! The stupid…." Alfie's mouth was on his and sweet fire pulsed down his backbone as he opened to Alfie's questing tongue. Gathered up in both arms, his head back, astonished and all the more aroused by his own deep surrender, he felt Alfie's knuckles dig hard into his back as the man snapped the tapes at the back of his waistband and shoved the suddenly loosened breeches down to his knees.

John's hand scrabbled at the wall as Alfie's full weight came down upon him, pressing him into the carpet. Prickly matting rubbed against his naked arse, skin dragged against his skin, sweat mixing slippery between them. He thrust up, Alfie's prick painfully hard against his own, and ecstasy gutted him. Surprised, he arched half off the floor, crying out something sharp. Remembering he had hands, he dug them into Alfie's arse, pulled him closer, and did that again, a hundred-score wet dreams coming true at once. He tasted salt and copper, then Alfie reached up, tugged him by the hair, and stopped the cries with another ruthless kiss.

Words melted in the wet heat. His heartbeat pulsed in throat and yard. His chest filled to bursting with a dark, erotic ache as the weight and kiss combined stole the breath from him. He tore his mouth away just as the fire reached the charge, exploding through him like the discharge of a cannon. His fingernails dug deep into Alfie's back, and all the things he meant to say coalesced into one frantic cry. "Oh God yes! Yes! *Alfie!*"

Chest heaving, slowly recognizing the little whimpers of shock as his own, John came back to himself, sticky, faintly uncomfortable, his back grazed by the matting. Alfie's sodden weight sprawled all over him as if to finally pin him down, but it was no longer so pleasant not to be able to breathe. He pushed at a shoulder still regrettably clothed in its prickly woolen uniform waistcoat. Obligingly, Alfie rolled onto his back, his eyes closed, his mouth lax as his breathing slowed and settled. John pulled his fallen muffler over by the tassels and used it to wipe up the mess.

Button-shaped bruises marked a trail down John's belly. He pulled his shirt further up to look at them, and pressed a thumb on the dark spot over his sternum. The little ache that resulted was pleasant as a kiss, and he frowned at it. *Is this really the sort of thing one could be happy about? Surely….*

Drawn like a needle to the North Pole he put the cloth aside, and lay back down, nestling into Alfie's side. Slipping his arm around Alfie's broad chest, resting his cheek in the hollow of his shoulder, John thought surely soon the horror would hit him. Perhaps in the next heartbeat it would come on him as it had in the Molly house. Shame. Shame for his need, shame for allowing Alfie to use him so, shame for the very marks of his debasement. Soon the full realization of his own vileness would return, just as it had after Bess. *Perhaps with the next breath….*

But moonlight seeped in under the door, the silence filled up with their shared breathing, and it did not seem to come. What came instead, filling him up until he felt it would spill from every pore in visible radiance, was happiness; warm, golden, heavy happiness that gilded even the ridiculous and messy act of sex with a strange beauty.

Finally he abandoned his wait for condemnation, pushed himself up onto one elbow and began to undo Alfie's white waistcoat, telling off each button opened like the bead of a rosary. Alfie lay still as a medieval knight on an unusually explicit tomb, breeches round his crossed ankles, his face relaxed in a sphinx-like smile. "If this is a sin," John said quietly, "is it wrong for me to cherish hopes that it will go on forever?"

"Is it wrong," Alfie opened an eye to smile at him, then shifted on the coarse fibre matting, "for me to hope there might be a bed in it somewhere?"

They kicked off their breeches and went upstairs. Still speechless—incapable of saying anything more meaningful than a joke—Alfie clung stubbornly to John's hand and refused to let go. It lay slender and strong in his grip, real. He needed its warmth and pressure, needed to feel the callous left by a sword and the faint pulse in the thumb. If he let it escape now he was sure to lose his way on the stairs, go stumbling through endless dark corridors only to wake in his own bed, alone.

He had suffered this dream before.

Wan light poured in from a window on the landing. The bare boards of the floor gleamed, scrubbed white as a quarterdeck, and as John lead him through into the bedroom, the sound of the ships in the harbor, ringing two bells in the middle watch, chimed sweet across the water.

The bed, almost exactly as Alfie had imagined it, sat neatly made in the center of a room bare and bright as the landing. In deference to the heat of the island, the colorful, home-made bed-rug sprawled on the floor beside it, its colors dimmed to shades of pewter and grey. His unwillingness to release John's hand occasioned much difficulty when it came to turning down the sheets, and John raised a skeptical eyebrow at him, tugging to get away.

Alfie looked down at their joined hands, his own tightening around John's attempts to escape, then looked up again to find the ends of John's full lips lifted in a fond, exasperated smile he'd never seen before, never even imagined. He let go reluctantly, and only so he could peel off the rest of his clothes, tugging his shirt over his head. Even to Alfie's lax morals it seemed indecent to be altogether naked, but he was shaken to the core. He felt... new, defenseless as a babe. It was appropriate, then, to enter his second life in the same state in which he had been born into the first.

Lifting the thin sheet, the linen worn soft as cotton, he slid into his lover's bed. *Who would have thought it?* Who would have thought some doors only slammed shut temporarily; that when you turned to trudge away they could be flung open again, and love come pelting down the path, shouting for you to come back?

He had thought himself prepared to achieve what he had spent his life hunting, but clearly he had only prepared for failure. Success left him stunned, close to frightened. "I'm finding this very difficult to believe," he said as John peeked out of the thin, white curtains, his gaunt beauty silvered by the moon.

John's head turned. He gave a smile of enormous innocence, then drew his own shirt off with blushing modesty, almost returned to the man with whom Alfie had fallen in love all those long months ago. "I too."

"Come over here and let me prove it to us both."

Shadows slid over skin pale as porcelain when John drifted closer, ghosted over his expression of mingled joy and amusement. He smelled of bergamot and salt. "You take a lot upon yourself, Mr. Donwell, assuming the man's part in this."

But he lifted the corner of the coverlet and slipped between the sheets, inching his way tentatively into Alfie's arms.

"It's not like that." Alfie closed his eyes against the rush of sweetness and pulled John's lean frame more closely against him until they were pressed full length together. *Oh! There* is *something to be said for being bare.* His skin could breathe in the touch of John's skin, soak him up like sunshine. The axe scar on John's side felt like exploring fingers, rougher, warmer than the silk of his flanks. He reached down and traced the shape of it, remembering Gibraltar, the usual stab of resentment transformed into nostalgia. He thought about soap and steam, *skin wet and slippery beneath him, John lying confiding and abandoned in his arms....* There would have to be more baths in their future.

Kissing behind John's ear, then at the angle of his jaw, Alfie mouthed along the long, elegant throat to the Adam's apple, licking at sweat and cologne. But as he pressed his lips there, John hissed in pain, his whole body tensing. The faint blue light, which sifted through the thin curtains, illuminated fear. Then a frown of determination. Alfie belatedly remembered the great black bruise, crawling with flies, that had swollen John's throat on Tobago to the point where Bentley had considered cutting into the airway to let him breathe. Long healed, it seemed the wound left still a phantom impression.

"What a pair we are," Alfie said gently, taking John's hand to kiss the palm and the thick bracelet of ridged scars. "Lucky to be alive."

"I bear the marks of my folly." There was no joy in John's smile now. "Was I punished enough, do you think?"

"Oh, *God!*" Collapsing back to the mattress, Alfie linked his arms about John's thin frame, and pulled him almost violently into a protective embrace, feeling a horror and indignation he could not fully express. *Beautiful man!* He was a beautiful man, and delicate like the best porcelain, half transparent, letting light shine through from elsewhere. But sometimes—from wherever it was he got his radiance—he also came out with the most terrifying ideas. "You didn't go through this for me. This is nothing to do with me. It never was."

"But still, it is in this bed with you."

"John," Alfie bent his head to whisper into John's dark hair, "did they…?" He didn't know what he would do; couldn't kill them all—it had already been done—didn't really want to know. John had been hurt, they had both been hurt, but it was over.

"You may not want to ask that question, Alfie. Or I will have to ask the same of you."

Thank God, they understood one another on that at least. "It's a new year. A new moment," he said, running a hand down the ridges and furrows of John's ribs, planning a regime of big meals. "And you have to admit it's a good one. We have better things to worry about now."

John laughed, his muscles softening from their stiff-as-a-board rigor. He heaved himself to his elbow, watching his own hand as it traced the lines of Alfie's shoulders, as though he was a naturalist, and Alfie some fascinating new creature, unknown to the learned gentlemen of the Royal Society. He watched it as though he didn't know what it would do next, and when it stroked down Alfie's neck to tweak the sparse hair on his chest, John's smile twisted into unexpected wickedness, astonished at his own actions.

His hand raised, hovering with curiosity and interest just above Alfie's nipple, but the absorbed eyes—grey as Toledo steel—flicked up to Alfie's spellbound gaze. "And this question of who is to be the boy?"

"You read too much Greek." Alfie mentally egged on the descent of those exploring fingertips, but still jerked with surprise and pleasure when they landed and pinched the little nub. "Oh! Um…they were very clever, I've no doubt. But I hope we are— *please do that again*—more enlightened nowadays."

"What do you mean?" John's head tilted, the same curious, almost dispassionate look on his face as his hand slid down Alfie's ribs to his belly, and found the trail of hair that lead like an arrow to his yard.

It raised itself, straining up to be touched, and he could sympathize with its frustration. *This is like a bloody lieutenant's exam, firing questions at you while you were disconcerted and….* But no, Alfie still remembered his lieutenant's exam with a shudder; all those lined leathery faces and squinting eyes peering at him. It was enough to wilt any man's ardor, but this? *Please just stop talking! Talk after, please, not….* "I mean you rescue me, I rescue you. You comfort me, I comfort you. I don't give a shit about anything else. Please just fuck me!"

"It seems a filthy act." Despite the faint tremble Alfie could feel sweeping through the fibers of John's boyish frame, the man paused, still as a marble statue, looking worried. If it had not been for his prick, which also resembled marble in its hardness, Alfie might have panicked. As it was, he groaned, aching. "Is it worth death? What we've done so far only earns us the pillory. I could be satisfied with nothing more than that forever, couldn't you? Why run the risk?"

Alfie shifted on the mattress, the very sheet beneath him making him itch with need as it slid across his skin. He lifted one hand to rub his thumb along John's cheek and lips. John's mouth opened obediently, he licked the end of Alfie's finger, and bit, and Alfie scrunched his eyes shut and whined.

"You'll understand…when you do it. John, I want you…in me. I want…*please!*"

The mattress ropes creaked beneath him as John leaned down for a kiss. John's scent and warmth enveloped him. Alfie twisted his fingers in the thick silk of John's hair, just as John wrapped his hand around Alfie's prick, and stroked down, tentative, amazing. Arching off the bed, Alfie yelped—"Oh, thank *God!*" which made the little bastard laugh—but at his rushing, tightening, frantic reaction Alfie abandoned all thoughts of leisurely foreplay—they had the rest of the night for that. He pushed John's exploring hand away and sat up to fumble for the tallow candle in the corner of the room. Taking the dish beneath it—full of warm fat—he pressed it into John's hands. "Grease. Goes on here. Then you just insert and push, understand? Nature does the rest."

Rolled over onto his stomach, he conceded that this was not the romantic coupling he'd put together in his daydreams for John's deflowering. That could be done another time, once the pledge was sealed; once they had both learned enough to be comfortable with one another. With careful strokes he kept himself just on the edge, and spread his legs further, the pull of his thigh muscles a burn of delicious tension, the vulnerability of the posture just on the pleasurable side of terror. Then John slid oil covered hands between his buttocks and the wave of sensation made him tilt his arse upwards in offering and bite the pillow rather than demand or plead, waiting for the…*oh god, yes,* the blunt, insistent probe at his hole.

"You could," he panted, "you could…use…." The word "fingers" came out as a squeak of surprised pleasure as his body yielded and the head of John's prick nudged inside, being held for a moment in the ring of muscle where he could feel it; the shape and heat and slickness. Then a careful thrust, and the tingling drag of sensation as John pushed further in, till he could feel balls against his balls, and his back was covered by the weight of John. His belly felt full, a core of hard heat within him. Even gasping for breath made little tremors race across his skin. He ground down against the sheet, eyes closed, mouth open, feeling bestial and glorious and on fire. A moan encouraged John to move.

Alfie twisted his neck round, forcing himself to haul up his heavy eyelids so he could watch John's face. The ferocity on it broke something cautious inside him, and opened new reservoirs of need. He let out a long, keening moan, raised himself on his hands again, and drove himself back to meet the febrile, possessed strength of John's thrusts. *"Hand!* Your hand—on me! God! *Please!"*

Long fingers on his cock squeezed him like a trigger and he went off, then collapsed, sobbing incoherent noises into the pillow. The hand around him smeared through semen before clamping around his hip like a vise. John thrust twice more and came with that cry of his that sounded as though his heart had broken.

If it had, however, there was no evidence of it when Alfie turned over and pulled him down onto his chest. The look he received was more shock than heartbreak, struck through by revelation. John held on tight to Alfie's shoulders as if to stop himself floating away. Basking in the aftermath, Alfie memorized his every throbbing ache with delight. Possessed. Marked.

At last.

He kissed John's sharp cheek, bone hard against his teeth, and belatedly it occurred to him to fear the religious backlash, the storm of self-reproach and shame. But as he stroked both hands down John's long back it softened beneath his palms, muscles unknotting, until John lay boneless and trusting against him, utterly relaxed.

"You were right." John shifted down, tucking his head beneath Alfie's chin. The movement of his eyelashes as he closed his eyes was a tickling caress against the hollow of Alfie's throat. "I understand now. I understand why God made us physical beings…why He gave us flesh…."

His drowsy voice wound through Alfie's state of drunken animal bliss like the enveloping wallow of the bed beneath him, their mingled scent, the prospect of sleeping, here, together, breathing one another's air, becoming one.

"It was because of this."

"If I'd thought this qualified as a consolation of religion," Alfie murmured, weary and happy, feeling the corners of John's mouth graze his throat as they lifted up in amusement, "I'd have long since become a minister."

"How will I live with your blasphemy?"

Though it almost felt his rough hands would tear the silken skin on John's half-hard prick, Alfie could not stop himself from touching again, stroking it like a responsive, affectionate pet. "You'll manage."

"I will." John raised his head and smiled dreamily, tousled and sated. "Yes, I will. And Alfie?"

"Hm?"

"Happy New Year."

Reaching up, Alfie tangled his fingers in sweat-pointed umber hair, pulled, and when John landed beside him with a *woomph* and a scattering of down from the pillows, he thought, *"A new year."* A new beginning.

Pray God the ending would be equally fine.

ACKNOWLEDGEMENTS

I'd like to start by acknowledging my immense debt to my mum, who, at the age of eighty-five, found out for the first time that her daughter wrote gay romance, with sex scenes. To her eternal credit, she said, "Well, everyone has to have love," before going around to her neighbours to boast of her daughter the author. Sadly, she died before this book could see the light of day, but I like to think she'd be as happy with it as I am.

I don't think it's any secret that I owe an enormous amount of inspiration, entertainment and information to Patrick O'Brian, the master of the Age of Sail novel. But for his Aubrey-Maturin series of books, I doubt if I would have written this at all. To N.A.M Rodgers and his in depth research into the Georgian navy, I owe Hall, the corrupt purser, as well as innumerable facts and figures that his fine scholarship made it fun to learn. And John Harland's *Seamanship in the Age of Sail* stopped me crashing into the reefs of my complete ship-handling ignorance.

I'd also like to thank my husband, Andrew. This must seem like a strange choice of career to him, but he's never been anything other than proud and supportive. I'm proud of him, too.

This is becoming a bit mushy, so I'll wrap it up quickly. Thank you to my internet friends who have been wonderful. Especially thank you to Ruth Sims, author of *The Phoenix*, and Erastes, the author of *Transgressions,* who put me in touch with Running Press in the first place, and urged me to submit *False Colors* for this series. Without them you wouldn't be holding this book now.

Thank you, to them and to everyone else who I have rudely forgotten to mention!

—Alex

About the Author

Alex Beecroft exists only intermittently in the real world. She can fight with spear and battleaxe and has helped to construct a Saxon manor house from the ground up. She has worked in an 18th Century kitchen, sewn her family a full set of Georgian clothing, can spin and weave and light a fire from flint and tinder. But she still can't operate a mobile phone.

Please visit her at www.alexbeecroft.com.